THE BLOOD
OF ROME

By Simon Scarrow

SIMON SCARROW

EAGLES·OF·THE·EMPIRE

THE BLOOD OF ROME

HEADLINE

First published in Great Britain in 2018
by HEADLINE PUBLISHING GROUP

1

Cataloguing in Publication Data is available from the British Library

ISBN 978 1 4722 5836 6 (Hardback)
ISBN 978 1 4722 5835 9 (Trade paperback)

Typeset in Bembo by Avon DataSet Ltd, Bidford-on-Avon, Warwickshire

Printed and bound in Great Britain by Clays Ltd, Elcograf S.p.A.

HEADLINE PUBLISHING GROUP
An Hachette UK Company
Carmelite House
50 Victoria Embankment
London EC4Y 0DZ

www.headline.co.uk
www.hachette.co.uk

For Colour Sergeants Coates and Hillary,
and all the other modern-day Macros.

CONTENTS

THE FRONTIER BETWEEN
ROME AND PARTHIA
IN THE FIRST CENTURY

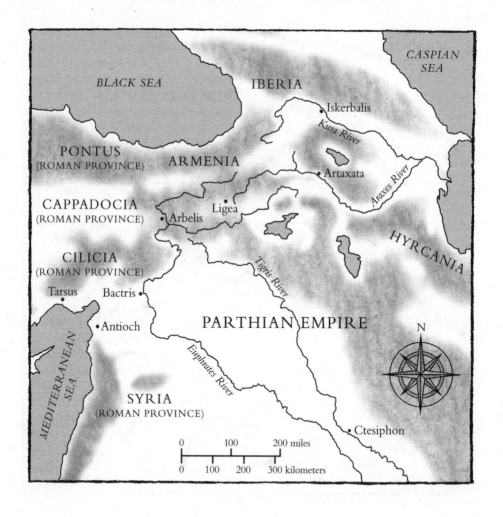

CASPIAN
SEA

BLACK SEA

IBERIA

Iskerbalis

Kura River

PONTUS
(ROMAN PROVINCE)

ARMENIA

Artaxata

Araxes River

CAPPADOCIA
(ROMAN PROVINCE)

Ligea

Arbelis

HYRCANIA

CILICIA
(ROMAN PROVINCE)

Tigris River

Tarsus

Bactris

Antioch

PARTHIAN EMPIRE

N

MEDITERRANEAN
SEA

Euphrates River

SYRIA
(ROMAN PROVINCE)

Ctesiphon

0	100	200 miles
0	100	200	300 kilometers

PRAETORIAN GUARD
CHAIN OF COMMAND

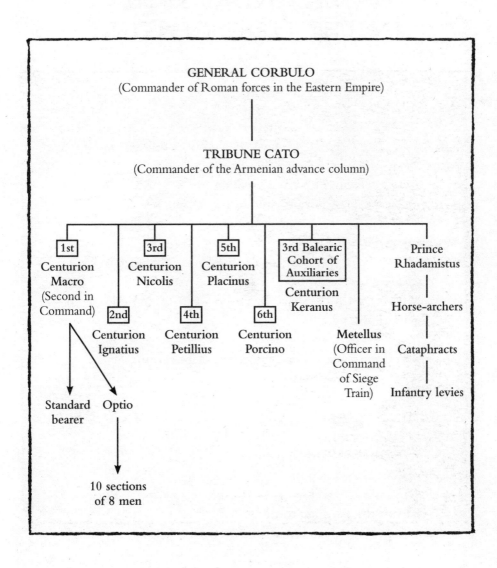

GENERAL CORBULO
(Commander of Roman forces in the Eastern Empire)

TRIBUNE CATO
(Commander of the Armenian advance column)

1st
Centurion Macro
(Second in Command)

2nd
Centurion Ignatius

3rd
Centurion Nicolis

4th
Centurion Petillius

5th
Centurion Placinus

6th
Centurion Porcino

3rd Balearic Cohort of Auxiliaries
Centurion Keranus

Metellus
(Officer in Command of Siege Train)

Prince Rhadamistus

Horse-archers

Cataphracts

Infantry levies

Standard bearer

Optio

10 sections of 8 men

CAST LIST

Quintus Licinius Cato: Tribune in command of the Second Cohort of the Praetorian Guard

Lucius Cornelius Macro: Senior centurion of the Second Cohort of the Praetorian Guard, a tough veteran

General Gnaeus Domitius Corbulo: Recently appointed commander of the armies of the eastern Empire

Ummidius Quadratus: Governor of Syria

Gaius Amatus Pinto: Quaestor in the governor's retinue

Praetorian Guard

Ignatius, Nicolis, Metellus, Petillius, Placinus, Porcino: Centurions

Marcellus, Gannicus, Tertius: Optios

Centurion Spiracus Keranus: Promoted by Cato to command the Balearic slingers

Rutilius: Standard-bearer

Auxiliaryman Gaius Glabius: A Balearic slinger

Titus Borenus: A legionary

Parthia

King Vologases: King of Parthia

General Sporaces: Parthian general

Abdagases: Royal treasurer

Prince Vardanes: Eldest and favourite son of King Vologases, and heir to the Parthian throne

Mithraxes: Armenian ambassador to the Parthian court

Armenia

Rhadamistus: Iberian prince, and the recently deposed king of Armenia

King Tiridates: Brother of King Vologases, and recently installed by him as the new king of Armenia

Arghalis: Chamberlain at Tiridates' court

Narses: One of Rhadamistus's retinue, appointed as interpreter and liaison officer between the Iberians and the Romans

Zenobia: Rhadamistus's wife

Bernisha: Servant girl in Rhadamistus's retinue, taken pity on by Cato

Iberia

King Pharasmanes: King of Iberia, father of Rhadamistus

Others

Lucius: Son of Cato, something of a handful . . .

Petronella: Nurse to Lucius, and a woman to be reckoned with

Yusef: Silversmith, and landlord to Cato

Graniculus: Quartermaster to the Roman garrison at Bactris

CHAPTER ONE

*Ctesiphon, capital city of the Parthian Empire,
March, AD 55*

The setting sun lit up the broad stretch of the Tigris river, so that it gleamed like molten gold against the pale orange of the sky. The air was still and cool, and the last clouds of the thunderstorm that had drenched the city had passed to the south, leaving the faintest odour of iron in the gathering dusk. The servants of the royal palace were scurrying about their duties as they prepared the riverside pavilion for that evening's meeting of the king and his council to discuss the latest Roman threat to Parthia. They were urged on by the impatient shouts and blows from the chamberlain, a thin rake of a man, prematurely grey with the anxiety that came from attending the irascible ruler of an empire that stretched from the banks of the Indus to the borders of the Roman province of Syria. King Vologases was a man bent on reviving the grandeur of Parthia and was not prepared to suffer anyone who stood in the way of his destiny, to the smallest degree. Neither rebellious noble, nor clumsy or inefficient servant. The last chamberlain had failed to ensure that the food served at a banquet had been sufficiently hot when it reached the royal table. For that he had been flogged almost to death before being thrown into the street. The current chamberlain was determined not to follow his example, and so he cursed and beat his underlings as they set up the divans, piled fuel by the braziers and hung thick embroidered screens on three sides of the pavilion. The fourth was left open for the king and his guests to enjoy the view of the river as the sun disappeared beyond the horizon and the stars came out and shimmered on the dark waters of the river.

1

When the last silk cushions had been carefully deployed, the servants backed to the side of the enclosed space and waited as the chamberlain scrutinised their work and bent to make a handful of minor adjustments until satisfied that there was nothing his master could take exception to. Not that Vologases was inclined to closely inspect every detail of the luxury he was accustomed to living within. Still, the chamberlain mused, better to be scrupulous than take the slightest risk of incurring the king's wrath. Having completed his inspection, he clapped his hands loudly.

'Away, you dogs! Bring the fruit and wine.'

As they began to trot away, he turned to his assistant. 'And you, tell the kitchen master to have the meal readied to be served the instant I give the word.'

His assistant, a younger, corpulent man who no doubt aspired to replace him, nodded and scurried away. The chamberlain cast another look round at the handiwork of his staff and then stood in front of the king's dais and narrowed his eyes as he inspected the large divan, cushions and covers minutely. He leaned forward to ease out a crease in the cloth and then stood back and folded his arms in satisfaction. Then, uncharacteristically, he gave a thin smile and glanced around warily. But he was quite alone. It was a rare moment in his life, consumed as it was with the myriad duties of his post. The interlude would be brief enough before the servants returned with the fruit and wine, along with the royal taster, who would sample each bowl and jar at the behest of the chamberlain to ensure that King Vologases would be able to eat and drink safely. Vast and enduring though Parthia was, the empire's rulers were less enduring, regularly falling victim to the plots of powerful nobles, or the ambitions of members of the royal family.

The chamberlain breathed deeply as he smiled at the royal divan and felt an almost irresistible urge to bound forward and throw himself upon its silk cushions, unobserved. It would be the act of a moment and no one would ever know. His heart quickened at the prospect of such an extraordinary breach of protocol, and for a few breaths he tottered on the brink of temptation. Then he drew himself back and covered his mouth in horror at the thought of what would become of him if the king ever discovered what he had done. Although the chamberlain was quite alone, the fear of his master ruled his heart and he quailed at his fleeting madness. With an anxious gasp he hurried to the top of the steps leading down to the gardens either side of the path that stretched towards the bulk of the palace. The first of the servants was returning, laden with a large silver platter of figs, dates and other fine fruits.

'Run, you idle dog!' the chamberlain snapped, and the man broke into a trot as he struggled not to upset the arrangement on the platter.

The chamberlain took a last look at the setting and offered a quick prayer to Mithras that his master would find nothing amongst the arrangements to displease him.

When the king and his small retinue emerged from the palace, the sun had slipped beyond the horizon and a band of bronze sky stretched across the shadowy landscape across the river. Above, the bronze gave way to violet and the dark velvet of night, where the first stars glittered like tiny specks of silver. A party of bodyguards marched in front, armed with lances and wearing their flowing, richly embroidered trousers tucked into their leather ankle boots. Scale armour cuirasses and conical helmets gleamed in the light of the torches and braziers burning either side of the path. But their appearance was as the basest metal to the purest gold compared to the magnificence of their master. Vologases was a tall, well-built man with a broad brow and square jaw, made to look more square still by the meticulous trimming of his dark beard. His eyes were equally dark, like polished ebony, which lent his gaze a formidable intensity. Yet there appeared to be humour in his expression too. His lips lifted at the very edges so that he smiled when he spoke in his deep, warm voice. And, indeed, he was capable of wit and kindness, alongside his wisdom and ambition, and his soldiers and his people regarded him with loyal affection. But those who knew him well were wary of the mercurial change in mood that he was capable of and smiled when he smiled and stood in rigid, fearful silence when he raged.

This night his mood was sombre. News had reached the Parthian capital that Emperor Claudius was dead, murdered, and that he had been succeeded by his adopted son, Nero. The question for Vologases was how the change of reign might affect the strained relationship between Parthia and Rome, a relationship that had soured in recent years. The cause, as ever, was the fate of Armenia, the hapless border kingdom caught between the ambitions of Rome and Parthia. Some four years earlier a pretender to the Armenian throne, Prince Rhadamistus of the neighbouring kingdom of Iberia, had invaded Armenia, killed the king and his family, and installed himself as the new ruler. Rhadamistus had proved to be as cruel as he was ambitious, and the Armenians had appealed to Vologases to save them from the tyrant. So he had led his army against Rhadamistus, who fled his capital, and placed his brother Tiridates on the throne. It was a provocation, Vologases knew, since Rome had regarded Armenia as within the Roman sphere of power for over a hundred years now. The Romans were not likely to regard Parthia's intervention favourably.

The chamberlain, who had been waiting at the entrance, bowed to the waist as the party climbed the steps into the pavilion. The bodyguards took their positions outside, except for the two largest men, who stationed themselves either side of the king's dais. Vologases eased himself down on to the divan and settled comfortably before he gestured to the members of his high council.

'Be seated.'

In a formal setting his guests would have remained standing before their master, but Vologases had deliberately chosen the pavilion and put court protocol aside to encourage his subordinates to speak freely. Once they were seated on the divans, the king leaned forward, plucked a fig from his platter and took a bite, thus giving permission for the others to eat as they wished.

Vologases tossed the half-eaten fruit back on the platter and gazed round at his guests: Sporaces, his finest general; Abdagases, the royal treasurer; and Prince Vardanes, the eldest son of the king and heir to the Parthian throne. An ambassador from Tiridates completed the gathering: a younger man, about the same age as the prince, Mithraxes by name.

'We've little time to waste, my friends,' Vologases announced. 'So you'll pardon me for dispensing with any small talk. You've all heard the news from Rome. We have a new emperor to contend with. Nero.'

'Nero?' Sporaces shook his head. 'Can't say that I recall the name, sire.'

'It's hardly surprising. He was only adopted a few years back. Son of Emperor Claudius's last wife by a previous marriage.'

'The same wife who happens to be Claudius's niece,' Vardanes added wryly. He clicked his tongue and raised an eyebrow. 'Those Romans, eh? Quite the decadent type. Never anything short of scandalous.'

The others smiled at his comment.

'What do we know of this Nero?' Sporaces continued. The general was a veteran who had little time for levity, a characteristic that suited his thin, almost gaunt features. Most of those in the royal court held his boorish manners in low regard, but Vologases knew his worth as a soldier and prized his talents. Moreover, as the son of a Greek mercenary and a whore from Seleucia, Sporaces was despised by the great nobles of Parthia and therefore posed no threat to Vologases.

The king nodded to Abdagases, who ran the network of spies that Parthia used to glean information about events within the Roman Empire. 'You've read the full report. You tell them.'

'Yes, sire.' Abdagases cleared his throat. 'Firstly, he's young. Only sixteen years old. Barely more than a boy.'

'Maybe so.' Sporaces tilted his head slightly. 'But Augustus was only eighteen when he set out to destroy his opponents and become the first emperor of Rome.'

'Nero is no Augustus,' the treasurer contradicted him tersely. 'He may become one, though the possibility of that is remote, according to our agents in Rome. The new emperor fancies himself as something of an artist. A musician. A poet . . . He surrounds himself with actors, musicians and philosophers. He has ambitions to make Rome some kind of beacon for such people, rather than turn his mind towards more martial matters.'

'An artist? A musician?' Sporaces shook his head. 'What kind of a bloody emperor is that?'

'One who will play into our hands, I trust,' said Vologases. 'Let us hope that young Nero continues to concentrate his efforts on his art and is not distracted by events in Armenia.'

Abdagases nodded. 'Yes, sire. We can hope, but it may be wise not to be guided by mere hope. Nero may be a dilettante, but it would be foolish to dismiss him out of hand. He is surrounded by advisers, many of whom have the intelligence and experience to cause us problems. Not least because they suffer from the Roman disease.'

'Roman disease?' Vardanes cocked an eyebrow, helped himself to a second fig and took a big bite. His jaws worked casually before he attempted to continue with a full mouth. 'What . . . disease . . . is that?'

'It's a term some of us at the royal court have used for those Romans obsessed by the pursuit of glory and their utterly inflexible sense of honour. No Roman noble of any standing ever passes up the chance to win acclaim for his family. Whatever the cost. Which is why Crassus attempted to invade Parthia and came to grief. And Marcus Antonius after him. It's a pity that they seem to measure themselves by outdoing the achievements of their ancestors, and are driven to succeed where others have failed.' Abdagases paused a moment. 'It would seem that the failures of Crassus and Antonius only serve to inspire Romans to regard Parthia as a challenge to be overcome. Reasonable men might have profited from the example of failure, but Roman aristocratic honour trumps Roman reasoning almost every time. Augustus was shrewd enough to realise that he could gain more from diplomacy than from military actions in his dealings with Parthia, and his heirs have followed his example in the main. Even if that meant frustrating the senators urging them to wage war on us. The question is, will this new emperor be able to resist the blandishments of his advisers, and the Senate?'

'I sincerely hope so,' Vologases answered. 'Parthia can ill afford the risk of war breaking out with Rome while we have enemies threatening trouble on other fronts.'

Vardanes sighed. 'You speak of the Hyrcanians, Father?'

Vardanes was the king's favourite son. He had courage, intelligence and charisma, qualities useful in an heir. But he also had ambition, and that was an attribute that was as much to be feared as admired. Particularly in Parthia. The king's expression darkened.

'Yes, the Hyrcanians. It seems that they disapprove of the increase in tribute I have demanded of them.'

Vardanes smiled. 'Which is no surprise. And not helpful at a time when we have provoked our Greek subjects by forcing them to put their language and traditions aside to embrace ours, even though Greek is the common tongue across the eastern world. Then there is the trouble brewing up with Rome over Armenia.' He sipped his wine. 'I fear we are overreaching ourselves. Particularly with respect to Armenia. Rome and Parthia are like two dogs fighting over a bone.'

The treasurer coughed politely as he interrupted. 'His Highness oversimplifies the matter. The bone happens to be ours, and those Roman interlopers have no right to attempt to seize it. Most of the nobles of Armenia share our blood. Armenia owed loyalty to the Parthian empire for centuries before Rome turned its gaze to the east.'

'I think we can all agree that Rome has no right to Armenia. Nevertheless, Rome lays claim to Armenia, and if it comes to war, she will take it. I have heard much about the might of the Roman legions. We cannot prevail against them.'

'Not in pitched battle, my prince. But if we can avoid a head-on clash, our forces can wear them down, weaken them and, when the time is right, tear them to pieces. Just as hunting dogs kill the mountain bears. Is it not so, General?' Abdagases turned to Sporaces for support.

The general thought a moment before he responded. 'Parthia has defeated the Romans in the past. When they have blundered into our lands without adequate intelligence of the lay of the land, or adequate supplies to sustain them. They march slowly, even without a siege train. Whereas our forces can cover ground far more swiftly, particularly our horse-archers and cataphracts. We can afford to trade ground for time in order to let them exhaust their supplies and their strength. But that is true only if they wage war across the rivers and deserts of Mesopotamia. Armenia is different. The mountainous terrain favours Rome's infantry rather than our cavalry. I fear Prince Vardanes is correct. If Rome wants to take Armenia, it will succeed.'

7

'There!' Vardanes clicked his fingers. 'I told you.'

'However,' Sporaces continued, 'in order to take Armenia, Rome will be forced to concentrate its forces. Her soldiers are the best in the world, it is true. But they cannot be in two places at once. If they march into Armenia, then they will leave Syria exposed. Not to conquest. We lack the forces to achieve that. Parthia will never be strong enough to destroy Rome, and Rome will never have enough men to conquer and occupy Parthia. And that is how it has always been, and always will be, my prince. A conflict neither side can win. Therefore the only answer is peace.'

'Peace!' Vologases snorted. 'We have tried to make peace with Rome. We have honoured every treaty made between us, only for them to be broken more often than not by the accursed Romans.'

Vologases' brow creased in frustration as he thought a moment. 'And for that reason we must be certain that we choose wisely in dealing with the situation in Armenia.'

He turned towards the ambassador sent by his brother. 'Mithraxes, you have not spoken yet. You have no opinion about the new emperor in Rome and his intentions towards Armenia?'

Mithraxes shrugged nonchalantly. 'It hardly matters what my opinion is, Majesty. I am an Armenian noble, descended from a long line of nobles, none of whom has ever lived to see our land free of the influence of either Parthia or Rome. Our kings have a habit of being deposed, or murdered. Your brother has been on the throne barely two years. He is no worse than some who have ruled Armenia and—'

'Choose your words carefully when you speak of my brother,' Vologases warned.

'Majesty. I was sent to report on the situation in Armenia and ask for your help. I believe that is best done if I speak honestly.'

The king regarded him closely, and noted that the Armenian did not flinch under his gaze. 'Courage as well as integrity? Are all Armenian noblemen like you?'

'Sadly not, Majesty. And that is the problem that besets your brother. As I said, he is no worse than many rulers, and better than many. Yet, he has been obliged to rule with a firm hand in order to establish his authority over his new realm.'

'How firm a hand?'

'Some nobles favour Rome, Majesty. Some resent having any foreigner imposed on them. King Tiridates determined that lessons were needed in order to discourage such disloyalty. Regrettably, it was necessary to banish some, and execute others. This had the effect of quelling most of the discontent.'

'I can imagine.' Vardanes smiled. 'But I dare say it might have inclined some to feel just a little more discontented.'

'Quite so, Your Highness. However, King Tiridates remains on the throne in Artaxata. His enemies are cowed for the present. Though I am certain they will soon appeal for aid in unseating the king. If they haven't already.' Mithraxes turned his gaze to Vologases. 'Therefore, your brother requests that you send him an army to ensure his control over Armenia. Enough men to defeat any nobles that conspire against him, and to dissuade Rome from invading his lands.'

'An army? Is that all he asks of me?' the king of Parthia scoffed. 'And does my brother think I can just pluck armies out of thin air? I need all my soldiers here in Parthia to deal with the threats I already face.'

'He does not ask for a large army, Majesty. Just a force strong enough to discourage any attempts to remove him.'

'The Armenian rebels are one thing, the Romans quite another. I doubt they would be discouraged by any force I could afford to send to Armenia.'

Mithraxes shook his head. 'I am not so sure, Majesty. Our spies in Syria report that the Roman legions there are badly prepared for war. They are understrength and poorly equipped. It has been many years since they have seen any action. I doubt they constitute much of a threat to King Tiridates.'

Vologases turned to his general. 'Is this true?'

Sporaces reflected a moment before he replied. 'It is consistent with our own intelligence, Majesty. But if the Romans should decide to intervene, they will bring more legions to Syria, and will be sure to find fresh recruits for the existing legions. Of course, they will need to be trained. Supplies will need to be stockpiled, roads repaired, siege trains massed. It will take time to prepare a campaign.

Years perhaps. But once the Romans have decided to act, nothing will stop them. It is the Roman way.' He paused briefly to let the others consider his words, then continued. 'My advice would be not to provoke our enemy any further. Rome already feels affronted by having Tiridates placed on the throne. But it has not yet decided on war. If we send troops to aid your brother, that may tilt the Romans towards action. Besides, we do not yet know the mettle of this new emperor, Nero. He may be swayed either way. So let's not give the war party in Rome any opportunity to persuade him to fight. Instead, I suggest we flatter him with warm words of friendship and congratulate him on his becoming emperor. If he questions our actions in Armenia, then tell him we were forced to replace a tyrant, and that we have no interest in any other lands that border Rome's territory.' He bowed his head in conclusion. 'That is my humble advice, Majesty.'

Vologases eased himself back on his cushions and folded his hands as he considered all that he had heard from his advisers. It was true that Rome's pride would endure being pricked only so far. Yet he could not risk sending any men to support his brother while he faced potential rebellion in Hyrcania in any case.

'It seems that I am forced to wait on events. The choice over what to do lies with Emperor Nero. He will decide whether we have peace. Or war.'

CHAPTER TWO

Tarsus, capital of the eastern Roman province of Cilicia,
two months later

'It's war,' Centurion Macro announced as he entered the quarters of his commanding officer and slipped his cloak off and slung it on to a chest by the door. He had returned from morning inspection of the troops guarding the silk merchant's house where General Corbulo was billeted.

'War?' Cato looked up from the floor where he was sitting with his son, Lucius. The boy was playing with toy soldiers carved from wood by some of the soldiers commanded by Tribune Cato and presented to the boy as a gift. The Second Praetorian Cohort had been sent from Rome to serve as the bodyguard for General Corbulo and his staff. Cato was still getting used to being addressed by the official rank of tribune, since the men and officers had previously addressed him as Prefect, the rank under which he had won so much renown in recent years. But General Corbulo was a stickler for protocol, and Tribune Cato it had become. During the long voyage from Brundisium the men had come to regard Lucius as a mascot and spoiled him at every opportunity. Cato gently ruffled his son's fine, dark hair and stood up. 'Where did you hear that?'

'Imperial proclamation. A messenger sent from Rome was reading it out in the Forum just a moment ago. Seems like the boy Nero has grasped the nettle and decided on sticking it to the Parthians and retaking Armenia.' Macro puffed his cheeks. 'War it is then.'

Both men were briefly silent as they contemplated the implications of the news. It had not come as much of a surprise as the decision to send the general to take command of the armies of the eastern Empire had already been taken some months before. Still, Cato

11

reasoned, Rome had often succeeded in getting its way by merely threatening to use force in the past, such was the awe in which the Empire was held by most of the kingdoms who had the misfortune to encounter its legions on the battlefield. Perhaps the emperor and his advisers had hoped that sending an officer of Corbulo's stature would be enough to convince Parthia to abandon its ambition to restore Armenia to its empire. It seemed as if Nero's bluff had been called. That, or the emperor had been persuaded that nothing short of war would satisfy the need to establish his reign firmly. There was nothing the Roman people liked more than news of another war successfully prosecuted.

'Well, one thing's for certain,' said Macro. 'We'll not be ready to march into Parthia for a while yet. Not until the general has gathered enough men and supplies. Could take months.'

'I'd have thought a year at the very earliest,' Cato replied. 'And that'll be time the Parthians won't be wasting. They'll be prepared and ready for us long before Corbulo crosses the frontier.'

Macro shrugged. 'Let 'em prepare as much as they like. Ain't going to make much difference. You know what those easterners are like, lad. A bunch of ponces parading around in flowing silk. We've faced them before and given them a good kicking.'

'True,' Cato conceded. 'But next time it may well be the other way round. Don't forget Crassus lost the best part of five legions at Carrhae. Rome cannot afford to repeat such a disaster.'

'Corbulo is no Crassus. The general's been fighting on the Rhine for most of his career and the enemy don't come any harder than those bastards in Germania. If the Parthians have any sense, then they'll come to terms as quick as boiled asparagus.' Macro crossed the room and ducked his head into the next chamber. The shutters were closed and the interior was dim, but he could easily make out the woman lying on her side on the large sleeping couch within. 'Ah, I wondered where you'd got to, my love.'

She stirred and let out a groan before pulling the covers more tightly about her shoulders.

'Let the poor woman sleep.' Cato eased him away from the door frame. 'Petronella was up most of the night with the boy. He's got toothache.'

'So why's he still awake and she's asleep?' Macro winked. 'I think there's something wrong with my woman, Cato. She's a slacker and no mistake.'

'Come here and say that,' Lucius's nurse growled. 'If you want a thick ear.'

Macro laughed. 'That's my love! Always up for a fight.'

He turned away and gently closed the door before crossing to the table, where the remains of the morning meal still lay: some bread, cheese, honey and the jug of spiced wine that the local people favoured. Picking up the jug, Macro gave it an experimental swirl and smiled happily as the liquid sloshed inside. He poured himself a cup, then paused and glanced at his friend. 'Want some?'

'Why not? Precious little else for us to do here besides getting drunk until Quadratus reaches the city.'

Macro shook his head. 'That's a meeting that won't go well.'

Cato nodded. Ummidius Quadratus was the governor of Syria, one of the most prestigious postings for any senator. At least, until Corbulo had arrived in the region with the emperor's authority to draw on all the resources, civilian and military, of the provinces bordering Parthia. The general had sent a message out ahead of his arrival, summoning Quadratus to Tarsus to confer on arrangements for the coming campaign. Cato could well imagine how the governor was going to react when Corbulo requisitioned most of his soldiers, equipment and supplies. There would also be the matter of ordering the provincials to stump up further taxes to pay for the repairs to the roads in the region, as well as providing draught animals and wagons for the baggage train and mounts for the cavalry units. Quadratus was going to be inundated with protests from angry town magistrates, claiming that they could not afford such impositions. Not that such complaints would have any effect. It was the duty of the provinces of the Empire to pay up when the army prepared to campaign in their region and there was no avoiding the obligation. Not unless those concerned were willing to face the ire of the emperor when word reached Rome of their parsimony.

'Quadratus isn't going to be happy,' Cato agreed. 'But that's the chain of command and he'll have no choice in the matter. Besides, Corbulo is not the kind of man who takes no for an answer.'

They exchanged an amused smile. In the course of the journey from Rome they had come to know the general well enough to recognise his type. Corbulo was a career soldier; an aristocrat who had a taste for the military life and the talent to go with it. So after serving out his time as a tribune he had remained with the legions rather than returning to Rome to submerge himself in the world of politics. One of the few virtues of the career path of Roman aristocracy, Cato mused, was that it permitted the weeding out of those with limited military potential, while making it possible for those who shone to remain in the army. Corbulo was a soldier's general. He often shared their rations, and hardships. When they slept in the open, so did he. In battle, once the soldiers had been positioned and given their orders, he led from the front. He pushed his men hard, and pushed himself harder still. That had won the soldiers' respect, and grudging affection. This, Macro and Cato had learned from the handful of staff officers Corbulo had chosen to bring with him from the Rhine frontier. The two friends had served under enough poor commanders to welcome being assigned to the general.

There were other reasons to be grateful to be heading far from Rome. A new emperor meant change, and those who had enjoyed the favour of Claudius now faced an uncertain future. New men would be appointed to positions of power and there were scores to settle. There always were in the seething pit of Roman politics. Inevitably powerful men would be accused of crimes committed under the previous regime and there would be trials; some senators would be exiled, some quietly disposed of, and their property would be divided between informers and the imperial treasury. Innocence was irrelevant when informers and lawyers scented blood and, more importantly, money.

Cato had no desire to be caught up in such matters. Especially as he had been rewarded with the estate of his father-in-law, who had been rash enough to be part of a plot to depose Nero in the early days of his reign. The surviving friends of Senator Sempronius had made little secret of their feelings about the source of Cato's recently found wealth, and he knew that his fortune had come at the price of making enemies who would seek to do him down as soon

14

as they were confident the time was ripe. And so he had been happy to join the general's retinue as it journeyed to the eastern frontier. Moreover, he had chosen to bring his son and the boy's nurse, rather than leave them as hostages to fortune back in Rome, a decision that had delighted Centurion Macro, since he had struck up a relationship with Petronella, a woman who could match him drink for drink and throw a punch that was the envy of any seasoned veteran of the legions.

So here the four of them were, in rented rooms at the home of a Jewish silversmith in a street just off the Forum in Tarsus. They had been here a month already, without sign of Quadratus, and, pleasant enough as Tarsus was, the city had soon grown weary of the novelty of having a Roman general and a cohort of Praetorians in residence. And still wearier of the loud drunkenness of off-duty soldiers. In the normal course of events Cato would have been fretting about the enforced inaction. But the delay had meant that he had time to spend with his son, and he was grateful for it. Just as Macro was grateful for the chance to enjoy Petronella's ample charms.

Macro poured them both a cup of wine and they sat on the stools either side of the table and looked down into the small, neat courtyard of the silversmith's house. A fountain splashed in a pool at the centre of the courtyard, around which were arranged a series of couches shaded by trellises. It put Cato in mind of the garden of his house in Rome and he wondered when he would next see it.

'This war with Parthia,' said Macro. 'How long do you think it'll take us to give Vologases a hiding?'

'Depends on Corbulo. If he does what's right, he'll ensure we get our man on the Armenian throne and be satisfied with that. If he gets a taste for glory, then who knows? We could end up marching in the footsteps of Crassus. And that would not be for the best. Either way, it's almost certain to come to a fight. Nero won't be satisfied unless there is a great victory to celebrate in Rome.'

Macro nodded and then indicated Lucius. The child was sitting, thin legs splayed, a wooden soldier in each hand, muttering in an excited low tone as he clashed them together and simulated a fight. 'What about them? Lucius and Petronella? What happens to them when the campaign starts?'

'They can remain here. I'll make sure our host, Yusef, is paid up long enough in advance to keep him happy. He's a decent sort. I'm sure he'll look after them when we head off. And keep them safe until we return. If we return.' Cato was glad that he had lodged his will with a lawyer in Rome before they had set off. At least Lucius's future was secure, even if his own was not.

'If? Tch!' Macro shook his head. 'Always the jug half empty with you . . . Speaking of which.' He topped up their cups. 'We'll be fine. Once we've given those Parthians a decent slapping, they'll be happy to return Armenia to us and bugger off back into the desert, or wherever it is they come from.'

Cato made a rueful expression. 'It's that kind of lack of hard intelligence that worries me, and should worry the general.'

Macro shot him a dark look before Cato shook his head. 'I'm talking about military intelligence, not yours.'

'Fair enough.'

'We don't know nearly enough about the terrain on the other bank of the Euphrates,' Cato continued. 'Where are the river crossings? Where are the rivers, for that matter? And the mountain trails, fortifications, towns, villages and so on. We have no idea about enemy numbers, their intentions or the disposition of their forces. We'll need guides to lead our armies by the safest routes, and yet how do we know we can trust them? It was the treachery of guides that led Crassus to disaster.' Cato took a sip and reflected a moment. 'I went to the imperial library before we left Rome to see what kind of references to Parthia and Armenia I could turn up.'

'Oh, yes. Books. You can solve every problem by reading books,' Macro said wryly. 'Bound to be an answer there, somewhere.'

'Mock them as you will, but there was some useful information. Not much, I grant you. There was an itinerary left over from Antonius's campaign. Didn't make for good reading. I had no idea of the scale of Parthia until I went over the distances between the towns and cities he encountered. And the man who drew up the itinerary left a note that our legions barely penetrated a third of the way into the region, according to his sources. He also records great swathes of desert and many days between opportunities to water the men and horses, and feed them. And then there was the

16

enemy. Rarely risking a pitched battle, while all the time harrying our columns and picking off patrols and stragglers.'

'Then let's pray to the gods that Corbulo doesn't get drawn into Parthia – just keeps his attention on Armenia and settles for carrying out the emperor's orders.'

Cato took a sip and looked down into his cup, gently swirling the contents. 'He wouldn't be the first Roman general tempted by the prospect of winning glory in the east.'

'And I'm sure he won't be the last. But there's not much we can do about it, lad. I'm just a centurion, and you're the tribune commanding his bodyguard. We're here to obey the general's orders, not quote advice from dusty scrolls back in Rome. I doubt Corbulo will look very kindly on that.'

'Well, yes. Quite . . . Whatever happens, I suspect our new posting will not be a short one.'

'I can live with that.' Macro drained his cup and wiped his lips on the back of a hairy hand. 'This part of the world is warm and comfortable for the most part. The wine's cheap and the tarts are cheaper still.' He glanced towards the door to the next room. 'Er, not that I'm on the lookout for that sort of thing these days.'

Cato grinned. 'Centurion Macro, what has become of you? Petronella has changed you into a new man. I barely recognise you.'

'With respect, you can fuck right off, sir.' Macro sat back and folded his thick arms. 'I'm the same soldier I ever was. No change there. Just a bit grey around the temples, and a few aches and pains. But I'm good for one last campaign. If it goes on as long as you fear.'

'Last campaign?' Cato arched an eyebrow. He knew that Macro had been serving in the legions for over twenty-six years. He was eligible for a discharge and the gratuity that went with it. If he wanted it. But Macro had put off any application and said the time was not yet right. Not while he had some years of good soldiering still left in him. And Cato was glad about that. He had an almost superstitious need to have Macro at his side when he marched off to war, and dreaded the day when his friend finally demobbed and retired to some sleepy backwater, while Cato continued his career alone. He forced himself to redirect his thoughts.

17

'I wonder what Petronella will have to say about that? If this campaign does drag on, she'll not be happy to be separated from you.'

Macro shrugged. 'That's what you have to accept if you hitch yourself to a soldier.'

'Very considerate of you, I must say.'

'It's the way of it. She knows that and understands it.'

'Then she's a fine woman indeed.'

'Aye, she is that.' Macro poured the last of the wine into their cups. 'And when I do finally quit the army, I'd be proud to have her as my wife.'

Cato smiled broadly. 'I wondered if you'd thought about that.'

'We've talked it through. Can't get married while I'm still serving. But the least I can do is guarantee her the wherewithal to get by if anything happens to me. I've drawn up a will. Just need a witness, if you wouldn't mind, sir?'

'Mind? I'd be delighted to do it.' Cato raised his cup. 'To a long and happy life together. Subject to the exigencies of military service, of course.'

Macro affected a frown. 'Get away with you!'

Then he raised his cup and tapped Cato's. 'And a long and happy life to you too. You and Lucius both.'

They turned towards the child and saw that he had slumped forward, resting his head on folded arms, eyes closed and breathing deeply and steadily.

'Asleep on duty?' Macro sucked his breath in. 'What's the penalty for that? No piggybacks round the courtyard or picnics with Uncle Macro tonight then.'

Cato shook his head. 'Anyone ever tell you you're a hard bastard, Macro?'

'Nah, not me. Soft as a lamb. Just ask the lads in my century.'

They laughed and drained their cups. The wine, the warmth of the afternoon, the companionship of his long-time friend and the peaceful slumber of his son combined to give Cato an immense sense of well-being, and he prayed that Governor Quadratus held off from presenting himself to the general for a few days yet.

Then he heard the sound of boots at the end of the corridor and a moment later there came a sharp knock on the door.

18

Cato cleared his throat. 'Come!'

With a soft grating of the hinges the door swung open and a Praetorian entered and saluted the two officers.

'Beggin' your pardon, Tribune, but the general wants you at headquarters.'

'What's up?' asked Macro.

'The Governor Quadratus's trireme has been sighted, sir. Should reach the port within a couple of hours. The general's calling out the cohort to form an honour guard.'

'Shit,' Macro sighed. He eased himself to his feet and looked down at the boy, still fast asleep. 'Like I said. No picnic today after all . . .'

CHAPTER THREE

'Cohort's formed up for inspection, sir.'

Macro squinted into the mid-afternoon sun as he exchanged a salute with Cato while the latter finished securing the ties of his helmet and adjusted it so that it sat squarely on his head.

'Very well, Centurion. Any absences?'

Macro consulted his waxed tablet and went through each of the six centuries in turn, his own, and those commanded by Ignatius, Nicolis, Petillius, Placinus and Porcino, before he gave his account: 'Three men excused duties on medical grounds. Eight on duty at headquarters. Two more guarding the pay chest. Six absent without permission, last seen at one of the inns behind the Forum. I've sent Optio Marcellus to find 'em and give them a roasting. I'll be docking their pay and giving them fatigues for a month, if you agree, sir.'

'Very good.' Cato nodded. 'Let's get this done before the governor's ship ties up.'

They both glanced out over the quay to where the trireme was passing the end of the watchtower, oars rising, sweeping forward and splashing down as the warship glided over the calm waters of the River Cydnus. The square leading off the quay had been cleared of civilians and the cohort was drawn up along three sides facing the quay, two centuries on each side, standing to attention in four ranks. Their shields were grounded for the moment, while they clasped the shafts of their spears in their right hands. Polished scale armour gleamed over their off-white tunics. At the rear of the square was a platform facing the temple of the divine Augustus, where General Corbulo and his staff officers stood waiting, in front of the cohort's standard, held by Rutilius, a burly veteran chosen for the honour.

The ceremonial welcome for the governor of Syria was an impressive enough sight, thought Cato, but no matter how assiduously the men had cleaned their kit, it would never be perfect enough for Macro's eagle eyes.

The two officers paced over to the First Century, Macro's own unit, and Cato slowed down, pausing every so often to scrutinise one of the guardsmen.

'This strap is loose . . .'

Macro noted the man's name and his misdemeanour with a few deft strokes of his stylus in the waxed surface of his centurion's tablet.

'Dirt on this man's scabbard . . . And rust on the cheek flap.'

So it continued down the lines of the cohort, notes being taken by each centurion in turn, until their commanding officer had completed the inspection. Cato turned to Macro and took a deep breath so that he could be heard right across the square. 'On the whole, a fine turnout, Centurion. These men would grace the presence of the emperor himself. Well done. Keep it up!'

'Yes, sir.'

Cato lowered his voice for Macro alone. 'Right, the show's about to start. Back to your men. I'll be with the general for the formal greeting.'

They saluted each other, and Macro turned about and marched across the square to the First Century while Cato climbed the steps to the platform in front of the temple and approached Corbulo.

'Cohort's ready, sir.'

The general gazed briefly at the neat ranks of the Praetorians and nodded. 'So I can see. A fine body of men you have there, Tribune Cato.'

'Yes, sir. Thank you, sir.'

'And from the accounts I've heard they acquitted themselves well in Hispania under your command. Not to mention that unfortunate business back in Rome recently.'

Cato said nothing. It was true that his men had been instrumental in the suppression of the plot against Nero to replace him with his younger stepbrother, Britannicus. That had involved a street battle in the capital itself, as well as an assault on the island of Capri, where the plotters had made their final stand. Since the capture and poisoning of Britannicus there had been a concerted effort to brush over the entire incident, which meant that the cohort had received no battle honours or any other official reward for its actions.

Corbulo patted him on the shoulder. 'Relax, Cato. We're well away from Rome and the politicians, informers and conspirers now. We're just soldiers here. Do your duty and don't worry about anything else, eh?'

'Yes, sir.'

'Now then. Let's see what Governor Quadratus has to say for himself.'

The officers on the platform stared out across the square, beyond the quay, to where the trireme turned gracefully to present its beam as the rowers hurriedly shipped their oars. On deck sailors stood ready with coils of ropes and heaved them towards the dockers waiting on the quay. They hurriedly looped the ropes around the mooring posts and heaved the warship in until the hull bumped softly against the cork fenders, then tied off the mooring cables.

At once a gangplank was run out and a party of marines dashed ashore, formed two lines on either side and stood to attention. A group of officers and men in togas stood towards the stern of the trireme, waiting. A moment later an individual wearing an elaborately crested helmet and silvered armour emerged from the small cabin at the rear and led his followers along the deck, across the gangplank and on to the quay. There he paused and briefly surveyed the Praetorians drawn up in front of him before he turned and snapped an order to one of his subordinates. Eight men carrying bundles of rods taped around them ran ahead and formed up in front of the governor.

'Lictors?' one of Corbulo's staff officers muttered. 'Bit over the top for a ceremonial at the arse end of the Empire, wouldn't you say?'

'Indeed.' The general chuckled. 'In any case, with this particular pissing competition I have the home advantage. A cohort of Praetorians trumps a pack of lictors any day. Especially here in my new command at the arse end of the Empire, as you helpfully point out.'

The officer's jaw sagged, then he made to respond, thought better of it and clamped his mouth shut as his face coloured with embarrassment.

There was a long pause as Quadratus stood motionless, waiting for the general to descend and greet him. But Corbulo did not move, standing as still as the Praetorians lining the square. At length the other man gave in and waved his party forward.

Cato smiled as he thought, *Round one to the general.*

As the governor's party reached the steps, Quadratus gestured for the others to halt and began to climb alone. Cato saw that Quadratus's features were far more lined since their last encounter. The responsibilities and strain of his office had taken their toll. He was clearly unused to wearing armour and was breathing hard by the time he stepped up on to the platform and held out his hand.

'Gnaeus Domitius Corbulo, welcome.'

'It is for me to welcome you, Quadratus, since I sent for you.' Before the governor could react to the barbed greeting, Corbulo stepped forward, smiled, clasped his forearm and gave it a brisk shake before he continued. 'I take it you have received word from Rome with respect to my purpose here?'

'I have been told you were coming, yes. And that you have been tasked with restoring Armenia to Roman control. But I have not been appraised of the precise scope of your authority in this region.'

'No? I find that something of a surprise. But never mind, all will be clear once we have had the chance to discuss the situation at my headquarters. I have arranged for food and refreshments for you and your retinue. And accommodation. Tribune Cato! Dismiss your men, and escort the governor's party to headquarters.'

'Yes, sir.'

Corbulo nodded and then turned back to the governor. 'Come.'

Without a further word he indicated the narrow stairs at the end of the platform, leading down to the main street that ran from the quay to the Forum, where the opulent merchant's house that served as the general's headquarters dominated the markets arrayed around the Forum. Corbulo's staff officers and clerks hurried after him while Cato returned to the square and cupped a hand to his mouth. 'Centurion Macro! Dismiss the cohort!'

'Yes, sir!'

Macro turned and called the men to attention, and then gave the order to fall out, and in an instant the neatly ordered ranks broke into clusters of men shouldering their spears as they ambled across the square. Cato turned to the governor's party. Behind the lictors stood a group of officers and men in togas together with a handful of men in flowing robes. One stood a head taller than his companions. Powerfully built with a light-brown beard and dark hair, he stood with folded arms, feet braced apart as he watched the departing guardsmen with a shrewd eye.

'I'm Tribune Quintus Licinius Cato, commander of the general's escort.'

One of the toga-clad men stepped forward and bowed his head just enough to be polite, but not enough to imply that he regarded Cato as an equal. 'Gaius Amatus Pinto, quaestor.'

'If you and your companions would follow me, sir,' Cato said politely and gestured towards the street at the corner of the temple. Pinto fell into step beside him as they set off.

'I trust your voyage was pleasant,' said Cato, by way of opening a conversation, trying not to be put off by the quaestor's disdain of a moment ago.

'As pleasant as any trip by sea can be. I don't find ships agreeable,' Pinto said with feeling. 'The motion of the deck under one's feet is rather upsetting to the stomach, not to make too fine a point of it.'

Cato felt his heart warm with sympathy towards the man. He suffered terribly from sea-sickness himself and spent most of the time on any voyage leaning over a side rail, waiting for the next bout of vomiting and retching to rack his slender frame.

'Still have your sea legs?'

Pinto hesitated and then nodded. 'Feels like I've had rather more wine than is good for me.'

'Is such a thing possible?'

They glanced at each other and shared a quick laugh, grateful for the chance to relieve themselves of the formal prickliness of first meeting. They turned the corner and saw Corbulo's party fifty paces ahead of them.

'So, Corbulo's been sent to tame the Parthians,' said Pinto. 'The best general in the entire army, I've been told.'

Cato pursed his lips. There were other fine commanders, but none with the length of experience and run of success of Corbulo.

'What do you make of him?' Pinto continued in a confidential tone.

'Too early to say with any certainty. I've not served under him before. But he seems confident. And he speaks directly to the issues at hand.'

'Which is why he has succeeded as a soldier rather than a politician.'

'Suits me. If we go up against Parthia, I'd rather be led by a man who knows how to face the enemy with a sword in his hand.'

'Rather than knowing how to wield a dagger and plant it in someone's back, eh?'

Cato glanced sidelong and saw that Pinto was grinning at him. 'Tribune, believe me, I know the difference between both types well enough. And Corbulo's military credentials are unimpeachable. Rest easy. You and your men are in good hands.'

'Glad to hear it . . . I dare say that your governor does not hold Corbulo in the same high regard.'

'Can you blame him? He was the most powerful official in the eastern Empire. Four legions under his direct command and scores of auxiliary units. Making a fortune from the sale of tax collection contracts. All until Corbulo pitched up. Quadratus is not used to playing the minor role. Especially when he feels he is the obvious choice to deal with Parthia. He knows the region. He knows the local rulers and he feels the job should have been his. Quite under-standable, really.'

Cato shrugged. 'What can I say? Nero made the appointment and sent Corbulo east. There's nothing left to be done but obey the orders. That goes for all of us.'

'I take it you were chosen for this role because you prefer to be a soldier and not a politician, like your general?'

'I didn't have a choice. My cohort was assigned to escort the general. Besides, I'm not a patrician. I don't get to play with the politicians.'

'Really?'

Cato was acutely conscious that he was being appraised by the other man, who was waiting for an explanation in lieu of having to pose pointed questions about Cato's background. That his father had once been a slave, and he himself had spent his childhood as a slave, was no source of shame for Cato. He was proud of his achievements. He had risen into the ranks of the equites, the second-highest class of Roman citizenry, purely by his own efforts. Few aristocrats could say the same. Of course, thanks to his lowly origins, he would never be admitted to the Senate. The pinnacle of his career, if he survived long enough and won the favour of the emperor, would be the post of Prefect of Egypt. That was the most senior post any member of the equites could aspire to. However, it was so unlikely that Cato rarely allowed himself to imagine such a prospect.

'Quintus Licinius Cato? I'm sure I've heard your name spoken when I was last in Rome a few years back.'

The opportunity to mention his achievements lay before him, but Cato refused to permit himself to boast. Instead he allowed himself the lesser victory of frustrating Pinto's curiosity, and glanced back over his shoulder at the group following them, and his gaze was again caught by the tall figure dressed in robes of the east.

'Who's the big man?'

'Him? Why, he's the reason we're all here and Parthia and Rome are at each other's throats again.'

'Oh?' Cato prompted.

'His name is Rhadamistus. Prince Rhadamistus. Heir to the throne of Iberia, a territory that borders Armenia. Only he was a bit impatient to inherit. So his father packed him off to Armenia at the head of an army so he could find his own kingdom to rule. Saved the old man the job of doing him in before he struck first. So he pitches up in Armenia, bribes the commander of the Roman garrison to hand over the previous king, butchers the entire royal family, and grabs the throne for himself. To make matters worse, the Roman governor of neighbouring Bithynia recognised his sovereignty without first referring the matter to Rome, which then made Rhadamistus our man.'

26

'So he's a liability, then?'

Pinto raised his hand and rocked the palm from side to side. 'He's a brave enough fellow, and strong with it, and his soldiers love him. Unfortunately, not enough of his subjects did, and they were happy to invite the Parthians in to kick him out. Only to discover that the Parthian replacement was almost as bad. Now we've got to put Rhadamistus back on the throne and make sure he stays there.'

Cato thought for a moment. 'There's no other candidate?'

'Not at the moment. It's down to our boy or the Parthian lad, Tiridates.' Pinto clicked his tongue. 'Can't say I envy the Armenians.'

'I'm sure that many foreigners regard Rome with similar sentiments, given some of the emperors we've had . . .' Cato coughed and continued quickly. 'Although I'm confident that Nero will turn out fine.'

'I'm sure he will.'

A short distance ahead the street opened out on to the Forum, burnished by the late-afternoon sunshine. Some of the traders were already packing up their stalls, but the main square was still bustling and the air was filled with the cries of tradesmen cutting above the hubbub of conversation and the clatter of hammers of metalsmiths. Directly opposite rose the columned facade of the merchant's house. It was built on a large scale and with such ostentation as to cause even the crassest of wealthy Romans to wince. A squad of Praetorians stood guard at the entrance and snapped to attention as Corbulo and Quadratus approached.

'I imagine you could use something to drink after your voyage,' said Cato.

'Too right. Be nice to have something to eat as well. And be sure that it'll stay down.'

Pinto picked up his pace and Cato lengthened his stride to stay at his side. Although the thought of a decent feast was welcome, the prospect of the tense meeting between his commander and the governor that would follow was not. With Parthia gathering its strength to hurl itself against the Roman frontier, now was not the time for Rome's leaders in the region to engage in a pissing contest to win glory and honour for themselves, Cato reflected. Not when so much was at stake. When empires clashed, victory was sure to go to the side that was not riven by division and competing ambition.

As they reached the entrance, Cato's chest heaved with frustration as he prepared himself for the coming encounter within the general's opulent quarters.

CHAPTER FOUR

Corbulo allowed his guests to drink and eat their fill before he called on the governor of Syria to join him in the merchant's study, which he had chosen to use as his office. Quadratus insisted on bringing Pinto with him.

'Very well, since you are insisting on witnesses . . .'

Quadratus shook his head. 'It's not that, my dear Corbulo. Of course I trust you, but I have reached an age when it is best to have an aide present, in case one loses track of details.'

Corbulo stared at him coldly before he rejoined: 'How wise. Then I shall do the same.'

He glanced round and raised his voice. 'Tribune Cato! Join us, please.'

Cato had been watching the by-play from the other side of the banqueting table that ran down the length of the main hall, and set down the seeded bun he had been eating absent-mindedly and made his way round to the others. Corbulo led them out of the hall, across a corridor and into his office, and closed the door behind them. The room was comfortably sized and there was plenty of space for the campaign desk set up for the general's scribes in addition to several cushioned stools used for briefings of his staff officers. A large window overlooked the garden in the centre of the house and a faint breeze stirred the fine material of the curtains on either side.

'Sit down, gentlemen,' Corbulo ordered and then, as the others eased themselves on to the stools, he remained standing, looking down on them. A neat ploy, Cato noted. The general had established his authority over Quadratus once again. And now he moved smartly on to addressing the governor as if he were a junior officer.

'Why did you not act upon my summons as soon as you received it? We've lost nearly a month when we should have been preparing for the campaign.'

'I came as quickly as I could. But there were matters that had to be attended to before I could leave Antioch. Syria is a large province, General. Its governance is complicated.'

'I don't require any lectures on administration, thank you. I summoned you to meet me here at once. Not at your leisure. In future, I expect a more timely response to any instructions I give you.'

Quadratus's expression became strained. 'You have no right to speak to me like that. I am a senator, as you are. I hold the governorship of one of the most prestigious provinces in the Empire. Indeed, thanks to my exemplary service, I have held the post for many years more than the previous incumbent.'

'That may change very soon,' Corbulo cut in. 'I dare say that if I reported that I considered it necessary to replace you, then Nero would readily agree. Of course, I hope that I will not have to. I'd rather make use of your extensive experience and contacts, as long as they are useful in planning and executing the campaign against Parthia.'

The governor could control his patience no longer and he stood abruptly. 'You go too far! By what authority do you act in such a high-handed manner? I have a good mind to report back to Rome myself and demand that you be recalled. I am certain that I can handle those Parthians myself, without any help from some soldier who has spent almost his entire career skulking around the forests of Germania . . .'

Cato watched his commander's face closely but saw not even a flicker of a reaction to the outburst. Instead, Corbulo calmly picked up a scroll from his desk and opened it out for Quadratus to see.

'There is my authority. Sealed with the imperial ring. "Gnaeus Domitius Corbulo is empowered to act in my name in all matters civil and military within the extent of, and including, the provinces stretching between Cappadocia and Judaea. I require all officials, regardless of rank, to obey his instructions as they would mine, on pain of being recalled to Rome to face charges of misconduct in public office, or treason, whichever is deemed appropriate to the individuals concerned." So, it seems that you have been placed under my direct command, Quadratus.'

The governor read, and then re-read, the imperial authority with a stony face before he clenched his jaw, nodded and resumed his seat. Corbulo turned to Pinto.

'Since the governor has had the foresight to insist on your presence, I require you to state that you have witnessed his reading and comprehension of the imperial authority. Do you agree?'

Pinto glanced at Quadratus for direction but the latter was staring directly ahead and gave him no sign. Pinto swallowed and nodded. 'Yes, sir.'

'And you, Tribune Cato. For the record.'

'I bear witness to that, sir.'

'Good. Then that's settled.'

Corbulo reached for a waxed slate on his desk and glanced over it before he continued. 'The first step will be to prepare our military effort. I will need up-to-date strength returns of every unit stationed within the provinces under my command, starting with Syria, since that is where most of them are concentrated. I want them as soon as possible. No further delays or excuses. Is that clear?'

'Perfectly clear,' Quadratus confirmed tightly.

'The backbone of my army will be the legions. You have four under your command based in Syria?'

Quadratus nodded. 'That's right. The Tenth, Twelfth, Third and Sixth. As soon as I received word of Nero's decision I moved some units to Bactris, on the Euphrates, to guard against Parthian raiders attempting to cross there.'

'A sensible precaution. Now, what of your other forces? Auxiliaries?'

'Eight infantry cohorts, but they're mostly dispersed in city and town garrisons across the province. Some are in forward outposts.'

'What about cavalry?'

'Five cohorts. Mostly on patrol duty.'

Corbulo did a quick estimate. 'Some twenty-six thousand men in all, then?'

'If they were all at full strength. I would be surprised if they numbered more than fifteen thousand as things stand.'

Corbulo made a note on his waxed tablet before he continued. 'Any special units? Archers, slingers?'

'One of the cohorts is from the Balearics. Slingers.'

The general made some more notes and then looked up again. 'So, as far as the legions go, which are the best?'

Quadratus paused before speaking and Cato saw a calculating look flit across his face for a moment. Then he shrugged as he replied: 'Oh, there's nothing much to choose between them. Of course, none of them have been in action for a long time. Aside from the odd punitive raid, or crowd control when things get out of hand at the chariot races. The only men with any campaigns under their belts are those who have transferred in from other legions. I'm sure they will perform well enough when called on to fight.'

'Hmmm, we'll see about that. As for their quality, from my own enquiries it seems that the Tenth and the Twelfth are in poor shape. So I'll be leaving those under your command for now. The other two I'll be taking under my direct command immediately, together with most of your auxiliaries. They are to march for Bactris the moment you return to Syria. I'll make sure you have their orders in writing before you leave us.'

Quadratus exchanged an anxious look with Pinto before he shook his head. 'But that will leave Syria open to attack. I barely have enough men to defend the province and keep the locals in line as it is.'

'That's nonsense, and you know it. There have always been far more troops than are required to maintain order. The legions are there to deter Parthia and to form the backbone of any army required to launch a campaign against the enemy. Now it's time for them to be put to use, and you will have more than enough left to hold Syria down. Besides, I am regarding the Tenth and Twelfth as my reserve, and it is more than likely I will be calling on them for replacements when the campaign gets under way. I may even require them to join the main army if the situation demands it. I would advise you to prepare your province for that contingency.'

'I protest!'

'Protest all you like. Put it in writing if that makes you feel better.

You can protest directly to the emperor if you wish. But given that my orders come directly from him, Nero may not appreciate having them called into question.'

Cato tried to hide his amusement as he watched Quadratus blanch and struggle to find any effective solution to his predicament. Corbulo gave him a moment to reflect before he continued. 'I am sure you will give me your full support for the duration of the conflict with Parthia. In turn I will be sure to keep you informed of any significant developments, and will confer with you regularly on the best way to proceed. Subject to my orders and the authority conferred on me.'

If it was meant as a sop of comfort then it had little effect, thought Cato as he regarded the governor's stony expression. It was more than likely that Quadratus would abide by the terms of Corbulo's authority to the absolute minimum, and would use back channels to his friends and allies in Rome to undermine his rival. To be fair, Cato mused, Corbulo would be sure to do the same. Even a successful general could not count on his indispensability and was obliged to play politics to cover his back.

'Moving on.' Corbulo nodded in the direction of the main hall where the other guests were still feasting. 'I take it the elaborately dressed giant in your retinue is Rhadamistus?'

'King Rhadamistus, yes.'

'A king without a kingdom is not much of a king, in my view. And since his father is not keen on having a potential rival return to Iberia, then he is barely worthy of the title "prince". The truth is, he is a tool of Roman policy. He will be returned to the throne of Armenia again only because Rome is prepared to force the issue at swordpoint. In return he will be our ally and will do our bidding henceforth. That is the price of our support. I dare say that some in Rome are already looking to ensure that Rhadamistus agrees to bequeath his kingdom to us on his death. At which point Armenia will become a fully fledged province of the Empire and that will put an end to Parthia's scheming.' Corbulo waved a hand dismissively. 'But that's work for the future. What matters now is getting him back on the throne as swiftly as possible. Aside from that motley crew of hangers-on that are with him, does he have any soldiers at his disposal? Or any allies he can call on to fight with him?'

Quadratus turned to Pinto. 'Well?'

His aide nodded. 'There's some men from the Iberian contingent his father provided him with to seize the throne in the first place. Five hundred infantry and perhaps two thousand mounted men. But that's all, sir. He was not on the throne long enough to make any firm alliances with surrounding kingdoms.'

'A pity,' Corbulo responded. 'Still, two and a half thousand men. That's something. Though not nearly enough for him to win back his kingdom alone. And that is the priority right now. I must have Armenia securely in our hands while I raise, equip and supply the army for any campaign against Parthia.'

Cato felt a chill of anxiety at the general's words. As far as Cato knew, the emperor's orders extended to retrieving Armenia. Was it possible that Corbulo intended on widening his remit? The prospect of yet another costly campaign across the vast expanse of unmapped Parthia filled Cato with foreboding.

Corbulo cleared his throat. 'I'll need to speak with Rhadamistus later. But for now, I'm pleased that we have established the basis of our working relationship, my dear Quadratus. Together, I am sure we will do the Empire proud. And while there's still wine and food to go round, I suggest you two return to the feast.'

It was a blunt dismissal and the governor and Pinto rose and made their way out of the room without another word. Once the door had closed behind them, Corbulo's features relaxed into a smile. 'I don't think I made any friends there. But he needed to be put firmly in his place.'

Cato nodded.

'I noted your expression at the end. When I mentioned a campaign against Parthia. I take it you disapprove of any wider operations?'

It was a very direct observation and Cato was discomforted that his superior had divined his feelings so easily. 'Sir, I have no say in the matter.'

'No say, but plenty of opinions, I'm sure. Speak freely, Cato. I value honest comments from my subordinates when the time is appropriate, and strict obedience once a matter is decided and the order is given.'

'Yes, sir. I share that philosophy.' Cato collected his thoughts. 'Very well. I can't help being concerned about the army being drawn into a wider conflict with Parthia. Rome has been down that road before and it has not gone well for us.'

'I am aware of that, and have no intention of repeating the mistake. I fully intend to limit the campaign to winning Armenia back for Rome. But if Vologases widens the conflict, then I have to be ready to meet any attacks across the Euphrates, as well as any attempt to seize Armenia once again. What I will not be doing is hurling myself deep into Parthia in an attempt to win deathless glory and fill my coffers with Parthian gold and silver.' Corbulo paused. 'I believe there is an unwritten contract between a general and the men he leads. An honourable general does not risk their lives unnecessarily, nor should he ever price his personal ambition above their lives. There, Tribune Cato. Does that reassure you?'

'Yes, sir. That's good to know.'

'And you can hold me to that standard. This I swear.' Corbulo moved round behind his table and sat down opposite Cato. 'I also believe in taking the initiative whenever possible. Keep the enemy off balance and the battle is half won. Which is why there must be no delay in restoring Rhadamistus to the Armenian throne. I dare say what's left of his army is little more than a rabble. Their ranks will need stiffening if he is to have any chance of success. He needs Roman soldiers behind him. And some siege equipment if his rival, Tiridates, decides to hold out in the capital city, Artaxata. The problem is, I have no troops directly to hand, except your cohort . . .'

Cato felt his heart beat faster. 'My cohort? But we were assigned to serve as your escort, sir. Who will guard you?'

'I don't need all of them to guard me. I'm quite safe here in Tarsus. A small party of bodyguards will suffice. Besides, I will have two legions and plenty of auxiliaries to hand once Quadratus sends them up from Syria. It will take many months to prepare the army for a campaign. It's likely I won't be able to move before next year. But a smaller force is much easier to provision and send on its way. That will be your command, Tribune. Your cohort and any auxiliary troops I can spare. Your orders will be to escort Rhadamistus and his forces to Artaxata and place him on the throne. Then you will assist the king in holding on until I am ready to bring the army up to deal with any threat from Parthia.'

'What if the Parthians reinforce Tiridates first, sir?'

'I doubt that will happen. Firstly, they too have to mobilise their forces and ready the necessary supplies. Secondly, I received some interesting intelligence from our sources in Parthia. It seems that King Vologases is facing a threat from one of his vassal states, the Hyrcanians. Better still, his son, Vardanes, has betrayed his father and thrown in his lot with the rebels.' Corbulo smiled thinly. 'The fact that he was handsomely bribed by Roman agents might have had something to do with it. In any case, he can afford the services of enough mercenaries to give his father plenty of trouble. More than enough to distract him from operations in Armenia for a while. Tiridates is on his own. So, you've no worries on that score, Tribune Cato.'

'I guess not, sir.'

'It should be a straightforward enough operation. It should take you no longer than three months from now. Get your man to the capital, get him on the throne and remain there until further orders. I'd say your biggest challenge is not to throttle the bastard before it's all over.'

'Sir?'

'I've heard enough about the man to know he's an arrogant individual with a cruel streak a mile wide.'

'Ah . . .'

'Just keep him out of trouble, Cato. I'm sure you can manage that. I've got to know you well enough these last few months to be confident you are just the man for the job.'

'If you say so, sir,' Cato said flatly.

There was a short silence before Corbulo gestured towards the door. 'That's all for now, Tribune. Best enjoy what's left of the feast. It'll probably be the last decent meal you'll get for a while.'

CHAPTER FIVE

'That's it.' Macro steadied the fishing rod in the boy's hands and patted him gently on the shoulder, as they stood on the edge of the river, not far from the city. 'You've got it, Lucius. Now you have to be patient. When the fish comes to the bait you must let it take a good bite. Not a nibble. You'll feel the rod move a little in your hands. But don't pull sharply yet. Wait for the fish to jerk the rod. Then you strike. Pull back hard to fix the hook and the fish is yours.'

Lucius looked up with an excited grin. 'Mine to eat for supper!'

'That's right. Of course, if you are really good, you'll catch enough for all of us to eat for supper.'

'Yes. I promise, Uncle Macmac.'

'Now then, young lad. You're old enough to stop using baby talk. No need for Macmac now. You can call me Macro when it's just you, me, Petronella or your dad about. Otherwise it's Centurion Macro, or sir. You understand?'

Lucius looked up seriously and nodded. 'Why?'

'If you want to be a soldier one day, you need to get used to it. Best start early, eh?' Macro reached down and repositioned his hand on the fishing rod. 'Now, concentrate. Uncle Macro's hungry and he wants fish for supper. Those are your orders for the day. Catch fish.'

'Catch fish,' Lucius repeated and pressed his lips together as he stared fixedly at the point where the line entered the flow of the river, creating a faint V on the surface of the water. Macro eased himself back and climbed through the reeds growing along the bank until he reached level ground, where Petronella was sitting in the shade of the trees as she unpacked the small hamper they had brought with them from Tarsus. The city, some two miles away, was just visible above a bend in the river, white stone and red-tiled roofs bright in the sunshine.

'I could use a drink,' said Macro as he sat heavily beside her.

Petronella handed him a flask filled from the public well outside the silversmith's house. They could have drunk from the river, but few people were prepared to do that downstream of a city. Macro pulled out the stopper, raised the neck of the flask to his lips and took several gulps before he set it down.

'Needed that. It's a hot day.'

'Too hot.' Petronella was fluttering a fan at the side of her face. 'I doubt I'll get used to it.'

'You will. I've seen enough of the Empire to know a person can get used to anything: the bitter cold and snow of the north, or the glare of the sun on a desert, so bright it hurts your eyes. You'll see.'

She glanced at him. 'Are we likely to be here some time?'

'Depends on the Parthians. If they're sensible, they'll see that Nero means business and they'll back off and leave Armenia to us. Once Rome makes a decision then everyone knows that we'll see it through to the end, whatever it takes. That's the reputation we've built up ever since the earliest times. Makes our enemies think twice before they take us on.'

'And yet the Parthians have decided to take Rome on.'

'Parthia's different,' said Macro. 'They think they're our equal. That's why they're prepared to take the risk from time to time.'

'And are they? As powerful as Rome?'

'Of course not,' Macro sniffed. 'Bunch of soft easterners. All flowing robes and eye make-up, as I recall.'

'And yet they're confident enough to defy Rome,' Petronella mused. 'Can't be that much of a pushover then. And if they're so soft, why haven't we made them part of the Empire already?'

Macro did not particularly like this line of questioning. It cast doubt on the proficiency of the Roman legions, of which he was inordinately proud. So he reverted to the standard line taken by soldiers keen to dispel the reputation of the Parthians.

'Oh, I suppose they can put up a decent fight from time to time. But the truth of it is that they're not proper soldiers. They don't fight fair. They're a crafty, devious, downright dishonest bunch. Full of tricks and traps. That's the only reason they've given us any trouble over the years.'

Petronella thought a moment. 'Sounds to me like they've found a successful way to deal with you and your legions.'

Macro laughed and patted her hand indulgently. 'Leave soldiering to the experts, my love. We know what we're talking about. I'm telling you. We'll sort the Parthians out without much trouble.'

'I hope so.' She stared at him and then cupped his bristly cheek in her hand. 'I'm just worried for you. That's all. You, and your friend Cato.' She nodded in the direction of Lucius, his head just visible amid the gently swaying tops of the reeds. 'And Lucius. He's already lost his mother. And his grandfather. Cato's all the family he has left.' She took his hand and squeezed it. 'I just want you both to come back from the campaign alive.'

'We've managed to survive so far. Been a few times when I thought we were done for, not that I'd admit to it at the time. But we'll be fine. I swear it, by Jupiter Best and Greatest.'

'Let's hope he's listening then. Macro, my love, I hate to say it, but you've been lucky. Luck doesn't tend to last. And there's, well . . .'

'Well?'

'Your age. You're no longer a young man. You've served out your enlistment, so why not retire, take your gratuity, and settle down somewhere quiet with me?'

Macro shifted uneasily. 'I'm still the man I was. And I've got some good years ahead of me. Besides, I have to look after the lads. They count on me. And there's Cato. He's clever and a gifted soldier, but he needs looking after too. A few more years in the legions for me, Petronella, that's all. I'll call it a day the moment I can't keep up with the rest. Anyway, this campaign should provide me with plenty of booty to pay for a decent home for us. The Parthians are as rich as Croesus. Easy pickings.'

'As long as you don't end up being pickings for them.'

'Pah!' Macro had had enough and pointed to the hamper. 'What did you bring for us to eat?'

'Lamb pastries, those falafel things the locals are keen on, and there's some fruit.'

'Sounds good.'

They stared out over the river silently for a moment, watching a cargo ship ease its way towards Tarsus under its sweeps, long oars with wide blades, handled by three men. Neither of them was keen to resume the earlier discussion about the coming campaign. At length Petronella spoke. 'Do you really think Lucius will catch anything?'

Macro shook his head. 'No. But it keeps the lad busy while I concentrate on you.' He put his arm round her waist and squeezed, drawing her closer. They kissed. Then again, longer this time, and then Petronella lay back and pulled him on top of her.

'No more talk. Make love to me.'

Macro eased the folds of her stola up, revealing her thighs. 'That's my girl . . .'

Lucius was getting hot under the noon sun and the fish weren't biting. No matter how hard he prayed to Fortuna or the local river god. Even though Macro had told him to keep the rod steady, he was getting bored and began to experiment by lifting it up so that the baited hook cleared the water and then letting it drop back again with a satisfying plop. But still there were no bites. He began to wonder if Macro had any further advice on how to catch fish. Macro seemed to know how to do everything. He could sharpen knives, carve wooden soldiers, tell rude jokes and spit further than Lucius ever managed. He recalled the phrase that Macro tended to use quite often in his company when things did not quite go as planned.

'Bollocks to this,' Lucius muttered with delight, then turned sharply to look up through the reeds. Petronella did not like him using 'soldier's curses' as she called them. She said that the son of a high-ranking officer must not use such language.

'Bollocks to that,' Lucius chuckled softly. 'Bollocks, bollocks, bollocks . . .'

He raised the rod and swung the line on to the riverbank and set it down before he climbed back through the reeds. As he approached the top he could hear Petronella letting out some soft cries. Pain or pleasure, it was hard to tell. Then he saw them, Macro on top, her legs wide, one tucked round his back.

40

Lucius shook his head. They were wrestling again. Just like the very first time he had found them at it and they'd hurriedly explained what they were doing. They liked to wrestle a lot. Macro always seemed to come off worse, letting out a deep groan and then rolling aside as he gave up the fight.

Lucius let out a soft sigh of exasperation as he turned away and made his way back down to the water's edge. They'd be wrestling for a while yet, he knew. And when Macro lost again they were always too tired to do anything for a while.

Lucius picked up his rod, checked that the small piece of gristle that served as bait was still firmly fixed to the hook and then cast it into the river. He squatted down, one hand holding the rod, the other supporting his chin, as he gazed across the water and waited for the first fish to bite.

Cato was waiting for them at the silversmith's house when they returned at dusk, tired but cheerful after their day by the river. In the end Lucius had caught three fish, late in the day when the cool air encouraged the fish to emerge from the shadier parts of the river. These he proudly raised for his father to see.

'I caught 'em! Once Uncle Macro showed me how.'

'Uncle Macro?' Cato smiled.

His friend nodded. 'We've moved things on from Macmac.'

'Pity, I had grown used to it. The men of the cohort will be disappointed as well.'

Macro's eyes narrowed. 'They wouldn't dare . . .'

'Not to your face.'

'The first one I catch will be digging the shit out of the centurions' latrines for the rest of the campaign.'

Cato's smiled faded as he considered the news he had to break to the three of them. But that could wait for a little while. He crouched down to admire his son's catches.

'They're beauties. Must have been a hard fight to land them.'

'Yes. Very hard.'

'Well done, Lucius. I'm very proud of you.' Cato tousled his hair. 'I can't wait to eat them for supper.'

'But they're mine.' Lucius looked crestfallen. 'I caught them.'

'Now, now, lad,' Macro intervened. 'Soldiers share their rations. If I'd caught them then I'd be sharing them with you.'

'But you didn't. Too busy wrestling with Petronella. That's why I caught them.'

'Wrestling?' Cato glanced up at the others. 'Oh, I see.'

Petronella darted forward, her face flushed, and took Lucius by the hand. 'Come, Master Lucius, we'll take those straight to the kitchen and cook up a feast for us all. How does that sound?'

'A feast! Yes, yes!'

Cato and Macro regarded them fondly as they disappeared down the corridor in the direction of the silversmith's kitchen.

'You have a fine son there, Cato.'

'Yes, I do.' He smiled proudly.

'I hope to have a son one day myself.'

'Petronella's not . . .'

'Not as far as I know. And not for want of us trying.'

'Ah yes, all that wrestling will pay off in the end,' Cato chuckled. 'I'm sure you'll have a son who will carry on in the same spirit as his father.'

Macro winced. 'The gods help me if he does. I was a right handful as a kid.'

'You do surprise me.'

The fish stew prepared by Petronella was sufficiently bountiful for Cato to suspect the surreptitious addition of other piscine matter from the pantry to bulk out the meal. The four of them were joined by the silversmith. Yusef was a rotund man with bulging eyes and a cheery face who bowed his head in gratitude when Cato indicated that he should take the seat at the head of the table. As the stew was brought in he rubbed his hands together and raised his nose to sniff.

'Ah! Superb!' He had been primed by Petronella and turned his gaze towards Lucius. 'I gather we have you to thank for furnishing us with this feast, young man.'

Lucius grinned with pride as Yusef waited until Petronella was seated before raising his cup. 'A toast to our skilled fisherman. To Lucius.'

'To Lucius,' the others echoed.

The boy raised his own cup. 'To me!'

The stew was a revelation to Cato. The fish had been diced and fried before being added to a thick base of onion, tomatoes and spices. There was a little heat to it that made him reach for some more watered wine, but the overall effect was delicious.

'One more reason to make this woman your wife, Macro.'

The centurion smiled happily and winked at Petronella.

The silversmith looked on with a mischievous expression. 'Indeed. But if he doesn't, then I'd be honoured to take your hand. If only to be certain of being served such divine food.'

Macro gave him a sharp look. 'I don't think the extra pounds would suit you.'

'I jest, Centurion. Truly. No one could ever replace my dear wife, rest her soul.' He reflected sadly for a moment. 'A sweet woman, but of a nervous disposition. I dare say she would have found our present circumstances rather frightening.'

Cato lowered his spoon. 'Oh?'

'The coming conflict with Parthia. Memories are long and the people of Tarsus still talk of the raids by bands of Parthians the last time Rome and Parthia went to war. The enemy scoured our lands, burning farms and villages, looting, murdering and raping as they went. There are few families in the city who did not suffer at their hands. Not to mention the damage to trade.' He raised his eyes. 'It took years to recover. So you will understand if I say that I hope cool heads and common sense prevail and war is averted between your glorious emperor Nero and the perfidious despot Vologases. Tarsus can ill afford such raids again.'

'No need to worry,' Macro responded. 'Corbulo knows his business. The eastern provinces will be safe in his hands. Besides, it'll be a while yet before the army's ready to march off to war.'

'I trust you are right, Centurion.'

Cato mentally winced at the exchange. With the cheerful homecoming of the fishing party and the warmth of the shared meal he had been putting off breaking the news about his orders from Corbulo. He cleared his throat.

'About that. I'm afraid we will be in action rather sooner than I'd thought.'

Everyone was looking at him, spoons poised. Cato set his down and leaned back as he continued. 'The general has given us our orders. The cohort will be leaving Tarsus in the next few days.'

Petronella swallowed. 'So soon? I thought it was going to take months to assemble the army.'

'So did I. I'm sorry that it isn't going to be that way.'

Yusef leaned forward with a frown. 'Is war that close?'

Cato was aware that he should not divulge any further details in front of his host. He liked the silversmith well enough, but there was a chance that he was the kind of man who might pass the information on socially and thereby inadvertently alert a Parthian agent to Cato's orders. 'I cannot say any more than that.'

'What's to become of us?' Petronella asked. 'Me and Lucius? Are we to go with you?'

Cato shook his head. 'I could not take the risk. You must stay here with Yusef.' He turned to the silversmith. 'That is, with your agreement. I will leave enough to cover their accommodation and food.'

Yusef nodded, his heavy jowls quivering as he smiled kindly. 'It would be an honour, Tribune.'

Lucius had been sitting in silence, and now he spoke up, his lip quivering slightly. 'Daddy and Uncle Macro are leaving us?'

Petronella put an arm round him. 'They have to, my pet. They need to help the emperor save us from the bad barbarians.'

'But I don't want them to go.' Lucius pursed his lips and blinked as the first tears pricked out of the corner of his eyes and ran over his small cheeks.

Petronella sighed as she rose from the table and picked the boy up. 'Come, it's time for sleep in any case. I'll tell you some stories if you're brave and dry those tears up.' At the doorway she turned and met Macro's gaze. 'We'll talk more about this later.'

'There's nothing to talk about, my love. We've got orders to obey. That's all there is to it.'

Her eyes narrowed. 'Hmmphhh.'

With Lucius gazing tearily over her shoulder she turned and left the room. As her footsteps echoed softly off the walls of the corridor Yusef stirred and lifted his ponderous bulk from his chair.

'I feel it is best I leave you two gentlemen to discuss the matter alone. No doubt there are things to be said that are not for my ears. I bid you a good night.'

He shuffled away and left Macro and Cato alone with the half-eaten meal.

'I'm not looking forward to having that talk with my beloved,' Macro puffed as he scratched his chin. Then he shifted round to face his friend with a gleam in his eyes. 'So where are we being sent, then?'

'Artaxata, capital of Armenia.'

Macro's eyebrows rose and he let out a low whistle. 'Just us? One cohort to invade an entire kingdom?'

'No, there'll be others. We're the spearpoint unit. I hope we'll be picking up some auxiliaries along the way. And there'll be another force of native troops, led by Prince Rhadamistus.'

'Who?' Macro's brow wrinkled as he concentrated. 'Oh yes, the pretender to the Armenian throne. How many men has he got?'

'A few thousand. No idea of their quality. But we'll find out when we join forces with them . . .' Cato reached for his cup of watered wine and took a sip. 'Same goes for Rhadamistus.'

'Any idea what's he like, then?'

'I haven't spoken to him yet. But from what I've heard, he's quite a character.'

'In a good way?'

Cato shrugged. 'We'll know soon enough.'

CHAPTER SIX

'Fuck me, he's a giant,' Macro muttered as the man who would be king of Armenia entered the general's office.

It was true, Cato noted, as Rhadamistus was obliged to duck his head to avoid the door frame. He was also broad enough across the shoulders to instinctively lead with his right in order to comfortably fit the width of the doorway. His bare forearms were like hams, and tanned almost to the colour of rind, so the comparison was apt. Jewelled rings glinted on his hands and his dark, oiled hair was held back neatly by a thin purple strip of silk.

He bowed his head to Corbulo and then eyed the other two officers carefully as the general returned the bow and gestured towards Cato and Macro as he spoke in Greek, the common tongue in the eastern Empire.

'Your Majesty, these are the two officers we spoke of yesterday. May I present Tribune Quintus Licinius Cato, commander of the Second Praetorian Cohort, and this is Centurion Lucius Cornelius Macro, his senior centurion and second in command.'

They bowed their heads as they heard their names. Cato, who could speak Greek fluently, had no difficulty following the introduction, but Macro, whose knowledge of the language was rusty struggled to keep up.

Rhadamistus made his way into the centre of the office and folded his arms as he looked down on the three Romans in front of him. Macro, who was already shorter than most, felt the flesh at the back of his neck bunch up slightly as he looked up at the Iberian prince. For the first time in his long career he felt himself to be in the presence of a man who would defeat him without question if

46

they ever met in a fight. Worse than defeat, thought Macro. Rhadamistus would crush him with his bare hands as easily as Macro could crush a tomato. He felt his stomach tighten anxiously at the thought. *Just as well the bastard's on our side . . .*

'It is a pleasure to meet you, Tribune.' Rhadamistus spoke in a voice that was higher pitched than Cato had expected. Nonetheless it was pleasant to the ear. 'And you, Centurion. My friend, the general, speaks highly of you both. I am pleased that you will be serving under me when I return to Armenia to kill that Parthian dog Tiridates and retake my throne.'

Cato stirred slightly at the implication that he would not be in command of the column. He met Corbulo's gaze and the general gave the slightest shake of the head to reassure him.

'And the centurion and I will be honoured to fight alongside you, Your Majesty.'

Rhadamistus smiled politely and turned back to Corbulo. 'I have already sent word to my soldiers in camp outside Antioch. They will march to Bactris as soon as they receive the order.'

'Good. I'm sure that they will make good use of the training I have arranged for them.'

Rhadamistus's smile faded slightly. 'I can assure you that they are already well trained. All they require to achieve victory is the support of our allies. We can do most of the fighting.'

'Of course. No one doubts the prowess of your Iberians. It's just that it would make sense for them to be familiarised with the way Roman soldiers operate, so that we can work together closely and effectively.'

'I understand and accept that, General. And now, what of my demand for siege engines? If Artaxata holds out against me I will need them to breach the walls.'

'I have given consideration to your request.' Corbulo laid just enough stress on the word for it to be noted. 'However, I have none to spare at present. They will be required to level the Parthian fortresses along the banks of the Euphrates when I cross the river and place my army between your kingdom and Parthia. Besides, most of the equipment is old and poorly maintained. It will be a considerable time before I have a siege train worthy of the name.'

Corbulo opened his hands. 'Believe me, Your Majesty, I would willingly provide it to you if I could.'

'Nevertheless, I must have bolt-throwers, onagers, towers and rams. Or my forces will be powerless before the least of the fortifications held against me in Armenia.'

'As I said, I wish I could help you.'

Rhadamistus drew himself up to his full height and stared back imperiously. 'I sense that you do not trust me with your precious siege weapons. If I am not given what I need, then there is very little point in me leading my men, and your soldiers, into Armenia. I will instead remain in Antioch and await the outcome of your campaign before I decide to act.'

Corbulo took a deep breath before he answered: 'Majesty, we have an agreement. You are to reclaim your kingdom as swiftly as possible, with whatever support I can furnish at this time. In return, when my army is ready to go into the field against Parthia, Rome has sworn to uphold your claim to the Armenian throne, whatever the cost.'

'My agreement is with your emperor. Nero has promised to give me the resources I need to take back my kingdom. I need siege engines. You will provide them. Or would you prefer that I send an envoy to Rome to take the matter up with the emperor directly?'

Cato watched as his general reflected on the threat and then accepted that he had been outflanked. If Rhadamistus did as he said, then, by the time the envoy returned with the response, there would be barely time to mount any operation in Armenia before winter fell across the mountainous landscape. Besides that, there was every possibility that the emperor would be infuriated at having his agreement with the prince questioned by one of his subordinates. Corbulo risked being recalled and his command handed over to Quadratus, a man who had very little military experience, while being desperate to win glory; a dangerous combination. It was in Rome's best interest, not to mention the general's, that Rhadamistus acted as swiftly as possible to recover his throne. All this Cato saw in an instant as his general wrestled with the dilemma and came to the same conclusion.

'Very well. For the sake of the sacred alliance between Your Majesty and the emperor, I will find some serviceable siege weapons to accompany your column.'

Rhadamistus nodded his gratitude graciously.

'But, as you will appreciate, the technical nature of the equipment requires specialists to operate and maintain it. Therefore the siege train will be entrusted to Tribune Cato and his men. They will ensure that it reaches Armenia safely and they will use the weapons to bring down the walls of your enemies, Majesty. I trust that is an arrangement that is acceptable to you?'

From his reading about previous wars in Parthia, Cato knew that the armies of the kingdoms of the east had limited expertise in siegecraft. Rhadamistus would be unlikely to make the best use of such equipment if the weapons were handed to him directly, and he knew it.

'Very well,' Rhadamistus replied. 'I accept your terms.'

'Thank you, Majesty,' Corbulo acknowledged as graciously as a man can who has been forced to give something up and be grateful for the privilege. 'I will see that the equipment is conveyed to Bactris as soon as possible. Well, then, I believe we have concluded our business now that you have been introduced to Tribune Cato and Centurion Macro. I will not impose upon you any further, Majesty. I am sure you have plenty of preparations of your own to make.'

'Indeed, General.' Rhadamistus exchanged a bow with the Roman officers and then nodded at Cato. 'I look forward to seeing you again at Bactris.'

'Yes, Majesty.'

Then Rhadamistus turned and strode from the room, ducking and slightly twisting once more as he passed through the doorway. At once the tension in the room eased and all three Romans breathed easily. They waited until his footsteps had retreated before Corbulo folded his hands together and sat back in his chair.

'I can guess what you are thinking, gentlemen, but we rarely get to choose our allies. That is what we have to work with and right now it is vital that we get our ally back into Armenia, where he can attempt to drive Parthia's usurper out.'

'Our usurper versus their usurper,' said Macro. 'May the best usurper win.'

Corbulo cocked his head. 'Are you in the habit of making such comments, Centurion? If so, please desist for the duration of our association, unless you would prefer to be broken back to the ranks.'

'Sorry, sir. Won't happen again.'

'Centurion Macro has a point, sir,' Cato intervened hastily to save his friend from provoking the ire of their commander any further. 'We need to make sure that our candidate has the best opportunity for success. We can't afford to leave anything to chance.'

'I don't intend to. Which is why I am sending you, and now a valuable siege train as well. I'll let you have sufficient onagers and bolt-throwers to take Artaxata. Our agents in Armenia report that almost all the Parthian troops have been withdrawn to deal with Vardanes and his Hyrcanian rebels. Now is the moment to strike and you will have more than enough men to do the job. So, in the centurion's words, the best usurper will win. Or there will be merry Hades to pay. For all of us.'

'Sir, may I ask what the plan is should Rhadamistus fail to retake his throne?'

'If failure looks certain, then you will extract your men from Armenia as swiftly and as safely as possible. It will be easier to replace our Iberian friend than an elite formation of the Roman army. I suspect Rhadamistus knows it and that's why he is obviously suspicious about the degree of our support for him. Who wouldn't be, in his situation? We have plenty of hostages of royal blood in Rome that we could use to replace him. If, for any reason, withdrawal is not possible, then you will ensure that the cohort's standards do not fall into enemy hands. Rome does not want to repeat the shame of the eagles we lost at Carrhae. That will be your responsibility as senior centurion, Macro.'

'Yes, sir. You have my word that the standards will not be taken.'

'Glad to hear that. It will also be your duty to train our friend's retainers as best you can before they march into Armenia. Time will be short and you will only have time for the rudiments. But they need to be able to act upon Roman commands if the column is going to fight as one.'

'Yes, sir. I'll drill the bastards into shape.'

Corbulo sucked in a breath. 'The preferred term is "esteemed allies". To their faces at least.'

'Esteemed allies, yes, sir. Not bastards. Right.'

Corbulo gave him a withering stare, but Macro did not flinch and gazed back, deadpan. The general turned his attention to Cato.

'Despite what Rhadamistus may think, and what I have just said to him, you will be the commander of the column. I will give you that authority in writing, and since my authority is conferred by the emperor himself, then that should be sufficient to keep Rhadamistus in line. In any case, you must make every effort to keep him on our side.'

'Even at the risk of endangering my men?'

'I will leave that to your judgement. And you'll have that in writing too.'

Cato tried to hide his sour reaction as he nodded. 'I understand, sir.'

'Don't take it that way, Cato. I have faith in your ability. You will do what is best. I took the time to ask around about you when I was passing through Rome on the way here. Seems like you have earned an enviable reputation for commanding men in the most difficult circumstances. That's why I have given you this job.'

'Yes, sir,' Cato replied flatly. It was in his nature to mistrust any flattery and to put most of his success down to contingencies over which he had no control. In his mind, he simply reacted as best he could. It would be the height of arrogance for him to even think in terms of mastering fate. Moreover, he was inclined to recoil from praise, suspicious of ulterior motives for it being offered. Almost the only person whose judgement of his abilities he trusted was Macro. The centurion never balked at calling him out on poor performance, and admitted any admiration grudgingly. And that suited Cato. He brushed the praise aside and turned to a matter that concerned him.

'Sir, while I can see that our ally may need to use a siege train, it occurs to me that making such equipment available to him might be a double-edged weapon. The one thing all the kingdoms of the east lack is an understanding of siege warfare, and siege weapons. It's what gives Rome a valuable advantage when we go to war in the

51

region. If Rhadamistus decides to change sides, then we'll be handing him the ability to destroy our frontier outposts and our fortresses. Worse still, if we are defeated and they fall into Parthian hands, then it may tilt the balance in their favour.'

'Then your orders are to make sure that does not happen. If Rhadamistus betrays us, or there is any danger of the siege weapons being captured by the enemy, you will destroy them, at all cost. Is that clear?'

'Yes, sir.'

'Unless there is anything else, I think matters are concluded here. You can requisition supplies from the procurator's stores in Tarsus to cover most of your needs for the march to Bactris. Anything else you can requisition on the way. Make sure you sign for it and direct the recipients to my headquarters. It may take them a while to be paid, but you may tell them that I will honour all requisitions. No point in alienating the people behind our backs when we face the Parthians.'

'Indeed not, sir.'

'I may see you at Bactris before you march on Armenia. Otherwise, the next time we meet will be at Artaxata, assuming your mission is a success. That's all. Dismissed.'

'That's all?' Macro growled as they descended the steps of the general's headquarters and started down the street towards the silversmith's house. 'If we see this thing through, put Rhadamistus on the throne and stay long enough to make sure he's secure, it could be a year or more before we're back from Armenia.'

'More than a year, I'd guess,' Cato responded. 'Given the time it is going to take Corbulo to concentrate his army and ensure it is equipped, supplied and trained for the campaign. He won't be able to reach Artaxata until after the coming winter. After that we'll be remaining in the field until the Parthians are defeated, or they sue for peace. That could take years.'

'Shit . . . Petronella's not going to like this.'

'Nor Lucius. I'm going to miss him badly.'

They walked on in silence for a moment, between the stalls that lined the street leading off the Forum, ignoring the appeals of the traders to stop and examine their wares. As they turned the corner into a quieter street, Cato spoke again. 'You had your chance to apply for a discharge. Perhaps you should have taken it while you could.'

'And miss all the fun?'

'Instead, you'll be missing your woman.'

Macro coughed. 'She'll understand. Once we get past the shouting and the tears, anyway. I'm hoping that me leaving her everything in my will might go some way towards saving my knackers tonight.'

'I think she might have another use for those, being the last night before the cohort marches out.'

Macro laughed. 'There is that. Just hope Petronella keeps it warm for me while I'm away.'

Cato looked at him. 'Come on. The woman's smitten. I've seen the way she looks at you. She'll be waiting and won't forget you, nor even look at another man. I'd bet on it.'

'Oh yes? How much?'

'I'd place a wager, but it would be like stealing cake from a baby. Come on, Macro, you know I'm right. Petronella and you were destined for each other. Never seen a finer match. Mind you,' Cato reflected bitterly, 'I felt the same way about Julia. And we know how that ended.'

Macro patted him on the shoulder. 'We don't know for certain, lad.'

'And we never will,' Cato replied through gritted teeth, and increased his pace so that he drew slightly ahead of the centurion in the narrow thoroughfare. Macro thought about catching up, but knew his friend well enough to leave him be when his thoughts turned to his late wife, whose fidelity he would never be able to be certain of now that she was dead. It would be good for Cato to get back in the field and have every hour filled with the duties and concerns of a commander, and leave little or no time for the things that tormented his soul and tipped him into that well of misery that was forever at his back.

As for himself? Macro shrugged. He loved Petronella like no woman he had encountered before. Not that he had ever been much of a one for love. Lust, yes. Nothing better than drink and a good fuck with a cheery whore when he was off duty in any of his postings around the Empire. Some of the women he had liked well enough, but not enough to miss when he moved on. But Petronella had cut her way through his tough hide right to his heart, and the thought of being without her for over a year brought on a pang of despair that was an entirely new experience for Macro.

'Fuck me,' he muttered as he thrust his way past a pushy orange seller, upsetting his basket and spilling the fruit into the street. His curses filled the air, but Macro ignored him and trudged on without the slightest inclination to turn on the man and give him a thick ear. He shook his head. 'What, in Jupiter's name, has happened to me?'

CHAPTER SEVEN

There were already plenty of signs of the initial preparations for the coming campaign as they approached Bactris eight days later. A short distance from the frontier fortress a road joined them from the south, upon which rumbled an escorted convoy of supply wagons. A large cloud of dust obscured all but the leading wagons and Cato gave the order to pick up the pace so that the cohort would get ahead of the convoy before it reached the junction. It was bad enough for his men with the dust their boots kicked up, and the fine powder and grit cloaked them in an ashen patina. Lips and throats were dry and the lines in men's faces were more clearly marked beneath their dusty fringes, so that each individual looked as if he had aged ten years or more since they had left the comforts of Tarsus. Cato and Macro rode at the front of the column and so were spared the worst of the dust.

Turning in his saddle, Cato glanced back over the column with a wry smile. This was a far cry from the luxurious conditions the Praetorian Guard usually enjoyed, cosseted in their barracks on the edge of Rome. Some might have accused them of having gone soft long ago. Such complaints were usually to be heard from the legions based on the Empire's frontiers, where life was harder, and usually more dangerous. But the men of the Second Cohort had proved themselves to be fine warriors when he had led them to put down a revolt in Hispania, and he had no doubts about how they would acquit themselves against the enemy here on the opposite frontier of the Empire.

It was late in the afternoon, the heat was slowly dissipating and he looked forward to making camp at the end of the day.

'Any stragglers to report, Centurion Macro?'

'None so far today, sir. Been three clear days since the last one fell out of line. The lads are in fine fettle. Grumbling of course, and the usual barrack room lawyers have said their piece, and I've said mine and I'm happy to say the matter is closed.'

Cato could imagine that more than words had been exchanged between Macro and the men, but then that was why centurions carried knotted vine canes. They tended to emphasise the officers' point very effectively.

Ahead, the road curved between low hills and there, not two miles ahead, lay the gleaming ribbon of the Euphrates river, flowing through the heavily cultivated land spreading out on either bank. The road descended in an easy slope towards the fortress town of Bactris, built on a slight bluff from where lookouts could see a considerable distance into the lands claimed by Parthia. Around the town looped the river, flowing swiftly between shingle beds for a stretch which permitted fording of the river. Because of this Bactris had a crucial strategic significance for both Rome and Parthia. Spread along the riverbank were the camps of three auxiliary units and the single cohort of legionaries Quadratus had sent. Macro frowned as he shaded his eyes with a hand and scrutinised the lines of tents without any surrounding ramparts.

'Lazy bastards haven't even set up marching camps. Someone might have told them we're at war.'

Cato nodded. This close to the frontier the units should have constructed the regulation 'camp in the face of the enemy' with palisade-topped ramparts at least twice the normal height, with watchtowers at each corner. If this was the approach adopted by the soldiers of the eastern frontier then they would be in for a rude shock when General Corbulo arrived to take personal command.

'And no sign of the siege train,' said Cato. 'Still on the road, I expect.'

'Assuming they have started out. I doubt that Quadratus is going to be happy when he hears that he's going to have to hand some kit over to Rhadamistus. A denarius to a sestertius he'll be kicking up a fuss and delaying sending the siege train on for as long as possible.'

56

'Maybe, but I suspect the general will have anticipated that and will be breathing down his neck to get the job done.'

'You hope . . . Look there.' Macro pointed to the other side of the town, where a large cluster of palm trees grew a short distance from Bactris's walls. A much larger camp sprawled amongst the trees and along the fringes. Lines of tethered horses were shaded by the palm fronds and here and there were clusters of brightly coloured tents.

'I expect those are our esteemed allies,' said Cato. 'We'll make camp just beyond them.'

'Not by the auxiliary lads?'

Cato shook his head. 'Might as well start setting an example to Rhadamistus and his men of what's required when we march into Armenia.'

He took a firm grip of his reins. 'You take charge here. I'll ride ahead and find our friend. One of those cohorts should be the slingers. Send a man to find their commander and have him report to my tent after the evening meal.'

'Yes, sir.'

They exchanged a quick salute, and Cato urged his mount into an easy canter and headed down the road towards the fortress town. Although he had said nothing to Macro, he was furious at the lack of precautions being taken by the auxiliary cohorts and was determined to give the commander of the slingers a dressing-down when they met later. He would pay the other units a visit as well, and make damned sure they followed suit and erected proper defences. After that, he'd tackle the trickier prospect of getting the Iberians to adopt Roman camp techniques. It would require a degree of tact and determination, since Rhadamistus would not take kindly to being treated as a subordinate. But that was bitter medicine he might as well have to swallow now before they marched to war. Better that than have unnecessary friction linger between the easterners and the Roman units.

As he left the road and angled towards the Iberian camp, the sun was low in the sky, bathing the landscape in a rich red-gold hue that Cato recalled from his last posting to the eastern frontier. That was when he had first met Julia . . . Her face briefly loomed in his mind's eye before he forced himself to dismiss any thought of her and concentrate on the preparations he must make to get his small column ready for war.

He rode straight into the camp unchallenged and reined in beside a cluster of tents. A handful of richly dressed men were lying on cushions drinking and talking as one of their servants laid a fire. They paused to look over the dusty rider, who raised a hand in greeting.

'Where can I find Prince Rhadamistus?' Cato asked in Greek.

There was a pause before one of the men replied in a thick accent: 'The king is beyond the trees, by the river. Through there.'

He rose on his cushion and indicated a path between the palms. Cato could see the gleam of water beyond and he nodded his head in thanks and slipped down from his saddle to lead his horse on. As he passed through the camp his keen eyes noted the details of the men around him. There was little of the uniformity of kit and dress of Roman soldiers, but the men seemed in good spirits and their mounts looked healthy and well-groomed. A few looked up curiously as he walked by. On the far side of the belt of trees the ground sloped gently to the reeds that fringed the Euphrates. Groups of horses were being watered and some of the men had stripped to splash around in the shallows. Others took the opportunity to wash clothes and rid them of the dust that was a constant discomfort of the region.

To his left, a hundred or so paces away, were several tents, one of which was the largest in the camp, and Cato made for it. This time he was challenged by the guards in green robes who stood in a loose ring around their king's encampment. Two men stepped into his path, spears in hand.

'I would speak with Rha—, His Majesty,' Cato corrected himself. 'At once.'

The two guards stared at him, then had a brief exchange. One gestured to him to remain where he was before turning and walking, unhurriedly, towards the largest tent. His companion watched the Roman visitor closely as Cato stood by his mount and patted its cheek as it loomed over his shoulder, champing gently. The inside of his thighs felt hot and sore from the long hours in the saddle and he looked longingly towards the men swimming in the river. At length the guard returned with a man in a black gown embroidered with golden stars and crescents. His skin was dark, his lips black, and he smiled as he stood in front of Cato, hands on hips.

'Who have we here?' He spoke in Greek as he tilted his head to one side. 'What manner of creature is this that has blown out of the desert?'

Cato glanced down at himself and saw that the medals on his harness and the finer accoutrements of his dress were dulled to a uniform grey grubbiness, along with every bit of his flesh exposed to the dust. Not a very favourable impression of Roman smartness, he conceded to himself. He cleared his throat to ensure that his response was comprehensible.

'I am Tribune Cato, commander of the Armenian column. I wish to speak with your king.'

'Commander?' The Iberian noble arched an eyebrow. 'I see. Please follow me. You can leave your mount with these men.'

Cato handed the reins over and followed the noble towards the main tent. A large slave in a turban held the curtains aside as they entered. It took a moment for Cato's eyes to adjust to the dim interior, and then he saw that it was fringed with cushions. In the middle sat Rhadamistus, and around him were arranged several men, dressed in the same fashion as the noble who escorted Cato. The king smiled a greeting and beckoned to his visitor.

'My dear tribune! Your presence honours my humble tent. Please, be seated.' He snapped a few curt words and one of his retinue scrambled off his cushions and backed away from the group. Cato sat himself down with as much decorum as his sore legs and backside permitted, and a small cloud of dust stirred from the folds of his tunic as he settled heavily.

'Do you require a change of clothes?' Rhadamistus asked solicitously. 'I can send for a silk robe while your armour and clothing are cleaned.'

It was a tempting offer, but grimy as he was, Cato did not feel it appropriate to disrobe or surrender to the comforts of an eastern potentate. 'I thank you, but that will not be necessary. I will not be interrupting your gathering for long, Majesty.'

'Something to drink then?'

This Cato felt he could accept without compromising the dignity of Rome's military. He nodded. 'Thank you, Majesty.'

Rhadamistus shot an order at the man whose place Cato had taken and he hurried out of the tent.

'I take it your Praetorians are not far behind you on the road from Tarsus?'

'They will be making camp within the hour.'

'Good! And the siege train also?'

'That is arriving separately, from Antioch. Within a matter of days.'

'Then we are almost ready to march against Tiridates.' Rhadamistus smiled briefly and Cato watched as the smile faded into a look of cruel amusement. 'And when I have the man in my hands, along with his family and all those in Armenia who call themselves his friends, the waters of the Araxes will run red with their blood.' Then he laughed and grinned at Cato. 'Apologies, Tribune. A moment's indulgence in the art of revenge. But we must not make our omelette before we have cracked our eggs. I believe that is the saying.'

'Yes, Majesty, something like that. Which brings me to the purpose of my visit.'

'Oh?'

They were interrupted by the return of the noble. Behind him came a slave, stripped to the waist, carrying a large silver tray bearing a glass beaker and a tray of honeyed pastries and dried fruit. He set the tray down beside Cato and backed out of the tent, bowing deeply. Cato gratefully lifted the glass and took a sip. The water was delightfully cool and scented with something sweet, and he savoured every drop.

'You mentioned the purpose of your visit,' Rhadamistus prompted.

'Ah, yes. Forgive me, Majesty.' Cato set the glass down and sat straight, hands folded in his lap. 'While we await the arrival of the siege train and the supplies bound for our column, we can begin training your soldiers in our ways of fighting, so that we might tackle the enemy in the most effective manner possible.'

'Training?' The Iberian prince shifted on his cushions and sat up.

60

'I thank you for the offer but I am confident that my troops will acquit themselves excellently when the time comes.'

Cato was tempted to remark that if that was so then they would be comfortably ensconced in the Armenian capital rather than in exile, living in tents along the banks of the Euphrates, protected by the frontier of the Roman Empire. Instead, he concentrated his weary mind on being diplomatic.

'I do not doubt their quality. I am fully aware of the potency of your horse-archers and cataphracts. Nevertheless, your troops and mine must work together if we are to defeat your enemies, Majesty. For example, I noted that your camp is unprotected. No rampart. No defences of any kind. If a band of Parthian raiders were to attack tonight then they would rout your men and carry away your mounts before I could lift a hand to help you.' Cato took the opportunity to drive the message home. 'Why, you yourself would be virtually defenceless, to be killed or captured. And Tiridates would remain on the Armenian throne. We cannot allow that to happen.'

'No, we can't.' Rhadamistus stroked his beard thoughtfully. 'Very well, Tribune. I will have my infantry mustered tomorrow for your men to train.'

'What of your mounted men?'

'Most are from noble families, the rest are paid retainers of their households. Are you suggesting men of high rank be trained alongside peasants? They would not stand for it.'

'But you are their king. They will do as you say, surely?'

'Yes, to a point. And if you humble or humiliate enough of them then you can be sure muttered complaints will lead to whispered plots and then no king is safe. I would hope that is not your intention, Tribune. It is better we do not undermine their pride. Therefore they will not be part of the training,' he concluded firmly.

Cato considered protesting, but realised there would be little purpose to it, and so nodded instead. 'As you wish, Majesty. I will have Centurion Macro take charge of drilling your infantry. He does not speak your tongue, though he has some Greek, so if one of your officers who knows some Latin could act as translator?'

'Of course.' Rhadamistus spoke quickly to the man who had given up his place for Cato. 'Narses will be at your service. You will find that Greek is widely spoken in the east, but Narses will be on hand for those who don't speak it.'

'Thank you.' Cato had concluded his business and stirred, ready to rise to his feet. But the audience was not yet over.

'One last thing, Tribune.'

Cato paused, halfway up, and then decided it would better to stand. 'Majesty?'

'My men require some additional training. Beyond obeying simple commands and digging camp fortifications.'

'I can arrange for weapons drill, or basic formations, Majesty.'

'That's not what I had in mind. It occurs to me that it would be useful for my men to become familiar with your siege engines, when they reach us. Together with the rudiments of siegecraft.'

Cato was silent for an instant while he considered his response. Mindful of his orders from Corbulo, he was reluctant to agree to the suggestion. 'Majesty, it is a difficult art to master, and we will be advancing to Armenia the moment the siege train arrives in any case. There will be no time available for such training.'

'I am sure that we can find time for a little instruction at the end of each day.' Rhadamistus smiled. 'After our camp has been constructed to your satisfaction. Surely it would only benefit our cause? If anything happened to your men then mine would be able to replace them. Otherwise the weapons would be quite useless. I am sure you see the good sense of my request.'

Cato saw the possible purpose of it clearly enough. In the event that the Iberians turned against Rome, they could take prisoner, or massacre, Cato and his men and use the siege weapons against their former owners. But for the present the prince's argument was sound enough.

'I will see what can be arranged, Majesty.' Cato bowed his head. 'Now, if I may, I need to return to my cohort.'

'A pity. I would offer you the hospitality of my humble tent. Perhaps I might entertain you, and your officers, another evening?'

'You are most generous.'

'It would be a pleasure.' Rhadamistus gestured towards the tent flaps. 'And now you may leave our presence.'

Cato backed away several paces before he turned and strode

outside. The sun had sunk behind the belt of palm trees and their fronds were dark against the brilliant orange glow of the sky. Swifts darted through the warm air hunting for insects and the river looked cool and inviting as it flowed languidly towards the bluff on which Bactris perched. Despite the beautiful tranquillity of the scene, Cato's mind was troubled. Already it was apparent that his ally would not accept that the command of the column should fall to a mere Roman tribune. Rhadamistus was determined to lead, with Cato relegated to an advisory role. Worse still, he was determined to learn the Roman way of siege warfare, the very thing that Corbulo was determined to prevent. Cato was caught between the orders he had been given and the need to maintain an alliance with the ambitious and headstrong Iberian prince.

'Fuck,' he muttered to himself as he approached the man holding his horse. He took the reins and swung himself up into the saddle, wincing as his thighs rubbed on the tough leather. With a quick jerk of the reins and a tap of his heels he wheeled his mount round, then trotted back through the trees and rode around Bactris to rejoin his cohort.

CHAPTER EIGHT

'What a bloody shower of utter wasters.' Macro scowled as he ran his eyes over the Iberians loosely assembled before him, some five hundred men dressed in blue robes and leather jerkins. Most had armour and helmets, though of widely varying pattern and quality. Some had no armour at all. They ranged in age from boys of fourteen or so up to a handful of wizened veterans who leaned on their spears as if they were walking sticks. The men occupied a patch of relatively flat open ground in the shadow of Bactris's walls. The sun had barely risen and the air was pleasantly fresh as the spearmen casually strolled out of their camp to the appointed place, chatting happily in small groups. Cato was also present, in order to make the introductions between Macro and Narses. After a brief exchange of greetings, Macro faced his new charges and stood with legs apart, gently tapping the vine cane in the palm of his spare hand. He had already prepared for the morning's drill by planting slender poles in a line across the stony scrub. A cart stood at one end, filled with picks and shovels. Two mules grazed nearby while a section of Praetorians leaned against the cart with amused expressions as they looked upon the men they would be helping their centurion to train.

'A more infamous-looking band of rogues I have rarely seen,' Cato agreed. 'But we must work with what we have. I need them to march at our pace, adopt our formations, respond to commands in Latin. But above all, I need them to be able to construct decent fortifications. The column is lacking in numbers as it is. If we run into any larger force then our lives are going to depend on fieldworks to even the odds.'

'That's fine, sir. By the time I'm done with 'em they'll be treating those pickaxes like an extension of their arms.'

'I have every confidence in you, Macro.' Cato slapped him on the back and raised his voice to conclude the exchange formally. 'If you need me, I'll be with the garrison quartermaster in Bactris. Carry on, Centurion.'

Macro saluted as his friend turned away and strode towards the town. Both of them had stripped and bathed in the river the previous evening, once the camp had been established and the passwords given to the duty officers. A change of clothing and a shave had made them both feel more comfortable and presentable. All to the background noises of the three auxiliary cohorts labouring into the darkness to construct proper fortifications to protect their camps. The Praetorian Guard might well be the most pampered formation in the Roman army, but they trained diligently and so were able to erect their camp in half the time of their auxiliary comrades.

Only the slingers had been up to the standard of the auxiliary units Macro and Cato had campaigned alongside in Britannia. The other cohorts had been stationed in Syria for far longer than was good for them. Garrison duty and escorting tax collectors meant that the nearest thing to combat that most of them had experienced was manhandling an irate taxpayer. Their kit was in poor shape and Macro could not help wondering how General Corbulo was ever going to mould this unpromising material into anything proficient enough to confront and defeat the Parthians. To Macro's mind, it was a toss-up as to who was more likely to break his heart: the auxiliaries, or the Iberians waiting in front of him.

He breathed in and turned to his translator.

'All right, Narses. Let's begin. I'll keep it brief. You translate when I pause. First thing is timing. We have to get these lads to do everything at the same time, or it'll all go tits up in no time.'

Narses frowned as he glanced at the birds circling overhead. 'Tits up?'

'Military term,' said Macro. 'I'll try and keep it jargon-free then. The term means it'll end in confusion. Which we do not want.'

'Ah!'

'So, when I give a command, I want the men to count to three very loudly and together before they carry out the order. That way, they'll do it at the same time. See?'

Narses nodded.

'Tell them to repeat exactly what I say.' Macro waited for Narses to translate, then filled his lungs, raised his hand to count off with his fingers and bellowed: 'ONE . . . TWO . . . THREE!'

There followed a ragged mumbling noise like a crowd gathering in a marketplace. Macro did not even wait until the noise had faded away.

'What the flying fuck was that?' he raged, then, as Narses struggled to find the right words to convey the colloquialism, he rounded on the translator. 'Stop!' He took a calm breath. 'Right, then, I will point at you when I need you to speak. You will not utter a single bloody sound until that moment. Clear?'

'Yes,' Narses said sheepishly.

'"Yes, sir" is the correct form of address when you speak to me from now on. Understood?' Macro gave him a warning look to ensure Narses got the point at once.

'Yes, sir.'

'That's better. Right. Let's try again. ONE . . . TWO . . . THREE!'

This time the Iberians at least managed to pause between each outbreak of cacophony.

'Holy fuck!' Macro shook his head in despair. 'Right, let's try one number at a time. ONE!'

It took most of the morning for Macro to drill them to get the timing right and repeat and act on basic commands. Then he divided them into centuries and chose those who seemed to be the best amongst them as their officers. Narses intervened to explain that they were usually divided into companies based on the regions they had been recruited from and were led by their local lord. But Macro was having none of it and insisted that they were organised according to the Roman model. The Iberians were happy to acquiesce, as any change from the norm was of passing interest to bored soldiers.

At length he told them to lay down their spears and watch as he turned on the Praetorians and ordered them to construct a ten-foot section of a marching camp rampart. The men had spent most of the morning watching in amusement from the shade of the cart, but rose nimbly and set to work with a will, keen to impress the Iberians with their professionalism. Once Macro pronounced himself satisfied with their efforts, he clambered on to the rampart and gave the order for the Iberians to line up to be issued with their pickaxes, which they examined curiously.

'In case you are wondering,' he began, 'you are holding in your hands Rome's secret weapon. This tool is what makes us all but invincible. Because it allows us to turn the terrain to our advantage and keep the barbarian bastards at bay while we cut 'em down with javelins, slingshot and every other nasty thing we can throw at them,' he explained with relish. 'In this world there are two kinds of men. Those who die and those who dig. You dig.' He indicated the sweating Praetorians. 'They've shown you the way. Now it's your turn. Line up!'

Narses translated and the Iberians formed up along the line of posts Macro had erected for them. When the last man was in place Macro raised his arm.

'On my command . . . Dig!'

'One, two, three, dig!' the Iberians chorused and then swung their picks into the hard ground and set to work.

Macro wiped the perspiration from his brow and reached for his canteen as he looked on with the severe expression he customarily used to hide his satisfaction from the men he trained.

'Not too bad,' he muttered grudgingly. 'I may make half-decent soldiers of 'em yet.'

The quartermaster's office enjoyed a fine outlook from the wall above the Euphrates, offering a panoramic view over the river and along the bank where the auxiliary camps stretched out across open ground. At one time, the room served as the magazine for the bolt-throwers and onagers that had been mounted on the platform outside. But during the long years since any Parthian army had been sighted from the fortress, the weapons had fallen into disrepair and then finally been dismantled and removed. In their place a canopy had been erected, and the quartermaster was cultivating tomatoes and oranges in large pots arranged about his well-appointed sanctuary. No doubt, thought Cato, an occasional gift to the commander of Bactris's garrison ensured that he retained his pleasant accommodation.

Graniculus was a slender man, as cultivated as his carefully tended plants, and he had a small library in his office along with the shelves laden with records of the supplies that came and went from the large granaries and storage cellars beneath the fortress town's citadel. He had welcomed Cato to his offices and plied him with good wine and such fine snacks as the local market provided. His posting, while comfortable, must have been frustrating in the dearth of companions with similarly elevated interests, and for the first hour or so he had insisted on discussing the news from Rome, political, cultural and intellectual, whenever the occasion arose. For his part Cato was happy to relate what he knew, before steering the conversation back to the matter at hand.

The document bearing the general's authorisation was read through once before Graniculus smiled and led the tribune through to his terrace, where they sat on cushioned seats either side of a cedar table inlaid with ivory geometric patterns. There, sipping his wine, Cato enquired about what stocks of food and equipment were being held at Bactris, and then proceeded to list his requirements. The quartermaster nodded as he took notes on his waxed slate and raised only one issue as he sucked a breath in through his teeth.

'Lead shot for your slingers is a problem, sir. We have very little on the inventory. There's been no need for it as long as I've been in this post. I did send a request to Antioch for fresh supplies when I did my first audit, but received no reply. Perhaps, given the situation, the clerks there might be more forthcoming now.'

'They might,' Cato agreed. 'But it's going to be a bit bloody late for my needs. Are there any forts or outposts nearby that might be able to send us their stock?'

'I doubt it, sir. They get their supplies from us. And I can't recall them ever asking for shot.'

'Damn. What about sourcing some supplies here in Bactris? There must be some metalworkers and forges. We'd just need the lead to melt and cast. Of course, they'd need to make the moulds, but that's simple enough.'

The quartermaster nodded. 'I know some of the local smiths. Let me talk to them, sir. See what I can do.'

He made another note. 'Is there anything else, sir?'

Cato reflected. He had already been guaranteed all the supplies he needed for the men, horses and mules for his column, together with spare leather for boots, jerkins and armour fastenings, javelin tips, shafts, caltrops, and ammunition for the siege train when it arrived.

'I think that's everything.'

Graniculus closed his tablet and set down the stylus before reaching for the wine jug to top up their cups. Cato could not help smiling.

'In all my years in the army I can't recall encountering a more helpful quartermaster. I must say, it makes a delightful change from having to beg or make threats to get just half of what I need.'

'That's because you are first in line, sir. It'll be different when the rest of the army turns up. Then I imagine you'll find I become more like those you have met before.' Graniculus sighed sadly. 'I shall miss this being a quiet little backwater. I've never known a more peaceful posting. I intend to remain here when I get my discharge. Even though there are few enough men of letters from Rome passing through.'

'What about merchants and traders from the east? Surely they have some learning of interest to you?'

'You may be right, sir. But I'll never know. They're strictly forbidden from entering Roman territory. They can bring their merchandise across the river to the landing platform to trade, but they are allowed no further. It's the same for trade going the other way. There may not have been war between Rome and Parthia, but there has always been deep suspicion and both sides have been anxious to limit the opportunities for spies to cross the frontier.'

'So there's no one I could speak to about the terrain on the other side of the Euphrates and the route to Artaxata?'

Graniculus shook his head. 'There are spies on both sides, to be sure. But I have nothing to do with that side of things. As far as the terrain goes, no Roman in Bactris knows more than what they can see from the top of our tallest watchtower. But that will change, of course, once Corbulo crosses the river.'

'True. However, I can't help thinking that advancing across unmapped ground with the vaguest idea where the next town, river or mountain range happens to be is a little chancy, to say the least.'

'An itinerary of the route would be useful, I agree, sir. But there is none as far as I know. I imagine there might be something useful to be found in the Great Library in Alexandria, or one of the libraries of Rome. If only there was more time or inclination to consult such resources. But . . .'

Cato caught the cautious look on the other man's face and completed the sentiment. 'But when the glory and honour of Rome are at stake our leaders tend to act before they think. That's what you were going to say, I take it?'

'Something like that, sir.' Graniculus smiled cautiously. 'Then again, it's not my place to question my superiors.'

'Nor mine, alas.'

They were interrupted by the thin blare of trumpets and Cato saw tiny figures scurrying from amongst the tents as those on duty made for their places on the walls. He rose to his feet and shaded his eyes. Away to the west he could see a column of horsemen trotting down the road from Antioch. Now and then there was a glint amid the cloud of dust kicked up by the horses' hoofs as the sun caught a helmet or armour.

'No point in asking if it's ours or theirs,' said the quartermaster, who was also on his feet now. 'Coming from that direction. Bound to be another cohort sent forward to Bactris. You'd better get your hands on those supplies while you still can, sir.'

Cato made no reply and continued straining his eyes to pick out details in the force rapidly approaching the Euphrates. Then he caught a glimpse of red at the head of the column, then more capes and crested helmets, and he realised he was looking at General Corbulo and his staff leading a small column of cavalry.

'That's Corbulo,' he muttered. 'I need to go. Make sure you and your clerks sort out my supplies. I'll have my men come and get them tomorrow morning.'

Their conversation had slipped into a more formal tone, and now Graniculus stood stiffly as they exchanged a salute before Cato strode across the terrace and back into the shaded interior of the quartermaster's offices. He had not anticipated the general's arrival coming so soon. Clearly Corbulo was not one to let the grass grow beneath his boots. The days of Bactris being a quiet back-water of the Empire were over. From now on, it would serve as the forward base for the Roman army. Soon the ground below the fortress would be swarming with tens of thousands of men preparing to cross the Euphrates and hurl their weight against the might of Parthia.

CHAPTER NINE

'It's beyond farcical,' Corbulo fumed as he strode up and down Cato's tent in the Praetorian camp. 'The information I had about the condition of the legions was true, up to a point. But the reality is shocking. The Tenth and the Twelfth are in a deplorable state. I doubt if half the men are even fit enough to lead into battle. Nearly a quarter of them should have taken their discharge many years ago. But they've got a taste for the comforts and pay that go with being a legionary, so why quit when Rome is putting a roof over your head, food in your mouth and money in your purse? Especially when there's no campaigning to be done. Their kit's a joke. Hardly any men have complete equipment, and what there is of it is in a poor state of repair. There are almost no stocks of spare weapons or armour. Discipline is poor. The centurions openly accept bribes in exchange for avoiding duties and the legates spend more time attending banquets and hunts than they do with their legions. The thing is that the Third and the Sixth are not that much better.'

He paused and clenched his jaw, then shook his head. 'Apologies, Tribune. But I have never seen the like. I tell you, if Vologases had the balls to invade Syria by himself and take on our legions single-handed, I'd give him favourable odds.'

Cato sensed that his superior's rage was fading to a level where he might tolerate hearing a word from another officer.

'It would seem that our preparations for the campaign are going to take a little longer than anticipated, sir.'

'Not half. The gods know what that fool Quadratus was thinking when he claimed he should be leading those men into Parthia. Our forces are in shit order and that is his responsibility. Frankly, I should send him back to Rome to be prosecuted for dereliction of duty. But he'd only use the opportunity to spread lies about the situation and try to pin the blame on me. So we're stuck with him for the time being. In the meantime, I'll have to send for kit to resupply the legions. The time-servers will have to be dismissed and fresh recruits found to fill their places. That means several months of training before they are ready to fight. Several months of lost campaigning time, which you can be damn sure the Parthians will make the most of.'

Cato cleared his throat. 'From what I've seen of the auxiliary troops here at Bactris, you're going to have the same issues with them. I would imagine that applies for most of the other units under your authority as well, sir.'

'I fear that's true.' Corbulo clasped his hands behind his back and looked down for a moment, deep in thought.

'Does this mean that you will be delaying sending my column into Armenia, sir?' asked Cato.

The general looked up sharply. 'Absolutely not! We must have Rhadamistus back on his throne as soon as possible. The longer we delay, the more opportunity we give Tiridates to consolidate his position. We have to take the initiative and strike fast and strike hard. Knock the Parthians off balance in order to win some breathing space to ready the army for war.'

'That won't be until spring next year, sir. At the earliest.'

'I appreciate that, thank you, Tribune. So you will be out on a limb for at least a year. An unenviable prospect, I agree, but we have to make the attempt. Even if that comes at the price of you and your men.'

Cato felt his respect for Corbulo cool. It was hard to hear the fate of his cohort dismissed in so few words. But the general seemed to be missing a wider issue.

'What about Rhadamistus, sir? The Empire might be able to risk and lose a cohort. But if Rhadamistus is taken prisoner or killed, then Rome will have lost its claimant to the Armenian throne.'

'Rome will have lost Rhadamistus, to be sure. But there are plenty of sons of eastern kings living at the emperor's pleasure in Rome. We can always rustle up another to place on the throne.'

So there it was, thought Cato. He and Macro were expendable. Along with the cohort, Rhadamistus, and all his retinue and soldiers. Mere stakes in Corbulo's throw of the dice to take the initiative from the enemy. He was tempted to feel bitter but forced himself to put himself in the general's place for a moment. He considered the forces in play and reluctantly concluded that he too would make the same gamble. All this passed through Cato's mind in a matter of heartbeats before he responded: 'I understand, sir.'

Corbulo stared at him searchingly, then nodded. 'I believe that you do, Tribune. It's a bad business, and if I thought there was any alternative, then I would not order you to go.'

'I believe you, sir.'

'Thank you. Then you'll need to be ready to march the moment the siege train arrives. I passed it on the road, two days ago. It should be here in no more than three days.'

'Three days . . .' Cato repeated as he reflected on all the preparations he must make. The supplies would be ready. Macro's training of the Iberians would have to be curtailed, or at least continued on the march as the opportunity arose. And there was another matter he had considered and needed to raise with his general. Now was the time, since Corbulo had voiced some sympathy for Cato's predicament.

'There's a cohort of slingers here, sir.'

'Yes,' Corbulo said wearily. 'What of it?'

'Given that my column is going to be isolated for longer than you anticipated, then we need to defend ourselves as best we can. It's not just a question of numbers. I have fought the Parthians before, sir, as you know. I have seen the damage their horse-archers can do. But I know that our slingers can shoot further. It should give us the edge if we run into any bands of Parthians that try to harass our column. I'd like to request the slingers be transferred to my command, sir.'

'And what if they are lost along with you if your column is defeated? It would be throwing good after bad, Tribune.'

'Conversely, it might just tip the balance in favour of my column achieving its mission, sir. You spoke of justified risk a moment ago. It's my belief that giving me the slingers is also a justified risk. But one that improves the odds in Rome's favour.'

74

Corbulo laughed dryly. 'You dare to play me at my own game . . . Very well, you may take them. One cohort more or less is not going to change things here in Syria. But that is all.'

'Yes, sir.'

The general was silent for a moment before he continued in a more emollient tone. 'Cato, there is one final matter. I could have raised it earlier, but I needed you to fully understand the strategic situation before I told you.' He reached for the saddle bag he had set down beside the tent opening when he had entered Cato's headquarters. Drawing the flap back, he took out a small waxed slate with a broken imperial seal. 'I received instructions from the emperor to send your cohort back to Rome once I had taken command of the army here. You were sent to escort me to Syria. That job is done and Nero wants his precious Praetorians back. My difficulty is that your men are far more precious to Rome here, not least because they are the only Roman soldiers worthy of the name available for the task I have given you. If I send you back now, then Rhadamistus will not be able to retake Armenia . . .'

He left it to Cato to complete the line of thought he had worked through on his ride to Bactris.

The tribune smiled faintly and nodded. 'Then it is a pity the dispatch from Nero only reached you after my column had marched and it was too late to recall me.'

'Yes. I will be sure to record that you were unaware of the dispatch and acted on my orders in good faith. I trust that you will back that version of events up if it becomes necessary in the future.'

'Yes, sir. Of course.'

'Sometimes it is the soldiers in the field who have to decide what is best for Rome, whatever their orders say.'

'I understand that, and accept it.'

Corbulo clasped his hand and shook it firmly. 'Good man. Now then, you've surely had the chance to scout out Bactris. Where can an old soldier find a decent drink and a comfortable bed for the night?'

Fortunately, the general stayed just long enough to inspect the facilities of the fortress and the state of the three cohorts that had already arrived, in addition to the cavalry cohort he had brought forward from its base at Zeugma. Then he and his staff and bodyguards rode back to rejoin the legions trudging to the assembly point at Bactris.

Over the next two days Cato laboured to ensure that his column would be ready to march as soon as the siege train arrived. Five days' rations were issued from stores, together with bundles of leather to repair boots and straps, and fodder for the mules that carried the baggage for the two cohorts, as well as all the supplies needed for the Iberians and their mounts. To which requirements were added fodder for the draught animals drawing the siege train as well as spare timber and nails for the inevitable running repairs. Carts and mules were bought from the local market to carry the extra rations and fodder needed to keep the column on the march. As was the custom, Cato intended to replenish his stocks at the end of each day's march while they were in friendly territory. Once they crossed the frontier region into Armenia, they would be obliged to forage and live off the land and its people. With luck there would be some towns that would welcome the return of Rhadamistus and resupply the column. Otherwise Cato and his men would be forced to take what they needed and risk turning the local people against them, where they could not be cowed.

Once the logistical arrangements were settled Cato turned his attention to the cohort of slingers. At first light on the second morning he had the Third Balearic and their commander assemble a short distance from their freshly erected ramparts. Tribune Pasito was a corpulent individual with a fringe of grey hair around his sunburned head. He was at least twenty years older than Cato and did little to conceal his resentment over Corbulo's decision to place him under the Praetorian officer.

'Where's your helmet?' Cato demanded.

'Helmet? Back in my tent.'

'Go and fetch it at once. You and any other officer who has failed to turn out without the proper equipment.'

'We are not in the habit of wearing helmets,' Pasito protested. 'Not unless battle is imminent.'

'I don't give a shit about that. Every officer under my command will carry a helmet with him at all times. And you will pay due deference to my rank from this point onwards. Is that clear?'

'Yes, sir.'

'Now fetch your helmet. I expect every man of the cohort to be properly equipped when he is called on parade from now on. Go.'

Once Pasito returned, sweating heavily and puffing, Cato had him stand at attention while he addressed him.

'What's the story with the Third Balearic? How long has the cohort been posted to Syria?'

Pasito swallowed and breathed deeply as he collected his thoughts. 'The cohort was raised in Palma twenty years ago, sir. The unit was sent straight to Syria to serve in a policing roll. Been here ever since.'

Cato eyed the cohort's bare standard. There was not even a single decoration. 'Any combat experience at all?'

'No, sir.'

'And you?'

'No, sir.'

'How long have you been in command?'

'Two years.'

'And before that?'

Pasito hesitated briefly. 'Assistant to the tax collector in Antioch, sir.'

'A lucrative position, I have no doubt. So the command of the cohort is a sinecure for an old friend of the tax collector, I take it? In exchange for providing a ready escort for any of his officials whenever he requires it.' Cato leaned forward and dared the man to contradict him.

Pasito wilted and nodded awkwardly. 'Something like that.'

'I see.' Cato straightened up to his full height so that he could look down at the other officer. 'Well, it seems that you and your men are now going to have to earn your keep. Let's have a closer look at them and see what they're made of.'

He turned and strode towards the end of the front rank of the cohort. The slingers, due to their specialism, were armed and equipped quite unlike most other cohorts. They were the lightest of infantry. Only the centurions and optios wore helmets and any kind of armour. The rankers had leather skullcaps with iron plates sewn on to give minimal protection from glancing blows of edged

77

weapons. Some had linen cuirasses, but most just wore light tunics, sandals, and sidebags to carry their sling and shot. A canteen, belt and sword completed their equipment. They would be cut to pieces in close combat, Cato thought. But then they were never intended for such a role. Slingers had come to replace most of the light infantry armed with javelins who once skirmished ahead of the legions. In the hands of a proficient user the sling had a far greater range than a javelin and most bows. Moreover, the lead shot was far more lethal, tearing through flesh and shattering bones with more destructive power than any arrow. Their function was to wear down the enemy and break up their formations before the legionaries charged home to finish the job.

Cato made his way along each line, building up an overall impression of the Third Balearic. Despite the duration of the unit's existence, it was still untried and unblooded. As natural wastage had thinned out the ranks, so local youths had been recruited and trained as slingers. Very few of the original islanders remained on the cohort's strength, and those who did were well past their prime. Cato noticed that most of the men had the darker skin and features of easterners and probably had not the slightest idea about the island after which their unit was named. Many of them looked too old or too out of shape to endure a long march, but there was only one way to find out.

Once he had completed his inspection, Cato gave the order to form columns of centuries, and when all the officers and men were in position he gave the order to follow him as he marched around the ramparts of the cohort's camp. He increased his pace for the next lap and then broke into a steady trot after the third, and continued lap after lap as the morning sun rose across the river and climbed slowly into the sky, bathing the landscape in its harsh glare. Despite the extra weight of his scale armour, Cato was able to keep up the pace thanks to his hard-won fitness over many years of campaigning across the length and breadth of the Empire. It took less than five laps for the first man to fall out. Others began to slow their pace so that the centuries started to lose their shape, and by the end of the first hour, as best Cato could estimate the passage of time, the cohort was a stream of men with laboured breath struggling to keep up with him. Pasito was an early casualty, staggering to a halt and then bent double as he vomited. Cato stopped briefly to order the rearmost centurion to round up those who had fallen out and take them aside. Then he ran back to the head of the remaining men and continued until he began to feel his own stamina starting to fail him. He called a halt once they returned to the original starting point.

Of the original strength of nearly five hundred men, just over three hundred remained, Cato estimated. Only three of the centurions were still with the unit. Almost all of them were blown and stood chests heaving, faces streaming with sweat. Some bent over, gasping or retching. But they had proved they had the ability to keep up, Cato conceded. As soon as he had recovered his breath sufficiently to give clear orders, he gave permission for them to use their canteens and called Pasito over.

'These are the men I want. You and those others are to return to Antioch at once and report to the governor for posting to garrison duties. That is all you are fit for. Return to camp, pack your kit and make ready to leave. I'll have your written orders prepared before you march.'

Pasito opened his mouth to protest but Cato raised a hand to forestall him. 'It's for your own good, Prefect. You and these others would only hold us back. And when we can't afford to delay any further, you'd be left behind, at the mercy of the enemy. Better you remain here in Syria where you can do some good.'

'But . . . but who will take my place?'

'One of the remaining officers shows some promise,' Cato said curtly.

'You have no right to do this.'

'Yes I do. I am acting on General Corbulo's authority. The matter is decided. Dismissed.'

He did not give Pasito a chance to object further as he turned and marched back to the waiting survivors. He already had his eye on one of the centurions, a wiry man who looked to be in his mid-thirties, light-skinned and with the straw-coloured hair of those of Dacian descent. He was one of the few who had kept pace with Cato.

'What is your name, Centurion?'

'Spiracus Keranus, sir.'

'Congratulations, Keranus. You're the new commander of the unit.'

'Sir?'

'The prefect, and those others with him have failed to meet the standard and I am sending them back to Antioch. I need someone to take Pasito's place. That's you, unless I am given reason to decide otherwise. Do you accept?'

'Er, yes, sir.' Then he stood to attention properly, nodded and repeated firmly: 'Yes, sir.'

'Good. Then get some targets set up. Five posts in a row, ten feet apart. I want three rows at one hundred, two hundred and three hundred paces from the shooting line. Then we'll find out how good the remaining men are. See to it.'

While Keranus called a section from his century and ran back to their camp, Cato took out a waxed slate from his sidebag and braced it against his left arm as he etched out a brief set of orders for Pasito and then pressed his seal ring into the wax. Snapping the slate shut he crossed to the prefect and handed it to him.

'There. Now take these men back into the camp to pack their kit and then get out of my sight.'

'But how do I know which tents to take down?'

'Leave the tents. I can always use spares. You'll have to make do without. It's not so far to Antioch. A few nights in the open will do you good.'

Pasito stepped closer and lowered his voice. 'You arrogant little bastard. I'll make you pay for this. I have friends who have plenty of influence with the governor and—'

'Lucky you. And by the time you have the chance to spill your guts to them, my column will be far away. If we're successful, then no one will care about your complaints.' Cato smiled grimly. 'If not, then I'll be past caring what you say. Now, if that's all, I have to deal with some real soldiers. Not men who are taking the emperor's coin and merely playing at being soldiers. Farewell.'

The rest of the morning was spent on the makeshift range as Cato watched closely as each group of five men loosed ten shots at each range. Only a handful reached as far as the furthest posts, but the vast majority were adept enough to shoot at two hundred paces and many managed to hit the targets at least once. At a hundred paces the slingers were far more accurate and tore splinters off the posts when they struck the targets. Only a few of the men failed to use their slings to Cato's satisfaction. One mistimed his release entirely and the shot whirred close by Cato's head. Accident or not, the man was a hazard.

'You there!' Cato bellowed. 'Put that bloody sling on the ground! The sidebag too. Then join the others in the camp. Go!'

He had Keranus gather the remaining poor shots and bring them over. Cato stared hard at them for a moment before he spoke. 'Looks to me that you men are in the wrong unit as things stand. You're more of a danger than the bloody enemy. Keranus.'

'Sir?'

'You will take personal charge of these men. I want them shooting as well as the others long before we encounter the enemy. You will drill them in the use of slings at the end of each day's march for an hour. Any man that still fails to meet the standard will be sent back to Antioch by himself.'

He paused to let them imagine the perils of trying to return to the province through enemy territory alone.

'We're done for the day. Have the cohort fall out.'

'Yes, sir.'

'You'll need to appoint some new officers to replace those I rejected.' Cato pointed a finger. 'No favouritism, mind. I'll have none of Pasito's habits any more. You pick the best men.'

'Yes, sir.'

'Dismissed.'

Cato planted his hands on his hips as he watched them march away to join the remains of the cohort. He had winnowed down their ranks considerably but was confident that those who remained would keep up with the Praetorians, and if there was a fight, they'd be able to unleash a deadly enough barrage of lead shot to thoroughly unnerve the enemy. He heard the crunch of boots and turned to see Macro striding towards him, a grin splitting his craggy features.

'I can see you've been having fun. Nothing like a bit of drilling to lift the spirits, eh?'

In truth Cato was exhausted by his efforts that morning, but was trying not to show it. 'It passes the time. But I can think of many things I'd rather be doing.'

'Pfft!' Macro sniffed, then nodded towards the slingers' camp, where a small column of soldiers was emerging from the gate and making for the road that led west towards Antioch.

'I heard that we were going to lose the wasters. But so many?'

'Word gets round quickly.' Cato shrugged. 'Much as we'll need every man we can get, I can't let that come at the price of us dragging our feet.'

'Maybe,' said Macro. 'But we'll still have the siege train to contend with, and you know what awkward buggers the larger pieces can be. Anyway, that's why I'm here. The siege train's arrived. The centurion in command, Metellus, sent a man ahead to report their arrival. I said I'd let you know. Look.'

Macro turned and pointed towards the line of low hills a few miles away. Cato shaded his eyes and squinted. He could just make out the shapes of the heavy wagons carrying the siege equipment, each vehicle drawn by a long team of mules.

'That's good. Find a space for them in our camp for the night. Then pass the word to our men, the slingers and our Iberian friends: in the morning we march on Armenia.'

CHAPTER TEN

Cato's modest force left Bactris in the cool air of dawn. The blinding heat of the midday sun dictated that the column marched in the early morning and late afternoon. During the hottest hours of the day Cato halted the column and ordered the men to fall out and rest. The soldiers found what shade they could, or made their own by propping their cloaks up with their marching yokes, or simply used their shields to block the sun's glare. The Iberians and the slingers were more accustomed to the climate and moved as little as possible as they rested. The Praetorians, however, had not yet got used to the east and were still marvelling at the arid harshness of the landscape in this part of the Empire that few of them had seen before. At first they failed to conserve their water and tended to drain their canteens too quickly, so they had to march with parched throats until they came across the next town or village well. Some rivers still flowed towards the Euphrates, but already many were starting to dry up as spring gave way to summer.

In order to conceal his advance from the enemy for as long as possible, Cato had chosen to take the less direct route along the west bank, keeping to a well-worn trading route that ran north through the hills a few miles in from the river. Progress was steady, and though the road avoided steep inclines as far as possible, there were still many occasions when the column had to slow down to allow the ponderous baggage and siege wagons to keep up. There were a handful of Iberian carts as well, reserved for royal tentage, wines and other luxuries, and the small group of women who accompanied Rhadamistus and his court. They were veiled and swathed in cloth, and Cato assumed they must be servants, or wives, or simply there to service the carnal appetites of Rhadamistus and his friends.

On the more difficult slopes the soldiers had to assist the mules by attaching ropes to the vehicles and hauling them forward. If the hill was high, then the officers had to call a halt from time to time and large rocks were jammed under the wheels to prevent them rolling back. Going downhill was even more gruelling as the soldiers had to use the ropes to control the wagons' descent as carefully as possible, while keeping their own footing. All the while the drovers shouted at their mules and the choking dust was split by the crack of whips. But the men swiftly got used to manoeuvring the wagons and Cato was content with the greater progress they made from day to day.

The siege train was of a modest enough size: four heavy bolt-throwers, four onagers, and two rams and their housings. In addition there were the six smaller bolt-throwers of the Praetorian cohort. Not enough to batter down and storm the walls of any formidable city or fortress, but adequate for the kinds of defences they were likely to encounter in Armenia. Certainly Rhadamistus was fascinated by the prospect of seeing the siege engines in action and plied Cato with questions whenever they rode together. Cato did his best to keep his explanations vague without causing any offence.

At the end of the day's march, the Roman soldiers and the Iberian infantry toiled together to erect a marching camp, while the nobles and their companies of mounted warriors arranged their horse lines and fed their mounts, disdaining the manual labour they deemed beneath them. For the first few days it took until after dark for the fortifications to be completed, but as the Iberians and the slingers became more proficient, urged on by the shouts and occasional blows from the officers, the work was completed in a respectable time.

When there was still an hour or so of light available after the camp was constructed, Macro continued his training of the Iberians and the slingers on alternating evenings. The former steadily learned to respond swiftly to formation commands, and even the veteran centurion was impressed. The latter lacked any combat experience, and Macro was determined that they should be as handy with their swords as their slings in case they ever ran out of shot, or closed with the enemy and had to resort to hand-to-hand combat. Once he had inspected their swords and ensured that the blades were thoroughly cleaned, sharpened and oiled, Macro introduced them to the 'spirit of the blade'. He had the frames of the onagers set up in the open ground between the tents and marching camp ramparts, and sacks stuffed with straw were suspended from the crossbeams. The slingers were lined up in front of the practice dummies as Macro went into the training routine he had learned by heart long ago.

'The two most important weapons in the army are the pickaxe and the sword. You have already met the first. Now I want you to meet my favourite.' He drew his sword and held it up for all to see.

'Here she is. She's been by my side in the mountains of Asturica. She was my constant companion in the freezing bogs and dark forests of Britannia. She looked after me in the deserts of Nubia. She has always been faithful and protected me from harm . . .' He tapped the flat of the sword on a livid scar on his forearm. 'Well, most of the time at any rate. The bitch has been known to be fickle, like most women.'

The men chuckled, some knowingly. Macro let the amusement die down before he continued. 'The reason she has looked after me is because I have learned the secret of keeping her happy. You see, she likes to grow grass. And I know that the secret of making grass grow well is to feed it blood. Lots of blood. And the blood of Rome's enemies is best of all.' He grinned cruelly and widened his eyes to emphasise his dangerous expression. 'So, when I ask the question, "What makes the grass grow?", what do you lads reply?'

There was a short pause before a handful of voices cried in a ragged chorus, 'Blood?'

'Bollocks!' Macro bellowed. 'I can't hear you! When I ask again, I want to hear it. Blood! Blood! Blood!' He paused. 'What makes the grass grow?'

This time the slingers were primed. 'Blood!'

'Louder!'

'BLOOD!'

'How much blood?'

'Blood! Blood! Blood!'

'That's it, lads!' Macro punched his sword into the air and then rounded on the nearest target and slammed the point home, cutting into the sacking and driving the tethered bag back in an arc. He wrenched his arm back so the sword was horizontal at hip level, his arm bent and legs braced, ready to strike again. Then he relaxed his posture and turned to the slingers. 'That's how it's done. Now draw your swords and line up. Officers, five good strikes for each man in turn. I want to hear 'em yell their guts out each time. Let's go! Move yourselves!'

He kept them at it as the light faded and the hills to the west cast long shadows across the camp. The air was filled with the constant din of men shouting their war cries as they struck the targets. Macro moved from century to century watching closely, nodding his approval at times and stepping in when some hapless individual, fatigued by drilling on top of a day's march, faltered or struck with insufficient force.

'What the fuck do you call that? That's a bloody Parthian you are stabbing, not a fucking winkle!' Macro stepped in front of the man he had singled out and squared up to him. 'Again. This time try me.'

The slinger looked surprised and hesitated, sword half raised.

'Are you deaf as well as a bloody pansy?' Macro screamed at him and punched him on the shoulder. 'Strike, you bastard.'

The slinger snarled angrily and lashed out with his blade, aiming the point at the centre of Macro's chest. The centurion reacted just in time and leaned to the side as the blade glanced off his mail vest. He grabbed the man's wrist with his left hand and landed a heavy punch on his cheek with his right. The slinger went down, dazed and helpless, and Macro helped himself to the sword and held the point to his throat.

'That happened because you didn't strike the target hard the first time. You don't get a second chance in battle. Understand?'

The man was still blinking as he tried to clear his head. He managed to nod. 'Yes, sir.'

'I catch you pulling your punches on target practice again and I'll have your balls for breakfast.' He raised the sword high and then stabbed it in the ground close to the slinger's head. 'There. Now get back in line.'

Macro moved to one side to oversee the rest of the men training, breathing carefully as the slinger's blow had bruised his chest and each breath he drew was accompanied by a sharp pain. Then he saw Cato approaching from the direction of headquarters. The tribune was bare-headed and without his scale vest, but still wore his sword belt. If they had been close to the enemy Macro would have frowned, but here in the hills on the friendly side of the Euphrates they were safe enough. Still, he thought, it was always a good idea for officers to lead by example and be ready for action at a moment's notice.

'How is the training going?' asked Cato as he joined his friend.

'Oh, not bad. The Iberian spearmen are good. Better than I thought they'd be. Not a patch on proper soldiers like our legionaries, of course. It's the slingers who concern me.'

'How so?'

'I know you picked the best of 'em, but they still fall far short of the standard of the auxiliary units we're used to. That's why I'm trying to get some fire into their bellies with sword drill.'

'And doing it well. I saw your little demonstration. You were lucky.'

'Lucky?'

'He just missed stabbing you in the guts.'

'But he didn't,' Macro retorted dismissively. 'Barely grazed me. It'll be a warm day in Hades before some ranker gets the drop on me.' He laughed and then winced.

'Right,' Cato nodded. 'Maybe you need to think twice about using that ploy in training again. I'd hate see you skewered, and then have to break it to Petronella. She would not be happy.'

Macro sucked his teeth. 'You can barely imagine. Still, credit to the lad who grazed me. He was quick.'

Cato eyed him warily. 'Or maybe you just aren't as quick as you used to be?'

'Stuff that. I can still deal it out.'

'You do that.' Cato looked round at the slingers as they stabbed their targets. 'Think you can make this lot into decent fighting men if we get in a tight spot?'

Macro grinned and clasped a hand to his side to press on his bruised ribs as he drew a breath and called out.

'Lads! Tell the tribune. What makes the grass grow?'

The slingers paused from their drill and brandished their swords. 'Blood! Blood! Blood!'

Macro turned to his superior with a happy smile. 'There!'

Ten days after leaving Bactris, they reached a small town at the foot of the hills giving out on to sprawling farmland alongside the Euphrates. As usual, Rhadamistus and a group of his horsemen rode ahead to make arrangements for billeting the men, stabling the horses and arranging for replenishment of the column's supplies. The townspeople would be assured that these would be paid for when the main column arrived. It was only when the supplies had been gathered that Cato made it clear that payment would be in the form of a promissory note, signed and sealed by him, that could be redeemed from the treasury at Antioch.

The ruse did not sit well with Cato, but it removed the opportunity for the towns they passed through to shut the gates in the faces of the Romans in an attempt to preserve their stocks of food, wine and fodder. In any case, it would have been a futile gesture as affronted Roman pride would demand nothing less than breaking in the gates and taking what was needed at swordpoint. Nothing else would have sufficed to make up for the failure of such towns to offer the hospitality due to the emperor's soldiers. It was simpler, and avoided any bloody unpleasantness, to present the townsfolk with a fait accompli instead. With any luck, Cato comforted his conscience, they would be able to reclaim most of the value of the requisitioned supplies from the sestertius-pinching treasury clerks serving the governor of Syria.

As he led the infantry and the baggage train towards the town, he saw a rider galloping back towards the column, whipping his horse on.

'Here comes trouble,' said Macro. 'I can feel it in my bones.'

A moment later horse and rider slewed to a halt in a spray of dust and grit, and Cato saw that it was Narses. He thrust a hand back towards the town.

'Sir, we have found the enemy!'

'Enemy?' Cato arched an eyebrow. 'In that town? On this side of the Euphrates?'

Narses nodded vigorously. 'We saw them! Riding away as we approached. Parthians.'

Macro muttered. 'Like I said, trouble.'

'How many Parthians?' Cato demanded.

'A hundred. Maybe more. The king took half his men after them.' Narses' eyes were gleaming. 'If we can catch them before they reach the river . . .'

But Cato was only half listening. Since the Parthians had been able to flee at such short notice, that meant that they had seen the Iberians approaching. More likely a scout had seen the entire column and dashed back to warn his comrades. Should they escape Rhadamistus, then they would warn their leaders of the presence of Cato's column. With Romans this close to the frontier with Armenia it could mean only one thing, that Rome was making an attempt to seize the kingdom from Tiridates.

'Shall I give the order for the men to close up?' asked Macro.

'No. No point. The Parthians have already gone. I'm going ahead. Keep the column moving. Once you reach the town, have the first and second centuries take the gates and post sentries on the walls. The rest can fall out and find billets. Narses, on me!'

Cato adjusted his helmet so that it was firmly in place and spurred his mount down the road. The dust raised by Narses was still in the air as the two pounded back through it. Closer to, Cato could see that the crudely constructed walls enclosed a settlement no bigger than the area taken up by the camp of a legion. A population of around five thousand then, he estimated. Enough to have some kind of militia, but not enough men to defy the Parthians when they arrived. A group of Iberian horsemen had dismounted by the gate, and while the handlers took charge of the horses the others had taken command of the gatehouse and ensured that the gates were kept open for the rest of the column. A wise step by Rhadamistus, thought Cato approvingly. His ally had had the presence of mind to order the precaution before taking off after the enemy.

He slowed his horse before he reached the gatehouse and entered the town at a steady trot. A narrow street led through tightly packed houses once whitewashed but now stained and streaked by sand blown in from the barren hills. Few people were about, and those that were scattered at the sound of hoofbeats and dived into alleys or doorways at their approach. Rounding a corner, Cato saw that the road opened out on to a large space, roughly square, and most of the riders that Rhadamistus had left behind had dismounted, tethered their horses, and gone in search of food and quarters for the night. A small party of horse-archers stood guard over an anxious-looking group of townspeople as Cato and Narses rode up to them.

Cato reined in and looked down on them. 'Anyone speak Greek?'

One, well-dressed in an embroidered tunic and silken headpiece, raised a hand.

'And you are?'

'I am the magistrate of Arbelis, sir,' he answered in Greek.

'Arbelis?' Cato could not recall the name on any of the itineraries he had examined before the campaign. But that was not so surprising, given the small size of the town and its location. 'Who do you answer to? Rome? Armenia? Parthia?'

'We send tribute to the governor in Cappadocia once a year, sir. When his agent comes to collect it.'

Roman then. But only just, here on the very fringe of the Roman province.

'I see. So what were those Parthians doing in Arbelis?'

'They came yesterday, at dusk, sir. Galloped in and seized our valuables, as well as food, wine and oil. Any man who resisted was killed.' The magistrate clasped his hands earnestly. 'Thanks be to the gods that you have come to save us.'

Cato felt a moment's guilty sympathy for the townsfolk as yet another band of soldiers descended on them to seize supplies. At least this time there should be no deaths, and the hope of repayment.

'My men need shelter for the night.'

'Of course.' The magistrate nodded, grateful that the presence of Cato and his men guaranteed that the Parthians would not return. That gratitude might prove to be rather short-lived, thought Cato.

'We will need billets for my soldiers, stabling and feed for the horses . . .'

'Yes, of course. As you wish, honoured sir!'

'I'll have one of my officers give you a full list of our requirements.'

The magistrate frowned. 'Full list?'

But Cato was already riding on, across the square and down the main street to the far gate of the town. There, another party of Rhadamistus's men had taken control of the gatehouse and they stood aside to let him pass. Cato continued a short distance and reined in atop a knoll, to one side of the track. Ahead, he could make out the great river, and saw that it was joined by a tributary, snaking into the hills to the east in the direction of Armenia. A faint trail of distant dust marked the path of the Parthians and their pursuers. Cato gestured to Narses to follow him and galloped on. Every so often he encountered a body, some attended by wounded or abandoned horses. Only one of the dead wore Iberian robes.

Three miles down the track, close to the west bank of the Euphrates, he saw the Iberians had halted. A smaller party, led by Rhadamistus, towering above his companions, was making its way along the riverbank. As Cato cleared the mass of horsemen and made for their leader, he caught sight of a small fort rising above the reeds on the far bank. It guarded the pebbled shallows of a ford.

'Ah, Tribune!' Rhadamistus smiled broadly, still excited by the pursuit of his Parthian prey. 'The Parthian dogs have gone to ground.' He pointed towards the fort and Cato could see the dull gleam of helmets and bright headcloths above the battlements, three hundred paces across the river. Small parties of Iberian horsemen surrounded the fort.

'But not before we slew scores of them,' the Iberian prince continued. 'The rest got away and shut themselves up over there. I had to pull my men back out of arrowshot. But we have them trapped, no?'

Cato eased himself up in the saddle and scanned the fort and the far bank. He could see more of the Iberians a safe distance beyond the fort. The Parthians were trapped, for the moment. But that presented a set of new problems. It was imperative that none escaped to spread the news about his column. And that meant reducing the fort and destroying the enemy inside. That would entail a delay and casualties that Cato could ill afford. But he had no choice. He turned back to Rhadamistus.

'Majesty, we will have to take the fort.'

'Good,' the Iberian beamed.

'May I request that you send more men across the river to ensure that none of the enemy escapes to raise the alarm? In the meantime, I'll bring the rest of our column forward to prepare for the attack.'

Rhadamistus nodded and quickly issued orders to his men as Cato turned back towards Arbelis. The Praetorians and auxiliaries were no doubt looking forward to the prospect of a comfortable night in the shelter and warmth of the town, rather than having to construct another marching camp. Instead they'd have to march by the town, into the gathering dusk, and construct a camp by the river in darkness. He would well imagine the grumbling that would ensue. But some, Macro more than most, would be delighted by the imminence of the first action of their campaign.

The Parthians had provoked this war, Cato reflected grimly. Now they were about to start paying the price for their hubris.

CHAPTER ELEVEN

'This spot will do nicely,' Cato decided as he and Macro emerged from the shallows, dripping. Ahead of them, a hundred paces from the eastern bank of the Euphrates, Cato could just make out the mounted pickets in the moonlight. He turned to look back over the river. The other bank was nearly a quarter of a mile away but he had managed to mark a passage across the pebble banks and the flows between that was no more than waist height. The wagons of the siege train and Porcino's century were waiting for orders to make the crossing. Centurion Metellus's men had already crossed and Cato could hear the sounds of their pickaxes as they laboured in the thin moonlight to complete the battery on a small rise just beyond the fort.

'All right, Macro, get back across the river and bring the siege train over.'

'Yes, sir.'

'And do it as quietly as you can.'

The centurion did not reply as he strode back into the current and Cato felt irritated with himself at the unnecessary admonition of his friend. Macro knew well enough the value of surprise. But Cato was tired, and anxious to take the fort as quickly as he could, question the prisoners, and discover if the Parthians had managed to send any message about his presence in the area. If Tiridates was warned, then he would have ample opportunity to ambush the column or lure them into a trap. All of which had prompted the remark to Macro. He tried to thrust the thought from his mind.

Cato comforted himself by reflecting that the Parthians must be feeling secure behind their wall as he climbed up through the reeds and on to the bank, his boots squelching with each step. After all, there was a good chance that they had fled the town after sighting Rhadamistus and his men, who had kicked up more than enough dust to obscure the main column, and more importantly the siege train. Horse-archers and cataphracts alone would never reduce the fort, and the enemy would be confident that they merely had to wait until the Iberians rode away before they could emerge again to continue their raids across the frontier. When dawn stole over the horizon and revealed the siege weapons, the Parthians would realise their mistake, moments before the first missiles struck the ramparts.

Making his way along the bank towards the chink and thud of the pickaxes, Cato saw the dark outline of the fort against the lighter night sky and hoped that the enemy would swiftly come to their senses and surrender. That would entail detaching half a century to escort the prisoners back to the nearest town garrisoned by Roman troops. He could ill afford to lose forty of his men, but still less could he afford losing as many men or more in an assault on the Parthian outpost. And the need to take it swiftly so that he could continue the advance meant that an attack would be necessary.

'Halt! Who is there?'

Cato instinctively grasped his sword handle and braced his boots before he took a calming breath and responded: 'Tribune Cato.'

A figure stepped out from behind a stunted tree and Cato could just make out the tip of the spear pointed at him as the Praetorian spoke again. 'Publius says . . .'

'Pour the garum,' Cato replied softly.

'Pass, friend.' The sentry grounded his spear and Cato released his grip on the sword and approached.

'Next time, whisper it, soldier. Better than blurting it out loudly enough for every enemy for miles around to hear,' he exaggerated to drive the lesson home.

'Yes, sir,' the sentry assented quietly.

'That's better. Centurion Macro will be bringing the siege train up shortly. Make sure you challenge him properly or he'll not be so forgiving.'

'Yes, sir.' The sentry retreated into the shadows of the tree, keen to escape back into anonymity before his commander could recognise him.

Cato continued towards the rising ground where the battery was sited and was pleased to see that the outer ditch and palisade were well under way, a precaution against any attempt by the defenders to sally out and attempt to damage or destroy the precious siege weapons. Behind the palisade other men were busy levelling the ground. A man with a crested helmet approached and saluted.

'Tribune Cato?'

'Yes. You and your men have done well, Metellus. No easy task to do this in the dark.'

'Thank you, sir.'

'Any trouble from the Parthians?'

'They sent a party out an hour or so ago, sir. Keranus and his lads allowed them to get on to some open ground before they let rip and sent the enemy running. They bagged two of the bastards. Not a squeak out of them since then.'

'Good. I don't want them getting wind of what we're up to. Once Macro arrives with the siege weapons, get 'em up quick as you can and ready to shoot the moment it's light enough to see the target. And, more importantly, for the target to spot us.'

Metellus chuckled. 'I wish I could see their faces when that happens.'

'You'll get your chance. Either when they give up, or when we go in.'

'My lads are up for it, sir.'

Cato shook his head. 'They've had no rest since we broke camp yesterday morning. If we have to assault the fort, I'll be using fresh troops.'

'Fair enough, sir,' Metellus conceded reluctantly. 'But if they need support then my mob will be ready.'

'I'm sure I can depend on you and your men.' Cato patted him on the shoulder. 'But for now, let's get the battery completed.'

The work continued through the night until they heard the low rumble of approaching wagons and Cato strode towards them to greet Macro.

'Any problems?'

'One of the wagons went over as we came out of the river, but the rest are fine.'

'Good.' Cato indicated the outline of the battery on the knoll. 'Metellus's men are just about done. Get the wagons up there and assemble the weapons as soon as you can.'

'Right you are.'

As Macro led the vehicles up the slight incline, the rumble of the wheels and the straining grunts of the men were added to by the braying of mules as their drovers used their switches on the animals' rumps. The noise seemed deafening in the darkness and Cato feared that it might prompt some sudden action by the enemy. Sure enough, a blazing arrow shot high into the sky and arced in the direction of the wagons, but it fell far too short to illuminate anything but the bare ground in front of the battery, and one of the mounted patrols which swiftly dashed a short distance away to avoid being subjected to a barrage of arrows from the fort. All the same Cato sought out Rhadamistus and found him on the track, three hundred paces to the east of the fort. No attempt was made to challenge him, he noted irritably, and he resolved to tackle the Iberian prince about the matter later.

'Tribune Cato,' Rhadamistus greeted him cheerfully. 'How are the preparations going?'

'We'll be ready before first light, Majesty.'

'I cannot wait to see my enemies pulverised by your siege engines.'

'Their walls won't last long. I intend to give them a good pounding before I ask for their surrender. I don't imagine they'll be keen for the bombardment to continue.'

'Surrender?' Rhadamistus edged his horse closer to Cato and loomed over him as he spoke in a low, urgent tone. 'Why give them the chance to live? Those are the scum who drove me from my throne. They deserve to die, if only to set an example to any who pass by the fort. Let no one doubt what fate awaits them if they dare defy King Rhadamistus.'

The vehemence in his voice took Cato aback and he had to think quickly before he replied in an emollient tone. 'Majesty, if they surrender then we will have no need to risk any of our men in an attack.'

'They are soldiers, Tribune Cato. Your men, and mine. They need to be tested so that they are ready for greater challenges when we march deep into Armenia. Their blood is up, and they want to get at the enemy. If we let the enemy surrender, then our men will feel cheated.'

'What they may feel is immaterial. As long as they obey my orders,' Cato insisted.

'Your men, maybe. My warriors are less cowed by discipline and wish to prove themselves. There will be no surrender. That is my command. The command of a king.'

Cato had known this moment would come at some point. His ally was headstrong and proud and no doubt did not relish having to go and beg for Rome's support in his bid to return to his throne. But Corbulo's orders were clear. Whatever Rhadamistus might think, or desire, Cato was in command of the column, and that needed to be established here and now with certainty, so that his authority would not be challenged again before the mission was complete.

Cato cleared his throat, eased his shoulders back and looked up at the other man unflinchingly, his bluff ready. 'Majesty, when you sit on your throne again, then you are king. Until then I have been charged by General Corbulo, in the name of the emperor, to do whatever it takes to ensure that you become king. That entails being the overall commander of our combined forces. If, in my judgement, your actions make it impossible for me to carry out my orders, then I will simply turn my men round and march back to Syria, with my siege engines. In which case, I think you may struggle to win back your kingdom by yourself.'

Rhadamistus was silent for a moment before he whispered harshly, 'You dare to defy me?'

'Majesty, I do not wish to defy you, but if you force my hand then I will do as I say, without hesitation.'

'Your emperor will crucify you when I tell him about this.'

'That may be, but you will have to make your case in person if you wish to resolve the matter as speedily as possible, and by then you will have wasted another year, maybe two, and it will be even harder to displace Tiridates the next time you march against him.

Would it not be better to work with me now and win your throne before this year is out?'

Bathed by the light of the half-moon, Rhadamistus's features looked like an anguished marble sculpture, then his lips pressed into a thin line and he nodded, barely enough for the gesture to register. 'Very well.'

'You accept that I am in command?'

'Until the throne is mine. After that I shall back in command and you will do my bidding without question.'

'As you do mine until then?'

'Yes . . .'

'Then the matter is settled. I will offer them a chance to surrender.'

'And if they refuse?' Rhadamistus asked.

Cato shrugged. 'Then there will be no quarter.'

'Good. And if they accept? What then?'

'Then I shall have them returned to Antioch to sell into slavery as spoils of war, while we march on into Armenia.'

Rhadamistus considered this briefly and nodded. 'That is good. I accept your proposal.'

It was a thinly disguised attempt to save a little face and Cato played along. 'I thank you, Majesty.'

Then he turned back to the fort. It was hard to be certain, but he felt that he could make out more detail than before. A glance to the east confirmed it; a pale hue was discernible behind the distant line of hills.

'When the attack starts, you and your men must prevent any attempt by the enemy to break out and escape, Majesty.'

Rhadamistus patted the hilt of his curved sword. 'Trust me, none will escape.'

The bolt-throwers had been mounted on their stands and trained towards the battlements just beyond the range of the enemy bowmen, as far as Cato had been able to calculate the distance under cover of darkness. Macro was overseeing the assembly of the onagers, and there was a steady series of sharp blows as the wedges were driven in to steady the uprights. As soon as the torsion cables were secured, and capped, and the locking pins tapped home, the men began to twist the cables, using long levers, and the loud clank of the iron ratchets carried for a wide distance. The keenest-eyed Parthians must be able to make out the battery by now, Cato decided. If they had not already guessed what their opponents were up to, the coming dawn would soon sweep away any remaining doubt.

'Get the ammunition up here!' Macro snapped and hurriedly directed his men to position the baskets containing two-foot-long bolts with heavy iron heads, sturdy shafts and wooden flights beside the weapons. The first bolts were carefully laid in the narrow troughs as one man in each crew worked the windlass that wound back the bowstrings. The others held back, in case the throwing arms snapped. It happened from time to time and the only warning would be a tell-tale creak before the wooden limbs splintered and hurtled back towards the man working the windlass, sometimes resulting in severe injuries. More men came up in twos, carrying strings of carefully chosen rocks for the onagers. As the first rocks were placed in the slings, the throwing arms were cranked back.

Soon all was ready within the battery and the slingers filed past on each side and then spread out across the open ground to the east of the fort. If the enemy attempted to charge out at them they would be able to run for safety behind the Iberians. There would be no escape across the river either as the rest of the Praetorians were formed up across the shingle bank to block any enemy attempting to break out in that direction.

For the last time Cato ran over his preparations and tried to envisage his enemy's possible responses, but every contingency that he could imagine had been considered. His men knew exactly what was required of them and he must trust them to do their duty.

The steadily growing light filtered over the landscape. It was quiet now that the siege weapons were ready and the crews stood silently waiting for the command to unleash their missiles. The first birds began to break into song, while others cried out mournfully and the dark, elegant shapes of swifts darted through the air, weaving around the frames of the onagers and over the battlements of the fort. Cato removed his helmet briefly, to mop his brow and brush any loose strands of hair away from his eyes, before he adjusted his felt skullcap. He eased his helmet on and grasped the cheek guards to work it firmly into position before he tied the straps and gave it an experimental wag from side to side. Satisfied, he shifted his scabbard so that it ran straight down the line of his thigh and then slowly exhaled now his rituals were complete.

'Finished fidgeting?' Macro clicked his tongue. 'Not long now.'

Cato smiled to himself at the unnecessary comment. So Macro was as tense as he was on the cusp of action. Glancing round the crewmen of the battery, Cato realised that every man in his command shared the sensation. Poised to act. Willing it to happen.

The cool blue tint of the morning air gave way to the first bright shaft of light as the sun edged above the crest of a hill and fiery orange spilled across the landscape and threw the stark shadows of the onager frames across the ground towards the battlements of the fort, where Cato could easily see the gleam of helmets and the glint of spears as the Parthians stared back, at last fully aware of their fate.

He raised his arm and took a deep breath.

'Onagers! Make ready!'

The section leaders braced their feet and grasped the levers, waiting for the order that would unleash the throwing arms.

There was a beat as every man held his breath. Then Cato swept his arm down.

'Onagers! Release!'

CHAPTER TWELVE

The quiet of the dawn was shattered as the stout timbers flew up and cracked against the padded leather buffers on the crossbeams. The rocks shot out of the slings and streaked up at a sharp angle, slowing as they reached the top of the arc they described towards the fort. Cato snatched a glance at the enemy and saw their faces raised towards the death and destruction now swooping down towards them.

The first rock landed with a large explosion of grit and dirt at the foot of the wall and then the others struck home in rapid succession. Another miss and a strike on the wall and the last went over the battlements and out of sight.

'What the fuck are you gawping at?' Macro roared. 'Get on them loading levers, you idle bastards! The emperor does not pay you by the bloody half day!'

At once the men threw themselves into action and the clanking of the ratchets rang in their ears as Cato attempted to recall the fall of shot for each weapon as best he could. 'Onagers one and two, adjust up for range! The others are good. Shoot at will!' He strode towards the optio in command of the heavy bolt-throwers and pointed towards the fort. 'Have your crews sweep the battlements. I want you to keep their heads down, and level the crenellations as much as you can to reduce their cover. Shoot at will.'

'Yes, sir. You heard the tribune, lads! Pick your own targets.'

An instant later the first bolt leaped through the gap between the throwing arms and swept towards the fort in a much flatter trajectory than the rocks hurled by the onagers. Cato saw it strike three feet below the top of the fort's gatehouse and there was an explosion of debris and the Parthian standing behind the wall was snatched from view.

Macro snorted with surprise. 'Bloody thing's made out of mud bricks. The bolt went right through it! Sweet Jupiter, we'll knock it to pieces in no time.'

Cato did not reply as he watched the other bolts smash into the fortifications with equally destructive results. He could imagine the helpless terror of the defenders as the vicious iron heads burst through the wall in front of them, showering them with grit. He watched for a little longer, until a swirling haze of dust hung over the fort.

'Keep them at it, Macro. As fast as the crews can work their weapons. I want the Parthians to be shitting themselves with fear.'

'Yes, sir!' Macro rubbed his hands gleefully as he paced along the line barking encouragement at his men.

Cato trotted out of the rear of the battery and made his way round the earthworks to find that Centurion Keranus had already given the order for his men to add their weight to the barrage. Slipping lead shot into their pouches the men swung the thongs in a loop, then quickly switched the movement overhead to build up speed before releasing their grip with a snap and sending their deadly missiles whirring towards the ramparts. Small explosions of dried mud marked their impact. Just a handful of faces were visible now as only the brave and the foolhardy dared to expose themselves. One of the Parthians was struck in the face and jerked back out of sight.

'Good shot!' Cato called out. 'Keep it up.'

For the next hour the bombardment levelled the battlements and the gates were shattered as one of the onagers scored several direct hits. The nearest corner of the fort had begun to collapse into the shallow ditch beneath. Returning to the battery Cato gave the order to slow the rate of shooting to conserve ammunition so that they would have enough left to batter open a breach if the enemy refused to surrender.

The blare of a trumpet drew his attention towards Rhadamistus and the main body of his horsemen. He could see the prince throwing back his robes as he reached for his bow case, drew the weapon out and fitted the bowstring over the horns. Around him, his men followed suit.

'What in Hades does he think he's doing?' asked Macro.

Cato felt a stab of anxiety in his guts as he looked on and saw Rhadamistus point a hand to his trumpeter. A fresh note cut through the dawn air, and with a ragged cheer of excitement the Iberians rippled forward into a walk, quickly accelerating into a trot and then a steady canter as they surged towards the fort. The slingers turned as they heard the cheers and the pounding of hoofs and ran out of the path of the oncoming horsemen. Macro saw the imminent danger at once and cupped his hands to his mouth and shouted.

'Cease shooting! Before you hit the bastards.'

The order came too late for one of the bolt-thrower crews: there was a final crack and the weapon lurched violently as the shaft flew towards the fort. Macro rounded on the crew at once and stabbed a finger at them. 'You! Yes, you lot! You're on a charge. Optio! Take their names!'

Rhadamistus and his men swept forward in a wave of flowing robes and flickering horse manes and tails. As they approached the fort, the first of the defenders reappeared behind the battered defences. Then, as soon as he saw that the battery was standing by, he called to his comrades and the wall was swiftly lined with men, many of whom were armed with bows, Cato noted, with sick apprehension of what was to come. Sixty paces from the outer ditch, Rhadamistus swerved his horse and his men followed suit as they began their ride around the fort, loosing arrows at the defenders. At the same moment the Parthians shot back and the first two riders toppled from their mounts, and several of the horses were struck, rearing or stumbling and crashing to the ground, crushing their riders beneath them. It was not an entirely one-sided exchange of missiles, and Cato saw one of the enemy topple from the wall into the ditch as the Iberians galloped round the fort.

'A magnificent spectacle,' Macro observed. 'But it ain't how war is fought, the foolish bastards.'

More men fell from their saddles as the Parthians concentrated on the leader of the horsemen recklessly galloping around them. Yet every arrow missed him, even as many struck his followers, and

Rhadamistus coolly aimed, shot, and nocked fresh arrows as he steered his horse with his knees.

'What are we going to do, sir? He's going to get them all killed at this rate.'

But there was nothing that could be done, Cato realised. If he gave the order to charge the fort, his infantry would most likely be trampled by the Iberians. Even if they managed to avoid the Praetorians, the two units would become hopelessly entangled and present a dense target for the Parthians.

'Damn him,' Cato muttered as he glared at the distant prince.

Then the Iberians' trumpet shrilled again, and they swerved away from the fort and let fly their final arrows across the rumps of their mounts. As Rhadamistus led them back to their starting point, Cato saw at least thirty men and horses writhing in the dust around the fort. He had to seize his chance to take back control of his unravelling plan.

'Macro, get your century down there in a line between those idiots and the fort, and don't let them get past you. Go!'

As the centurion called to his men, Cato grabbed Narses and made for their horses, which had been brought up to the rear of the battery. Swinging himself up into the saddle, Cato took a tight hold of the reins and kicked his heels in. The two riders galloped round the edge of the battery as Macro led his century obliquely across the open ground to cut the Iberians off. Cato could see that Rhadamistus was already readying for another fruitless charge and hoped that Macro and his riders would have time to place themselves between the Iberians and the fort. He himself steered his horse directly towards the gatehouse. As soon as he was within bowshot distance he slowed to a trot, then a walk, all the while feeling an icy tingling in his spine as he watched the enemy on the wall intently. Most stared at him, some held their bows ready and a handful took careful aim at the two riders. Fifty paces out, Cato reined in and raised his empty hands for the enemy to see.

'Narses, tell them I have come forward to demand their surrender.'

The Iberian nobleman's chest swelled in readiness, and then he called out to the defenders.

'Tell them that if they refuse, I will order my siege artillery to level the walls and then everyone still alive will be put to the sword. That is what will happen. No one is coming to their aid. I have all the time I need to wipe them out,' Cato bluffed. 'Ask their commander to make himself known.'

There was a brief delay before one of the splintered gates was forced open just far enough for a man to squeeze through. A slender figure wearing a scale vest over a dark tunic and breeches emerged. He wore a conical helmet with a strip of black cloth tied about the rim. As he approached warily, Cato saw he had a narrow beard and a thin face with deep-set eyes. He did not appear to be armed as he stopped ten paces away and addressed Cato in a high-pitched voice.

'He says he is Baltagases, the senior surviving officer,' Narses translated.

Cato looked more closely and saw that the Parthian was no more than a youth. 'I don't believe him. Tell him I demand to speak to the commander of his band.'

There was a brief exchange, and Cato noted the anger in the young man's tone.

'Baltagases says that his father was the leader. Until he was killed within moments of your attack starting. So he is in command now.'

Cato nodded. It was unfortunate that he was dealing with an inexperienced youth who had shortly before had the responsibility of command thrust upon him. Moreover, Baltagases' mind was bound to be clouded with grief at losing his father. That could well affect his judgement, and place many lives at risk, Roman as well as Parthian. Cato felt little compassion for his loss. After all, Baltagases and his father had led the raid across the river and had killed some of the townspeople and looted their valuables. Thanks to the timely arrival of Cato's men the people of Arbelis had avoided worse treatment at the hands of the Parthians. No, there was no cause for pity, he decided.

'Then I'll address my demands to him. Tell Baltagases he is to surrender, immediately. There will be no second chance.'

The Parthian heard the stark instruction and then stared at Cato in silence for a moment, seeming to weigh him up. Cato stared directly back, his features fixed and his expression implacable. Then the youth's gaze wavered and he clasped his hands together at the end of his loose arms as he made his reply.

'He asks what terms you will offer him. He wishes for free passage if he gives his word to return to his estate near Nisibus.'

'Nisibus?'

'A city far to the east,' Narses explained.

Cato shook his head and Baltagases spoke again.

'He says he gives his word that they will not take up arms against Rome. Until the present war is over.'

'No.'

'He says they will give up their weapons and all their valuables as well.'

Cato smiled cynically. Whatever valuables they had had belonged to the people of Arbelis only the day before. 'My terms are simple. He orders his men to surrender and lay down their arms. Their lives will be spared, but that is all I will guarantee. But only if he surrenders now.'

Cato glanced round and saw that Rhadamistus and his men were edging towards them. Macro shouted an order and the Praetorians advanced their spears. The youth listened to the translation and his face twisted into an anxious expression. He began to speak again, quickly, but Cato raised his hand.

'Enough! I will not waste another moment. Will he surrender? Yes or no? I want the answer at once . . . Do you wish for you and your men to live, or die? If you surrender, I give you my word that your lives will be spared.'

Baltagases visibly flinched as the final terms were translated, then he lowered his head and muttered a few words.

'He will give the order to surrender,' said Narses.

Cato hid the relief that flowed through his body. No more men would need to die this day. 'Very well, he is to order his men to lay down their weapons.'

He did not wait for confirmation but turned his horse and galloped over to Macro.

'The fort's ours,' he announced. 'Their commander has agreed to surrender.'

'Thank fuck for that.' Macro nodded towards Rhadamistus,

who had ordered his men to halt and now rode towards them alone. 'I was worried I might have to stick it to one of them before they came to their senses. The situation could have become ugly.'

Cato gritted his teeth as he watched the Iberian prince approaching. 'Last thing we need is a divided command. If that happens then we're all going to be easy pickings for the Parthians. Let the men know that if there is any trouble between us and that lot, then it won't be because a Roman started it.'

'Yes, sir. I'll make sure the lads behave.'

Rhadamistus slowed as he approached the line of Praetorians and Macro barked an order for the men to part to let him pass through.

'What is the meaning of this?' The prince gestured angrily at the Roman soldiers. 'I was preparing to charge again.'

'There is no need for another charge,' Cato interrupted. 'The Parthians have agreed to surrender.'

'Surrender?' Rhadamistus looked aghast. 'But we've barely started the attack. The cowards!'

'Cowards or not, they're my prisoners now. I gave my word that their lives would be spared. They will be escorted to Antioch while we continue our march without the enemy being any the wiser about our plans.' Cato pointed towards the Iberian casualties scattered around the fort. 'And no need for us to lose any more men. I call that a good day's work, Majesty.'

Rhadamistus rested his hands on his saddle pommel and leaned closer to Cato. 'And what if one of the prisoners should escape and carry news of our column to the enemy?'

'I doubt there is much chance of that happening.'

'Nevertheless, it might. Is it worth the risk? Then there's the matter of the men required to guard the prisoners on the way back to Antioch. How many will that be? Thirty? Fifty? Men we can hardly afford to lose.'

'I agree, Majesty. Any more than we can afford to lose men in attacks by your horse-archers on an enemy protected by fortifications. If I had not been able to persuade the Parthians to surrender, then I am sure we would have lost at least as many men in taking the fort as I now have to send back to Antioch to guard the prisoners. And how many more of your men would have become casualties?'

'Tribune Cato, there is a way to ensure that you do not have to deplete your ranks, or mine.'

Cato narrowed his eyes. 'What exactly are you suggesting, Majesty?'

'Kill the prisoners. All of them. That way there is no possibility of any of them escaping to raise the alarm, and no need to assign any men to guard them.'

'I gave my word, Majesty. Their lives will be spared.'

'Your word?' Rhadamistus laughed. 'What is a word? A mere sound that is gone the instant it is spoken. If the enemy think your word matters, then they are fools indeed, and deserve to die. This is war, Tribune. All that matters is surviving long enough to win. Everything else is a mere detail. Kill them, and let's continue into Armenia.'

'No,' Cato replied firmly. 'My word matters to me. And it matters to Rome. I am an officer acting in the name of my emperor. If I give my word and break it, then I dishonour not just myself, but the very name of Rome. I would not be forgiven for that.'

'Who is to know? I will not speak of it. The only other witness is my servant, Narses. If I command it, he will not speak of your breach of faith. But if it pleases you, I will have his tongue cut out, or have him disposed of.'

Cato felt a wave of revulsion sweep through him and it was a struggle to keep his composure as he swallowed to ensure he spoke calmly and clearly. 'I would not ask that of you, Majesty, as I need his services as a translator. In which case his tongue will be required.'

Rhadamistus pursed his lips and nodded. 'This is true. Very well, my point still stands. Who will ever know that your word was broken, eh?'

'I will, and that is enough.' Cato was weary of this exchange, and greatly tired by the night's exertions. 'The Parthians will not be killed.'

Rhadamistus sniffed with disdain and straightened up in his saddle. 'As you wish, Tribune. But I fear you will come to regret your decision. And now I must see to the burial of my dead.' He nodded curtly, gave his reins a sharp tug and turned his mount back towards his waiting men and spurred it into a gallop.

Cato let out a sigh of relief. 'Did you follow that?'

'Most of it,' said Macro. 'Not sure that I care much for our ally's disregard for Roman honour.'

'He's got a point, from a purely pragmatic point of view,' Cato reflected. 'But if people in this world start breaking their word, then we can kiss goodbye to any treaties or trust of any kind. That's not the kind of world in which I'd be happy to live.'

'Nor me,' Macro muttered. 'Guess we'd better be very careful in our dealings with Rhadamistus from now on. I'd trust the bastard just as far as I could comfortably shit him.'

Cato laughed, grateful for the release of the tension that had been building inside him. 'Better be careful what you eat then.'

He pointed to the fort. 'Take four sections, go in there and disarm the prisoners. And see if there's anything in there we can use to secure the Parthians. Chains, rope, whatever comes to hand. Narses can translate for you.'

'Yes, sir.'

'Then get the siege weapons broken down and loaded back on to the wagons. I'm going back across the river to fetch supplies from Arbelis and then bring up the baggage train. With luck, we'll be able to resume marching this afternoon. We'll be in enemy territory from now on. Best we strike out for the Armenian capital as quickly as we can and get this business over with. I'll be a lot happier when we no longer have any dealings with our Iberian friend.'

Macro cast a glance towards Rhadamistus and nodded with feeling. 'I fear he's going to prove as much of a danger to us as the bloody Parthians . . .'

CHAPTER THIRTEEN

Macro led his men over the packed earth ramp and shoved the ruined gates aside. He paused to survey the interior of the fort. Most of the battlements had been smashed in and large sections of the walkway had collapsed. Several bodies lay sprawled over the debris. Some of the rocks shot from the onagers had landed amongst the horse lines and struck down at least twenty of the Parthians' mounts. As many men were injured and being tended to by their comrades. Macro strode forward, aware that every eye was on him, but he felt no fear. If any of the enemy attempted treachery Macro would deal with them without mercy.

'Tell them to hand over their weapons. Swords, daggers, bows, arrows, axes, the lot. I want them put over there.' He indicated the well. 'Anyone who tries to conceal any weapon will go down the well and be left to rot. Make sure they get that.'

As Narses translated, Macro ordered the four sections of Praetorians to surround the interior of the fort and the Romans trotted into position and turned their shields towards the enemy and held their spears ready.

'Keep a good watch on them, lads. If anyone tries to make a break for it then cut 'em down, no questions asked.'

Narses finished talking and for a moment all was still, and none of the Parthians made a move. Macro strode over to the nearest group and thrust his vine cane towards a tall soldier standing defiantly with his arms crossed.

'You're the first, my friend,' he said loudly so all could hear. Even if they did not understand his words, there would be no mistake about his intent. 'Take your sword and that gaudy-looking bow case of yours and drop them by the well.' He jerked his thumb to emphasise the direction. 'NOW!'

The Parthian stared back and stood his ground, unmoving.

'Very well, then.' Macro stepped forward and reached for the man's sword handle. At once the Parthian slipped his arms apart and his hand snapped towards his scabbard. Macro's move had been a feint, and he had fully expected this response and now made his enemy pay for his defiance. Up shot the vine cane, the gnarled knob at the top slamming under the man's chin and jerking his head back. Macro followed up by throwing his weight behind his spare hand as his fist struck the Parthian on the side of the jaw. He staggered back a step and collapsed on to his knees. Bracing himself, Macro delivered a firm kick to the man's collarbone and he landed heavily on his back, dazed and winded. Calmly helping himself to his victim's sword and bow case, Macro handed it to Narses and then glared round at the remaining Parthians.

'Who wants to be next?'

Before Narses had even finished translating, the first of the enemy hurried towards the well. More followed, regarding the Roman centurion warily as they passed by. The light clatter of deposited weapons echoed off the walls as the pile steadily built up. With a nod of satisfaction Macro turned and beckoned to the optio of his century.

'Tertius!'

The Praetorian trotted over. 'Sir?'

'Take over. Once the last of them has handed over his weapons, start binding them. Use whatever you can. If need be, you can tear strips from the clothing on the bodies. Just as long as they're secure and won't be able to make a break for it when they are marched back to Antioch.'

The optio's expression brightened. 'They're to be sold as slaves?'

Macro nodded. 'A nice little bonus for the lads, eh? And the campaign has barely started. Carry on.'

He took a last look over the prisoners, daring any man to defy him, then turned about and made his way out of the fort and over the open ground towards the earthworks surrounding the battery. The other six sections of his century and Metellus's crews were

111

standing or squatting around the siege engines, cheerfully celebrating their easy victory with wine and good-humoured conversation. Macro scowled as he tapped his cane sharply against his greave.

'And what in Hades is this? A fucking public holiday? Well no one told me about it, ladies. Now get off your arses and get this kit packed on to the wagons.'

The Praetorians leaped up, hastily replacing the stoppers of their canteens, and set to work knocking out the wooden pegs and working the timber frames loose before carrying them off to the wagons behind the battery. Macro paced up and down making sure that no one slacked off. It was too bad that the men had lost a night's sleep, and they might curse him for being driven on, but he had little sympathy. In fact, he was inclined towards quiet satisfaction as he watched the emperor's most pampered soldiers being obliged to work as hard as the men of the legions.

It would be good for them, Macro told himself. There was nothing like proper soldiering for making proper soldiers and he was pleased with the way the men of the Second Cohort were shaping up. Despite his doubts, they had performed well in Spain the previous year, and he had few complaints about their professional approach to this latest venture. He was even inclined to hope that one day they might match the standard of his beloved Second Legion – the unit he had first served with, and where he had met Cato. The memory of his first encounter with the scrawny youth who was far too educated and unworldly made Macro smile. He would never have guessed that young Cato would rise to command a cohort. He had even doubted whether the recruit would survive his first fight. But Macro had been proved wrong and he had long since learned to respect Cato's judgement and soldierly qualities.

He paused, mid-stride, conscious that he was still smiling, and looked around sharply, catching the eye of one of the men nearby. 'What are you gawping at, my lad? Got a thing for centurions, have you?'

'No, sir.' The Praetorian tried to hide his amusement.

'Are you saying you don't like me?'

'Yes, sir. I mean . . .'

Macro leaned his head closer to the man, eyes wide with staged hostility. 'You don't like me? Me, who treats his men like he was their own fucking mother? What kind of ungrateful bastard are you?'

The Praetorian's amusement evaporated like morning dew in the desert and he opened and closed his mouth helplessly as he struggled to compose a reply that did not deepen his centurion's anger.

'Pah! I'll be watching you, my lad.' Macro straightened up. 'Now put your bloody back into it and get that bolt-thrower broken down. Before you break my bloody heart any further.'

He stalked off with a scowling expression, daring anyone else to meet his gaze as he passed by. As the sun rose and warmed the arid terrain the siege weapons were dismantled and loaded on to their wagons. Over by the fort the Iberian horsemen walked their mounts towards the river so that they could be watered. Macro watched them for a moment and clicked his tongue. They were fine riders, and fine archers, no doubt. But their prince was as foolhardy as he was courageous, and Macro had served long enough to know how dangerous a combination of qualities that could be. Hopefully Cato had Rhadamistus in hand now and there would be no more unnecessary loss of men in futile attacks. It would be a relief when the man was securely on his throne and the Romans could leave Armenia in the hands of their ally. For Macro that would mean a return to the arms of Petronella, a prospect that warmed his heart and firmed his resolve to complete his mission as soon as possible.

Once the last of the siege engines had been dismantled and loaded on to the wagons, amidst much cracking of whips and braying of mules, Macro ordered the siege train to move back down to the track a short distance from the fort. The Praetorians took up their shields and spears and marched alongside the vehicles. It was then that Macro noticed a movement on the wall of the fort and stepped to one side of the dust being stirred by the heavy wheels of the wagons. Now he could clearly make out one of the Praetorians, bare-headed and unarmed, clambering over the crumbling battlements and dropping down to the base of the wall. He hit the ground and rolled out of sight into the ditch. An instant later, Macro saw the man scramble over the lip of the ditch and come running towards them.

Macro felt his guts give a slight lurch and at once he filled his lungs and bellowed the orders for the siege train to halt and then for his century to form up.

'Stay here!' he shouted, then trotted to meet the man half running, half stumbling from the fort. They met some fifty paces from the siege train, as the man drew up, gasping for breath.

'What's happening, man?' Macro demanded. 'Speak up.'

'It's them . . . Iberians, sir. They're killing the prisoners.'

Macro looked beyond him towards the fort. In the absence of the grinding rumble of the wagons' wheels he could hear the distant shouts and cries for the first time. He grasped the Praetorian's shoulders and gave him a savage shake. 'What in fucking Hades is going on? I left Tertius in charge. Where is he?'

'In . . . the fort, sir. With the . . . rest of the lads.'

'Then why are the prisoners being killed?'

'Rhadamistus, sir. He came into the fort with some of his men. Went up to the optio and some of the lads with him. Then . . . quick as you like, they had 'em pinned . . . knives at their throats. Ordered the rest of us to lower our spears or . . . they'd cut the throats of the optio and the others. Tertius told 'em to do as he said.'

'Did he now?' Macro glowered. 'And then?'

The Praetorian tried to take even breaths, so that he could speak clearly. 'Rhadamistus had his men bring the prisoners to him one at a time, and he cut their heads off with his sword. I had been taking a piss behind one of the stables when the trouble started. Knew I had to get out and find you, sir. Came across the entrance to one of the watchtowers so I climbed up, crawled along the wall until I found a gap I could use to get down the outside.'

'All right.' Macro nodded. 'Good work. Join the wagons.'

The Praetorian saluted and ran off, leaving Macro staring towards the fort. The screams carried to his ears clearly now. He must act at once. Glancing over his shoulder he raised his arm. 'First Century! On me, at the double!'

He ran across the open ground, hearing the drumming of boots and the chink of loose kit behind him. Ahead, he saw a figure rise up above the gatehouse, watching the Romans for a moment before turning to gesticulate down into the heart of the fort. As he ran,

114

Macro switched the vine cane to his left hand and drew his sword. Then, conscious of the danger of drawn weapons making matters worse, he returned it to the scabbard and gritted his teeth furiously. Macro and his Praetorians were no more than fifty paces from the shattered gates when they saw one of the Iberians clamber on to the wall to one side, spear in one hand and a fist full of hair in the other from which swayed a dripping head. He planted the spearhead securely into the rubble and then jammed the head on to the iron point of the butt, before standing back to admire his work. More of Rhadamistus's men appeared along the wall, each carrying a spear and head as they proceeded to follow their comrade's example.

'Fuckin' barbarians,' one of the Praetorians behind Macro grunted.

'Shut your mouth!' Macro snapped over his shoulder. 'No one breathes a word. No one but me.'

He halted the century just in front of the ramp and had the men close up. Through the open gate he could see a pile of corpses heaped in the courtyard before the doors of the barracks. A pair of Iberians dragged another headless body, bound hand and foot, to the heap and dumped it on top. Macro sighed inwardly and muttered to himself: 'Time to put a stop to this.'

'Advance!'

At the head of his men he marched across the ramp and under the arch above the gates. On the far side he was met with a scene from a slaughterhouse. To the left the surviving Parthians were crowded together at spearpoint, while the Romans stood helplessly to the right, also under guard. To one side of the gatehouse was a raised platform, waist high, from where the garrison's commander had once reviewed his men. Now Rhadamistus stood in his place, surrounded by heads and pools of blood. Even as Macro watched, two of the Iberians thrust another prisoner on to his knees. The Parthian was wailing pitifully as he struggled and had to be held down. The prince grasped the man's hair in his left hand and pulled hard, forcing his exposed neck down. Then his sword rose high, paused for a beat and slashed down in a blur. Head and body parted in a burst of crimson with a sound like an axe head burying itself in wet sand. Rhadamistus, splattered with gore, smiled with satisfaction and tossed the head aside as he caught sight of Macro and his men. Before he could speak, Macro turned and shouted an order to the Praetorians under guard.

'Stop standing there. Pick your kit up and fall in! Move!'

His men hesitated briefly before Tertius pushed his way between their Iberian guards and strode towards the shields, spears and swords piled at the side of the barracks. One of the Iberians fitted an arrow to his bowstring and swung round to take aim at the optio's back.

'Don't you fucking dare!' Macro roared and ran across to the man and slashed his vine cane down on the bow arm, and the weapon fell from the Iberian's numbed fingers. Macro lashed out again at the man's head and he staggered back. At once his comrades raised their spears and bows, but Rhadamistus barked an order in a loud, booming voice that echoed back off the walls of the fort. His men backed away and the Praetorians hurried to follow the optio and arm themselves before they joined their comrades at Macro's back.

There was a brief stillness in the fort as the Romans and Iberians stood in silent confrontation either side of the heap of Parthian corpses. High above, a handful of buzzards spiralled lazily as they waited for their chance to descend and feed.

'Tertius,' Macro spoke quietly, 'go and find the tribune. Tell him what's happened. He should be with the baggage wagons, close to the river by now. Be quick about it.'

'Yes, sir.' The optio turned and ran out through the gatehouse.

Rhadamistus stepped down from the platform and strode casually towards Macro, then paused at the pile of corpses to clean his blade on the clothes of one of his victims before he sheathed the sword. He stood in front of Macro and folded his arms.

'Centurion Macro, I sense that you do not approve of my actions.'

Macro stared back, trying his best to conceal his disgust at a man who could butcher defenceless prisoners for sport. His voice was strained as he replied in halting Greek: 'Those men are captives of Rome. You have no right to kill them. Especially since my commanding officer gave his word that they would live.'

'They are our enemies. Yours and mine. We are at war with them. It is our duty to kill them until the war is over. You Romans can't be trusted to do your duty, so I am doing it for you instead.

116

This way we don't waste any time, nor food nor water on these Parthian scum. Nor do we have to waste any of our men guarding them. Now, take your men out of the fort and let me finish my work.'

'Work?' Macro arched his eyebrows. 'Is that what you call this? I can think of a better word for it.'

'Really? And what would that be?'

Macro forced himself not to reply, anxious that the situation did not spark off a fight between the two sides that would destroy any hope for the wider mission's success. Rhadamistus watched his troubled expression closely and smiled.

'Come now, Centurion, surely this is no way for friends to speak to each other? I suggest that you take your men out of the fort and wait outside if the sight of blood distresses you.'

'We'll leave once you hand the prisoners over.'

The Iberian prince took a step closer, so that he towered over Macro. 'You will address me by my title. I have overlooked this for the sake of our alliance. I will not do so again. Do you understand?'

'Yes,' Macro swallowed bitterly. 'Majesty.'

'That's better. Now take your men outside.'

Macro shook his head. 'Not while those prisoners are alive, Majesty. They come with us. I insist on it.'

'I see.' Rhadamistus nodded, and backed off a few paces. 'Very well, I have grown tired of killing those dogs in any case. I shall take no more heads.'

Macro let out a relieved sigh and immediately felt the edge taken off the tension in his muscles. He bowed his head to the Iberian prince before the latter turned and paced towards his waiting men who stood ready with their weapons. Macro saw him wave in the direction of the Parthians and issue some instructions in a calm, casual tone. At once the Iberian archers turned on the prisoners and loosed their arrows into the dense target. They shot swiftly, nocking arrow after arrow, and the range was too close to miss. The Parthians cried out piteously and shrank from the barrage of lethal shafts, but there was no refuge, no cover, and the cries quickly died away as bodies fell, one upon the other, until there was a fresh mound of corpses and the twitching of the wounded, accompanied by their agonised moans.

All this happened under the eyes of Macro and his men, before he could even think how best to act. Then it was too late. As soon as the last of the prisoners went down the archers closed in and drew their daggers to cut the throats of those still living, and there was none for Macro to save.

Rhadamistus took a sip from his wineskin as he surveyed the scene and then called across to Macro.

'Like I said, Centurion, I have taken no more heads.' He laughed. 'You see, I too am a man of my word.'

CHAPTER FOURTEEN

'I'm telling you, Cato, he seemed to be having the time of his life.' Just standing there and butchering the prisoners. That Iberian lad is not quite right in the head. Oh, sure, he's a brave one. Leads from the front and all that, but he's dangerous. He's got a taste for blood, and woe betide anyone who crosses him.' Macro shook his head. 'For a moment there, back in the fort, I was sure he might even turn on me and my boys.'

'Then it's as well you did nothing to provoke him any further,' Cato replied tersely as he shielded his eyes and peered into the distance. A mile ahead he could pick out the small groups of horsemen screening the advance of his column. To his right rose a range of hills that overlooked the narrow strip of level ground on each side of the tributary of the Euphrates that the local people called Murad Su, according to Narses. There was arable land on either bank, and farms and villages dotted the landscape. Rhadamistus and his horsemen ensured that they seized every decent mount along the route to ensure that no warning of their advance could be given.

It was two days since they had taken the fort guarding the crossing, and an uneasy mood had settled on the column as they entered Armenian territory. The Praetorians and the auxiliaries kept themselves apart from the Iberians. Before the massacre of the prisoners, there had been an amicable enough relationship between the allies, with some trading of rations and trinkets, and good-humoured attempts to learn each other's tongues. Now, they marched apart, ate apart and no attempt was made to mix within the camp at night. Rhadamistus did not seem concerned about the tension when Cato had cause to confer with him each night about the next day's advance. The Iberian prince spent each evening in his comfortably appointed tent, drinking and feasting with his inner circle of noblemen. When the drinking was done, Rhadamistus retired to his sleeping tent, along with one of the veiled women from his entourage. It was not, Cato reflected, how he himself would have acted as a king returning to claim his throne. Far better to win the people's hearts rather than behave like a common bandit, looting their meagre stocks of food and wine, and abusing their wives and daughters.

'Provoke him?' Macro repeated. 'I did nothing of the sort. The bastard jumped my men and disarmed them, and then started lopping off the prisoner's heads. Prisoners, I might add, who would have fetched a nice price in the slave markets. I'd say he did rather more to provoke me.'

'And you did the right thing by keeping a cool head.'

'I should have put a stop to it,' Macro continued in a sour tone.

Cato leaned on his saddle horn as he half turned to his friend. 'And what would have happened then? What could you have done differently that would not have ended in a fight between you and his men?'

'We could have taken them on.'

'Maybe. But at what cost? You'd have lost most of your century and Rome would have lost the chance to place our man on the Armenian throne. We'd have had to abandon Armenia to the Parthians. Put that in the balance against a little loss of face and I think you can guess how the emperor and his advisers might view things. Even if you survived the fight in the fort I doubt that Nero would have let you live another day once he heard what had happened.'

Macro thought for a moment and scratched his head. 'I suppose you're right.'

'Besides,' said Cato, 'if you had the worst of the encounter, I'd have lost a good friend.'

They shared a brief laugh, and Cato was glad to have lightened the grim mood of his companion. He was feeling the burden of command weigh down on him more and more the further they marched beyond the frontier of the Empire. Even though Armenia was nominally an ally of Rome, the people had far closer blood ties to the Parthians. The hostile demeanour of the natives and the overbearing behaviour of Rhadamistus and his followers wore away at Cato's conviction that he could see this mission through successfully. It was a calculated risk in any case. Corbulo had wagered he could wrest the initiative back from the enemy with a quick strike into Armenia. And he had dispatched Cato with just enough men to warrant the risk, but not so many that the general could not afford to lose them. It no longer mattered whether it was a calculated risk or a mere gamble, Cato concluded. They were committed. That meant their fate was bound to that of Rhadamistus. Whatever Cato or Macro might make of their ally's untrustworthiness or cruelty, they must ensure that he reached Artaxata alive and triumphed over his Parthian rival. Armenia was the prize, he reminded himself. His superiors deemed the kingdom strategically vital to Rome's influence in the east. And that was all that mattered.

The column continued its advance, and each day the hills increased in scale until the horizon was bounded by mountains in every direction, with the river forced to conform to the increasingly rugged terrain as it flowed through the foothills. The rate of advance was dictated by the heavy wagons of the siege train, which ground and bumped along the stony track. The slightest of inclines slowed progress to a crawl and the column was forced to halt to allow the wagons to catch up. Even though it was early summer and the trees were green with fresh leaves and the grassy hills were speckled with bright flowers, the nights were cold and Cato was obliged to send out forage parties for firewood as well as food. But there were no attacks on the foragers, and as darkness fell the camp was illuminated by ruddy pools of firelight that bathed the men warming themselves in a lurid glow.

With every mile they advanced, Cato felt that he and his men were more exposed to danger as they tramped across a landscape that was utterly unknown to him, about which he had read only the scantest details before leaving Rome. He was made acutely uncomfortable by the need to rely on the guides of Rhadamistus, who led the column further and further into the mountainous region. It was difficult to hold his suspicions in check, especially as he knew that false guides had caused the ruin of previous Roman expeditions against Parthia.

On the evening of the tenth day they made camp on the edge of a dense forest of pine trees which provided a plentiful supply of fuel for the campfires. Beside the rampart the river flowed by and the men were able to take the opportunity to wash clothes and bathe as twilight settled over the Armenian countryside and the scent of pine needles filled the air. It was a peaceful enough scene, and once Cato was satisfied that the camp was secure for the night he went down to the river for a swim. Removing the leather cuirass he wore on the march, his sword belt, tunic and boots, and lastly his loincloth, he stepped into the shallows and gasped at the coldness of the water. A short distance upstream a group of Praetorians stopped larking about and watched him curiously, amused by the sight of a senior officer stripped of any trappings of rank and as naked as them.

Feeling exposed and slightly ridiculous, Cato waded a few steps further and submerged himself. The shock of the cold water on his skin felt like fire for a moment as he struck out lustily for fifty paces in a bid to get used to the temperature. Then he turned and trod water, and saw that the men had returned to their amusement and no longer regarded him as being of any interest. The river flowed slowly at this point, and Cato was able to observe the camp with a practised eye and was pleased by the neatness of the ramparts, the palisade and watchtowers at each corner and the horse lines beyond the outer ditch. Smoke rose lazily in the still evening air and scored a series of faint lines against the violet sky. The dull gleam of the sentries pacing along the wall and keeping a lookout in the towers was reassuring proof that his men were vigilant and ready for any emergency.

The current had carried him a short distance beyond the fort, and so Cato began to swim directly for the bank rather than fight the current in a more direct line towards his kit lying on the bank. As soon as his feet could touch the bottom he surged into the shallows and emerged dripping water and feeling refreshed and hungry as he paced up stream. The air felt comfortable after the chill of the river and he pulled on his tunic and tied his boots and bundled the rest of

122

his kit under his arm before striding down to the men splashing in the shallows.

'Time to get out, lads. It'll be dark soon and I want everyone safely behind the ramparts before then.'

The men returned to the bank as he strode off towards the nearest gate and exchanged a salute with the sentries standing guard at the entrance to the camp. Within, most of the men were busy cooking their evening meal over the fires, and away to Cato's right, beyond the neat lines of tents of the Praetorians and the slingers, he saw the Iberians tents, massed with no apparent order, other than that they were erected around the much larger tent of Rhadamistus. There was a stretch of open ground between the two forces which underscored the residual lack of trust that still lingered.

When Cato reached his tent he found Narses waiting for him outside.

'My king requests that you join him for dinner.'

'Requests?' Cato smiled slightly. 'I imagine the original wording was that he commands me to join him.'

Narses smiled back. 'Indeed, Tribune. I merely wished to couch the invitation in more diplomatic terms out of respect for your sensibilities.'

'I appreciate your tact and will attend His Majesty directly.'

'As directly as convenient would be greatly appreciated, sir,' Narses said anxiously.

'I'll do my best.' Cato paused a moment. Rhadamistus was not in the habit of inviting him to his evening feasts. 'What's the occasion?'

Narses sighed. 'The prospect of imminent action, I should think. Knowing him as well as I do.'

'Imminent action?' Cato arched an eyebrow.

'You'll find out for yourself soon enough, sir.' Narses bowed and hurried away. Before Cato could call him back and demand a more detailed response, the Iberian had ducked between the tents and disappeared.

Rhadamistus and his circle were already eating when Cato arrived. The Iberian prince greeted him effusively and beckoned him over to the couch to his right, the place of honour. Some slaves brought him platters of spiced mutton and bread and a jar of wine. As Cato settled, Rhadamistus rolled on to to his side to face him.

'Feast well, my friend. Tomorrow we will reach the town of Ligea and my revenge against those who betrayed me will begin.'

Cato had been about to eat a strip of mutton but now replaced it on the platter as he looked at the Iberian prince. 'This is the first I've heard of any town nearby, Majesty.'

'That's because you and your men march like snails and you have no cavalry. My advance patrols first observed the town two days ago.'

'And you did not see fit to inform me that we were approaching this town, Ligea?'

'Would it have made a difference if I had? We are here now and Ligea is a short march beyond the forest. You will see it for yourself tomorrow and the enemy are sure to surrender once you demonstrate the power of your siege weapons.'

'The enemy? There are Parthians in Ligea?'

'I doubt it. If there are any Parthian forces in Armenia then they are most likely to be protecting that coward Tiridates skulking in my capital.'

'I see, so the people in Ligea are Armenians, rather than our enemy.'

Rhadamistus frowned. 'They are *my* enemy, Tribune. Ligea closed its gates to me when I was forced to flee. They declared for the usurper and refused my followers and myself any shelter or succour. And for that they will pay with their lives. Like all those who betrayed their king. I mean to teach the people of Armenia a lesson about the price of treachery.'

Cato listened to his words with a sinking heart. He could easily imagine the circumstances under which the hapless people of Ligea were confronted with a king on the run demanding their help, and knowing that if they answered the call then they would inevitably incur the wrath of the new ruler sitting on the throne in Artaxata. They had chosen the safest path at the time. Cato would have done the same himself. And now they would be living in abject terror when they realised the man they had spurned as a fugitive had returned at the head of a small army. But there was an opportunity to be had here, Cato realised.

124

'Majesty, would it not be wiser to show mercy to the Ligeans? Perhaps they acted out of fear of Tiridates, rather than animosity to you. Pardon them and their gratitude will reward you many times over as they spread word of your magnanimity. Punish them and they will become your implacable enemy and the fate of their town will act as a beacon to unite other towns and cities against you.'

Rhadamistus shook his head. 'Fear is the key. You made that point yourself just then. They feared Tiridates and so turned against me. So I must make them fear me even more to make them turn against my rival. That is the secret of power. I learned that from one of your emperors, Caligula. "Let them hate, as long as they obey me." Wise words.'

Cato kept his mouth shut. He remembered the years of terror under Caligula and was not inclined to regard that emperor as anything other than dangerously insane.

'Wise words,' Rhadamistus repeated with emphasis. 'Wouldn't you agree?'

'I'm not sure, Majesty, since the author of the aphorism was murdered by his own bodyguards, and most of his family along with him. I would hate for the same to happen to you should your actions turn your people against you.'

Rhadamistus laughed. 'They will do as I wish, or they will face the consequences. Let Ligea be an object lesson for them all.'

Cato steeled himself before he spoke again. 'I do not think it is wise to take unnecessary risks. Ligea may be a small town. It may be easily taken, but that will come at the cost of lives and time, neither of which it would be wise for us to squander if we are to have the best chance of capturing Artaxata. I suggest we bypass the town and continue our march, Majesty. At least, if we must halt before the town gates, then offer them the hand of friendship. Who knows? You may win new recruits to our force. We could use more men.'

Rhadamistus stared back a moment and then nodded. 'Very well, there is some wisdom in your words. I will give the matter some thought. It is true that we need to reach Artaxata quickly. Besides, I am keen to be with my wife, Zenobia . . .' He reached for his cup and took a thoughtful sip before he continued speaking, but without meeting Cato's gaze. 'My Zenobia. She is the most beautiful of women, Tribune. The partner of my labours. There is nothing she would not do for me. She is as worthy of being a queen as any woman in this world. All men desire her, yet she is mine. Mine alone.' His expression darkened. 'And she is in hiding. Waiting until it is safe for her to emerge.'

Cato could not help expressing his surprise. 'You left her behind?'

'Tiridates' assassins would kill her as eagerly as they would me. It is better for her to remain hidden until my return. Somewhere she will not be found.' He glanced shrewdly at Cato before he continued. 'You know the effect that such a woman can have? Sometimes it is like staring at the sun. Which is why I need the company of lesser women from time to time.' He clapped his hands and called out loudly in the Armenian tongue. At once a flap lifted at the rear of the tent and three young women were ushered in by one of his bodyguards. Cato was dimly aware of the sound of a trumpet sounding above the hubbub of conversation, but his attention was drawn to the women, each one a beauty. They wore simple flimsy linen tunics and shuffled across the tent until they stood before Rhadamistus, eyes cast down with fear. He ran his gaze over them and then pointed to the woman in the middle.

'I'll have her.' He spoke in Greek. 'You can take one of the others to enjoy, my friend. My men took them from a local village just the other day. I gave orders that they were not to be touched by the common soldiers. So I offer you a gift. Which one shall it be?'

Cato shook his head. 'A Roman officer is always on duty, Majesty. I have no time for such pleasures. I must take my leave of you and do the rounds of my sentries.'

It was a bald lie, but Cato was tired and he had spent as much time as he could bear in the company of the Iberian prince.

'So soon? A pity. Then perhaps I shall have them given to my bodyguards for their pleasure.'

Just then, the woman on the right glanced up and caught Cato's eye and he thought that she looked terrified. He could imagine her fear at being torn from her home by the Iberians. It was only for a moment that their eyes met but there was something in her expression, a plea, and Cato resolved to do what he could to save her from the abuse at the hands of Rhadamistus's bodyguards.

'You are right, Majesty. A soldier needs such diversions. I'll take that one.' He pointed.

'Bernisha? A good choice. I'll have her sent to you. With some wine. Enjoy them both, my friend.'

Cato bowed his head and eased himself up from the couch, just as a guard ducked through the main entrance to the tent. He lowered his head as he addressed Rhadamistus, who then turned to Cato.

'It seems your centurion Macro is outside. He wishes to speak to you urgently.'

Cato hurried under the flaps and into the cool air outside. Night had fallen and the stars pricked out above the jagged lines of the surrounding mountains. Macro stood to one side, vine cane resting on his shoulders. In the glow from a campfire nearby Cato could clearly see the anxiety in his expression.

'What's happened?'

'It's one of the forage parties, sir. Centurion Petillius and twenty men. They haven't returned to camp. They were due back well before dark, but there's been no sign of them. I've ordered a man to sound the recall at intervals, but there's been no response, no sighting of Petillius and his lads.'

The effects of the wine and the prospect of female company for the night were thrust from Cato's mind as he took this in. It was possible, but unlikely, that the centurion and his men had ventured too far and become lost. Petillius was too experienced to make such a mistake. A niggling fear crept into Cato's mind as he became more certain that there was a sinister reason for the failure of the foraging party to return.

'Shall I get Ignatius to call out his men to look for them, sir?'

'No,' Cato replied instantly. There was no point in sending more men out there in the darkness, to blunder around and possibly fall into the same trap that might have caught Petillius. 'Have Ignatius's century stand ready to man the palisade, if there's any trouble.'

'Do you think there will be?'

Cato thought for a moment. 'I hope not. I hope the fools are just stumbling around in the forest, but if they're not, then we'll need to be ready for anything. Give Ignatius his orders. I'll be at the gate facing the forest. Find me there.'

'Yes, sir.'

They exchanged a salute and Macro turned to trot back towards the Roman tent lines while Cato strode towards the gate. He was inclined to rush, but did not wish be seen by his men as anything other than a calm and unruffled commander. By the time he had climbed up on to the rampart he could hear Ignatius bellowing orders to his men and the soft chink of kit as the men moved to take up their positions. A moment later his century marched up to the gateway and halted as Macro joined Cato.

'Anything, sir?'

'Nothing.' Cato had scanned the shadowy treeline but could detect no movement, no sign of the missing men. The bucina sounded the recall three times and fell silent. The quiet around the camp was eerie and Cato felt his skin tingle with expectation in the cold night air. Something had happened to Petillius and his men, he was sure of it now. Time crept by, like a caterpillar picking its way across a flagstone, and at length he was aware of some men approaching from behind and turned to glance down into the fort, where he saw Rhadamistus and four of his bodyguards. The Iberian prince climbed up to his side.

'Narses told me there was something going on amongst your men. What's happening, Tribune?'

Cato explained briefly and then the three of them continued to squint into the darkness, ears straining for any sound of movement. Aside from the occasional mournful cry of some birds down by the river, and from time to time the noise of an animal picking its way through the undergrowth, unnerving enough in itself, there were no other sounds. No voices, no sign of a body of men blundering through the pitch darkness of the forest.

At length Rhadamistus growled softly. 'This is foolishness. If your men are out there, we should find them. I'll take some of my men, and torches, and look for them.'

'No, Majesty. We wait until they return, or until dawn comes. Then we'll start searching. Not before,' Cato concluded firmly.

Rhadamistus was about to protest when a sentry a short distance along the rampart called out. 'Something's moving! Over there!' He thrust his arm out to where the track entered the forest and Cato narrowed his eyes as he looked towards the spot. Then he saw them, barely, dark shapes shifting against the even darker shadows.

Macro cupped his hands to his mouth and bellowed. 'Petillius!'

There was no reply, and a moment later no further sign of movement, as though whoever, or whatever, the sentry had spotted had dissolved into the night. Macro called out again.

'Who goes there? Petillius?'

His challenge was greeted with silence and stillness and it seemed as if everyone in the camp was holding their breath in anticipation of some dreadful event. All that could be heard from that direction was the faint rustle of a light breeze blowing the topmost boughs of the trees.

'What are your orders, sir?' Macro asked quietly.

Cato hesitated. Part of him reasoned that the right thing to do would be to avoid any risk and wait until dawn before sending any men out to search for Petillius. It was possible that the enemy were out there preparing to attack the camp, waiting for the order to rush from the trees. But if that was so then they must know that they had been spotted and so the element of surprise had been lost. In which case there was no need to conceal their presence. Even if it was not the enemy, there had been somebody, or something, out there, watching them, and maybe they were still there, lying in wait. Another part of his mind was anxious to resolve the fate of Petillius and his men. Cato's instinct demanded to know the answer. In the end his instinct, tempered by the calculation that if a large body of enemy soldiers was out there, then they would surely have revealed their presence by now, won out and he cleared his throat.

'Macro, I want torches for Ignatius and his men. The rest of the cohort is to stand to. The slingers as well. You'll take command here.'

'Yes, sir,' Macro acquiesced reluctantly and then hurried down from the wall to carry out his orders. Shortly after, the bucina sounded the stand-to, strident notes carrying over the camp, and instantly the quiet of the night gave way to shouted instructions as the officers roused the men and figures, illuminated by the dying campfires, rushed to form up into their units. Macro returned with a squad bearing flickering torches in each hand. These were handed over to the Praetorians waiting inside the gate as Macro approached Cato.

'I can lead them out, sir.'

'No.' Cato rejected the suggestion firmly. Then he relented. 'Not this time, my friend. You've taken more than your share of risks in the past. Look after the camp. If anything happens to me, then you take command of the column and continue the mission. If anything happens to Rhadamistus, get our men back across the frontier as quick as you can.'

Cato went down to join Ignatius, borrowing a shield from one of the sentries manning the gate. As he hefted the shield, Rhadamistus joined him. The Iberian took a spear from the same sentry and stood beside Cato.

'Majesty, you should stay here.'

'I will come with you, Tribune. The dark holds no fear for me. If the enemy are out there then it will be my pleasure to deal with them.' He patted the hilt of his sword.

'Majesty—'

'No more protests, Tribune. If there is a fight, I want to be at your side. Let us go.'

Cato nodded reluctantly and gave the order. 'Open the gates!'

The sentries removed the locking bar and hauled the hewn timbers aside on their rope hinges. Cato raised his shield and drew his sword. 'Advance!'

The distance from the fort to the forest was just beyond bowshot and they covered the ground at a measured pace, all the while straining their eyes and ears for the slightest hint of danger. The torch-bearers held the torches aloft, and the wavering flames lit up the Praetorians and cast a glow over the ground around them. It made them easy targets, Cato knew, but if the forest fringe was to be searched, it would be possible only by torchlight. They reached the track at an angle and then followed it towards the point where it entered the forest. That was where there now seemed to be some obstacle arranged across the track.

'Steady boys,' Ignatius intoned. 'Keep shields up and eyes open.'

It was an unnecessary comment, Cato realised, and hinted at the nervousness of the centurion.

At the front of the formation, Cato's keen eyes were the first to see what he had thought was an obstacle. As the light of the torches revealed the bodies, he ordered the century to halt and advanced cautiously with Rhadamistus. Petillius and his men had been bound to wooden frames set up across the track. Each man had been crudely flayed and strips of flesh still clung to the red muscle tissue beneath. Worse still, their genitals had been cut off and hung from thongs about the stumps of their necks. Having inflicted the mutilation the enemy had put an end to their lives by cutting their heads off and these were impaled on spikes on the top of each frame. All save one. Petillius had been set up a short distance in advance of the rest and now his head lifted slightly as he let out a keening cry.

At once Cato set down his shield and hurried to the man and lifted his chin gently, keeping his eyes off the bloodied flesh and small sack hanging upon his chest.

'Petillius . . .'

The centurion's eyes flickered open and he blinked weakly as he tried to respond. His mouth opened but only a gargled croak emerged from his lips and Cato saw that his tongue had been scorched to a blackened stump. He took half a step back in horror and disgust. Petillius's expression twisted into one of agonised frustration as he tried to speak again but all he could manage was a series of bestial groans. There was nothing that could be done for him, Cato realised. The centurion was a ruin, tortured and tormented by the agonies he had endured at the enemy's hands. Death was now only a release from suffering. Cato raised his sword and looked into Petillius's eyes. 'I'm sorry, brother . . .'

The centurion stared back, shaking his head slowly as the ghastly noises from his throat rose in volume. Cato hesitated, unable yet to bring himself to end the man's agony.

Rhadamistus stepped forward and spoke gently. 'Let me do this, Tribune. It will be done swiftly. He will not suffer any more.'

'No.' Cato shook his head. 'No. I have to. He was one of my men.'

The Iberian moved aside and Cato raised his sword to the vertical and rested the point in the soft tissue just behind Petillius's collar bone. Then, grasping the handle firmly in both hands, he drove it down deeply into the centurion's chest, tearing into his heart. Petillius convulsed, shuddered powerfully and then again more weakly as his head lolled back and his jaws opened and closed and then hung slack. Cato worked the blade free as hot blood coursed from the wound. He wiped the blade on the grass quickly before returning the sword to the scabbard. It took a moment before he was in full command of his wits again and called out.

'Cut the bodies down and take them back to the fort.'

While Ignatius instructed his men in their grisly duty, Cato looked on, a cold fury building in his heart. It seemed likely that word of what had happened to the Parthians in the fort had reached the enemy. This was their revenge. He had lost one of his officers and twenty good men, butchered like sheep. They would be avenged, he swore to himself. No one could commit an atrocity like this on Roman soldiers and be allowed to go unpunished. No one.

'Tribune.' Rhadamistus spoke quietly. 'This is the handiwork of my enemies in Armenia. Now you see what these craven savages are capable of.'

'Yes,' Cato replied numbly.

'There is no question of showing them mercy. Not after this. You agree?'

'Yes.'

'They must be punished, Tribune.'

'Yes.'

'They must be put to the sword, every single one of them. How else can we teach these dogs to respect Rome? Ligea must be burned to the ground and its people slaughtered. Let their bodies feed the crows. Let that serve as a warning to all who defy us.'

Cato felt his numbed outrage steadily twisting into a dark, implacable wrath as he watched Ignatius and his men cut down the bodies and remove the heads from the spikes. Petillius was the last to be dealt with, and as the cords around him were cut, his body fell limply to the ground at Cato's feet. He swallowed bitterly and cleared his throat.

'Tomorrow, Ligea dies.'

CHAPTER FIFTEEN

'A nd who are those fellows?' asked Macro as a small party of horsemen in fine robes were escorted towards the main column by a squadron of Iberian horse-archers.

Cato said nothing as he regarded the strangers' approach. He was still profoundly absorbed by the funeral that had taken place that morning. The bodies of Petillius and his men had been laid upon a long corduroy platform of logs and the pyre was lit by Cato himself. The Second Cohort had stood in silence as they formed up on three sides around the pyre and watched the flames catch and spread until the wooden logs and bodies were engulfed in a swirling inferno. Above, the smoke billowed into the sky and the air was filled with the acrid tang of roast meat and burned pine resin. At one point, as the corpses began to contort in the heat of the blaze, one of the bodies rose slowly into a sitting position and seemed to look directly at Cato as he stood in front of the other officers and the standards of the cohort. It had unnerved him for a moment and he felt as if the figure was demanding something of him. Demanding vengeance. Slowly, too slowly, the flames consumed the body and the remains collapsed amid the charred logs as the pyre settled and steadily burned itself out, leaving a pile of glowing embers and thin trails of smoke.

'Remember our comrades!' Cato had called out. 'Never forget that they were denied a soldier's death and they passed into the shades with hearts filled with the desire for revenge. Praetorians, they were slaughtered like animals by our enemies. Subjected to torture and humiliation that went far beyond what is tolerable in war. Their spirits cry out to us from beyond the grave, demanding

133

vengeance! Demanding that we visit fire and fury and ferocity upon the enemy! We shall not rest until the Parthians responsible for this outrage are hunted down and butchered without mercy. Only then will our brothers, Centurion Petillius and his men, know peace.' Cato raised his arms and face towards the smoke-stained heavens. 'This I swear, before Jupiter, Best and Greatest! Brothers, swear it with me!'

The Praetorians chorused the oath with an angry roar. 'This we swear, before Jupiter, Best and Greatest!'

As the cohort formed up to march, Cato had seen the bitter determination in their faces and he felt cold satisfaction at the prospect of the wrath they would unleash against the enemy when the chance presented itself. The deaths of their comrades would be avenged many times over before their thirst for blood was slaked. The column had progressed in silence all morning, with none of the customary banter and occasional marching songs that usually accompanied them.

Now, just after noon had come and gone, Cato and Macro were riding a short distance behind Rhadamistus and his coterie when the prince halted and sat tall in his saddle, reins in his right hand while his left rested on his hip, with his elbow projecting imperiously. The two Romans caught up and waited until the newcomers approached. Close to, Cato could see that they wore gold chains and jewelled rings, and their robes had a silky sheen to the material. Clearly men of some worth, but also men who feared Rhadamistus, judging by their nervous expressions. They dropped from their saddles and bowed low, before their leader stepped forward and addressed the prince in the native tongue. He spoke in a humble tone and gestured frequently towards his colleagues and beyond in the direction of Ligea, still hidden from the main column by a low ridge.

Rhadamistus listened in silence and when the man finally dried up and stood, head down, awaiting the response, he turned to Cato.

'Our friends here are the leaders of the town's ruling council. They have come to tell me that there is a small force of Parthian soldiers in the town, besides their militia. These men claim that they have arranged for the gates to be opened for us, and that the council has voted to take my side and swear to be loyal to my cause.' He smiled thinly. 'It is a pity that their loyalty was not offered when I needed it most. So, Tribune, it seems that we may not need to fight our way into Ligea after all. Nevertheless, some example will need to be made to ensure that they know the cost of defying me. What would you suggest? That I decimate the council? That has a nice Roman touch about it and will please Emperor Nero, I should think. But decimation is a game of chance, and I want those who gave the order to close the gates against me last time to be the ones to pay for it with their lives. Namely, most of the men sitting on Ligea's ruling council, skulking behind the walls in Ligea. Well, Tribune? What do you say?'

Cato stared coldly at the men from Ligea before he spoke: 'Majesty, I want the heads of those responsible for the capture and torture of Centurion Petillius and his men. Ask them who butchered my Praetorians.'

Rhadamistus addressed the council members and Cato noted the fearful glances they exchanged before their leader answered. Rhadamistus listened and then translated for Cato in a low voice.

'He claims it was the Parthians. Their patrols have been watching us for the last three days. As soon as they saw your soldiers enter the forest they decided to wait until they were busy cutting trees before the trap was sprung. The Parthian officer tortured them before they were killed and displayed in front of the fort as a warning to Rome not to interfere in Armenian affairs. This man swears it was nothing to do with the townspeople. They are peace-loving, he says.'

'Then I want the Parthian officer handed over,' said Cato. 'And every man in that patrol.'

'That may prove difficult. They say the Parthians are determined to fight, but the militia is not, and since the militia hold the town gates, their commander has said they are ready to open them for us when we reach the city. After that we can have a free hand with the Parthians. You may punish them as you see fit, Tribune. These men say the Ligeans have always been friends of Rome and loyal to me. The men responsible for spurning me were forced from their posts by the people. They say the ruling council regards the Parthian presence in their town with hostility.'

Cato regarded the Ligeans with a faint sneer on his lips, then turned to Rhadamistus. 'A word with you, Majesty, out of earshot of the council members.'

The two moved a short distance away before Cato continued quietly. 'And do you believe them, Majesty?'

'Of course not. They are craven liars, trying to save their skins. But that will not save them. Once we have entered Ligea they will be amongst the first to be put to the sword.'

Cato nodded. 'Meanwhile we must make good use of them. We must agree to spare them and accept their protestations of loyalty, so that they betray the Parthians and open the gates. Once we have destroyed the enemy, we can punish those who betrayed you, Majesty, and those whom I hold equally responsible for the deaths of my men. Let the fate of Ligea serve as an example to all those who fail in their loyalty to you, their king, and Rome, their ally.'

The last words were leaden with irony and Rhadamistus raised an eyebrow.

'Very well, Tribune. I will speak to them. I will tell them we are glad to be welcomed as friends, and in return we pledge to rid their town of our mutual enemy.'

Cato was already thinking about the next step. Although he felt confident that the Ligean envoys were genuine in their offer to betray the Parthians, it was possible that they might be setting a trap instead. He had no wish to let his two cohorts suffer the consequences of any double-dealing by the Ligeans. 'We'll need to approach the town as if we were preparing to lay siege. When the militia act we'll have to move fast, before the Parthians are wise to the danger. Your horse-archers have the best chance of taking and holding the gate before the Parthians counter, Majesty. I'll bring the Praetorians up as quickly as I can to support you. With luck we'll catch the Parthians by surprise. Of course, once they realise they have been betrayed they'll try to flee. In which case it would be prudent to position my slingers and your cataphracts on the far side of the town to block their escape.'

Rhadamistus had listened closely and nodded his approval. 'A wise plan, Tribune. Truly, I am fortunate that your general chose you to serve me.'

136

Cato gave a modest bow of the head.

The Iberian glanced towards the waiting Ligeans. 'Now, we must tell those curs what they want to hear and send them back to their accomplices.'

'No. We only need to send one man, their leader. The rest can stay with us. If the commander of the militia fails to keep his word then we can make an example of them. Show the Ligeans what happens to those who try to deceive their king.'

It was late in the afternoon as the column resumed its advance and approached the town. The cataphracts and slingers had already set off on a roundabout route behind the hills to the south to block the road on the other side of Ligea. The baggage and siege trains were interspersed with the Praetorian centuries, and the dust raised by the mules and heavy wheels helped to conceal the size of the column, so that the enemy would not realise that the force approaching the town directly was smaller than that observed a few days earlier. For the infantry, the dust was an acute discomfort, and the men grumbled through the wool of the neckcloths most had raised to cover their nose and mouth. At the head of the column, and on either flank, rode the horse-archers. The largest group of riders was in the centre, led by Rhadamistus and Cato, with the Ligean envoys close behind, under guard.

A mile from the town they encountered a small group of Parthian scouts who watched the column for as long as they dared before turning their horses and galloping to safety. The gates of Ligea closed behind them and along the wall Cato could see the occasional flash of sunlight reflecting off helmets and the tips of spears. The column advanced unhurriedly and Cato gave the order to halt while they were still beyond bowshot. Behind him he heard Macro bellow the order for the men to set down their marching yokes, so that they would not be encumbered when the moment came to rush the town's gatehouse. Cato called for his trumpeter and Narses to ride at his side and then turned to Rhadamistus and Macro.

'Once the gates are opened, Majesty, send your horse-archers forward to take the gatehouse. Macro, you come up with the Praetorians at the run. The rest of the cohort will come up after you.'

'My lads are ready and keen to go, sir. After what happened to Petillius and the others, we'll let nothing stand in our way.'

'Good.' Cato took a last look round at the men of the cohort, forming up and waiting for the order to attack. Then he took a deep breath and urged his mount into an easy trot, gesturing at the trumpeter and Narses to follow him. Ahead there was a slight incline as the road approached the low mound upon which the town had been built. To the left of the town a trip of irrigated land spread along the bank of the river, while to the right the ground gave way to a range of steep-sided hills, sparsely covered with trees. Cato reined in and walked his horse towards the gatehouse.

'Sound your bucina,' he ordered.

The trumpeter spat to one side then raised the mouthpiece and blew three sharp notes, a pause and three more notes, as was the custom for those seeking a parley. Fifty paces from the closed gates Cato stopped and ordered the trumpeter to lower his instrument. On the tower above the gatehouse he could see a cluster of faces staring down at him. Then one man leaned forward, hands braced on the battlement, and called out to them.

'He demands to know why Rome has violated the border of the kingdom of Armenia,' Narses translated.

'Is he a Parthian?' Cato asked.

'From his accent, I would say so, Tribune.'

'Then tell him that Rome demands to know, what business has a Parthian in the land of an ally of Rome? Why has Parthia broken the longstanding agreement between our empires to acknowledge Armenia as a Roman protectorate?'

The response came a moment later.

'The people of Armenia demanded the help of Parthia to rid themselves of the tyrant Rhadamistus, he says. Armenia no longer looks to Rome. He orders us to turn our column around and march back across the frontier.'

Cato's gaze switched between the man on the tower, and the gates, which remained closed. His heartbeat quickened. Any moment now the militia should be flinging the gates open . . . But there was no sign of movement.

'You will surrender Ligea to us,' he commanded, trying to

prompt the militia to act. 'Surrender at once. If we are obliged to take the town by force then none will be spared.'

As Narses translated, there was a swirl of movement amongst those on the tower and then a figure was thrust up on to the wall and shoved hard in the back. Arms flailing, he fell a short distance before the rope around his neck snapped taut and his body spasmed and then hung limp as it swayed from side to side. It took a moment and then Cato recognised the leader of the town's council. Another figure was forced on to the wall and over the parapet to tumble and jerk to a halt, swinging against the other body. This one wore a mail vest and greaves and Cato guessed that he must be the commander of the militia. It was clear that the treachery of the Ligean envoys towards the Parthians had been uncovered by some pro-Parthian element in the town and the traitors had paid with their lives.

The Parthian officer called out again.

'He orders us to leave, before we share the same fate.'

Cato stared at the swaying bodies for a moment, then made his reply: 'I will lay siege to Ligea. You have until the ram first touches the wall to surrender. After that, no life will be spared. Rome has spoken.'

As soon as Narses had translated, Cato turned his horse about and the three men galloped back towards the column, Cato's face set in an expression of cold determination as he formed his plans to storm the town and burn it to the ground, along with its inhabitants, down to the last living thing. Starting with the remaining envoys.

'I take it the enemy isn't keen on the idea of surrender?' Macro greeted his commander.

'No. But they will be.' Cato glanced at the Ligeans under guard close by. They had followed the brief exchange outside the gatehouse and were stricken with fear.

'Majesty, if you have no objections, I'd like to use them to demonstrate to the Ligeans what happens to those who defy their rightful king, and Rome.'

Rhadamistus chuckled. 'Of course, Tribune. I would be delighted to see them put to good use.'

One of the group stepped forward, clasping his hands round

Rhadamistus's foot as he spoke quickly. The king kicked him away with a sneer.

Cato regarded the prisoners with contempt before he turned to Rhadamistus. 'What is your pleasure, Majesty?'

Rhadamistus edged his mount over to the Ligean and leaned forward to pat him on the head, as if he were showing affection to a faithful hound. The Ligean looked up hopefully and gave an uncertain smile. Then Rhadamistus straightened up.

'We should return them to their friends and families inside the town. Once you have set up your onagers, you can return them, one piece at a time. Starting with their heads.'

CHAPTER SIXTEEN

The command post was on the spur of a hill that stretched out towards Ligea and offered good views over the ground that surrounded the town. A path had already been worn through the stunted grass clinging to the slope and Macro paused just below the crest to catch his breath after the steep climb in full armour. He removed his helmet and mopped the sweat from his brow before he turned, chest heaving, and braced his hands on his hips as he looked back. There was perhaps an hour of light left and the landscape was washed in the warm glow of the setting sun. Long shadows stretched out over the ground and the heat of the day had started to abate, much to Macro's relief.

To his left was the camp, with its neat tent lines of the Roman troops and the less ordered sprawl of the Iberians. The ditch and rampart were deeper and higher than was usually the case with a simple marching camp, since the men had had more time to prepare the defences. Another ditch and rampart stretched from the camp down to the riverbank, and to the right of the town a similar fortification ran across the level ground to a rock outcrop below the hill. All of which had been constructed within a day of the column's arrival outside Ligea. Those inside the town were now cut off from the outside. They had no access to the water from the river as the channel used to supply the town had been dammed. Thirst would be their biggest danger in the days to come, Macro mused. While for the besiegers the greatest danger would be the approach of any relief column. But with Iberian patrols keeping watch from high vantage points, there would be little possibility of the besiegers being caught by surprise.

The faint crack of one of the onagers releasing another rock drew Macro's attention to the siege weapons secure behind earthworks just beyond bowshot of the walls. The battery was garrisoned with a century of slingers, as well as the crews of the onagers and bolt-throwers. Under Macro's instructions the weapons had been assembled shortly before, and he had come up to the command post to report to Cato. Before the battery took aim on the gatehouse there had been the distasteful duty of sending the heads and body parts of the Ligean envoys over the town walls to drop amongst the townsfolk. Macro shook his head at the thought. Killing a foe in battle was one thing, cutting down a bunch of unarmed cowards was demeaning to all concerned, and had left him feeling sullied. He only hoped that the short bombardment of bloodied body parts might undermine the enemy's desire to resist. If not, the steady battering down of the gatehouse should weaken their will. The question was, would the defenders seek terms before the ram was brought up?

Macro looked down to where Centurion Ignatius's men were assembling the ram and the wooden frame of the mantlet that would protect the crew. Already men were fastening lengths of timber, cut from the nearby forest, to the frame and covering them with hide. Once the ram was suspended beneath the mantlet the latter would be ready to be hauled forward to complete the job of breaking into the town. That would be the last chance the defenders had to surrender, according to the customs of war. If they forced the attacker to make an assault, with the risk of casualties that entailed, then it was deemed that the defenders had only themselves to blame for the consequences when the attackers sought revenge for the loss of their comrades. No quarter could be expected.

Tucking his felt cap into his helmet and holding the latter under his arm, Macro continued up the final stretch of the path and approached the command post. A company of Iberian spearmen guarded the tents and awnings occupied by Rhadamistus and his closest followers. The spearmen waved Macro through the perimeter and he crossed to where Cato was seated on a stool as he observed the scene below and made notes on a waxed slate. He looked up at the sound of Macro's boots crunching across the gritty soil. His friend looked exhausted, Macro thought, his eyes listless and his face lined where the dust had settled into the smallest creases of his skin and scar tissue.

'Sir, beg to report the siege battery is complete and is targeting the gatehouse and the walls on either side, as you ordered.'

'And the prisoners' bodies?'

'Cut up and returned to the town like you wanted.'

Cato sensed a hardening of his friend's tone and enquired evenly: 'You disapprove?'

'Not my place to comment on orders given to me by my commanding officer, sir.'

Cato smiled wearily. 'When you speak to me as formally as that, then I know you disapprove.'

'Well, aside from the mess it's made on the onager pouches, not to mention having to dispose of the offal, I am not quite sure what good it has done. After all, they had come to us to offer help. Not their fault it didn't go the way they planned. By killing the envoys and lobbing them back to their families in pieces, I don't think we are going to win much support down there.' Macro jerked his thumb in the direction of Ligea. 'The townsfolk weren't too keen on their Parthian guests before, and now we've given them reason to form a common cause. Strikes me we should be practising a little more divide and conquer, if we want this over as quickly as possible.'

Cato listened in silence and then thought a moment before offering a reply: 'It's too late for that. We have to take the town now. Can't afford to leave any hostiles across our lines of communication.'

'What lines of communication? We're out on a limb here, sir, living off the land. Our best hope of success is to get the Iberian lad on his throne as quickly as possible. This siege is going to waste time and lives. Every day we spend here gives the Parthians time to prepare their defences in Artaxata.'

Cato nodded thoughtfully. 'That's one argument. But there's another. Once knowledge of the fate of Ligea spreads through Armenia, then I doubt we'll have any trouble from any other towns we march through.'

'That's not what you were telling me the other night, after you'd spoken to Rhadamistus.'

143

'Then I've changed my mind. Perhaps he is right after all.'

Macro ground his teeth. 'This isn't like you, lad. Not at all. This is to do with what happened to Petillius and his boys, isn't it? Blood for blood?'

Cato stared back. 'Is there anything wrong with wanting to avenge your comrades?'

'Plenty, if it means putting the rest of the column at greater risk than was already the case.' Macro raised his hand and ran it through his hair. 'Look, I can see this has shaken you, and no doubt you're bloody exhausted. We all are. But you have to keep your head and think clearly. You of all people.'

Cato stood up suddenly and looked down at Macro, his voice strained. 'You forget yourself, Centurion Macro. I am in command here. I give the orders. I do not have to explain those orders to anyone, least of all those who serve under me. You will not question me again, do you understand? Just do your duty.'

Macro took a deep breath before speaking. 'Cato . . . Sir, I know my duty. It is to serve Rome, serve the officers Rome places above me, and to serve my brothers-in-arms. I have always been dutiful to Rome . . . and to the closest of my comrades and friends. That is why I speak as I find.'

'Then perhaps you should speak less, Centurion,' Cato suggested tersely.

Macro's jaw sagged open in surprise. Then he stood to attention. 'Will that be all, sir?'

'Yes.'

'Then I'll return to the camp and set the evening watches.'

'You do that. Dismissed.'

They exchanged a formal salute, then Macro about-turned and marched away, towards the path leading down the hillside. His face was flushed with suppressed anger and hurt that his views had been so curtly dismissed and derided. At the same time, he had seen the weariness eating away at Cato, compounded by the loss of Petillius and the others. Cato was not himself, Macro decided, but there was nothing he could do to help his tribune if the latter refused his advice and, more tellingly, his friendship.

★ ★ ★

Cato watched his friend stride off. It was a pity that their brief exchange had been so fraught, but the plain truth of it was, Cato was not prepared to have any subordinate criticise his orders. Not even Macro. As for his change of heart over the best way to win the people of Armenia over to Rhadamistus's cause ... He paused to reflect over the contesting trains of thought that had plagued his mind for the last two days. While he had previously pressed the case for mercy as the most persuasive means of winning support, it was possible that Rhadamistus had been right all along, and fear and terror were the best guarantees of loyalty, or more importantly, obedience. If so, then the fate of Ligea would be the proof of it. Besides, it was too late to try any alternative. They were committed now and it would be unwise to leave a force of Parthians in their wake. The siege must be seen through to its conclusion, he told himself. And then the Parthians and their Ligean allies, whether the latter were willing accomplices or not, would pay the price for their slaughter of a veteran centurion and twenty of Rome's finest men.

Cato looked over his notes for the disposition of his forces and his plan of attack once the town was breached. Despite what he had said to his friend, time was a pressing issue. The sooner the siege was resolved, the better. Balanced against this was the need to preserve as many of his men, and those of Rhadamistus, as possible for the final stage of the campaign: the capture of Artaxata. The best way to achieve victory was to pound away at the enemy's defences, day and night, crushing their will to resist before the assembled ram was brought forward to smash through the gates. That would require a prodigious supply of rocks for the onagers and would exhaust the supply of heavy darts for the bolt-throwers. He had already given orders for the latter to be used only when a viable target presented itself on the town's walls. Meanwhile, Porcino's century had been assigned to find ammunition for the onagers, an exhausting task of scouring the hills for exposed outcrops, chipping away at them and loading usable rocks on to the mules before leading them down to the battery to unload.

A soft crunch of footsteps behind him interrupted his thoughts and he turned to see Rhadamistus approaching. The Iberian was wearing a green silk tunic, cut long and loose so that it allowed the

145

air to flow around his body. He carried a stoppered jar in one hand and two silver goblets in the other.

'Drink with me, Tribune?'

Cato stood up respectfully. 'I would be grateful for a drink, Majesty.'

Rhadamistus set the goblets down, took out the stopper and filled the first goblet and handed it to the Roman as he spoke in a warm tone. 'You do not have to defer to my title when we are alone, Tribune. We may have met as allies of convenience, but I feel that we have a much better understanding of each other now. Wouldn't you agree?'

He filled his own cup and raised it in a toast. 'To allies, comrades and friends.'

Cato nodded and took a sip. He had thought it might be wine, but it was the juice of some fruit, or fruits, sweetness and bitterness combined in a refreshing blend. He drained half his goblet and felt far better for it.

'How is our siege progressing?' Rhadamistus continued.

'Well enough. The onagers will keep up a steady bombardment. However, Ligea is not like the fort we took earlier. That was merely an outpost and it was never intended to withstand siege engines. Ligea, on the other hand, is protected by a wall of stone. The lower courses are dressed blocks. Above the first ten feet or so, the stonework is irregular and set in mortar. At some point it must have been decided that the wall was not high enough and the Ligeans needed to complete the improvement either quickly or cheaply. The results look impressive from a distance, but are no match for our siege weapons. The onagers will destroy the upper works easily.'

They watched as two of the weapons swung their arms almost at the same moment, the pouches flicking forward and releasing their rocks. The tiny black dots inscribed a gentle arc towards the wall and plunged down, one striking the top of the gatehouse with a puff of dust and dislodging a small shower of debris, while the second rock smashed into the solid base with a smaller burst of dust and grit, but no other visible effect.

'How soon until your men create a practicable breach?'

Cato thought for a moment before he answered. 'It depends on a number of things. We need a ready supply of rocks for the onagers, then there's the wear and tear on the weapons. A throwing arm may split and need replacing. Same goes for the receiver bar. The torsion ropes will be under a lot of strain and may need to be renewed. Then there are the defences and defenders to consider. If I am right about the construction of the wall, then we may be able to sweep the top of it away within two or three days. But it'll take far longer to create a breach in the lower courses. We may have to scale those if the enemy attempt to clear the debris slope in front of the wall. I'll give orders for ladders to be constructed tomorrow. By keeping the bombardment going through the night, we'll deny the defenders the chance to make repairs, but if I were them I'd be hard at work on the construction of an inner wall, behind the gatehouse and the sections we are attacking on either side. If they do that, then we'll have to attack the inner wall as well.' He summed up his thoughts. 'So, if all goes well, I reckon we should be in a position to bring the ram up in three or four days. The gates will be broken in within a few hours at most, then my cohorts and your spearmen will launch their assault through the gate and the breaches on either side. If there's an inner wall, you can add a day or so to reduce that. Seven days at the outside is my best estimate.'

'Seven days . . .' Rhadamistus repeated thoughtfully. 'That is an acceptable delay. Of course, when our men make their attack they will be instructed to spare no one.'

'Yes, if that is still your wish?'

'It is. There will be no mercy.'

There was a brief silence as both men regarded the town below them. They could see figures on the walls either side of the area under attack, and behind the walls Cato could pick out women on the roofs, laying out washing as children played at their feet.

'Why did you change your mind, Tribune?' Rhadamistus asked. 'Was it because of the killing of your men?'

'Partly that,' Cato admitted. 'Partly because I have come to think that it is quicker to win people's obedience by fear than win their loyalty through gratitude. Although I believe that the latter is more inspiring and enduring. But we are short of time and must cut our cloth accordingly. It is a calculated risk.'

Rhadamistus laughed. 'Now that is a Roman speaking. There is a saying here in the east, you know. In peacetime Romans drill their men as if they are fighting a bloodless battle. In war they fight battles as if they were conducting a bloody drill.'

'I have heard that said. And it is true. That is why there is none to rival the power of Rome.'

'Except Parthia.'

Cato mused briefly. 'Even Parthia. Given the right strategy.'

'You think so?' Rhadamistus thought briefly before continuing. 'It would appear that you Romans have failed to find the right strategy so far. I wonder when you will? For my sake, I hope it is sooner rather than later.'

CHAPTER SEVENTEEN

The ram and mantlet were ready the next afternoon, and stood idle as the onagers continued their ceaseless routine of lobbing rocks at the gatehouse and the wall on either side. From time to time one of the bolt-throwers lurched on its stand as it unleashed a shot when any defender unwisely revealed himself in the target area. On most occasions the shot either slammed into the battlements or passed too high and dropped out of sight in the heart of the town. As Cato had anticipated, the effects of the bombardment were mostly felt above the height of the dressed blocks, where the defences were steadily beaten down. The lower courses remained intact, and the Romans prepared a supply of assault ladders accordingly. Since there was no let-up in the rocks dropping out of the sky, the defenders' efforts to repair the damage under cover of darkness lasted only two nights before they lost enough men to discourage any further attempt.

The dim glow of torches behind the gate told of other efforts made by the defenders to prepare for the coming assault, but the spur upon which the command post was positioned was not high enough to afford any view of the activity behind the gatehouse. Attempts were made by the Parthians to send messengers out of Ligea by night, but they were captured or killed by Romans patrolling the siege lines. Those that were taken alive were interrogated but only divulged that they had been sent to request a relief force. They kept tight-lipped about the situation in the town, even under torture, and were eventually tied to stakes posted around the town and left to die from their injuries, or thirst. Their pitiful cries carried over the wall to undermine the spirit of those within. As their

149

strength failed, their voices died away to mere croaks and then they hung silently from their bonds as their lives gave out.

On the third day, as Cato was standing in the battery with Macro observing the fall of shot against the gatehouse some two hundred paces away, there was a sudden splintering crack and a shouted warning. Spinning round, he saw that the throwing arm of one of the onagers had split apart and the rock had been flung down instead of sailing towards the town. One of the slingers had been hurled against the inside of the earthworks as the rock struck him between the shoulder blades, shattering his spine so that only his arms responded to his will as he tried to ease himself up on to his feet and failed each time, before collapsing face down.

'Get that man back to the dressing station in camp!' Macro snapped at the nearest of the slinger's comrades, even though it was obvious that the casualty was finished as far as the army went. If he lived, and survived the return journey to Syria, then the auxiliary would spend the rest of his days as a wretched street beggar.

They hurried over to the onager to inspect the damage. The throwing arm was ruined and would need to be replaced from the limited stock of spare seasoned timber carried in the wagons. That would entail carefully unfastening the pins that locked the torsion ropes in place and easing them round so that the stump of the arm did not swing wildly and cause any further injuries, a ticklish business that was best handled by a small party of men covered by shields. It would also mean that the crews on the onagers on either side would have to retreat to a safe distance while the work was done.

'Look at that.' Macro tapped the shaft close to where it had split. 'Something's been eating away at it.'

Cato leaned closer and saw that the exposed interior of the throwing arm was riddled with the trails of boring insects. Because the outside of the wooden shaft had been bound with ropes at intervals, it would have been impossible to tell that the throwing arm had been weakened.

'It's a miracle the bloody thing lasted as long as it did,' Macro commented. 'Could have gone at any time. Makes you wonder how much of the rest of the weapon is unfit to use.' He gave the frame a kick with the toe of his boot.

150

Cato glanced round at the other onagers. 'I want them all checked over, inch by inch. As well as the spare timbers on the wagons. If any more rot is found, or even suspected, I want the carpenters to make repairs or replacements as need be.'

Macro sucked in his cheeks. 'That means we'll lose the use of them for a day or so. Worse still, the enemy will make good as much damage as they can while there's no danger of being hit.'

'I worked that out by myself, thank you.'

Macro raised his eyebrows briefly. 'Yes, sir. I don't doubt it. I'll need to get the carpenters down here from the camp. Permission to carry on?'

'Yes . . .'

Macro cupped a hand to his mouth as he bellowed the length of the battery. 'Cease shooting! Artillery crews stand down!'

As the centurion made his way to the opening at the rear of the battery, Cato felt angry with himself. He had not meant to be so terse with his friend. He was even angrier with the quartermaster back in Antioch who had allocated him siege weapons that were barely fit for purpose. No doubt the pick of the onagers and bolt-throwers had been set aside for the local units. Given that General Corbulo had decided to leave most of them in Syria, it was likely that the best siege weapons would never see action throughout the entire campaign. Meanwhile, it was the likes of Cato and his men who would have to rely on worn-out and unserviceable kit when they found themselves facing the enemy. It was an intolerable state of affairs, and Cato made a mental note that he would represent his views in person to the quartermaster if he returned from Armenia.

He took a moment to try to calm his bitter frustration and glanced towards the town. A few heads had popped up behind the defences to investigate the pause in the bombardment. As they caught sight of the shattered throwing arm and the crews seeking shade, more of the defenders joined them and began to jeer and whistle.

'Sir?'

Cato turned to see one of Metellus's optios salute him. 'What is it?'

'Let me have a crack at them bastards with my bolt-throwers, sir. I'm sure I can hit one of 'em. At the very least it'll shut them up.'

Cato nodded. Anything that nibbled away at the enemy's morale was worth the effort.

The optio jogged back to the nearest of the weapons he commanded and had his men ratchet back the torsion arms before he carefully sighted the weapon and made some careful adjustments. Rising up, he ordered: 'Stand clear!'

He paused long enough for the crewmen to step away from the weapon and then tugged the firing lever. The throwing arms snapped forward and the bolt zipped in a dark blur towards the gatehouse, the trajectory low enough for it to be missed by the small crowd that had gathered to mock the besiegers. Cato followed the line of flight and was rewarded with the sight of two of the defenders being plucked off the top of the ruined tower, snatched from sight as the iron-headed shaft pierced them through and carried their bodies away with the impetus of the shot.

Now the Romans and slingers let out a loud cheer and made crude gestures at the defenders as the latter scurried back into shelter.

'A fine shot, Optio!' Cato called out to him. 'If any of those Parthian bastards thinks he can take the piss again, you have my permission to shoot him down.'

'Yes, sir! My pleasure, sir.'

'But only clear targets. Understood?'

'Yes, sir.'

Cato scrutinised the town for a little longer, assessing the damage that had already been achieved. As things stood, the gatehouse was well on the way to being a ruin and unable to protect the gates below. The battlements on either side had been largely destroyed. It would take no more than another day before an assault could be made with a reasonable expectation of success. Now there would be a delay, and the enemy would make good use of the time to effect repairs.

Unless the besiegers took action.

It was an hour after nightfall when Cato reached the position he had chosen during the afternoon, using the bed of a stream that must have dried out many years ago. With him he had half the force selected for the spoiling attack: forty Praetorians from Macro's century, and forty slingers. Each man was wearing a brown cloak over his tunic and exposed skin had been smeared with mud and ash to help conceal them. The Praetorians carried only their spears. The armour, shields and swordbelts had been left in camp to avoid any clink of kit that might give away their position as they crept towards the gatehouse. A hundred paces away Macro was lying with a similar force to the right of the gatehouse but there was no sound or movement to give away their location.

A similar distance ahead lay the wall, and the sounds of men carrying out repairs carried clearly to Cato and the others. The enemy were working without any kind of illumination and doing their best to talk as little as possible, and even then in low voices. But the faint shifting of rubble and the grunts of men carrying heavy loads were impossible to muffle. A handful of Parthian skirmishers stood or crouched a short distance from the wall, keeping watch, and it was these who had made Cato's progress so slow as he and his men moved into position. As long as the skirmishers dared not venture too far forward they posed no danger.

'Sir,' Rutilius, the cohort's standard-bearer, whispered. 'They're lighting the braziers.'

Cato glanced back towards the battery and saw that there was a glow from behind the earthworks, over and above the flicker of torches. 'Pass the word to make ready.'

The men lying on either side turned to their neighbours and spoke as softly as they could. Cato was recalling the orders he had left with Centurion Metellus in charge of the battery. The bolt-throwers had been half-cocked at dusk so that the final loading would not be accompanied by too much clanking from the ratchets, while at the same time not overloading the torsion bars. Incendiaries had been prepared by tightly tying strips of linen soaked in pitch around the shafts of the heavy darts. And now the crews were stoking up the braziers and lighting up the ammunition for the first volley.

It was then that Rutilius nudged him and pointed towards the town. For a moment Cato saw nothing, then his eyes caught the movement. A figure was approaching cautiously. It stopped and squatted, there was a pause, and then Cato heard the sound of someone emptying his bowels.

The metallic sound of ratchets being levered back came from the battery, and Metellus's voice called out clearly: 'Release!'

A series of sharp cracks broke the quiet of the night and bright flares of light carved through the night sky, streaking over the heads of the Romans pressed into the ground, briefly illuminating the Parthian, who saw some of Cato's men in almost the same instant. He jumped up, turned and ran back towards the town as the first shafts crashed into the shattered walls in bursts of sparks that lit up the figures crouched over their work. They froze in the sudden harsh glare and Cato snatched his spear and jumped to his feet as he filled his lungs.

'Up men, and get at 'em!'

The plan was simple enough. The slingers were to cause the most damage. The Praetorians were there to protect them in the first instance and then do what they could to undo the defenders' repairs if the opportunity arose. Cato ran forward, dark figures rushing up on each side. To his right he heard Macro bellow the order to charge, and from behind came the clanking din of the next volley being prepared. Aside from orders, no man was to make a sound. Cato wanted to unnerve his enemy as much as possible and the dark shapes with darkened faces rushing from the night would present a frightening spectacle.

Another series of cracks sounded, then there was the crackling whoosh of projectiles flying above to fall a moment later amongst the enemy, striking down several this time as one landed squarely amongst a chain gang bringing up blocks of stone to build a new breastwork on the wall. As the Romans came within forty or so paces of the wall Cato shouted the order to stop.

'Slingers! Forward five paces and loose at will!'

At the sound of Cato's voice Metellus ordered the bolt-throwers to cease shooting. As the Praetorians held back, the slingers moved up, slipped lead shot in their pouches and whirled their thongs overhead before sending the deadly little missiles hurtling towards the enemy. One of the first shots struck the Parthian who was still struggling to hold up his sagging breeches as he ran to safety. His head snapped forward and his arms jerked outwards, causing his breeches to drop and trip him up, and he fell headlong. More shot whirred and zipped towards the men clambering back over the wall, knocking down several more, and as the last disappeared into the gloom Cato called on the slingers to lower the weapons and for the whole force to double forward. He was the first to reach the foot of the rubble to the left of the gate and began to scramble up as his men followed suit on either side, pausing only to finish off the enemy wounded and to gather the burning incendiaries.

As they reached the half-completed breastwork, Cato snatched up one of the flaming bolts, lodged between two stones and hurled it to the other side. Then he glanced over the breastwork and the light of enemy torches revealed hundreds of men milling about below. Many were Parthians, armed with bows and spears, but most were clearly townspeople, formed into repair gangs to work on the defences. All looked up, their fearful expressions caught in the glow of the flames. Behind them, as he suspected there would be, rose a low internal wall, topped with a crude palisade.

Once more the slingers set about their work, sending lethal shot down into the compact mass. It was almost impossible to miss, and cries and screams of pain and panic filled the air. Cato felt consumed by the wild exhilaration of the spectacle before him and shouted for the Praetorians to throw down the breastwork. There would be only a short opportunity to do as much damage as possible before the Parthians counter-attacked in force. Already some were shooting arrows back from the heaving mass below. More Parthians were appearing along the inner wall and letting fly shafts from there. Nearby a slinger threw out his sling hand and was instantly struck down by an arrow through the throat and toppled back on to the rubble slope behind him. More arrows struck home, taking down two Praetorians and another slinger. Then one struck a block of stone close by and ricocheted close to Cato's face so that he felt the rush of air at its passing. He dropped his spear, snatched up a rock the size of a small melon and hurled it down at the enemy below. He did not wait to see where it landed before picking up another and throwing it as far and as hard as he could.

There was a grunt as the man next to him was struck and Cato glanced round to see the standard-bearer, Rutilius, stumbling back with the shaft of an arrow piercing his shoulder.

It was time to leave.

'Fall back! Fall back!' He turned to his right and shouted again to be sure Macro heard the command, then picked up his spear in one hand and took the standard-bearer's good arm in the other.

'Can you manage on your own?'

'Yes . . . Yes, sir.'

'Back you go then.'

Rutilius stumbled down the debris and away from the wall, but some of the Praetorians and slingers were still feverishly throwing down the barricade. Cato cursed them under his breath before he yelled again. 'Fall back, damn you!'

This time they obeyed at once, abandoning their work, grabbing their weapons and clambering down the ruins of the wall to safety. Cato took a last glance at the inner wall to fix the details in his mind, then saw an archer swing his bow round to take aim at him, and turned and bolted as the arrow whirred over his head. At the foot of the wall the men were carrying out the orders they had been given at the briefing just before dusk. The Praetorians dashed back towards the camp, dark shapes streaming through the night. The slingers followed them a short distance before turning about and loading fresh shot. Cato was the last man to pass through the skirmish line and stopped, chest heaving. The shouts of the defenders reached him, above the pounding of blood in his ears. They let out a ragged chorus of shouts as they set off in pursuit of the raiding party.

The first heads appeared above the crest of the rubble – Parthians armed with bows and spears, lit up by the wavering flames of the incendiaries. The slinger next to Cato began to swing his arm.

'Wait for it!' Cato snapped at him, then louder for all to hear, 'Slingers! Only on my order!'

The enemy rose up and over the rubble, their shouts taking on a strident, triumphant tone as they saw most of the Romans running from them. In amongst the Parthians were some of the townspeople, armed with an assortment of swords, axes and spears, Some just had rocks in their hands, ready to hurl them at any Roman who came within reach. Cato waited until the target was hard to miss, slowly raising his arm, heedless of the fact that it would be invisible to most of his men. Then he swept it down as he roared.

'Slingers! Loose!'

Thongs whirred, then snapped as the shot spat out towards the enemy, and Cato was rewarded with the sight of several men tumbling down and others spun round by the impact.

'Pour it on, boys!' he yelled with excitement. 'Kill 'em!'

The slingers needed little encouragement as they unleashed their lethal missiles from the darkness, in amongst their targets, clearly visible by the glow of the flames still burning on the incendiaries. Once again the enemy faltered, frozen by fear of shot whipping out of the night. Those with cooler heads raised their bows and strained their eyes to try and pick out a target in the night before releasing their shafts. Some shot at shadows, and the air around Cato was filled with the soft drone of slings winding up and the sigh of arrows cutting through the darkness. He heard an oath as one of the slingers was struck, and then a voice shouted out.

'I'm hit! I'm hit!'

'Keep your bloody mouth shut!' Cato called out. 'Get to the rear, damn you!'

He allowed the slingers a moment longer to take down as many men as possible while the situation was in their favour. Then one of the Parthian officers grasped the need to keep pushing forward and get out of the light cast by the incendiaries. He drew a curved blade and bellowed at his men and waved them on, and the Parthians and their Ligean allies rushed at the slingers.

'Fall back to the battery!' Cato ordered, turning to run with the slingers as the enemy took fresh heart and raced after them with wild cheers. Inside the battery the glow from the braziers was swelled by fresh orange blooms, and the two onagers that had been checked and found to be sound released tightly packed bundles of brushwood doused with pitch and set alight. These roared high in the air and then plummeted to earth to provide light for the remaining slingers and the Iberian archers shooting from within the battery. It was then that Cato realised he had waited too long before falling back. The first of the bundles reached its apex and then swept down towards him like the blazing sun falling from its place in the heavens. Cato just had time to hurl himself aside before the faggot struck the ground close by in a burst of flames and sparks that showered over him, singeing his exposed skin. His first thought was fury over the mistake in setting the onager's range. If he discovered who was responsible for nearly cooking his commanding officer there would be more than a little trouble for the individual concerned.

He rolled aside and on to his hands and knees. Then he felt someone grasp his arm and haul him up on to his feet.

'Come on, sir. No dawdling,' Rutilius grunted painfully through clenched teeth. Then he clamped his spare hand back round the shaft of the arrow as he applied pressure to staunch the flow of blood.

Cato could not suppress a grin. 'Good man, Rutilius. Let's go.'

They ran out of the pool of light, sprinting with the others towards the sides of the battery to get out of the direct line of sight of the archers and slingers. Two arrows thudded into the ground to Cato's side and he swerved a short distance before changing direction in an effort to put off the aim of any Parthian picking him as a target. He heard Rutilius breathing hard to one side as the standard-bearer ran with him.

The earthworks loomed ahead and Cato angled to the left, calling Rutilius to follow him. He slowed as he reached the corner of the battery and turned to look back. The walls and the ground in front of the town were lit up by the blazing faggots and he could see that there were many bodies, dead and wounded, on the ground and scattered across the debris slope. Much of the breastwork was in ruins and already most of the defenders had scurried back into Ligea to take cover. A few brave souls still stood their ground and shot arrows in the direction of the attackers, and then fell back. A satisfactory result, Cato decided.

'Ah! There you are, sir!'

He turned to see Macro striding up to him, just visible in the glow of the braziers inside the battery. The centurion was rubbing his hands together in delight. 'Bloody good night's work that! Knocked down most of their wall my side. And took out a score of the bastards at least! They'll not be thinking about repairs again, I bet.'

'You saw the inner wall?'

'Of course. That won't keep us out for long.'

'No, but it'll cost us some more men to get over it.'

Macro shrugged cheerily. 'That's sieges for you, sir. Now tell me that scrimmage didn't get you out of that dark mood of yours.'

As they gazed towards the town, Rutilius came out of the darkness, staggering. Blood covered the hand he clutched to the wound.

'Let's get him to the camp,' Cato said urgently and started forward.

The standard-bearer stopped and shook his head wearily as he tried to stand to attention. 'I can . . . manage . . . sir.'

'Nonsense, man. Here, let me—'

As Cato reached out, the standard-bearer spasmed wildly. His jaws snapped open and his eyes stretched wide, then his legs gave way and he sank on to his knees. Another arrow shaft stretched out almost vertically to one side of his neck, the fletching no more than six inches from the entry point – a freak of fortune as some Parthian had shot his last arrow at a high angle before turning to flee. Cato realised at once that the point had torn its way deep into Rutilius's vitals and the wound was mortal. Blood pulsed up round the shaft and Rutilius groped at it as he let out a low groan, more blood spraying from his lips on to Cato's face.

'Rutilius . . .' he began, but there was nothing he could say that would help.

The standard-bearer suddenly grasped Cato's tunic and drew him close. He swallowed and tried to speak, but spittle and gore clogged his throat and he coughed desperately to clear it away as he whispered.

'My girl . . . Back in Rome . . . She . . .' He choked again, and this time the sound was accompanied by a guttural gurgling as blood filled his lungs and he began to drown. Rutilius shook his head desperately and his hands trembled violently as the fingers clenched into the cloth of Cato's tunic. Cato put his arms around the standard-bearer and drew him close and whispered in his ear.

'The gods watch over you in the afterlife . . . Farewell, brother Rutilius.'

The standard-bearer's strength faded steadily and then he was limp, his head lolling against Cato's shoulder.

'He's gone, lad,' Macro said softly. 'Rutilius has gone.'

Cato eased the body away and laid him down gently, then reached to close the man's eyes, before he straightened up and stared towards Ligea.

'One more to be avenged . . .'

CHAPTER EIGHTEEN

At dawn, two days later, the Praetorians quietly formed up a short distance from the ruins of the gatehouse and the wall. The men carrying the scaling ladders stood behind the First Century, whose shields would protect them until the ladders were set against the inner wall. The ram had made short work of the gates the previous afternoon and the Iberian spearmen and the slingers had occupied the ruins, erecting hoardings to protect them from the defenders' arrows as they hurled shot at any defender who dared show his head above the inner wall.

The air was thick with the sharp tang of burning, and smoke still trailed into the pale sky from the fires that had raged the previous night. Having battered down the defences around the gatehouse, Cato had brought the onagers forward to unleash a steady rain of incendiaries on the town for most of the night, forcing the defenders to concentrate their efforts on putting out the fires started by the blazing faggots. Meanwhile, the men chosen for the assault had been fed and rested and would be far fresher than their grime-streaked and weary opponents. Macro's and Ignatius's centuries would spearhead the attack, while Porcino and Placinus and their men would form the reserve, ready to follow up, alongside the slingers and Iberian spearmen, the moment the inner wall was taken. The Praetorians had been ordered to leave their spears in the camp. The kind of scrambling close-quarters fight ahead was best conducted with their short swords.

'Morning, sir.' Macro greeted Cato brightly as the tribune approached. 'The lads are keen to tear into those bastards in the town. Right, boys?' He turned to the men immediately behind him and they grinned and nodded.

'That's good,' Cato acknowledged flatly, not sparing them a glance as he stared towards Ligea. He had found it almost impossible to sleep since the siege had begun and now had to force himself to think clearly. Every time he had lain down on his camp bed and closed his eyes, his mind refused to stop going over the details of the siege, and his wider mission, as the serving girl, Bernisha, cleaned his boots and armour. Even when sleep came, it was disturbed by dark dreams about the fate of Centurion Petillius. Sometimes it was Cato himself being hunted through the dark forest, until he was run to ground by the Parthians and forced to share the terrible deaths of his men. He awoke sweating and trembling, and frustrated. He had endured sleepless spells before, but not accompanied by the nightmares that haunted him now. But why should the fate of Petillius have so unsettled him when he had seen the horrors of war many times? He could not quite fathom it: other than a vague sense that something had changed within him, and that he felt a perpetual weariness with being a soldier, and the overwhelming burden placed on him by the responsibilities of command. He had known other officers to falter under the strain, and had tended to put it down to some defect of character. And now he feared that he too had some flaw in his nature and he dreaded the shame of being found out by Macro and the other men he commanded.

Macro's smile faded as he saw the tribune's haunted expression. He had been aware of the recent moroseness in his friend, but it was impossible to attribute it to any particular cause. The present campaign was no worse than the bitter fighting they had experienced in Britannia. Close friends and comrades had been lost too, and the icy cold and constant rains of the island's mountains had been utterly exhausting. Macro had known far tougher men than Cato who had broken under such strains and he was concerned for his friend. All the more so as Cato had rebuffed his attempts to speak about it.

Cato turned to the two centuries standing ready. He could see the eager anticipation in some faces, and the tight anxiety in others, and prayed that his courage would not fail him, nor would he suffer some agonising wound which he would not be able to endure with the affected indifference of veteran soldiers. He had to force such

162

thoughts aside. His men looked to him. As did Macro. He must not fail them.

He coughed lightly to clear his throat and then addressed them, as loudly and clearly as he could.

'The enemy in the town are the ones who slaughtered our comrades. No one does that to the men of the Praetorian Guard. We are the emperor's chosen. The finest soldiers in the Empire. A soldier's death is ours by right.' He paused and let an icy tone of anger fill his next words. 'Our comrades were denied that right by the cowards who captured them, tortured them and finally killed them for their sport. The spirits of our comrades call out to us from beyond the grave to return the deed in full. By the end of this day, let no one dwelling in the town be left alive. No man, no woman, no child. Nor any beast. No living thing shall survive. They are yours to dispose of as you will. Yours to use before you cut them down. But there will be no prisoners. None to be sold as slaves. When we continue our march towards Artaxata we will leave Ligea behind us as a tomb. So that all the enemies of Rome, and the allies of Rome, will never forget the terrible price paid by those who dishonoured our comrades. This I swear, by Jupiter, Best and Greatest.' Cato signalled to the Praetorian holding his shield and helmet and the man handed them over one at a time before Cato drew his sword and raised it. 'For Petillius, and all our fallen brothers!'

The men echoed his cry and rattled their swords against the trim of their shields in a deafening clatter. Macro looked on with conflicting emotions. There was his usual thrill of imminent action, but also an unsettling feeling about his longtime friend. He had never heard Cato speak in such cold, bloodthirsty terms. In place of the usual desire to win the battle with the minimum loss of life on all sides, which Macro fondly excused as the result of reading too much poetry and philosophy, Cato thirsted for death and destruction with a depth of sentiment that exceeded even Macro's lust for combat.

Cato rocked his head to either side to loosen the muscles in his neck and then took his place at the head of the assault troops. Macro fell in beside him.

'Sir,' he said in a low voice. 'There's no need for you to go in with me and the lads.'

'You know me, Centurion. I'll not ask men to do anything I'm not prepared to do myself.'

Macro sighed. 'You have nothing to prove. Not to them. Not to me. Not to anyone. Besides, we can't afford the risk.'

Cato smiled grimly. 'Risk? Since when were you worried about risk?'

'Since we first pitched our tents on the Parthians' turf. If we're going to see this folly through and get back to Syria with our hides intact, we're going to need you to lead us, sir. Get yourself killed now, and there's a good chance the rest of us are fucked.'

Cato stared at him blankly and then gave a dry chuckle. 'It is not for you to question my decisions. Do your job and lead your men.'

Before Macro could even consider protesting, Cato called over his shoulder, 'Praetorians! Advance!'

He set off at a steady pace and the men rippled forward behind him. They passed through the gaps between the onagers and the faggots piled behind them. As soon as they moved on a safe distance the onager crews set light to the faggots and unleashed a final few volleys over the wall and beyond the inner wall to harass those sheltering behind. Cato walked towards the gatehouse, followed by Macro and his century, while Centurion Ignatius and his men brought up the rear. Ahead, some of the spearmen and slingers on the ruins either side of the gate glanced back and cheered the Praetorians on as they approached. The rubble and the shattered remains of the gates had been removed during the night and there was a clear path leading through into Ligea.

Cato raised his shield and tightened his grip as he stopped just short and called out the order.

'First Century! Form testudo!'

Cato slipped back into the front rank, and Macro and one of his men closed up on either side, while those behind held their shields to protect them from the flanks and overhead. Once the thud of shields coming together had ceased, Cato gave the order to continue the advance. With Macro shouting the time, they moved slowly through the arch and emerged into the rubble-strewn space beyond. In the daylight the inner wall was clearly visible over the rim of his shield and Cato saw that it stretched round in a gentle curve from where the walls had not been damaged by the siege weapons. There were still scorch marks on the ground from the incendiaries shot over the wall and the dark patches and smears of dried blood from the spoiling attack. One way or another, Cato thought briefly, far more blood would be shed before the day was over.

As soon as the Romans entered the town there was a blast of horns from beyond the inner wall and at once the defenders rose up from behind the low parapet and unleashed a hail of arrows and rocks as the slingers along the debris of the main wall returned the barrage. Cato halted the column halfway across the open ground and then saw one of the defenders topple down directly in front of him, his forehead caved in by a lead shot. He rose unsteadily on his knees, blood running from the wound, his nose and his ears as he let out a piercing scream that made Cato shudder and freeze.

'Sir,' said Macro. 'We should deploy into line.'

Cato heard the words but he could not think clearly.

'Sir, what are your orders?' Macro glanced sidelong at Cato's blank expression. 'Cato?'

The centurion snatched a deep breath and bellowed: 'First Century! Deploy into line.'

The Praetorians peeled away on either side, the front rank extending the line of shields as the second rank raised theirs to provide overhead shelter. Behind them the men carrying the ladders kneeled down and waited for Ignatius's men to take up position to their rear.

Reassured that the plan was being carried out, Macro leaned closer to Cato and whispered harshly as he shook his arm, 'For fuck's sake, sir, take control of yourself. Before the men notice. Do you hear me?'

Cato shuddered, blinked and then nodded. 'Yes . . . Yes.'

'You'd better pull back, sir. Outside the wall, where you can take overall command of the attack. That would be for the best.'

'No. My place is here. With my men.'

'Not when you're in this shape.' Macro ground his teeth. He

could see that his friend was badly shaken. 'All right, then. I'll give the commands. Just stick close to me until this is over.'

He did not give Cato a chance to protest and looked round. Ignatius's men were inside the wall and formed up behind the First Century. Macro drew his sword and called out as clearly and loudly as possible.

'Praetorians! Make ready! . . . Advance!'

The First Century paced forward, directly into the storm of arrows and rocks being hurled at them, cracking off shields and splintering where they penetrated. Macro spared Cato a glance and saw the tribune's fixed expression. There was fear there too. The mortal fear of battle to be sure. But perhaps a far greater fear of humiliation. And that could be dangerous, Macro knew from experience. He had seen men be reckless in combat in order to cover up their failure of nerves. Most of them had paid for it with their lives. But there was no time to think of that. The inner wall was directly ahead.

'First Cohort! Shields up!'

The men lofted them over their heads to protect them from the point-blank battering from above. The man to Cato's right was too slow and a rock the size of a mutton joint crashed on to the crest of his helmet, driving him down, senseless. At once the Praetorian immediately behind him stepped forward, covering them both with his shield.

'Ladders!' Macro bellowed.

The men carrying the assault ladders hurriedly raised them all along the wall with a rolling clack and clatter as the stiles struck the stonework at an angle that made it just possible to climb without using either hand. As the defenders focused their attention on the Praetorians the slingers took advantage of the diversion to rise up and pick off the enemy packed along the parapet before the first Romans climbed the rungs to fight their way on to the wall. Bodies tumbled down to join the first Praetorian casualties and the enemy wounded were quickly finished off without mercy. As soon as the ladders were raised and kept in place by their carriers, the first of the Praetorians began to clamber up. Cato placed a foot on the lowest rung but Macro thrust him aside and took his place. He raised his shield with his sword held up and out and surged from rung to rung as he made for the parapet.

A Parthian was struggling to push the ladder aside, but abandoned the effort as soon as he saw Macro, drawing a curved sword and slashing downwards. The centurion thrust himself up behind the shield, catching the blade before thudding into the Parthian and knocking him back off the walkway to drop out of sight. The defenders to each side of him turned to strike him down and the press of bodies was so tight neither they nor Macro could wield their weapons effectively. To his right there was a Ligean, with a simple iron cap trimmed with cloth. He held a spear in his hands which was quite useless, but he clung to it desperately as he shoved the shaft at Macro. Gritting his teeth, the latter drew his head back and then slammed his forehead into his opponent's cheek, gashing his skin and momentarily stunning the Ligean. Throwing his right shoulder forward Macro shoved hard and opened enough of a gap to work the point of his sword up to his enemy's stomach and drive the blade home. Cloth and flesh held for an instant and then gave way and the metal cut through.

The Praetorian behind Macro saw the slim space behind his centurion and made to jump down into it, only to collide with a Parthian and both men came down on the walkway in a tangled heap. A townsman carrying a heavy butcher's cleaver hacked at the exposed neck of the Roman, nearly severing it, but continued to strike in a frenzy until the blood covered both men below him and he began to strike at the Parthian as well. So intent was he on slaughtering his foe that he fell victim to the next man up the ladder who slashed at the side of his head and cut him down. At once he jumped astride the butcher's victims and thrust his shield in the opposite direction to Macro and hurled his weight behind it to gain another two steps before the packed bodies of the defenders held him up. But a space had been won and more Praetorians joined the fight.

Further along, several more Romans were battling to win space on the wall. A handful of ladders had been shoved aside, as the men on them crashed down on to their comrades below. The slingers and Iberian spearmen were climbing down to join their comrades pushing towards the ladders, eager to join the fight, crush the enemy and sack the town.

Macro, now that his back was covered, concentrated on the enemy to his front, alternately slamming his shield forward and stabbing with his sword. This was exactly the kind of fighting that favoured the heavy armour of the Romans and the short blade designed for close work. Each pace along the walkway he progressed opened the way for more of his men to gain the wall and join the battle.

'Drive 'em back, lads!' he yelled as his lips curled into a frenzied grin. He was in his element now, and already scented victory. With a lung-bursting roar he braced his boots and hurled himself forward again, battering the curve of his shield against his foes. Suddenly the shield splintered close to the left edge as an arrow point burst through and sent shards pinging off Macro's cheekguard. Around him he heard the sound of impacts and the grunts of the injured. Risking a glance, he saw a small body of Parthian archers standing ten paces back from the inside of the wall. They were already nocking arrows for the next volley. It was a desperate measure as they stood as much chance of hitting one of their own men as a Roman.

'Watch out for the archers!'

Most of the Praetorians heeded his advice and did their best to cover themselves as the next volley lashed into the melee raging along the wall. Macro saw two of his men injured in the legs, and several of the enemy struck down. As they realised that the arrows were coming from behind them, the nearest defenders turned and fled, dropping down from the wall and running for the immediate safety of the streets beyond. Macro smiled grimly to himself. Once panic gripped men, it spread like a forest fire on a high wind. Now was the time to exploit the enemy's mistake. He turned to look down the other side of the wall and cried out to his men.

'What are you waiting for? The bastards are on the run!'

His men let out a triumphant chorus of shouts and rushed up the ladders and threw themselves at the shaken defenders. Within moments it was clear that the wall had been won. And now the

Romans presented a clearer target for the archers. Macro found a crudely constructed flight of steps and raced down them as he called to the closest men to follow him. There were perhaps thirty Parthians shooting at the Romans on the wall and as soon as Macro had been joined by ten or so of his men, he pointed his bloodied sword at the archers.

'That lot need killing! On me!'

Shield to the front, and head hunched down, he broke into a dead run, his men following him in a loose group. At once the officer in charge of the Parthians shouted to his men to turn and aim at the new threat. The first volley was unleashed quickly and aimed too high, so that the arrows glanced harmlessly off the shields, or lodged quivering where the points struck squarely. Macro had closed half the distance as the first shafts of the second volley streaked towards him. This time there was a cry from his left as one of the Praetorians went down on one knee, his ankle pierced through by an arrow. He staggered to a halt and looked down and was instantly hit again in the thigh.

Macro sprinted on, blood pounding in his ears, and he was on the nearest Parthian just as he raised his bow. Macro slashed at his extended arm before he could shoot the arrow and the edge of the blade splintered the shaft before cutting into the archer's forearm. The bow slipped from his grip and shot back towards the string and struck him a dazing blow in the face. Macro followed up with his shield, smashing into the archer and sending him down. He stabbed him between the shoulder blades, twisted and ripped the sword free as he looked for his next opponent. On either side the rest of the Praetorians piled in, using shield and sword with savage abandon. It was a one-sided affair, despite the unbalanced numbers, and with half their men downed the rest of the Parthians turned and ran.

Macro drew up, chest heaving, eyes wide and glaring, teeth bared, as he looked round and assessed the situation. The last of the defenders had been driven from the wall and chased back into Ligea's streets as a steady stream of Praetorians, and the most eager of the slingers and Iberians, clambered up the ladders and dropped down into the open space behind the wall. Their blood lust was up and those enemies who had been wounded were slaughtered on the ground where they lay before the attackers raced off into the streets to kill, rape and loot.

'Where's the tribune?' Macro called out as he looked round anxiously. 'Has anybody seen the tribune?'

CHAPTER NINETEEN

Cato was running down a street, thinking of nothing but the need to find and kill his enemy. After Macro had shoved him aside he was forced away from the ladder, and by the time he came to the foot of another and pulled rank to get on it, the fight on the wall had developed into a frenzied blur of flashing blades, crimson droplets and bodies pressed up against each other, all accompanied by the grunts of men striking and receiving blows, the thud of blades landing on shields and the softer sound of metal striking flesh. He jumped down from the ladder and one foot caught on a body and caused him to stumble, lose his grip on the shield and then roll over the edge of the walkway and down on to the ground below. The impact winded him badly and he sat hunched against the wall, holding his sword out in front of him, until his breath returned. Thirty paces to his right he saw Macro gather his men for the charge against the archers. Then one of the Parthians saw Cato, and started to swing his bow towards him. Macro's order cut across the noise of battle and the officer in charge of the archers snapped a command and the bowman turned away from Cato.

Heart beating hard inside his chest, Cato rose to his feet and saw the opening of a street directly opposite the wall, perfect cover to save him from the archers if they survived Macro's wild assault. Ahead of him he saw several of the enemy, Ligeans, and as the nearest slowed slightly and glanced back he saw Cato and shouted a warning, then he and the rest of his companions raced towards the heart of the town. Not knowing what else to do, Cato pursued them as fast as he could, determined to strike down those who shared responsibility for the deaths of Petillius, Rutilius and the others.

His prey ran round a corner a short distance ahead. Cato followed and almost ran straight into the man who had spotted him a moment earlier. He had a club in his hand and swung it wildly at Cato. There was barely time to react and Cato rolled aside as the sturdy length of wood swished over his head. Then, continuing the roll, he was back on his feet, crouching low, sword moving side to side as he sized up the Ligean. His opponent was a heavy-set man, but no fighter, and he knew it. He backed off as he called out to his companions. Some of them had stopped a short distance further on and now that they saw Cato was alone they ran back to confront him. Four of them, ranged across the width of the street, armed with swords and an axe to add to the first man's club. Like him they were not soldiers, but the advantage in numbers more than made up for that, Cato realised, as he backed away, towards the corner.

There was the sound of more men approaching from behind and he felt a rush of relief before glancing back to see some Parthian bowman running towards him.

'Oh shit . . .'

There was an alley to his left, shadowy and narrow, where he would stand a better chance of fighting it out. If he could down one of the Ligeans he might discourage the others. Two would cause the others to flee. Cato picked the man with the club as his target. He had turned back to fight and had more guts than the rest of them. Best to take him out first. Feinting at the man's face caused his opponent to sweep his club up to block the blow as he stumbled back a step. Cato launched himself forward and stabbed up, tearing into the underside of the man's weapon arm, and then sprang back, ready to defend himself against the others. It was a flesh wound, but it bled profusely and the clubman stepped away as he clutched his spare hand to the torn flesh.

For the moment, none of the others dared to risk an attack and Cato continued to edge back towards the alley entrance. A sidelong glance showed that the Parthians had seen him and were nocking fresh arrows to their bows even as they ran. Cato turned on his heels and sprinted into the alley, running as fast as possible, expecting any moment to feel the barbs of an arrow tear through his back and burst out of his chest. There were shouts from behind and footsteps as the remaining three Ligeans raced after him. Cato felt some small relief that they would obscure the target for any of the Parthians.

Then a piercing shout echoed down the alley and two arrows passed close by Cato, struck the stained wall of a two-storey building to his right and clattered off on to the street. He realised at once that the Parthians valued the lives of the townspeople so little that they were prepared to shoot them down to get at the fleeing Roman. A narrow street opened up to his right and Cato's boots scraped and slithered to a halt as he changed direction and ran out of sight of the archers. At once he turned again and lowered into a crouch, sword raised. The footsteps of his pursuers loomed loudly and then the first burst into sight and ran straight on to the point of the sword that Cato slammed into his guts. He folded over the blade and the impetus of his charge knocked Cato back enough that for an instant he thought he might fall. But he staggered and stayed on his feet and thrust the man's shoulder back with his left hand as he tore his sword free. The Ligean swayed and then reached for the wall of the building on the corner to steady himself, just as the two remaining Ligeans rushed round the corner and collided with him. All three went down with panicked cries.

Cato stared down at them, smiling cruelly now that he had them at his mercy. Then he heard the shouts of the Parthians only a short distance behind and he snarled with frustration and ran off again. He took the first alley to his left, then left again in what he hoped was the direction of the main gate and the safety of his comrades. He realised that he was heading back in the direction of the street along which the Ligeans had chased him, and he stopped. Cato pressed himself into a doorway and tested the handle. The door was securely fastened.

He looked both ways and saw that all the doors were closed along the street, and then it struck him that the streets were unnaturally still and silent, apart from the sounds of his pursuers, and the fainter sounds of the shouts and clatter of weapons from further off. He was in what seemed to be an impoverished quarter of the town, cut off from his men and surrounded by terrified townspeople who thought that locking themselves out of sight might save them from the wrath of the Roman and Iberian soldiers who had started the sacking of Ligea. For now, he was as doomed as the townspeople if he failed to escape his pursuers.

A door creaked open a short distance along the alley and Cato readied his sword, sweat dripping from his brow and running down his cheek. A head poked out, then a woman emerged dressed in a dark cloak over her tunic. She clutched the hand of a young girl as they stepped into the street looking warily from side to side. Then she saw Cato and her mouth opened in horror.

'Wait!' he said as loudly as he dared, holding his left hand out, palm first. 'I won't harm you.'

Even though his words would not be understood, Cato hoped his tone would be. But the woman grabbed the girl in her arms and ran off in a panic, sandals clacking on the paved street. Sucking air through his teeth in frustration, Cato made for the door she had left open and ducked inside as the sound of the Parthians' footsteps swelled in the narrow alley. He shut the door quickly, reached for the sturdy bolt that fastened it and slammed it home, then backed into the gloomy interior of a small room with a bolted, shuttered window. The only light came from an opening in the ceiling in one corner, where a ladder led up to the next floor. As the sound of footsteps swelled outside in the street Cato grasped his sword and readied himself for the door to be battered down. He was gasping for breath now and his heart seemed to be beating so loudly he feared it would give him away. Shadows flickered across the strip of light at the bottom of the door and there was shouting from outside. The footsteps stopped and there was a brief heated exchange and then the door was battered from the outside and a demanding voice called out. Cato stood quite still, hardly daring to breathe as there was a pause, then the door was struck again. This time it shook on its hinges as the Parthian threw his weight against the outside. But the bolt held.

Cato's attention was so fixed on the door that he did not hear the soft padding of footsteps behind him. He felt something touch the back of his leg and instinctively swung round, low, sword tip raised as it cut through the gloom and bit through flesh and bone. There was no cry of pain, no sound at all for a terrible frozen instant as Cato stared down into the wide eyes of a young boy, the same age as Lucius. The resemblance was so striking, save for slightly darker features, that Cato's lips formed the name of his son as he stared into the boy's face. Then his gaze fell to where the sword blade entered the bottom of his small ribcage. Blood was already seeping out around the metal.

The boy was quite still and stared back in shock.

Then the Parthian kicked at the door again and cursed loudly. The boy's eyes widened as he made to cry and Cato instantly reached down and clamped his spare hand over the child's mouth to muffle him. Both sank down on to the floor, facing each other on their knees.

'Don't make a sound,' Cato whispered soothingly. 'For Jupiter's sake, please don't.'

He eased his sword free and set it down beside them as the blood flowed freely from the wound. It was mortal, Cato could see that at once. Yet he unwound his neckcloth with his right hand as he continued to press the left over the boy's mouth. Balling the cloth up he pressed it to the wound to try and staunch the flow of blood.

The rattling of the hinges and the bolt sounded deafening in the hot, still gloom of the room and the boy started to struggle. Cato pulled him on to his lap and held him close, his left hand curled around the child's head and covering his mouth.

'Shhh. Please, be still. Be quiet . . . It'll be over soon.'

With a final, loud kick to the door the Parthian uttered a curse and moved on and the crack of light at the bottom of the door flickered a moment and then glowed clear.

The boy began to moan and Cato rocked him gently as he eased his hand away.

'There, he's gone. We're alone now. Safe.'

The child's wide eyes gazed up at him, his lips moving slowly as he breathed with difficulty. Cato stroked his hair for a moment, stricken by the similarity between the boy and Lucius. Guilt and intense self-loathing filled his heart. He looked round the room desperately and saw there was little, apart from some pots, a stool and a bedroll. Gently lifting the boy he crossed to the bedroll and laid him down and lifted the neckcloth away from the wound. For a moment the wound looked like a mouth, then the blood welled up and oozed over the boy's smooth stomach as he whimpered and began to writhe. Cato saw a pile of rags at the end of the bedroll and quickly reached for one to press back on to the wound and then tied his neckcloth around the stomach to hold the wad in place. Then he eased himself back against the wall and rested the boy's head on his lap. There was a dim shaft of light from the hole leading up to the next storey and faint motes of dust swirled lazily. Outside the sounds of the Parthians faded and then only occasional shouts broke the silence. Cato no longer cared if he was discovered by the enemy or not. Time seemed to have slowed to a complete stop and there was only himself and the dying boy, and the gloomy hovel in which they lay. His heart was leaden and filled with despair at what he had done and he no longer felt he wanted to live, still less deserved to.

He looked down and stroked the fine curls as he spoke comfortingly.

'I've done what I can for you . . . It's not much, but all I know . . . There, hush.' He smiled as he looked down. 'I'm sorry. You came up behind me . . . I thought you were my enemy. I didn't have time to think. I . . . I'm sorry.'

The boy stared back uncomprehendingly as his breathing became steadily more shallow. Then he smiled gently and reached a small hand up and traced his fingers over the bristles of Cato's cheek and then his lips. Cato felt his throat tighten and tighten until there was a raw ache and he could not trust himself to speak as he was overwhelmed by mortal horror at what he had done. At the life he had ended. At his powerlessness to save the child and avert this tragedy that was his own creation. Of all the evils that he had experienced in the long years of military service, this, he felt, was the greatest. And he was its perpetrator.

The boy's fingers stopped moving, and a moment later his hand slipped away as his arm slumped by his side. His chin rose, his jaw sagged and he gasped two or three times and then there was a slow, soft outward breath as his life left him.

Cato stared at him, paralysed by grief. Then he lifted him tenderly and cradled the lifeless little body in his arms as he began to weep uncontrollably.

'That is the good stuff!' Macro sniffed then smacked his lips as he tapped the stopper back in the large amphora and stepped back to admire the rest of the row leaning against the side of the merchant's storehouse. 'Enough garum here to last us the rest of the campaign if we go easy on it.' He turned to the four men of his century who had found the storehouse. 'Find a cart and some mules to carry these. I want them packed safely in straw.'

There was no need to tell them to take care with the valuable sauce. Garum was a luxury, and now the men of the Second Cohort were going to enjoy having it added to their cooking every day. Macro was already working out how much he might get for one of the jars from the auxiliary cohort. Of course, it would be necessary to keep their find secret from the Iberians in case Rhadamistus demanded a share of the spoils from his allies.

Macro patted the biggest of the jars affectionately before he turned to leave his men to carry out their orders. There were other valuables there to be sure, but he was wary of overburdening the column with loot and slowing down its advance. Besides, he had been diverted from a more pressing issue: discovering the whereabouts of his commanding officer. The last time he had seen Cato was at the foot of the assault ladder. Some of the men claimed to have seen the tribune climbing on to the wall but no one knew what had happened to him since then. Macro had searched the bodies piled along the wall and on the ground either side, and amongst the wounded propped up in the shade of the inner wall, but Cato was not amongst either the dead or the injured. So Macro had sent parties of men to search for the tribune, men who were disgruntled at not being allowed to join their comrades ransacking Ligea. That was tough on them, Macro accepted, but he would soon need a cadre of sober men to round up the remainder at the end of the day so that they could rest and recover from their debauchery in time for the column to resume its advance into Armenia.

Outside the storehouse he saw smoke billowing across the end of the street and three Iberians came staggering through the haze coughing as they clutched small wine jars under their arms. A fourth man followed them, dragging a large woman by the hair. She was naked and her breasts swayed heavily as she screamed and tried to break loose. The Iberian turned and slapped her violently and the screams ceased. They got a safe distance from the smoke and then kicked in a door and the soldiers entered. The last man thrust the woman through the door and followed her inside. A moment later the screaming resumed, this time accompanied by drunken laughter and guttural chanting.

For all his long years of service in the army Macro had never been involved in the sacking of a town. Forts and villages, yes. But never a town on even the modest scale of Ligea. Of course he had heard all the veterans' tales of the rich takings and entertainments to be had in the bacchanal chaos that followed the taking of an enemy town or city and had hoped one day to be a part of such an occasion himself. But now that he was, he felt unsettled by the drunken disorder of those who had made it their priority to find wine, and the cruelty, bloodlust and actual lust that ensued.

He turned in the opposite direction to the smoke and took the first street that he came to, a wide thoroughfare that led into the main square of the town. Here there were bodies lying in the street. An old man lay on his back, spread-eagled, his bowels opened from crotch to ribcage, and a cloud of flies was already feeding off his tacky blood and greasy-looking intestines. Further along Macro had to step round a group of bodies that seemed to be a family. An infant had had its brains dashed out against a wall and the body lay on the steps outside an open door. Two young boys had been cut down with swords and lay nearby. An older man, their father, Macro guessed, had been decapitated and his head left neatly upright in his lap with the body propped against the wall beside the doorway. A bloody trail led up the steps inside and Macro leaned across the threshold and called out on the off-chance.

'Cato?'

There was no reply. Just the buzzing of more flies. In the light shining in from the street he saw three more bodies. A naked woman lying on a bedroll, her head rolled to one side, dark eyes staring directly at Macro. Her legs were wide apart and dried blood matted her pubic hair and stained her thighs. On the floor nearby were two more naked bodies. Girls, no more than ten or twelve.

There was a loud belch from the rear of the house and the sound of a chair or table leg scraping on a stone floor.

'Who is there?' Macro demanded.

A moment later one of the Iberians stumbled into the room. He clasped a wineskin in one hand and his spear in the other. The point and the first two feet of the shaft were covered with dried blood and he grinned drunkenly as he saw the Roman officer. The Iberian began to babble in his own tongue and gestured towards the bodies with his spear, mimicked a woman's cry and then laughed.

'Fucking barbarian,' Macro growled.

The Iberian was too drunk to recognise the dangerous tone in the Roman's voice and strode clumsily towards him and offered up his wineskin.

Macro slapped it away and thrust the man back. 'I'm not drinking with you, you murderous little bastard.'

The Iberian's cheeriness vanished in an instant and he took his spear in both hands and turned the gore-encrusted point towards the centurion.

Macro sneered. 'Fancy your chances against some decent opposition, do you? Well go on, then, my friend.'

The Iberian hesitated and Macro slapped his hand on his chest and roared, 'Go on! Right there if you think you're hard enough! Brave bastard like you who can kill women and kids? Come on!'

The man's lips peeled back in a snarl and he lunged at the Roman. Macro swerved, snapped out his right hand and grasped the shaft and thrust it to one side, causing the man to lose his balance. Then he smashed his left fist into the side of the Iberian's head, knocking him cold. He let go of the spear and dropped to the ground and lay still for a moment before he groaned. Macro stood over him and raised the spear, ready to strike down into the man's throat. The Iberian blinked and then his eyes opened wide as he saw the point of his spear only inches away. He started babbling and begging piteously and Macro's resolve turned to contempt.

'You're not fucking worth it.'

He raised his arm, and the Iberian shrieked in panic, then Macro hurled the spear through the doorway at the back of the room and heard it crack into some stonework. He spat on the man in disgust as the latter curled into a ball on his side, knees pressed against his chest, then Macro turned away and returned to the street and marched off as quick as his legs would carry him.

As Macro entered the main market square in the heart of the town he saw another centurion catch sight of him and come running.

'Sir!' Centurion Ignatius waved a hand to attract Macro's attention. 'I've found him. I've found Tribune Cato.'

Macro felt a surge of relief sweep through him, banishing his morose thoughts.

'Alive?'

Ignatius hesitated 'Yes, sir. Alive.'

'What is it? Speak up!'

'Best you see for yourself. Come. Follow me.'

They left the square and entered the streets, passing more bodies and parties of drunken soldiers, and more sober individuals searching for valuables as the officers trotted past. Then Ignatius drew up outside a doorway where two Praetorians stood guard.

'He's in there, sir.'

Macro stood on the threshold and looked round the small room, seeing his friend slumped against a wall with a child curled up on his lap.

'Cato, thank Jupiter you're alive. You had me worried there, my lad, I don't mind telling you.'

Cato did not seem to notice him, and then he frowned. 'Hmmm?'

'Cato? Are you wounded?'

Macro entered the room and saw that there was a small shuttered window to one side. He slipped the bolt back to reveal an iron grille through which bright light pierced the gloom and fell squarely on Cato and what Macro could now see was a boy. The latter's skin was pale and there was no sign of movement. Then he noticed the blood smeared on Cato's armour and staining his tunic and hands.

'Ignatius! Send for the surgeon. The tribune's wounded.'

The light had caused Cato to shrink away from it, squinting, and now he murmured: 'I'm not injured . . . I'm fine. Quite fine.' His right hand began to stroke the hair of the dead child and Macro saw that it was trembling. He squatted beside his friend and saw the distracted expression on his face as Cato continued: 'I'm just tired . . . Very tired. That's all. I just need some rest.'

His words were slurred and half mumbled and there was a vagueness in his manner that Macro had never seen before. He reached out and touched the tribune's shoulder. 'We'll sort that out. Let me get you back to camp. Then you can rest. I'll see to everything for you.'

There was no protest from Cato, as Macro had anticipated, just a nod.

'Here, let me . . .' Macro leaned forward to pick up the boy. Instantly Cato snatched at the body and held it close as the child's limbs and head swung lifelessly.

'Don't touch him! Leave Lucius alone!'

'Lucius?' Macro frowned. Even though he knew it was impossible, he looked closely and shook his head. 'Cato, that's not Lucius. Just some boy. Here, let me take him from you.'

'Don't touch him, I said!'

Cato's eyes were red-rimmed and staring madly, so Macro eased himself back and raised his hands.

'All right . . . But Cato, that isn't Lucius . . . Look at him.'

Cato was still for a moment, then lowered the boy's body and looked down, his face creasing up in grief as he choked. 'I killed him, Macro . . . Killed him with my sword . . . He surprised me. I turned and stabbed . . . I killed him.'

Macro sighed. 'It was an accident. You didn't mean to kill the kid – I get that. Come, let's put him down, eh?'

This time he waited for Cato's assent, and the tribune nodded. Macro lifted the little body away tenderly, as if it were a newborn, and set it down on the floor beside Cato. He arranged the limbs tidily and closed the child's eyes before turning his attention back to Cato.

'Come on, sir. There's nothing we can do for the poor mite. It's too bad, but you're not to blame. In fact, you mustn't blame yourself. It's what happens sometimes. An accident of war. It's not your fault.'

'But I killed him,' Cato insisted and swallowed hard. 'Me. No one else.'

Macro thought of all the dead and dying in the surrounding

181

streets and of the casual rape, slaughter and mutilation being carried out by his men, the auxiliaries and the Iberians, and for a moment he was tempted to be angry with Cato's self-indulgence. But there was more to it than that. This was not one of his friend's flights of poetical and philosophical fancy about the nature of good and evil. Something in Cato had broken. What he needed at this moment was not a stiff talking-to, a harsh shaking to bring him to his senses. He needed time to rest and recover. Macro could only pray to the gods that he recovered swiftly. The men needed Cato. So did Macro. With a shock he realised that he had grown so used to following his friend that he wondered how he would cope now that he might have to assume command. For a while at least.

He took hold of Cato's arm and lifted him on to his feet, and then put his friend's arm over his shoulder as he supported Cato's weight with his other hand.

'Come on, lad. We have to get you away from here.'

CHAPTER TWENTY

'I will be taking command of the column until the tribune has recovered from his injury,' Macro announced to the officers at the briefing that evening. The sun had only just set and there was still plenty of light to see the faces of the centurions and optios sitting around the headquarters tent. The sides had not yet been unrolled and the air was already cool, which suited Macro as it would discourage anyone from making the briefing last any longer than necessary.

'For now, you are all in my tender care, not that that should concern you unduly.' He forced a smile. 'It will only be a temporary measure. Until the tribune is back on his feet.'

'What happened to him?' asked Centurion Porcino.

It was the question Macro knew was coming and yet he still felt uneasy about lying to the others. The cohort's surgeon, Ignatius and the two men he had set to guard Cato had all been sworn to secrecy, and now Cato was in a deep sleep in his private tent, and orders had been left that no one was to disturb him under any circumstances.

'The tribune received a blow to the head,' Macro announced. 'It's scrambled his brains for a bit, according to the surgeon. So that should give the rest of us a chance to keep up with him for a while.'

There were a few smiles from the officers who had long since recognised the quality of their commander's intellect and grasp of nearly every detail of administration off the battlefield and sound grasp of tactics on it.

'But he will recover?' Porcino persisted. 'He won't be left, you know, simple. I've seen it happen often enough when someone gets a hard knock.'

'Even simple, Cato is smarter than most,' Macro replied. 'For now you will have to put up with me. I'll do my best to run things as he did.'

He paused a beat to see if anyone challenged his version of what had happened to their commanding officer, and was relieved when Porcino let the matter drop.

'Very well, our first order of business is the butcher's bill. Twenty-eight dead, thirty-four wounded, twenty of whom are fit enough to walk. We lost twelve men from Keranus's cohort, and eight wounded. The Iberians are counting their own casualties, but that will be less than ours since they supported the attack. We have also lost one of the onagers. The cross beam has begun to split and we haven't got time to make a repair, so once it is broken down we'll use the parts for spares.' Macro nodded. 'Not bad losses considering the nature of the action. But we won't have the final figure on the strength returns until Marcellus's squadron rounds up the last of the men still looting the town. I'm not best pleased that they did not respond to the recall. The lad on the bucina nearly burst his lungs for the best part of an hour so there's no excuse for them. If any of them are in your units, then I want them disciplined. Loss of a month's pay and latrine duties until we reach the Armenian capital. No exceptions,' Macro said sternly. 'I don't care what they offer you. I'll not have men ignoring the signal and getting away with it. That clear?'

The officers nodded, some reluctantly since accepting bribes was an accepted way of supplementing an officer's income, especially in the Praetorian Guard, where there were plenty of opportunities to extract bribes from soldiers. They in turn were flush with silver from the bribes they were handed by the emperors ever keen to buy their loyalty.

'Anyone else still not back when we march tomorrow will be left to the enemy, and treated as a deserter if he tries to rejoin the column.' Macro let his words sink in so there was no doubt about the seriousness of his intent. 'We have lost several days dealing with Ligea. The men have had their fun, and now they're going to have to be soldiers again. Not a rabble of drunken thieves and rapists. You'd better make sure they understand that. I hope the

184

spectacle that took place in the town will not be repeated. It was my understanding that Rhadamistus persuaded the tribune that an example needed to be made of Ligea. Now it has been, and so we don't stick it to any civilians we meet from here on. Not unless the tribune orders it. Another thing. This is a Roman column. The Iberians are allied troops and that means we're in charge. Rhadamistus is a king in name only until we put him back on the throne. Until then, he is in our charge and we must not forget it, even if *he* does from time to time. If you have any dealings with him and he gives you any orders then you clear them with me first.'

Macro drew himself up as he concluded. 'Any questions? . . . No? Then the cohorts will assemble at dawn for the funeral for our fallen brothers. We march straight after that. Dismissed!'

Once the last of them had gone, Macro made his way to Cato's tent and found the surgeon waiting for him. Cato lay on his side on his camp bed, curled up in a ball, asleep.

'How is he?'

'No change, sir. Been out since you last saw him. Hasn't stirred once.'

'I suppose that's good. Let the lad have a decent rest and he'll be right as rain when he wakes up.'

The surgeon puffed his cheeks. 'I'm not sure it is as simple as that, sir. I've seen this kind of thing before.'

Macro arched a brow. 'What kind of thing would that be?'

'There's no medical term for it, sir. At least none that I am aware of.' The surgeon stroked his jaw as he gathered his thoughts and continued. 'It's a kind of nervous exhaustion. If a man takes on responsibilities and refuses to take the rest he needs, then he's storing up trouble. It's worse if he is on campaign and facing the stress of battle, and the loss of friends and comrades.'

'Bollocks,' Macro exclaimed. 'I know him. He's been through far worse than this without getting into such a state.'

'All men have a breaking point, sir. Most of us are lucky that we are never pushed beyond it. Some men I've known, men both of us would regard as heroes, have coped for years and then something happens. It could even be something that seems quite trivial to you and me, but not to them.' The surgeon looked at Cato thoughtfully.

185

'I see he has quite a few scars on his body. There will be others too. Scars of the heart and mind. Experience does that and we all cope with it differently. I've served with you for a couple of years now, sir. We've seen plenty of action together. We both know that the tribune never spared himself. It's also no secret that he was troubled by the loss of his wife.'

'That's none of your damn business.'

'I'm just saying, sir. The tribune has endured more than most men have at his age. Are you really surprised that this has happened? I wonder what it was that tipped him over the edge?'

'He killed some kid in the town. An accident. Something about the boy reminded the tribune of his own son.' Macro shrugged. 'That's as much as I can make of it, anyhow.'

The surgeon nodded. 'And did he?'

'What?'

'Did the boy look like the tribune's son?'

Macro did his best to recall the details. 'No. Looked nothing like him. Not to me.'

He regarded Cato sorrowfully for a moment before continuing. 'How long until he gets over this black mood of his?'

'Who can say?'

'Well you bloody well should be able to. You're the surgeon. You said you've seen this before. So what's the answer? How are you going to cure him?'

The surgeon looked indignant. 'I said I've seen it. Never said anything about curing it. This isn't a cut or a broken bone. It goes deeper. The tribune needs to cure himself. Rest will help, I am sure. I can give him something to help him sleep, but that's all.'

'You're not much good then, are you?' Macro sniffed. 'Rest it is. I'll have a covered cart prepared for him. Hopefully he can get some sleep on the road to Artaxata. You'll have to keep an eye on him, I've got duties to take care of.'

'I have other patients too.'

'So deal with them,' Macro snapped. He was starting to lose his patience with the surgeon. 'We'll let him sleep then. You'd better go.'

The surgeon bowed his head and left the tent. Macro stayed a

186

little while longer, watching his friend as Cato's chest rose and fell with a steady rhythm. Once he stirred suddenly, as if disturbed by a dream, then the mumbling subsided and the tension eased and he slept on.

Outside the tent Macro saw the girl that Cato had brought back from the Iberian encampment several days before. She had been given food and water and slept outside Cato's tent each night. He had given strict orders that she was not to be touched and was to be regarded as a servant of the tribune. Since when Cato had seemed to ignore her, as far as Macro was aware. He had put it down to that aspect of Cato's character that insisted on protecting the weak and vulnerable. A shame, he reflected, as she was attractive enough to be welcome in any man's bed. Still, Cato was Cato and he was not just any man. Even so, the girl could make herself of some use to him.

The girl stirred as she saw Macro looking at her and sat up and hugged her knees as she stared back anxiously.

'Bernisha? Right?'

She nodded shyly.

'The tribune did you a favour, taking you out of the Iberian camp. You could look after him, you know,' Macro said gently. He pointed at Cato's tent and mimed sleeping, then mopping his brow. She did not react.

'Fuck this . . .' Macro stepped over to her, grasped her wrist and dragged her to her feet and into the tent. She struggled for a moment and then gave up when she realised it was futile. Macro pointed to Cato. 'I want you to see to his needs.'

She looked at him blankly. Macro sighed and mimed mopping his brow again, then drinking and feeding and pointed at Cato. Bernisha opened her mouth and spoke in her own tongue and nodded.

'Good.' Macro smiled. 'Then you see to it. Mind you . . .' His eyes narrowed. 'If anything happens to him, if you do anything to harm him or get in the way of his recovery, I'll have you flogged and thrown back into the Iberian camp for them to use you as they want.'

His threatening tone was unmistakable, even if she did not appear to follow any of the details of his words. Macro pointed at Cato, then at her and then at his eyes and pointed at her again.

'Get on with it.'

With that, he left the tent and stood outside for a moment to collect his thoughts. Macro was disturbed. If this had happened to almost any other man he'd have said the man's nerve had failed him and that he'd given in to that sentiment that all soldiers dreaded: cowardice. But he knew Cato better than most men knew their own family. He knew that Cato never lacked for courage, and even when the odds were daunting he forced himself to fight on. He was the bravest soldier Macro had ever known. And if this could happen to Cato, then it could happen to anyone. Including Macro himself. That was a frightening enough thought in itself. All the more reason to do whatever he could to help his friend recover. Their roles might be reversed one day if Macro ever discovered his own break-ing point. He shuddered at the prospect, then made himself think about his most pressing responsibilities: to do the rounds of the sentries, ensure the column would be ready to move at dawn, and oversee the preparations for the morrow's funeral. The burdens of command were his now, he mused, as he strode towards the area of the camp occupied by the Iberians. Before he saw to anything else he decided that he must inform Rhadamistus he had taken temporary command. That was a task he did not relish. Not one bit. Cato was better at handling that sort of thing.

Macro steadied his breathing, and prepared himself to be firm but polite. 'But,' he muttered to himself, 'if that Iberian ponce thinks I am going to toady up to him then he's in for a fucking big disappointment.'

'Wounded?' Rhadamistus frowned.

'Yes, sir. A head injury. It'll take a few days before he recovers. Meanwhile, I'm the senior officer in the column, so I'll be taking command, temporarily.'

'You?' Rhadamistus seemed suspicious. 'Please pardon me, I hardly know you, Centurion Macro. Not as well as I have come to know your superior at least.'

'I can't help that, sir. But that's the situation. Just thought you should be informed.'

'Quite right. And as we will no doubt have to confer regularly over the coming days, until your tribune is well enough to resume command, it would be best if you addressed me as "Majesty". Just to prevent any further awkwardness.'

Macro's mouth opened, then he shut it quickly. He had no idea that there had been any awkwardness. But if the Iberian wished to be called 'Majesty', then 'Majesty' it would be, if only to keep the peace. He cleared his throat and bowed his head.

'Yes, Majesty.'

Rhadamistus nodded condescendingly. 'From what I understand of the Roman military, you centurions are the backbone of the army. You are chosen for your courage, your willingness to be the first into battle, and the last to leave the fight. Is that so?'

Macro could not help but be flattered by the observation, swiftly followed by wariness at the purpose of such praise. 'I wouldn't know about all that, sir. It is an honour to be chosen to lead other soldiers. We centurions just try to be the best soldiers we can.'

'The modesty of the true hero,' said Rhadamistus. 'You are a man after my own heart. A fighter and leader of men.'

Macro said nothing in reply, and just wished to remove himself from the Iberian's presence as soon as he could. So he cleared his throat. 'Well, yes. Thank you, Majesty. Now, I mustn't impose on your valuable time any longer.'

Rhadamistus's benign smiled faded. 'You'll quit my presence when I say so, Centurion. I have not finished with you quite yet. As I said, I am sure you are a fine warrior. And your main duty is to lead the men of your century into battle. You are the senior centurion of your cohort, but the tribune is the commander.'

'Unless he is unable to command. Then the responsibility falls to me.'

'. . . Majesty,' Rhadamistus reminded him.

Macro nodded. 'Yes, Majesty.'

'So, in the normal run of things, you are not used to the command of a cohort, let alone two cohorts, or even a column of men as numerous as ours. Is that right?'

Macro could see at once where the exchange was headed and chose his words carefully. 'All Roman centurions must be ready to assume greater responsibilities as the need arises, Majesty.'

'I understand that. But such responsibilities are assumed only in the absence of an officer of higher rank. Correct?'

'Yes, Majesty.'

'And would you not agree that a king ranks higher than a centurion?'

Macro placed his hands behind his back and flexed his fingers anxiously. 'It depends—'

'It depends? Centurion Macro, you are clearly a veteran with many campaigns behind you. No doubt you have fought across many different provinces of your Empire. Tell me, in all that time did you ever once encounter a situation when a centurion was accorded more authority than a king?'

'No, sir, I did not. But—'

'But what? There is no but anything that contradicts my point.' Rhadamistus leaned closer and stared intently down into Macro's eyes. 'I am a king, and you are a centurion. Moreover, I am king of the very land under your feet as we speak. This is my kingdom. I am its ruler. You are here on my sufferance. By every measure we care to apply, I am your superior and therefore I should command this column in the absence of Tribune Cato. I agreed with your General Corbulo to accept Cato as commander of our little army. I made no such undertaking with regard to you. Therefore I tell you now that I will lead the column. Do you understand?'

'I understand, Majesty.'

'Good, then I will expect you to follow my orders, just as you followed those of Tribune Cato.'

'No, Majesty. I will not.'

Rhadamistus's jaw sagged momentarily before he recovered from the shock of being addressed so directly. 'I warn you, Centurion, do not cross my path.'

Macro pulled his shoulders back. 'Majesty, my orders ultimately come from the emperor. And the emperor of Rome outranks any man alive. Whether they be a king or a humble centurion. As things stand, you are not a king. Nor will you be until Roman soldiers place you back on your throne. I serve Tribune Cato because the tribune was appointed over me by the emperor. In his absence my duty is to serve the emperor directly. Not you. Not unless my orders specifically require me to. Which they don't. It is my intention to take command of the column.'

'You will not command me! Nor my men.'

Macro stared back as he organised his thoughts while struggling to control his rising temper. 'I command the Praetorian cohort. I also command the auxiliaries. And I command the siege train. It is in both our interests that your men and mine march together, Majesty.'

Rhadamistus glared back. 'If you value your life then you will do as I say.'

'Majesty, I value my life dearly. But I value duty and honour even more. And my duty is clear. Until Tribune Cato recovers, I am in command. That is the end of the matter. I bid you goodnight.'

Macro turned and strode towards the entrance to the tent. The two Iberian bodyguards standing there crossed their spears in front of him, forcing Macro to draw up. He felt his fingers move towards the handle of his sword before judgement prevailed over instinct and he lowered his hand. He half turned towards Rhadamistus and raised an eyebrow.

There was silence and a stillness that seemed to last far longer than a few heartbeats and then the Iberian barked an order and the bodyguards grounded their spears. Macro marched between them as he growled: 'You won't be so lucky if you try that on me next time, lads.'

Then he was outside in the cool evening air. The sky was purple along the horizon and shaded into velvet darkness above, pricked by the glimmer of stars. He exhaled slowly as he marched back towards the Roman half of the camp and offered up a quick prayer.

'Jupiter, Best and Greatest, I pray that you do everything in your power to return Cato to his senses. Before I do anything else I may fucking well come to regret.'

CHAPTER TWENTY-ONE

An hour after dawn, once the wounded had been loaded on to the wagons, the column continued its advance into the mountainous heart of Armenia. Behind them the Romans and Iberians left two blazing funeral pyres. The first consumed the bodies of their fallen comrades, and thick greasy smoke billowed into the air and the morning breeze blew the smoke after the column so they choked on the acrid tang of woodsmoke and roast meat, and it clung to their clothes for many hours afterwards. The second pyre was the town of Ligea, which had perished in all but name the day before. Fires had been set in every street and the flames, fanned by the breeze, had spread rapidly. Looking back, Macro could see that the blaze was almost continuous, bounded by the walls so that the town looked like a vast fire pit. Tongues of flame lashed the morning sky and the roar and sharp reports of bursting timbers carried clearly for the first mile of the march. When the column halted briefly at noon, the soldiers looked back in hushed awe at the thick pillar of smoke that rose into the heavens.

Macro regarded the spectacle as he took out his canteen and took a swig of water. That smoke, he knew, was going to announce their presence for a considerable distance and soon the curious would be coming to investigate. When word of the devastation of Ligea spread across Armenia, they would discover if the act had chastened the people Rhadamistus aimed to rule once again, or so inflamed their passion that they would rise in arms against him. That remained to be seen, Macro reflected. Besides, he was concerned with more immediate matters.

The Iberians had broken camp first and, disdaining the routine of shovelling the rampart back into the ditch, they packed their tents and marched away. The Romans regarded the departure in silence as they formed up for the funeral rites. The Iberian dead had already been buried during the night, but their refusal to stand with the Romans and honour the dead of their ally was taken as a calculated insult by every man of the Praetorian and auxiliary cohorts. Macro had considered challenging Rhadamistus directly and demanding that he halt his men, but such a confrontation could have escalated out of control very easily, given the previous evening's fraught encounter. So he had let them march off, and then concluded the funeral rites as swiftly as possible before setting off in their wake.

The Iberians had a two-mile start on the Romans and as the distance between them grew, thanks to the slow progress of the baggage and siege trains, Macro sent the slingers ahead with orders to bridge the gap between the two forces and keep both in sight. It was a highly unsatisfactory state of affairs for the column to be divided on a march through what it was prudent to regard as hostile territory. But it was better to march divided than be at each other's throats, Macro reflected. He hoped that Rhadamistus's wounded pride would soon give way to reason and that he would accept Macro's command over the combined force. It might take a day or more, but the Iberian must surely come to realise that his ambitions stood a better chance of coming to fruition with Roman soldiers and siege weapons at his side.

Macro's attention turned to the covered cart that rumbled along the crude track a short distance behind the men of the First Century tramping along beneath the burden of their marching yokes. The flaps of the goatskin cover were untied and through the gap Macro caught a glimpse of his friend lying on his bedroll, the girl sitting beside him, atop the folds of Cato's tent. He dropped back and fell into step at the rear of the cart.

'How's he doing?'

Bernisha turned and looked down at him, guessed the nature of his query, mimed sleeping, then raised her palm and rocked it from side to side. Macro groaned with frustration. Cato was needed now more than ever. Grasping the side of the cart Macro pulled himself up and waved the girl forward and took her place. Beside him Cato lay on his back, his body jolting as the cart rumbled and lurched beneath him. He was shaded from the bright sunshine but the dust covered the interior in a grey patina, and occasionally he coughed as he slept. Other than his exhaustion there was not a mark on him. No wound. Macro still struggled with the idea that his friend could be so stricken by some sickness of the heart and mind. He was tempted to give the tribune a firm shake and tell him to pull himself together, but was concerned that such action might hinder his friend's recovery.

One of the cart's wheels crashed down into a deep rut and the cart lurched violently. Cato's eyes snapped open and he glanced around anxiously before he saw Macro sitting at his side.

'What's happening? Where are we?'

'Back on the road to Artaxata, lad. If you can call this bloody glorified goat track any kind of a road.'

Cato frowned, struggling to concentrate. 'And the town? What happened to Ligea?'

Macro eased aside the flaps to reveal the column of smoke in the distance. 'Burned to the ground, as you ordered.'

Cato flinched. 'I ordered? Yes . . . Yes, I did. And the people?'

'All killed. We took no prisoners.'

'All dead?'

Macro nodded heavily. He had derived no satisfaction from obeying the orders and, in truth, believed that the destruction of Ligea and its people was a stain on the reputation of Rome, and on the honour of the Second Cohort in particular. Worse still, it was a mistake, in Macro's opinion. But the orders had been given and it was not his place to question them. Besides, it was too late.

'I shouldn't be lying here,' Cato continued. He tried to rise up but found that his body felt utterly leaden and the effort exhausted him. The arm he had used to prop himself up trembled like a leaf in a gale. Bernisha regarded him with concern and eased herself round Macro so that she could support Cato's shoulders. She spoke soothingly and gently eased him back on to the bedroll. Cato did not resist her and lay back with a deep sigh as he looked up at his friend.

'What happened to me? Was I wounded?'

194

Macro shook his head. 'Not as such, lad. You're just sick. The surgeon says it's exhaustion and some kind of malady of the heart. I can't tell you any more. You'd best hear it from him when we make camp tonight. I'll send him to you.'

Even though he was struggling to think coherently Cato heard his friend's words with a growing sense of shame. He was weak when his men needed him to be strong. If there was no wound and none of the sicknesses that soldiers were prone to while on campaign, then there was no excuse for his incapacity. Certainly no excuse he would have accepted from any man under his command. He would have called them malingerers, the kind of soldier others regarded with knowing looks that led to contempt. Men who let their comrades down and invented illnesses to excuse themselves from labour or, unforgivably, from taking their place in the battle line. Cato's thoughts turned in on him and he dreaded to consider what Macro might be making of all this. He rolled his head to the side and stared fixedly at the wooden plank just inches from his face.

'I am sorry, Macro. I am failing you. Failing the men . . .' Cato could imagine the snide comments that the rankers would be making about their commander's weakness and the thought filled him with even more intense self-loathing. 'They'll not think me fit to lead them again.'

'That's bollocks, lad.' Macro forced himself to sound cheery. 'Why, they'd follow you through the gates of Hades without a thought, and be sure you'd lead 'em out the other side.'

'Not after this. Macro, I've served long enough to know how their minds work.'

'They'll be fine. Besides, as far as they know you received a head injury and you'll be back in charge as soon as you've recovered. I should think they'll be grateful not to have me bellowing at them any more.'

Cato felt a mixture of gratitude to his friend and vulnerability. Even if the men never guessed the truth, Macro would always know. And that would be a burden for Cato to carry evermore.

'I'm tired. I need to rest.'

'Of course you do. Best I stop bending your ear then, and let you get on with it.' Macro patted him on the shoulder and turned to

Bernisha. 'And I'm sure this one will do her best to help you recover. Think she's taken a bit of a shine to you. Right, lass?'

Bernisha smiled and dampened a cloth with some water from Cato's canteen before folding it into a compress and placing it over his forehead.

'You're in good hands, lad. I'll see you later, in camp. For now, you get some more rest.'

Macro eased himself on to the tail of the cart, dropped down to the road and strode ahead to catch up with his men.

Inside the rattling cart Cato did his best to settle into a comfortable position and closed his eyes. His brief moment of wakefulness had tired him out, and once more his thoughts came with difficulty, and even then they were random and rarely coherent. More like a dream, he mused. As the tension drained from his limbs, restless, unordered images and impressions flickered through his mind: the stark terror of the attack on the inner wall of Ligea – the first time he and Julia had ever made love – the conviction that he would be killed when he had swum to a wrecked ship off the coast of Britannia to rescue the survivors years ago – the dread of losing Macro when his friend had been wounded by an arrow in the same campaign – the nervousness of the occasion when he had first been introduced to his son, and the depth of love he had felt for Lucius thereafter – then the face of the boy he had stabbed in Ligea . . . So like Lucius, it had seemed. So much so that it felt as if he had murdered his son. And then darkness and oblivion as he finally fell once more into the deep sleep of the utterly exhausted and distressed.

Bernisha sat by him, occasionally refreshing the compress and gently tamping it down over his forehead and eyes. When he stirred and shifted, and mumbled anxiously, she took his hand and held it until the moment passed, and then stroked his dark curls. This seemed to ease his mind. She muttered in Greek: 'Rest, tribune. Rest . . .'

For the next four days the column marched as two forces. The Iberians never advanced so far each day that the Romans could not keep up with them, Macro was relieved to discover. Each night he gave orders for the camp to be constructed on a scale that would permit their erstwhile allies to join the Romans if they chose. But they remained apart, at least a mile off, and erected their tents in the open, to Macro's professional disapproval. If the enemy took the opportunity to attack them now, then they would raise havoc amongst the Iberians. Much as he was tempted to ride over to their camp and try and persuade Rhadamistus to unite the columns, Macro could not bear the thought of such an approach being taken as a sign of weakness. And so the two forces spent each night apart, their campfires forming two pools of light amid the dark masses of the surrounding mountains.

The additional duties that fell to Macro tested his endurance, and he began to understand the strain his friend had suffered since the start of the campaign. Each evening he came to Cato's tent to report on the day's march, the condition of the men and the location of the Iberians. He was relieved to find the tribune recovering steadily, and by the fourth evening Cato announced he was ready to resume command the next day.

'Are you certain, sir?'

Cato hesitated a moment before he nodded. 'I am.'

Macro watched him closely and saw the faint tremor in his limbs as Cato stood up and crossed to the open tent flaps and looked out across the camp.

'Looks like you could still use some rest, sir.'

'I said I am ready,' Cato responded firmly. 'Well enough to ride, and my head is clear now.'

'If you say so. If you need me to continue taking on some of your duties, then just let me know.'

Cato glanced back over his shoulder and smiled. 'Thank you, brother. I am grateful.'

'Pah! It's been fun to be the ranking officer these last few days.'

'I sincerely doubt that.' Cato's experienced eyes and ears scrutinised the rows of tents stretching out around him. The pleasing sounds of singing and some laughter carried to his ears. It was good that the men's spirits were still high despite being abandoned by the Iberians. A quiet camp would have indicated dissatisfaction and faltering morale. Along the rampart he could just make out the figures of the sentries, moving slowly along their beats. All was well.

At least here in the Roman camp. The glow of distant campfires was visible to the east and Cato wondered about the mood amongst the Iberians. Was Rhadamistus regretting his hubris? Were his men anxious about abandoning the security of a Roman marching camp to sleep in the open? Or were they simply waiting for the Romans to come to them and agree to accept Rhadamistus as their commander? Either way, he concluded, it would be increasingly perilous to permit the present situation to continue. He turned back and returned to his camp bed and sat down heavily.

There was a clatter of pots outside and a moment later Bernisha entered the tent with Cato's mess tin. She set it down on the small table beside his camp bed and looked to Macro, miming eating.

He nodded and gave her a smile. Once the girl had left the room he cocked an eyebrow at Cato. 'Pretty one, that.'

'I suppose she is.' Cato took a sip of the gruel, but it was too hot, so he set the mess tin and spoon down. 'What of it?'

'Oh, nothing.'

'For fuck's sake, Macro, do I look like I am up for it? Well, do I?'

'I guess not. But . . .' Macro clicked his tongue, ' . . . be a shame to let her go to waste. Just saying, if I were in your boots . . .'

'Well, you're not. She looks after my needs and keeps my kit clean, that's all. It'll remain that way as long as I want and that's the end of the matter.'

'Yes, sir.'

Bernisha returned with a spare mess tin and handed it to Macro.

'You must eat too.' Cato pointed to her and raised his mess tin and nodded towards the tent flaps. She smiled at him quickly and scurried away. Macro eyed her departing figure appreciatively.

'Not one word, Macro,' Cato warned him. 'Just eat, eh? We could do with a bit of peace and quiet for a while.'

The midnight signal had barely sounded across the camp when Macro tore aside the flaps of Cato's tent and rushed over to his bed. Out of the corner of his eye he saw the girl rise from the ground to one side with a frightened gasp.

'Sir! Wake up!'

The tribune was slow to respond and Macro shook his shoulder roughly. 'Wake up.'

Cato's eyes snapped open and he propped himself up on an elbow. 'What is it?'

'The Iberian camp, sir. It's alight.'

Swinging his legs out, Cato slipped his feet into a pair of light sandals and stood up. He was already wearing a tunic due to the coolness of the nights in the mountainous terrain they were marching through. He hurried from the tent and with Macro at his side they ran to the gate tower closest to Rhadamistus and his men. Cato was out of breath when they reached the ladder and sent Macro up first before steeling himself for the climb. His heart was beating swiftly and his limbs were shaking as he heaved himself on to the platform and stood with Macro and the sentry, gasping for breath to ease the fire in his lungs.

Just over a mile away the Iberian camp lay on slightly lower ground, beside a bend in the river that the road followed as directly as possible. From their vantage point Cato could see that scores of tents were ablaze, and by the light of the flames he could make out hundreds of men and horses dashing in every direction. A short distance from the flames he could just see the dark outlines of riders on swift ponies racing around the camp loosing arrows. Further out, a handful of small fires burned and near them arrows cut fiery arcs through the night before plunging down amongst the Iberian tents.

'Parthians,' said Macro. 'They must have been tracking the column. Given that fool's arrogance, this was bound to happen. What are your orders, sir? Shall I tell the men to stand to?'

Cato thought for a moment and shook his head. 'No. Have the duty century moved on to the rampart, together with fifty of the slingers. I doubt the Parthians will attempt any attack on us, but best to be safe.'

'What about the Iberians, sir? Should we send men to help them?'

'There's nothing we can do now.'

While Macro climbed down to the ground to give the orders, Cato watched the raiders set light to more of the camp. But Rhadamistus was already reacting to the raid. Several bands of horse-archers and cataphracts had already mounted and now cantered out of the camp to chase down the enemy. The light barrage of fire arrows abruptly ceased and the dark figures of the mounted Parthians disappeared into the night. The Iberians remaining in the camp did their best to fight the fires, beating out the flames with lengths of brush and water drawn from the river. One by one the blazes were extinguished and the horses that had been scattered by the raiders were rounded up. Only when Cato was sure that the attack was over did he leave the tower and pick his way wearily back to his tent.

Come the morning, he resolved, he would ride over to the Iberians and confront Rhadamistus and put an end to this foolish division of their forces.

CHAPTER TWENTY-TWO

As Cato and his escort rode into the camp it was clear that the Iberians had suffered badly during the previous night's raid. Scores of tents had been burned to the ground and the charred skeletons of their frames and shreds of blackened tent leather on the scorched ground were all that was left. Where the extensive spread of Rhadamistus's personal tentage had stood little remained, and his slaves and servants were picking over the ruins to salvage what was left of the cushions, rugs, furniture, and the stocks of wine and other luxuries. The Iberian prince was standing with his small court of noblemen observing the scene of devastation when Cato reined in and dismounted. The ten men he had brought with him on the only horses in the Roman column remained in the saddle.

Rhadamistus turned to greet him with a sour expression. His face and robes were smeared with scorch marks and grime and a blood-stained dressing was fastened about his forearm. The nobles behind him were similarly marked by the consequences of the raid.

'Tribune Cato, I am glad to see you have recovered. I imagine you have come to gloat at my misfortune.'

'I would hardly do that, Majesty. You are an ally of Rome. I feel your losses as keenly as you do. I merely came to see what assistance we can offer.'

Rhadamistus sighed. 'Unless it is within your power to conjure up fresh tents and supplies, and raise the dead, then there is little that you can do for us.'

'How many men did you lose, Majesty?'

The Iberian turned to his followers and there was a brief exchange before he replied. 'Over fifty were killed. Many more were wounded. We lost over a hundred mounts. As well as those that bolted into the night and are still being recovered. Then there are the tents . . .' He waved a hand over the surrounding scene and shook his head slowly. 'Almost a third of them destroyed or damaged beyond repair. The Parthians lost a handful of men in return. I doubt there were more than fifty of them in the band that attacked us.' His face darkened as he continued. 'They would not have taken us by surprise if my sentries had been alert. They will pay the price for failing me.' He gestured towards a party of men sitting on the ground a short distance away, their hands and ankles bound. 'Those curs will be left to burn alive when we continue our march today. It is a fitting punishment, no?'

Even at this distance Cato could see their terrified expressions and guessed that they had already learned their fate.

'Majesty, you have lost enough men. Men who will be needed to win your throne. Why waste the lives of any more? Punish them, yes. If they were my men I'd have them flogged in front of their comrades. That would be a lesson on the consequences of poor watch-keeping that would not easily be forgotten.'

'Perhaps, but burning them alive would be even more memorable, I think,' Rhadamistus speculated coldly. 'I do not tolerate the mistakes of those who follow me.'

He scrutinised Cato for a moment. 'You think I am being cruel, Tribune?'

Cato replied calmly: 'I think you are being wasteful, Majesty. I believe that there is a place for discipline and punishment at the heart of any army, but that has to be balanced against the effect it has on the army's ability to fight.'

'You Romans have a punishment called decimation, do you not? I have read that when your generals have been poorly served by cowardice or incompetence they have ordered that every tenth man is beaten to death by his comrades.'

Cato had once been a junior officer in a cohort taking part in the invasion of Britannia that had been subjected to the most draconian penalty meted out in the Roman army. He nodded. 'There is such a punishment, but it is rarely used. And the soldiers that survive it are demoralised for a long time afterwards. I would not advise

202

employing such a measure, Majesty. It is a luxury that you can ill afford at present. Punish those men, flog them, but spare their lives. I am convinced you will need them before this campaign is over.'

'I will consider your advice, Tribune,' Rhadamistus concluded. 'There is some merit in what you say. I will decide their punishment later as I have more pressing concerns. We must salvage what we can before resuming our advance, and attend to our dead and wounded.'

Cato spotted the opportunity to start repairing the alliance. 'Majesty, I would be happy for our surgeon to treat your wounded. And they can be transported, along with our sick and injured, in the wagons.'

Rhadamistus was silent and Cato sensed pride battling with pragmatism within the heart of his ally. At length he simply nodded and spoke as if giving a command: 'See to it then, Tribune.'

'Have them placed beside the road and my men will load them on to the wagons.'

The Iberian nodded.

'There is still the other matter, Majesty.'

Rhadamistus eyed him warily. 'Other matter?'

'After last night, it is clear that it would be best for our men to march together and make camp together.'

The other man's lips compressed into a thin line and Cato knew he had to press the point. He decided to sweeten his offer. 'We can spare you some tents to make up for your losses. I think you and your men will appreciate the shelter since the nights are cold.'

'As you wish,' Rhadamistus said quietly. 'And no doubt you will insist on exercising command over my troops as well as yours in exchange for your generosity?'

'I should not have to insist. The danger of dividing our column has been demonstrated clearly enough.' Cato gestured at the smouldering remains that surrounded them. 'From now we must march together and fight together, and the best means of achieving that is to have one commander. General Corbulo's orders were for me to command the column. He also told me that it would be best to exercise command with as much diplomacy as possible. I have done my best to carry out his orders. But the time for diplomacy is over. The situation is too dangerous for that. So I will tell you now: accept my command, without question, until you have regained your throne '

The Iberian prince winced and folded his arms as he glared back. Then he exhaled with a hiss and looked down at his feet. 'Very well, I agree.'

Cato hid his relief as he continued in the same firm tone. 'Thank you, Majesty.'

'I place myself under your command, Tribune. But I warn you now: if, as a consequence of your orders, I fail to regain my throne, then I will have your head.'

'Majesty, if I fail then it will cost me my head one way or another. I have no illusions about that. You will have your throne, or you and I, and every man in our column, will perish in the attempt.'

Rhadamistus stared back and then smiled. 'I could not ask for more.'

He extended his hand and they grasped forearms briefly before the Iberian bowed his head. 'Tribune Cato. I am yours to command.'

Cato nodded, but wondered how long Rhadamistus would stick to his word this time.

An hour later the Roman column reached the remains of the Iberian camp and the vanguard glanced over the ruined tents and the burial mound standing to one side. The Iberian wounded lay along the side of the road and at first they and the Romans regarded each other with cool suspicion – until a Praetorian stepped out of line to hand some of his dried meat to one of the injured. More followed his example, and Iberians responded to their kindness with smiles and thanks. Macro was about to bawl at the men to return to the ranks, but Cato stopped him.

'Now and again a little tolerance is more effective than discipline.'

'If you say so. But if I was still in command . . .' Macro began, then clamped his mouth shut and tapped the end of his vine cane against the side of his boot.

'And there you prove my point about being tolerant,' Cato laughed, for the first time in many days.

'Tolerance?' Macro muttered. 'Who fucking needs it? A quick kicking works better every time, if you ask me.'

'I will be sure to ask you, brother. But that's as far as I go. Now, let's keep the men moving.'

Macro forced himself to keep his tone neutral as he ordered the Praetorians to rejoin the column. As he stood at the end of the line of wounded Iberians the man nearest him caught his eye and reached out with his palm.

'If you bloody well think . . .' Macro began, then muttered bitterly. 'Fucking tolerance, eh?'

He reached into his sidebag, fished out a dry crust of bread and tossed it to the Iberian.

'There you go. Don't choke on it, friend.' He forced a smile and strode off to take his place at the head of the cohort.

The cataphracts and horse-archers had already ridden ahead to the front of the reunited force, and the spearmen fell in ahead of the Praetorians. Cato reined in to wait for the baggage train and oversee the loading of the wounded. He waved down the leading vehicle, where the surgeon was sitting on the bench beside the driver.

'Have the Iberians loaded up. Do your best for them, same as you would for our men.'

'Yes, sir.'

The surgeon's orderlies, aided by the drivers and muleteers, began the task of lifting the injured on to the carts and wagons, some settling alongside the Roman wounded, who greeted them with the light-hearted grumbling that was characteristic of veterans. Before long the last of the men were loaded and the baggage train began to rumble forward once more.

Cato turned at the sound of hoofbeats and saw a small party of Iberians riding off from amid the tattered remains of the camp. The distant crackle of flames reached his ears as a fresh column of smoke rose up.

'What's that?' the surgeon asked nervously. 'More Parthians?'

'Not Parthians,' Cato replied with a sharp sense of dread.

Then they heard the first cries of terror and screams of agony and all doubt was banished from Cato's mind. He thought of racing over to try and save the men, but from the density of the smoke and the flames licking up into the morning air, he knew it was already too late.

The surgeon stood on his bench. 'By the gods, what's happening?'

Cato pulled himself up into the saddle of his horse and picked up the reins as he spoke to the surgeon. 'What you hear is the price of failure. Remember it well.'

He tapped his heels in and urged his mount into a canter as he made for the head of the Praetorian cohort, keen to get as far as possible from the sound of men burning alive as their screams followed him down the road.

In the days that followed, the column continued its advance following the course of the Murad Su river without any further attacks from the enemy, although the Parthians kept them under observation every step of the way. Small bands of cavalry followed them from the safety of the hills to their right, and along the far bank of the river. The Iberians and the Romans watched them warily for the first day but soon came to accept the distant enemy as part of the landscape and resumed the usual banter between comrades and the occasional bursts of marching songs. Once in a while the Parthians ventured close enough for Rhadamistus to send out a body of his horse-archers to try and engage their opponents, but they instantly turned and galloped away until the Iberians gave up the pursuit. Nor were there any attempts at further raids now that the entire column retired behind a ditch and rampart each night.

Cato ordered that all forage parties went out in strength and were screened by an equal number of Iberian horse-archers, more than enough men to deter the largest band of Parthians they had seen. As the days passed he kept a note of the enemy numbers and calculated that no more than two hundred men were shadowing the column. Unless a far larger force was being concealed by the enemy then there was no immediate risk to the column, and nothing stood between them and Artaxata. Not yet.

Cato's strength returned with each day, and each night Bernisha cooked him a large meal and cajoled him by looks and comments in her own tongue to eat every spoonful. In return Cato taught her a

206

few words of Latin to aid the minimal communication that was possible between them and was delighted when she seemed to learn quickly. Twice, Rhadamistus visited Cato's headquarters, now reduced to a single tent as he had surrendered the others to the Iberian prince. Nor was Cato's the only such sacrifice. Macro and the other centurions were now sharing a single tent, and all the spare goatskin tents on the wagons had been turned over to their allies.

On each occasion that Rhadamistus visited him to confer on their progress, Bernisha had fled as soon as she was aware of the Iberian prince's approach. Cato could only guess at the cause of her apparent fear, but, without the means to ask her for an explanation, there was nothing he could do to understand or reassure her that she was safe under his protection.

At the second visit, as they shared a jug of heated wine with Macro, Rhadamistus informed him that the column would soon reach a place where the road divided; one fork continuing along the river to the south, while across an easily forded stretch of the river another road struck out into the mountains towards the final river crossing before they reached the Armenian capital.

'How many more days until we arrive before Artaxata, Majesty?' Macro asked.

'Two days to the ford, and then we must cross the mountains. It would take my men another two days, but with your baggage wagons and siege train I would guess at least twice as long. After that there is another river to cross and then three days to the city.'

'And this mountain route,' said Cato. 'What do you know of it?'

'I have travelled it many times. It is well used by merchants and open for most of the year. Only in the worst of winters do the snow and ice make it impassable for wagons.'

'What about choke points? Could the enemy block our way, or ambush us?'

Rhadamistus recalled the route for a moment before he replied: 'There are a handful of places where the road passes beneath cliffs or runs along a defile, but my men can clear the heights in advance of your cohorts and wagons. I see no danger we cannot deal with.' The Iberian drained his cup and poured himself another. 'It is not the enemy that will pose the greatest challenge, but cold and hunger.

Even at this time of year the nights will be bitter, and there will be little food for our men to forage.'

Cato nodded, and then asked: 'What of other routes that avoid the mountains?'

Rhadamistus shook his head. 'We could skirt round them and approach Artaxata from the south, but that would add at least twenty days of marching.'

Cato considered all this swiftly and reached a decision. With every day spent on the road the initiative passed more fully to the enemy.

'We shall take the mountain road.'

'I agree, Tribune. It would be best.'

Cato stifled a smile at the other man's attempt to share the decision. Since the two forces had been reunited, Rhadamistus had not directly challenged his authority once, and so Cato was content to let him save face from time to time. He began to consider the arrangements that would be needed for the coming days, frustrated by the slowness of his thoughts as a consequence of his continuing weariness. His recovery was not going nearly as well as he would like, or was needed.

'Centurion, I'll need an inventory of all the rations we are carrying with us. We will need to halt at the river tomorrow, then spend the next day foraging for sufficient supplies to see us through the mountains. And we must have fodder for the horses, fuel for campfires.'

As Macro took out his waxed slate and made notes Cato raised his cup to Rhadamistus. 'Majesty, all being well, this time in ten days, our soldiers will be in camp outside Artaxata. And then we will settle this affair in a final battle with your enemies. To victory!'

CHAPTER TWENTY-THREE

Cato made a last inspection of the men, horses and wagons in the pale light of the dawn. The sun had not yet risen above the crests of the mountains to the east, and all was in shadow, and the air was suffused with a blue tint that seemed to make it feel colder. They had crossed the river in the hours before dawn, Rhadamistus and his horse-archers leading the way to clear the far side of any bands of Parthians who might be tempted to interfere as the infantry and wagons struggled through the freezing current flowing swiftly across the shallows of the ford. The men had emerged on to the far bank dripping and shivering, before being formed up by their officers into the line of march.

In addition to the wounded, each wagon was heavily laden with bags of grain, cured meats, bread and cheese from the villages and farms the forage parties had looted the day before. Nets of fodder hung from the saddles of the Iberian cavalry, and their spearmen carried yet more supplies, as did the Praetorians and slingers. Cato paused to check the traces of the mule teams drawing the siege weapons. There could be no room for careless preparations amongst the muleteers when the column climbed the road that led into the mountains. Looking at the rough track that wound its way up the nearest slope he wondered how anyone could describe it as a road. And yet Rhadamistus had assured him the route was well used by camel trains and merchant convoys. If that was true and they encountered anyone, then Cato intended to relieve them of any food and useful supplies in passing.

As before, Rhadamistus and his men would scout ahead of the column, clearing away obstacles and dealing with any of the enemy who might attempt to make a stand. The wagons of the baggage and siege trains had been distributed amongst each of the Praetorian centuries, who would be tasked with adding their muscle to the mule teams whenever the road negotiated a steep slope. Returning to the small cart carrying his personal kit, Cato indicated his fur-lined cape to Bernisha and addressed her in Greek.

'Hand me that.'

She reached a hand towards it, then stopped abruptly and pointed to the cape, then at Cato, and arched an eyebrow. He nodded and she handed the cape over before huddling in the corner of the cart and covering herself with one of Cato's spare tunics.

Pulling the cloak about his shoulders and fastening the clasp he felt a little better protected against the elements and rubbed his hands together briskly before blowing into them to stave off some of the numbness creeping into his fingers.

'Cold enough to freeze your balls off, ain't it?' Macro grinned from where he stood by the colour party at the head of the cohort. 'Still, we'll all warm up soon enough once you give the order to advance.'

Cato glanced round at the nearest men, who, like him, were trying to warm their hands. Some were using strips of cloth tied around their hands as makeshift mittens and Cato wished he had had the foresight to purchase the real thing before he left Antioch. A thin haze of exhaled breath swirled around the men, mule teams and horses, and for the first time in many days Cato felt a spark of joy. Yes, it was cold and his boots squelched, but there was something thrilling about the spectacle of a body of soldiers formed up and ready to march as a new day dawned. More than that, there were feelings of affection for, and belonging with, these men, mostly hardened veterans who had seen as much action as he had. In some cases more. There was also the sense of privilege at being in command of the Praetorians, the slingers and mule-drivers, over a thousand men all told. They were a force to be reckoned with, Cato felt, and given the chance he would prove it.

'Let's hope so,' he replied to Macro as he looked up at the sky. It was mostly clear, promising a bright day, but clouds clustered above the mountains on the road ahead. If it was cold down here beside the river then there was a good chance that there would still be snow lying higher up, even this late in the year. He prayed that it would not be heaped in drifts across the road.

'Just waiting on the last of the Iberians now,' Cato continued. 'Ah, here they come.'

Both officers turned and looked back across the ford as the cataphracts and spearmen marched down the bank and plunged into the cold waters of the Murad Su. The horses tried to highstep at first, kicking up a fine spray, and then gave up as the river reached their barrels and then their chests surged through the current, directed by the armoured men sitting astride them. The spearmen waded through a short distance downstream, using the warhorses as a breakwater to make their passage easier. As they joined the waiting Romans on the far bank, the riders passed along the column and set off after the horse-archer contingent, already well advanced along the road. The spearmen fell in at the rear of the column, and when the last of them had emerged from the river, Cato mounted his horse and gave the order to march.

At first the road wound through the foothills with an easy gradient that permitted the wagons to rumble along unassisted, and Cato was pleased with the rate of progress. The clearly defined ruts proved that Rhadamistus had spoken the truth about the frequent use of the road, and there were few rocks that needed to be moved aside to avoid them bringing any of the vehicles' wheels to a jarring halt. The last of the spring wildflowers were blooming on the hillsides in clusters of yellow and purple amid the boulders and outcrops of rock. Swifts flitted overhead and filled the air with their screeches, while the morning sun appeared above the mountains and flooded the landscape with its ruddy glow. Though they were trudging along under heavy loads, the men were in good spirits, happy to have left the dusty plain and to be breathing clear air scented with the odour of the heather and pine trees on either side.

Macro was marching along a short distance behind Cato's horse, whistling happily as he indulged himself with raunchy memories of Petronella and occasionally swiped the heads of flowers with his vine cane. He was glad to see Cato emerging from the dark gloom that had laid him low at Ligea. It was a side of his longtime friend that he had never seen before and it had shaken Macro, since he had been unable to understand what Cato had been going through. Exhaustion of the body he was familiar with, and the passing dullness of mind that came with it. Cato's physical and mental collapse had been far more severe and accompanied by a darkness of the soul that found its expression in the destruction of the town and the slaughter of its inhabitants. As he recalled the details of the sacking of Ligea Macro's whistling faded from his lips and he breathed in deeply and sighed.

'Oughtn't to have done that,' he muttered to himself. To his mind it was fair enough to loot a town, since given a bit of time the people would have recovered from their loss and put it down to life serving up one of its reverses. But the destruction of a town was wasteful. Ligea would never rise from the ashes. Her streets would never again know the hubbub of people going about their business, nor the shrill cries of children at play, or the chants of the local priests. Ligea was nothing more than a charred memorial now, blackened ruins to be slowly overgrown by weeds while wild dogs and crows picked over the bones of the dead. Such thoughts weighed heavily on Macro. He could not help thinking that whatever gods the Ligeans worshipped would surely be angered by such an outrage. Who knew what misfortunes they had in store for the desecrators of their temples?

He offered a quick prayer to Fortuna to deliver him and his comrades from any misfortune then clicked his tongue and repeated: 'Oughtn't to have done that . . .'

As the sun reached its zenith the gradient began to increase and their progress slowed as the Praetorians had to frequently down their packs and put their shoulders to the wagons to help the mule teams haul their vehicles up steeper stretches of the road. More onerous still was the need to carefully control the descent of the wagons on the downward runs. The men used ropes trailing from the rear of the wagons to slow the pace, while others stood ready with chocks in the event that the wagons' speed presented any danger of crushing the mule teams beneath their heavy wheels, or lurching to the side and threatening to overturn. It was a tricky business and sorely tested the judgement and patience of the optios and centurions overseeing the process.

Rhadamistus and his horse-archers were untroubled by such concerns as they scouted ahead and watched for any sign of the enemy lurking in ambush. The Parthians continued to hang about them, falling back before the Iberians and appearing from time to time on the crests of the hills and ridges that flanked the road. Their presence did not worry Macro unduly, but lingered on the fringes of his thoughts like some persistent nuisance, and his initial cheery mood began to give way to a weary and wary watchfulness as he kept half an eye on the enemy and half on the progress of the wagons in his charge.

At the end of the first day, Cato calculated that they had advanced no more than eight miles, half the distance they had managed each day down on the plain. They camped on the crest of a hill above the treeline, surrounding their position with sharpened stakes as the ground was too strewn with boulders to permit the digging of a ditch. As the sun set, the temperature dropped sharply as the men huddled in their crowded tents and tried to sleep. The horses had no shelter, and as the wind rose they turned away from it and kept their heads down as it moaned through the rocks and rippled the tent leather and whipped any poorly tied flaps open with a sharp crack accompanied by the protests of the men within.

Once he was satisfied that the camp was secure and that the sentries were keeping a good watch, Cato retired to his tent. A single candle, sheltered by a glass sleeve, provided barely enough light to make out the interior as he removed his armour and sword-belt. He saw that Bernisha had prepared his camp bed and laid his spare cloaks over it. There was also a small bowl set out on the table with cheese, bread and dried fruit. She gestured to it with an apologetic expression. This was the best meal that could be had under the circumstances. He ate hungrily and then took off his boots and eased himself beneath the covers. Bernisha took the bowl and finished off the crust and morsel of cheese Cato had left and then put the bowl away in his travel chest before taking a blanket and lying down in the corner of the tent.

Cato rolled on his side, towards the candlelight, and though he was exhausted, sleep did not come to him. Instead his mind retraced the events of the campaign, always circling round the image of the boy dying in his arms. At length he was aware that the girl was also restless, shivering beneath her blanket. He watched her for a while before clearing his throat.

'Bernisha . . .'

She lowered the blanket a fraction and peered over the hem as Cato flicked back the covers and beckoned to her. After a brief hesitation, she rose and scurried across and climbed in beside him. The bed creaked as Cato made room for her and pulled the covers back. She continued to shiver and there was a light clicking from her teeth as she burrowed into his chest. He caught the unfamiliar scent of her hair, recalling that it had been over a year since he had lain with a woman, the wife of a senator who had a taste for decorated soldiers when she couldn't find a gladiator to suit her appetite. He slipped his arm round her back and once Bernisha had stopped shivering they settled into an easy breathing rhythm as their bodies became warm. Cato felt a light tingle in his loins and shifted away slightly so that his groin was not pressed against her. He sighed. He felt tired, and tempted, and the two feelings did not sit easily together.

'Mmm?' Bernisha purred, edging herself up a fraction and looking up at him beneath the fringe of her dark hair.

'Go to sleep,' Cato whispered.

She smiled and he felt her hand reach down and slide up under his tunic.

'I said, go to . . .'

Cato paused as her fingers curled lightly around his penis and applied the slightest of pressures. The tingle of a moment earlier intensified as Bernisha purred again in a deeper tone. 'Mmmmm.'

Cato was tense at first, and then slowly he relaxed into the bedroll and closed his eyes in bliss as she worked him into a state of arousal and erection. Then, shifting herself to straddle him she felt between her thighs and guided him inside her and began to ride him gently. This was against the usual custom for Roman men, most of whom regarded allowing a woman on top as degrading. But it felt good, and Cato let her continue without interruption. There was something

214

about the fit of her that was different to the handful of other women Cato had known, something that fired up his sensitivity and which became more intense still as she increased the pace of her movements. Soon he felt the familiar tightening of his abdomen and then the release that flowed through his body like some divine sigh, before he slumped back into the bedroll.

Bernisha rolled her hips gently as she stared down at him, her lips lifting in a saucy smile. As he became limp, she lifted herself, let him slip out, and then settled back at his side, pulling the covers up. Now they were warmer than ever and Cato's previous troubled thoughts were banished and he felt calm and more content than he had been in a long time. But there was one issue he could no longer ignore.

'Bernisha, you understand Greek, don't you?'

He felt her go tense and still beside him. Then she stirred but did not meet his eyes. 'Hmmm?'

'Don't try and fool me any more. I've watched you when Greek is being spoken. You know the tongue.'

She did not reply for a beat and then spoke cautiously. 'Yes . . .'

'Why have you been hiding that from me?' Cato demanded, propping himself up on an elbow and turning her chin towards him. 'Are you a spy, Bernisha?'

She flinched. 'No, my lord! I swear it.'

'Are you spying for the Parthians, or for Rhadamistus? Did he send you to spy on me?'

'I am not a spy.'

'I don't believe you.'

'But, my lord, you chose me. In his tent.'

That was true, Cato admitted to himself. She had been his pick. He searched his memory of the occasion for any hint that his choice had been surreptitiously directed towards selecting Bernisha, but could not think of anything. He nodded slowly, but his suspicions were still fully aroused. 'Then why did you hide your ability to speak Greek from me? What possible reason could there be for you to do that? You have been able to follow exchanges between me and Rhadamistus. That smacks of espionage. Who are you working for? Tell me!' He took her by the throat. 'Tell me, or I'll have you flogged.'

She gasped, and then replied tremulously: 'Lord, I swear I am no spy. I am simply a captive, taken by Rhadamistus's men. That is all.'

'Bollocks. You are no simple captive. Who are you?'

'My father is a merchant. He trades between Armenia and Aegyptus. I often travelled with him, that is why I speak Greek . . . Greek and Latin.'

'Latin?' Now it was Cato's turn to be still as he rapidly pondered her fresh admission. What had he said to Macro in her hearing? What of any significance?

She nodded, still in his grip, and spoke in fluent Latin this time. 'My father had me taught, so that he could deal with Roman merchants.'

Cato's mind was still reeling with the implications of what he had discovered. If she was not a spy, then she might have overheard things that made it impossible not to treat her as one. He would not trust her explanation because she had already deceived him. On the other hand, if she was a spy then she should be put to death.

She had watched his expression closely and now spoke again. 'If I was a spy then surely I would have done you harm? I had plenty of opportunity. But I looked after you. I cared for you, fed you, cleaned you . . . let you use my body. Because you saved me from Rhadamistus and that pack of animals he calls friends. Because I came to realise you are a good man. Have I done you any wrong, Tribune?'

'Apart from deceive me?' Cato removed his hand from her throat and sat up, making a little distance between them. 'So why do that? Why hide from me your knowledge of Greek and Latin?'

She pulled her tunic down to cover her nakedness. 'When I was young, my father taught me never to reveal any more about myself than I had to. Sometimes, it served him well to have a daughter who could overhear the words of other merchants without anyone suspecting that she might understand. It is a lesson I have not forgotten.'

Cato nodded. He could see the use of that and imagined a wily eastern trader using his daughter to gain intelligence from those he traded with. 'A spy of sorts, then?'

216

Bernisha nodded sheepishly.

'And you have understood all of the conversations you heard in my tent, and that of Rhadamistus.'

'Nothing I would ever repeat, I promise, Lord.'

Cato stroked his jaw for a moment. 'Does Rhadamistus know you speak other tongues?'

'No. He knows nothing.'

'Why are you afraid of him then?'

'Afraid? Why would I not be afraid? His men took me from my home. He used me, and was about to hand me over to his officers as their whore, before he offered me to you instead.'

Cato felt a stab of shame over what had passed between them earlier, now that he knew her story. Perhaps it was just a story, he mused. After all, she could be telling him anything, for any reason.

She continued speaking in a low, husky voice. 'I wanted to give myself to you. You saved me from Rhadamistus's men. You have treated me well, and I have come to care for you, Tribune. I hoped you wanted me. I hoped it would please you. Instead you call me a spy, throttle me and threaten to have me flogged. If that is how you feel, then you might as well send me back to Rhadamistus.'

It was a challenge and Cato decided to call her bluff. 'I might do just that. In fact, I will.'

He swung his legs out of the bed and stood up and strode towards the entrance to the tent, where he stubbed a toe on a rock. 'Shit!'

Standing on one leg he lifted his foot and rubbed the spot. He heard Bernisha laughing and glanced back angrily and she covered her hand with her mouth.

'Guard!' Cato called out.

An instant later, one of the duty Praetorians entered the tent and snapped to attention. 'Sir?'

'I want this woman taken to the tent of Prince Rhadamistus.'

'No!' Bernisha cried. 'You can't!'

'Get her out of my sight,' Cato ordered, stepping aside for the soldier. He approached the bed and Bernisha cringed in front of him. The Praetorian grabbed her wrist and hauled her to her feet. She struggled like a wild animal and then bit his hand, hard.

217

'Why, you fucken' slut!' The soldier balled his spare hand into a fist and drew it back.

'Wait!' Cato snapped. He stood over Bernisha and grasped her by the shoulders.

'You tell me the real reason why you are afraid of Rhadamistus, and you tell me now. Or I swear, by all the gods, I will send you back to him.'

She glared at him for a moment and then lowered her head as her body slumped into a resigned posture. 'Very well, Lord. I will tell you. If you give me your word you will keep me here.'

'That depends on what you tell me.'

She was silent and then sighed. 'I will tell you the truth. Tell you everything. But only you.' She glanced at the Praetorian, still grasping her wrist firmly, even as a dribble of blood rolled over his knuckles from the neat half-circle of the bite mark.

'Wait outside,' Cato ordered.

Once the soldier had left the tent he sat Bernisha back down on the bed and stood in front of her, arms crossed.

'Speak . . .'

CHAPTER TWENTY-FOUR

Cato could see the anguish in Bernisha's face as she carefully collected her thoughts before she explained. He prepared himself to hear her words with a high degree of caution and suspicion, until he was able to determine for himself if what she said turned out to be true. She had already concealed the truth from him once. By the same token she had tricked Rhadamistus as well, unless this was an elaborate double game and she had been spying for the Iberian all along to determine if his Roman allies were deceiving him. As he briefly considered this, Cato felt all the more vulnerable for himself and his men.

'Tribune.' Bernisha spoke softly, looking up at him with imploring eyes. 'I bear you no ill-will. I swear that on the lives of my mother, my father, my sisters, and all the gods that I worship. Please believe me.'

Cato said nothing and just stared back at her fixedly, his face a mask of severity.

'I wish no harm to come to my family,' she continued. 'And that is why I hid my knowledge of Greek and Latin from you, and for no other reason. I wish, with all my heart, that I could have been honest with you, for I see that you are a good man. Despite what happened in Ligea. It is not in your nature to order a town to be destroyed and its people to be massacred. You were goaded into it by Rhadamistus. He poisoned your mind, Tribune, and directed your hand towards revenge and cruelty. The fate of Ligea was crafted by him, not you, and the blood that was spilled is on his hands and not yours.'

'How is telling me that you speak other tongues placing your family in any danger?' Cato demanded. 'And how exactly did Rhadamistus manipulate me, as you claim?'

The Armenian girl's brow furrowed as she held a loose fist over her mouth and then lowered her head into her hands as she let out a sob.

'Enough of this!' Cato growled. 'Tell me straight. Or I swear by my gods that I will drag you over to Rhadamistus's tent myself, and I will tell him that you have been spying on him.'

She looked up, her face a mask of fear, as tears gleamed in her eyes.

'If I tell you, then you will become angry . . . enraged. If I tell you the truth, then you will be a danger to yourself, and your men.'

'Speak!' Cato shouted.

She recoiled, as if struck a hard blow, and shook her head. 'I cannot. Not while your passions are aroused. Please, Tribune, do not make me.'

Cato's frustration was fast turning to anger, and he felt fire in his veins. He steadied himself, took a long, deep breath, and forced himself to be calm and continue in a low, level tone as he addressed her again.

'Bernisha, I have to know everything you can tell me. Right now. I will give you a fair hearing. If you have good reasons for concealing the truth from me then I will not punish you. If not, or you refuse to reveal all, then I will return you to Rhadamistus, immediately.'

Her shoulders slumped and she nodded. 'Very well. What I said about not letting him know I spoke your tongue is true. When his men took me from my home I hoped that if I played along with them, and endured what they had in store for me, they would eventually let me go. If they knew I could speak Greek and Latin then they might find a use for me, and I would never be released. My father had taught me the value of silence, a lesson I have never had any reason to regret, until now. You see, I overheard things in Rhadamistus's tent, exchanges between him and his closest followers. Powerful men always seem to think that their slaves and servants are dumb beasts and often speak without caution in front of them. But I overheard nothing of note. Until that night you came to the tent

220

and he offered me to you.' She paused and met Cato's gaze. 'You may recall how frightened I looked?'

Cato nodded. 'I remember. It's the reason I chose you.'

'The reason for my fear is because shortly before, I had heard Rhadamistus giving orders to one of his officers . . . Orders to take a squadron of his horse-archers out of the camp to hunt down and kill some prey.'

'A foraging party,' said Cato. 'I remember. We sent out quite a few parties that day. Nothing unusual about that.'

'But, Tribune, the prey these men were sent to hunt were your soldiers . . .'

Cato felt an icy chill creep up his spine. 'My soldiers?'

'I thought they were talking about animals. But then Rhadamistus said something about Roman pigs, and the need to kill them in order to stiffen the backbone of their commander. Those were the very words.' She looked up at him fearfully.

Cato's mind was a foment of ghastly images as he recalled the fate of Centurion Petillius and his men.

'It's not possible,' he said softly. 'Surely not?'

Bernisha remained silent, not daring to say anything more for the present as she watched his reaction, and the realisation dawning in his face.

Cato recalled the details of the night. He had taken Rhadamistus's insistence on joining him to investigate the suspicious movements on the edge of the forest as a further display of his bravado. But if Bernisha was telling the truth, then Rhadamistus would have known there was no danger waiting for him in the darkness. And then there was the matter that had troubled Cato when he played the event over in his mind. How was it possible for Petillius and his men to be taken by surprise so that there had not been any sounds of fighting, or cries of alarm, to alert the other forage parties? It was obvious now. Why would they be on their guard against another forage party from the camp? They would have seen the Iberians as allies, as friends, and that would have made them easy enough prey to the killers sent by Rhadamistus.

Cato felt nauseous about the scale of the betrayal and the scheming of the Iberian prince. Rhadamistus had wanted him to share in his

221

ruthless ambitions to cow the Armenians and make them so terrified of him that they would not dare stand between him and the throne in Artaxata. Cato had refused to co-operate, so the Iberian had devised a way to fill him with wrath and a thirst to avenge his men. The manipulation did not stop there, Cato reflected bitterly. When the Ligeans had sent that deputation to discuss the surrender of the town, Rhadamistus had seen an opportunity to add fuel to the rage burning in Cato's heart. That was why he had been so keen to translate their words for Cato, why he had said that Petillius's killers were hiding behind the walls of the town, knowing full well that would inflame Cato's wrath still further.

He burned with shame that he had been so completely duped. Rhadamistus had manipulated him like a cheap street entertainer's puppet, pulling every string to make Cato dance to the Iberian's tune. As a result, Ligea had been reduced to ashes and the charred remains of its slaughtered people left buried beneath the ruins. Not only that, but good men had been killed and wounded in the attack. And there was the matter of the darkness and anguish that Cato had been dragged through in the days that followed. All of it at the hands of Rhadamistus.

No doubt the king thought that the ends justified the means. A reasonable enough philosophy to apply, Cato reflected, as long as you were not the means.

He hissed with frustration and anger and sat himself down on the opposite end of the bed to Bernisha.

'What are you going to do, Tribune?'

Cato turned to her and had to refocus his thoughts before he could respond. 'Nothing, as far as you are concerned, if that's what is worrying you.

She looked hurt. 'I was more worried about you. About what you will do now that you know.'

'Do?' Cato ran a hand over his head, ruffling his curls. He had no desire to share his thoughts with this woman who had already given him enough reasons not to trust her. So he kept his silence as he considered the dangerous situation. He could order Macro and his century to follow him over to the king's tent and cut down Rhadamistus and his nobles, but then the rest of the column, Iberian and Roman, would be at each other's throats in an instant and the force would be destroyed. The Parthians would make mincemeat of what was left . . . He could abandon Rhadamistus, return to Antioch and report his murder of Petillius and the other Praetorians. Cato doubted the emperor would be very pleased to hear that his ally had murdered Roman soldiers. But Nero might well mourn the loss of his men somewhat less than he would mourn the loss of the chance to reclaim Armenia as a Roman protectorate. And for that Cato would be held responsible. Besides, what proof had he got that Rhadamistus really was responsible? All he had was his suspicion and the word of some serving girl.

He glanced at Bernisha. 'I have no idea what to do.'

'But do you believe me?'

Cato hesitated before he gave a cautious nod. 'At the moment, I think so. It makes some sense of what has happened. I wish it didn't. It would be easier if you were a liar, or a spy. But, as it is, I believe you, and that means that my mission here in Armenia is more dangerous than ever. Rhadamistus has proved to be as ruthless as he is ambitious. Such men cannot be trusted, and I'll have to watch my back at every moment. If he discovers that I know the truth then I am sure he'd lose no sleep over having me go the same way as Petillius. Better that, and cover his tracks, than let me live to report his crime back to Rome.'

'Then you are in danger, whatever you do.'

Cato smiled wearily. 'That's the story of my life . . .'

'You could get away from him. Go now. Take your men and return to Syria,' Bernisha suggested. 'What's stopping you?'

Cato leaned forward and rested his chin on his folded hands for a while before he replied: 'No. I have to continue with the mission What else can I do? For now, at least, I must continue as if you never told me what you have. I will do all that I can to help Rhadamistus take his throne. Though it revolts me to the very core, this is what I must do. It is in the best interests of Rome and my emperor.'

'You would let him kill your comrades with impunity?'

'I did not say that. If the situation changes, and that bastard ever becomes of no further use to Rome, I swear by Jupiter, Best and

223

Greatest, and by Nemesis, that I will do whatever I can to take his life with my own hand, so that he knows his crime has not been forgotten, nor forgiven. Until then, this must remain our secret. You have not told anyone else of it, I trust?'

'And put my life at risk?' She arched an eyebrow. 'Why would I?'

'Quite . . . Then let's keep it that way. For all our sakes.'

'And you will not tell anyone?'

Cato shook his head.

'Not even your friend, Centurion Macro? I have seen that the two of you are very close.'

Cato felt uncomfortable about any exchange that she might have listened to and which might have given her any knowledge that she might later use against them. 'And now that confidence has been betrayed,' he told her pointedly. 'As it happens, there is no one in this world that I trust more than Macro.'

'Really? Not your family? Not any wife?'

'Especially not my late wife,' Cato said through gritted teeth. 'And, apart from my young son, Macro is the closest thing I have to family. You'd do well to remember that. If you do anything to cause harm to him, or deceive him, then I will make you answer for it. Understand?'

'Yes, Tribune.' She nodded. 'What happens to me now?'

'You stay close to my tent and my bodyguards and keep out of sight as much as possible. Hopefully Rhadamistus will overlook you, even if he doesn't forget about you. And you don't speak to anyone.'

'And what about Centurion Macro?'

Cato thought briefly. It was important to him that Rhadamistus's deed was reported back to Rome so that there was a chance that Petillius and the other victims might be avenged one day. There would be a better chance of that if knowledge of the Iberian's treachery was shared. Yet he knew that Macro's blood flowed even more hotly than his own. At some point he might need to tell Macro, in case anything happened to him. Cato had little doubt that his friend might be inclined to ensure that vengeance came swiftly, rather than waiting for the emperor to act, a process that might well take many years. Macro was also not a great keeper of secrets and there was a risk he would give himself away. Then Rhadamistus would be sure to put an end to them both before knowledge of his crime spread any further. No, it was not fair to tell Macro, and thereby put his life in danger, Cato concluded.

'I will tell him when I judge the moment is right. I cannot afford for him to be distracted when the campaign is reaching the decisive moment. Once we're over these mountains and across the river, then we'll be laying siege to Artaxata in a matter of days.' He paused, suddenly aware that he was sharing so much information with a woman who had deceived him, and suddenly a flood of memories and suspicions about Julia filled his mind and he realised that he must keep on his guard. There was no good reason to trust Bernisha any more than was necessary.

'There's nothing more to be discussed. The hour is late and the road ahead will be exhausting. We should sleep.'

Bernisha nodded and eased her legs back under the blankets and furs. She edged to the far side of the bed and propped herself up on an elbow as she held the covers back for Cato to return to his place beside her. He recalled the arousing warmth of her body and the soft touch of her skin from earlier. She was undeniably pretty. Some might even call her beautiful and seductive. At that, Cato felt himself recoil from the prospect of enjoying her charms that night. He cleared his throat and shook his head.

'No. I said I believed you. But I still don't trust you. That has to be earned, and you have some work to do there, my little Bernisha. So, I'll have you out of my bed. You can take one of the coverings and sleep the other side of the tent. Over there.' He indicated a patch of ground just inside the tent flaps.

She looked at him as if he were joking and laughed. 'Surely not . . . Tribune. It's a cold night. We can keep each other warm. Just like we did before.'

'Out you get.'

When she still did not move, Cato hardened his tone. 'Get out of my bed, or I'll have that guard come and drag you outside to sleep in the open. Move!'

She recoiled from the sharpness of his tone, then slithered out from under the covers, pulled a cloak around her shoulders and scowled as she walked past him. Cato eased himself down and pulled back the covers. He thought about blowing out the candle, then thought it best to have some light, so he could see her. Bernisha slumped down and huddled herself into the fur covering so that only her eyes showed beneath her dark fringe. She muttered something that Cato could not make out.

'What did you say?'

'That you are as cruel and ruthless a swine as Rhadamistus,' she spat back defiantly.

'You think so? Then you'd better start praying to your gods that you are wrong. Better still, get to sleep.'

Cato turned on his side, facing her, and they glared at each other for a while, as the wind grew outside and stirred the flaps and shook the sides and ridge of the tent. After a while she lowered her head, and only when he heard the faint rasp of her snoring did Cato relax and close his eyes before falling into yet another troubled sleep.

CHAPTER TWENTY-FIVE

For the next two days the column battled along the narrow track that climbed through the mountains. The condition of the route steadily worsened and at times Cato had to halt his men where the slope was steep enough for the wagons to have to be hauled up one at a time, for fear of having any of them breaking loose and mowing down the men and mule teams immediately behind. Each delay weighed on Cato's mind, for it meant that the rations would have to stretch for that bit longer before they reached the gentler landscape at the foot of the mountains and could more easily forage amongst the farms and villages once again. Here, in the mountains, there were scant pickings, and what goats, hovels and passing merchants they encountered had already been looted by Rhadamistus and his men riding at the head of the column. At night, as their allies cooked mutton over the handful of campfires they had managed to build, the Romans ate their rations cold and tried to ignore the aroma of roasting meat wafting from the direction of the Iberian tents. Those men with sufficient coin, and the willingness to spend it, bargained for some of the meat, and the dissent that had been sown between the Iberians and the Romans then spread amidst the ranks of the Praetorians and slingers as others looked on while their comrades feasted.

Cato approached Rhadamistus on the second evening to request that his men share their bounty but was curtly rebuffed, as the Iberian prince explained that it was not the tradition of his people to share the spoils of war.

'Spoils of war?' Macro sniffed when Cato returned to his tent following his fruitless encounter. 'It's not as if the bastards have had to fight for it. The only enemy they're going to find in these bloody mountains is some knackered old shepherd and his young goatherd. And I doubt even Rhadamistus's lads are going to have much of a struggle overcoming such tough opposition.'

He shook his head and broke off another chunk off the stale bread in his mess tin and dipped it into his wine beaker to soften it before eating.

'I tell you, we should put the Iberians at the back of the column for a day and send our lads to scout ahead. In this terrain, a man on foot is just as effective as cavalry.'

'It's a nice idea,' Cato agreed. 'But the truth of it is that we need them to keep the Parthians at bay. Last thing I want is any arrows raining down on the wagons while they're caught on a slope.'

Macro pursed his lips and conceded the point. 'I suppose. In the meantime we'll just have to make do with dried meat, stale bread and cheese so hard you could build a bloody aqueduct with it.' He looked up as Bernisha entered the tent. 'More wine here, girl.'

She looked at him blankly, and then Cato raised his own beaker and spoke a few halting words of Armenian. She nodded and left the tent, and returned a moment later with a stoppered jug to top Macro up.

'So, you're picking up a bit of the local lingo then?'

Cato nodded. 'I'm teaching the girl a few words of Latin and she's returning the favour.'

As she turned and headed to the corner of the tent, Macro cast an eye over her shapely body. 'I bet she is. And I'll bet you are a willing student, eh? Well why not? I would.'

'It isn't like that,' Cato objected.

'Well, maybe it should be. Fine-looking girl like that going to waste. You could use a little female company. It's been a while.'

'That's my business, Macro. I'll thank you not to tell me what I do and do not need.'

Macro dipped some more bread in the wine and popped it in his mouth as he mumbled: 'Suit yourself.'

Cato was angry with himself for being so terse with his friend. He was tired but that was no excuse for the way he had treated

Macro recently. 'Look, I know I haven't been the easiest of comrades since that business at Ligea . . .'

'Really? I can't say I fucking noticed.' Macro chuckled briefly. He was just happy to have Cato return from the black trough into which he had fallen. 'It's nothing. What's done is done.'

Cato decided to turn the conversation to less troubling ground. 'How are the men holding up?'

'They're fine. The usual grumblers making a song and dance of it, but no one pays them much attention. A few days on hard rations out in the open up here will remind 'em what proper soldiering is about. These Praetorians are good lads, but they're inclined to whine about what they're missing back in Rome.'

'Can you blame them? It's why appointment to the Guard corps is top of every soldier's wish list.'

'That's as maybe, but I can't help feeling we'd be better off with some legionaries. Not those wasters who have gone soft in the Syrian garrisons. I'm talking about proper legionaries, like the lads of the Second Legion.' He smiled fondly at the memories he shared with Cato of their former unit, then raised his cup. 'To the Second Augusta. Best legion in the army by a bloody mile.'

Cato raised his beaker and tapped Macro's vessel. 'To the Second Augusta.'

They each took a sip and reminisced in silence for a moment before Macro caught a bit of bread in his throat and coughed, and coughed again to dislodge it. 'Seriously, though, once this job is over, we should look at getting transferred back to the legions. Much as I like the privileges that go with being a Praetorian, I'd rather put some distance between me and Rome. That place is too dangerous for my liking.'

'Easier said than done,' said Cato. 'Easier for you, anyway. Any legion would be proud to have you on its strength, but there's no opening for a tribune like me. Best I could get is command of another auxiliary cohort. Unless I took a demotion to the centurionate.'

'That's a possibility,' Macro mused. 'That, or you go the whole distance and try and get yourself the prefecture of Egypt. Now that would be something.'

229

'It would indeed.' It was the kind of ambition that Cato tempted himself with in more reflective moments, but was reluctant to speak of for worry that such hubris might be held against him. The people of Rome, especially the senators, were hidebound by tradition and considered it distasteful for an individual to enjoy too much social advancement. For a man of his equestrian rank the highest office he could achieve was Prefect of Egypt. That province alone was considered so vital to the interests of Rome that no emperor would ever bestow it upon a member of the Senate in case it tempted the office-holder to higher ambitions. On the other hand, Cato reflected wryly, the emperors had a habit of creating their own traditions, and breaking others, as the whim took them. If Caligula could decree that his favourite horse, Incitatus, be elevated to the Senate, then anything was possible.

Then his thoughts returned to his immediate concerns and his levity faded like a field of brilliant flowers cast into gloom as a dark cloud swept over, veiling the sun. He smiled cynically at the poetic image he had conjured up. He felt veiled by black, threatening clouds sure enough.

'What's so funny?' asked Macro.

'Funny? Not much. Not much at all,' Cato replied morosely. He wondered, once again, if it might be better to share his knowledge with his best friend. Then he dismissed the notion. It would only place Macro in the same danger as himself. Better to wait until the mission was over. So he took a strip of dried beef from his mess tin and began to chew in order to forestall any more conversation for the moment.

Macro finished what remained of his own food, drained his beaker, held a fist to his chest and burped loudly. At the sound, Cato and Bernisha looked at him and Macro raised his hands. 'What? Better out than in, eh? Anyway, I'd best do the rounds, sir. The men are tired and cold, and if any sentry is going to take the chance for a quick nap, now's the time. If I catch any of them at it, they'll be feeling my vine across their shoulders.'

Cato winced mentally at the prospect. He remembered his time as a fresh recruit and how often he had incurred the wrath of Centurion Bestia, and bore the bruises from his cane for many days

230

afterwards. 'Very well, but as soon as you are done, get some sleep.'

'Look who's talking,' Macro chuckled. 'You look like shit, sir.'

'Thank you for that,' Cato muttered.

Macro's expression became more serious. 'I thought we'd seen the back of that mood. What's up?'

'Nothing.'

They stared at each other in silence briefly before Macro raised his eyebrows. 'If you say so. But—'

'I think you'd better get going,' Cato interrupted.

Macro shrugged. 'Please yourself. I'll see you in the morning.'

The centurion rose from the table and gave Bernisha a knowing wink before he left the tent and the flaps slid together behind him. She waited a moment before she spoke in an undertone. 'It seems your friend would willingly have me in his bed. Why won't you?'

'Because I don't trust you, my dear. Besides, Macro already has a woman. Someone far better than you, so don't go getting any ideas about seducing him as well.'

She scowled. 'I am not a woman of easy morals.'

Cato laughed dryly. 'You are not a woman of many morals at all, as I have discovered.'

'But not to your cost.'

'No?' Cato rounded on her. 'If you had told me what you knew before, then the people of Ligea would have been spared. The men who died taking it would still be alive. The boy . . .' He paused and drew a breath. 'And all along you could have prevented that. I'd say that any person with morals would struggle with all that on their conscience. But you? It's hard to say. I wonder if you regret any of it at all.'

She looked away and spoke in a low voice. 'I know what I have done, and I have told you why. There is nothing more to be said. If you have no further need of me, then I'll sleep outside.'

Without waiting for a reply, Bernisha stood up, took a fur from Cato's bed and left the tent without a backward glance. He stared at the flaps as they settled into place and then continued his meal in silence.

★ ★ ★

231

It took another three days before the column reached the far side of the mountain range and descended towards the last river crossing before the Armenian capital. Two of the wagons had been lost the day before. The first had suffered a split axle and had been abandoned. The second had been at the rear of the baggage train when a section of the road had given way and the wagon, its driver, several of the wounded, and the entire mule team had plunged into a gorge. Aside from the deaths of some of those wounded at Ligea the rest of the column had emerged from the mountains unscathed but exhausted and hungry, as they had endured half-rations over the last two days.

Ahead of them the river flowed like a great silken ribbon across a plain of rich farmland. Small homesteads and villages spread out towards another mountain range, hazy grey in the distance.

'Rich pickings,' Macro grinned as he stood beside Cato, who had dismounted for a moment to relieve himself at the side of the road.

'Not this time.' Cato contradicted him. 'We're only a few days' march from Artaxata. It's best that we treat the locals well and pay for our supplies if we don't want to find ourselves surrounded by enemies. I'll make sure our Iberian friends do the same.'

'You've changed your tune.'

'Oh?'

'Not so long ago you were as happy to kill and destroy as our friend down there.' Macro pointed far down the road to where Rhadamistus and his cavalry were watering their horses on the near bank of the river. He glanced at Cato. 'Change of heart?'

'Something like that,' Cato admitted as he surveyed the landscape spread out before them.

Macro watched him for a moment, wondering at the changes he had seen in his friend over the course of the campaign: the spiral down into the black mood during and after Ligea, a slow recovery and now this stand-offish demeanour of the last few days. He wondered, had there been some kind of falling-out with the slave girl? She had seemed to be a devoted enough nurse to Cato when he needed caring for. For his part, Cato had appeared to be pleased by her attention and her company, and Macro guessed that their relationship went much further than patient and carer. Or, at least, it had until the last few days, when Cato had adopted a cold disregard towards Bernisha. And that was a waste of a fine opportunity, Macro decided. His friend badly needed to indulge himself in the arms of a pretty woman. It did not require any special degree of insight to work out that Cato was still coming to terms with the loss of Julia. Not that it was grief exactly, more an abject sense of betrayal of all that he had been so confident about in his wife. But then Julia had been cunning and ambitious and Macro wondered if perhaps she had come to regret her choice of a low-born husband. While Cato was fighting far away in Britannia, Julia had been immersed in the high society of Rome, with all its sophistication, temptation and intrigue.

Macro gave silent thanks to Fortuna that he himself would face no such concern over Petronella. Hers was a far simpler life and Macro had absolute faith in her fidelity and firmness of character. Her strong voice and loud, honest laughter warmed his heart, and he suddenly realised just how much he was missing her and yearned to return to her embrace, and what would inevitably follow on a necessarily robust bed. He shook his head in amusement at this side of his character that he had not guessed at before. He actually needed Petronella.

'What the fuck has become of me?' he muttered under his breath. If he was not careful, he'd end up writing poetry at this rate, and the gods knew what a bunch of useless pansies those bloody scribblers were, he frowned.

He hurriedly put his feelings aside and turned his attention back to his friend. 'Care to explain your change of heart?'

Cato looked at him shrewdly for a moment before he responded: 'No, Centurion, I don't think I do.'

He took the reins from the Praetorian looking after his horse and swung himself up into the saddle. 'I'm going ahead. Get the rest of the column down to the river as quick as you can. It'll be dark by then but we'll still need to fortify the camp. I'll try and buy some goats for the men to cook tonight. Should lift their spirits.'

'I'll say.' Macro's eyes lit up at the prospect of roast mutton.

'Carry on, Centurion Macro,' Cato concluded formally and they exchanged a salute before he clicked his tongue and spurred his horse into a trot as he rode down the track towards the distant Iberians.

As a new moon rose above the mountains and bathed the Armenian landscape in a ghostly silver veil, the night was pierced by the campfires of the Romans and their Iberian allies. Despite the arduous labours of the day, the men of the two cohorts were in a cheerful mood now that they were out of the cold and wind of the mountains and had plenty of firewood to warm them, and roast meat to fill their bellies. There was plenty to drink too, thanks to the cart filled with jars of wine Cato had purchased from a nearby village, along with a score of goats. All of which he had paid for with silver from his personal strongbox. The locals had been nervous as he approached with Narses and a squadron of Rhadamistus's horse-archers. Once the Roman officer had announced his intentions they had swiftly recovered, and gouged him after a brief bout of haggling. Cato had little doubt he was paying over the odds but was content with the knowledge that his generosity would be handsomely repaid by the gratitude of his men.

And so the air was filled with the aroma of roast meat and the cheery exchanges and bursts of song from the men warming themselves around the fires. As Cato strolled through the camp in the company of Macro, he was pleased to see that some of the Praetorians and Iberians were fraternising, and some of the former were even introducing their allies to the joys of dice games.

'Our boys will skin the Iberians if they get the chance,' Macro smiled. 'You know what they can be like when they find an innocent mark.'

'Then it might be an idea for you to have a word with the officers. If the men are going to play at dice, then they'll do so fairly, or they'll regret it.'

'I'll make sure they know, sir.'

As they passed the end of the tent line of Macro's century and turned towards headquarters, one of the men stood up and saluted them.

'Excuse me, sir.'

'What is it?' Then the man's name came to Cato. 'Tertius . . .'

234

'Yes, sir.' The Praetorian smiled with pleasure at his commanding officer remembering his name. 'Well, sir, the lads heard you'd paid for the meat from your own purse. We was wondering if you would care for a bite of food by our fire.' He stood aside and waved his comrades to their feet. The men looked at Cato expectantly. In truth he was keen to return to his tent and rest, but knew that he would be a fool not to humour the men on this occasion. There was a time for being stern and insisting on hard discipline and driving the men on, and another time for treating them like comrades. Some officers switched deftly between the two roles, but Cato was reluctant to be too familiar with his men. He had known other unit commanders who had tried to treat them more like friends than comrades and had only won their contempt and ridicule as a result.

'Very well. Centurion Macro and I can spare a moment.'

'Thank you, sir. If you please?' Tertius indicated a log bench set close to the fire and Cato sat down cautiously, making sure the bench was stable and unlikely to slip and cause him to fall into an undignified heap.

Macro sat beside him. 'Let me guess what's on the menu, boys.' He made an elaborate show of sniffing the air. 'Could it be goat, perhaps?'

The men around the fire smiled and some laughed.

'Not just any goat, sir. We've done it special, like. Hirtius over there used to be a cook's boy in Senator Seneca's place at Baie before he joined the Guard. He knows a thing or two about preparing decent grub, sir. Tell the tribune and the centurion what you've cooked up.'

A round-faced Praetorian with a spotty complexion picked up two mess tins close to the fire and came over. He paused to try and salute, but frowned in confusion as he raised the two tins. Cato could not help chuckling at his discomfort and took mercy on him.

'Here, hand me that one.' He angled the mess tin towards the fire to illuminate the contents and saw chunks of meat swimming in a dark, glutinous sauce. 'What's this?'

'The mutton you got us, sir. I've stewed it in wine and prepared a garum and honey glaze.'

235

'Garum and honey?' Cato arched an eyebrow. The idea of the pungent salty condiment being mixed with sweet honey struck him as an unlikely combination.

'What the fuck would you do that for?' Macro demanded.

Hirtius stood his ground and offered the other mess tin to Macro. 'Just try it, sir. It is one of the senator's favourite dishes.'

Macro drew his dagger and speared a piece of meat. 'Just because some bloody snooty aristocrat likes his food fancy . . .'

He popped the dripping meat into his mouth and chewed. Then his jaw slowed and his eyes widened. He swallowed and looked at Hirtius in awe. 'That is the most fucking delicious thing I have ever eaten. Cato, the lad's a prodigy! Try it.'

Cato took out his pocket-tool and unfolded the spoon attachment and chose a small piece of lean meat to sample. As soon as the sauce touched his tongue he knew Macro had not exaggerated. The rich flavour was overwhelming and he hungrily began to work through the rest of the contents of the mess tin as Hirtius rested his hands on his wide hips and beamed with pride.

Macro finished first and proffered his tin. 'Any chance of seconds?'

Before Hirtius could reply, there was a sudden burst of angry shouting from the direction of the Iberian section of the camp. Everyone turned towards the sound and for a moment no one moved. Then, as the shouting grew louder, Cato put down the mess tin and stood up.

'Macro, on me.'

At first Cato restrained himself to striding through the tents but as the shouting swelled he broke into a run. Close to the gap between the Roman tents and those of the Iberians they came across a small crowd. More men were coming from amongst the tents to see what was happening.

'Make way there!' Macro bellowed. 'Commanding officer coming through!'

The soldiers at the rear of the crowd glanced round and peeled aside to let the two officers past. Cato led the way, shouldering through those too slow to obey Macro's order. Then they were through the press of bodies and emerged on to open ground. In front of them was a campfire. Two men were facing each other, knives drawn: a slinger and one of the Iberian spearmen. The latter was clasping his spare hand to his side, and blood was oozing out between his fingers as he swayed on his feet. The slinger was in a crouch, eyes fixed on his opponent as he swept his blade slowly from side to side, daring the Iberian to strike. Neither of them registered the arrival of the two officers. The slinger moved in and feinted and the Iberian slashed desperately and caught the other man on the forearm and opened a gash just below the elbow. The slinger let an angry roar and braced himself to spring forward and land a final, fatal blow.

'Enough!' Cato shouted. 'Stand down!'

The crowd, who had been shouting their support for the two men, fell silent as the slinger paused and glanced towards the tribune, then backed a safe distance away before he rose to his full height and nursed his wounded knife arm.

'What in the name of Jupiter is going on here?' Cato demanded.

The slinger stiffened to attention, still holding his wound. 'A fight between me and that barbarian bastard, sir.'

Macro moved round so that he stood between the two men.

'A fight? About what?' Cato continued.

'He accused me of cheating, sir. Me and some of the lads had a dice game going, and some of the Iberians wanted to play. Only they was losing money. When I tried to take me winnings, he ups and starts shouting his nonsense and slaps my hand away from the coins.' He gestured to the ground near the fire where a small scattering of silver gleamed in the light of the flames.

'How do you know he was accusing you of cheating?'

The slinger opened his mouth, hesitated, then shook his head. 'That's what I assumed he was doing, sir.'

'And then?'

'He draws his knife, I go for mine and he has a go at me. Only I got him first, sir.'

Cato looked round at the crowd. 'Is this true? Anyone see what happened?'

An optio stepped forward. 'I was in the game, sir. It was like Glabius says. The Iberian started it.'

Before Cato could ask for further corroboration, the Iberian slumped to his knees, breathing heavily as he continued to hold up his curved dagger with a wavering hand. Two of his comrades hurried forward and kneeled at his side. One gently took the weapon from his hand while the other pulled the wounded man's tunic up, moving his hand aside, and exposed the wound. Blood pulsed over the exposed flesh and the Iberian's companion pressed his hand against the wound and held it in place.

Cato pointed to the optio. 'You go and find the surgeon. Now!'

As the man turned and forced his way back through the press, Cato glanced round at the curious and hostile expressions. Already the Iberians were moving off to one side, with their backs to their tents, and the mood was becoming dangerous.

'Macro.' He spoke calmly. 'Get our men out of here. Except him – Glabius. He's got some answering to do.'

'Yes, sir.' Macro nodded, then drew a quick breath before he addressed the Roman soldiers. 'Back to your tents! Centurions! Optios! Get these men moving! At the bloody double!'

The tense quiet of a moment before was shattered as the officers yelled orders at their men and pushed and shoved them away from the scene.

Cato turned to Glabius. 'And were you cheating?'

'No, sir! It was a fair game. Ask anybody. Glabius runs a fair game, they'll say.'

'Oh, I'll be sure to ask. In any case, you know the regulations, and what the penalty is for drawing a weapon on a comrade. If he dies, you die.'

The slinger shook his head. 'He ain't a Roman, sir. He ain't any comrade of mine. Just some fucking barbarian, that's all!' He spat in the direction of the Iberian.

'Shut your mouth!' Cato snapped fiercely. 'Not one more word, you hear?'

The crowd was dispersing quickly and then there was the optio, the surgeon close behind him with his sidebag stuffed with dressings and the immediate tools of his trade. He saw the slinger's wounded arm and hurried over.

'Not him. He'll live.' Cato nodded towards the Iberian instead, who was struggling to stay upright and was supported by his companions. 'That one needs you first. See to him.'

The surgeon nodded and set his bag down beside the injured man and wiped the blood away to examine the wound briefly before reapplying the makeshift dressing.

'He's bleeding badly, sir.'

'Do what you can for him,' Cato ordered and looked round at the Iberians, who were still standing in a half-circle, their expressions hardening as they regarded their stricken comrade. The surgeon eased the wounded man on to the ground as the latter began to tremble. More figures emerged from the tents behind them and Cato felt his heart sink as he saw Rhadamistus and several of his entourage striding towards them.

'Oh, bloody terrific,' Macro muttered. 'Just what we needed.'

Rhadamistus snapped an order and the Iberians hurried out of his way. He stopped and quickly surveyed the wounded man on the ground and the slinger, and then fixed his dark eyes on Cato. 'What's happened here, Tribune?'

Cato explained briefly and Rhadamistus nodded towards Glabius. 'He's the one who stabbed my man?'

'Yes, Majesty. But he says your man started the fight.'

Rhadamistus turned to the small group of Iberian soldiers and interrogated them sharply, then faced Cato again. 'They say your soldier was responsible. He tried to cheat this man out of his silver.'

One confrontation was leading to another, far more serious, and Cato forced himself to deal with the situation calmly, even though he could feel his heartbeat increasing and his shoulder muscles tensing, as if he was about to go into a fight.

'We can lay the blame for this at a later time. Right now, both men need to have their wounds seen to. Glabius, get yourself to the surgeon's tent. Have one of the orderlies see to your arm.'

Before the slinger could act upon the order, his opponent gave a deep groan and arched his back for an instant before going into violent convulsions. The surgeon did his best to hold the man down, and the dressing slid off and a fresh gush of blood welled out of the puckered flesh around the wound and spilled on to the ground.

'Hold him!' the surgeon ordered. The Iberian's companions

needed no translation and grasped his limbs to try and hold him still as the surgeon groped for a fresh dressing from his bag. The wounded Iberian began to gasp for breath, a horrible rasping sound, and his eyes opened wide and began to roll in mortal terror. There was one last convulsion, and his jaw hung open, and then with a slow release of tension his body sagged as the air sighed from his lips and he lay still, eyes staring up at the stars.

For a moment no one moved or spoke, then the surgeon leaned forward to close the Iberian's eyes and rose to his feet.

'He's gone, sir. There was nothing I could do to save him,' he added with an anxious glance at Rhadamistus.

Cato jerked his thumb towards Glabius. 'Get this one to the hospital tent and have his wound seen to.'

'Yes, sir.' The surgeon closed the flap on his sidebag and approached the wounded Praetorian.

'Stop there!' Rhadamistus stepped up to the dead Iberian and thrust a finger towards the corpse as he glared at the Roman officer. 'My man is dead. His murderer must answer for it.'

'Now wait a moment,' Macro interjected. 'He accused Glabius of cheating and drew a knife on him. He started it. The fight was fair and he lost. That's too bad for him, but Glabius is no murderer.'

Rhadamistus spared him a glance before he addressed Cato again. 'Tell your underling to still his tongue, before I order my men to cut it out.'

'Underling?' Macro's eyes bulged.

'Centurion,' Cato intervened. 'I will deal with this, if you please. For now, I want you to place Glabius under arrest and keep him in your custody. Understand?'

'Yes, sir,' Macro grumbled and then added a curse under his breath. He moved to Glabius's side, as ordered.

Cato turned to confront Rhadamistus. 'As Centurion Macro says, Majesty, it would appear that some of your men chose to play dice with Glabius. When the dead man lost, he accused Glabius of cheating and attacked him. Glabius was acting in self-defence.'

Rhadamistus listened and then questioned the spearmen standing by the body. Satisfied by their answers, he turned back to Cato. 'They say your soldier was the first to draw his blade and struck

240

my man before he could defend himself.' The Iberian pointed towards Glabius. 'This man is a murderer, and a coward. I demand that justice and vengeance are satisfied. And so he must die.'

CHAPTER TWENTY-SIX

'This is bloody absurd!' Macro protested. 'Those bastards are lying. You heard what Glabius said, and his optio backed his account up.'

They were standing a short distance away from Rhadamistus and his men as they conferred. Two men were carrying the body away into the Iberian tents, while the Iberian prince and a handful of his nobles stood waiting for Cato's response to the demand for Glabius's execution. The wounded slinger stood to one side as the surgeon stitched his wound by the light of the fire. Glabius winced now and again as the needle went in and through his flesh but his gaze switched anxiously between the two Roman officers discussing his fate and the Iberians looking on with hostile expressions.

'The optio would back him up,' Cato countered. 'Same as he'd back the word of any Roman over that of a barbarian, as he'd see them.'

'I don't think there's much doubt about that lot being barbarians. You saw what they did at the fort. Are you going to believe them before you believe one of our own?'

'Of course not. But it's his word against theirs. It was done in the heat of the moment, and anything could have happened.'

'Then you should err on the side of our man,' Macro insisted. 'That's what I would do every time. If I was in command I'd tell that lot of sand monkeys to fuck right off.'

'But you're not in command, Centurion,' Cato replied firmly. 'I am, and it's my responsibility to see that anyone who breaks regulations is punished. It really doesn't matter who struck the first blow, or why they did it. The rules are clear enough. If a soldier pulls a blade and wounds a comrade he is given a beating by the men of his century. If he uses the blade to kill another soldier then the penalty is death. You know that well enough.'

'It's death if the man kills a comrade, but these Iberians are not Romans. Why, they're not even in the same army.'

'You're wrong. They are our allies, and as such they are subject to the same regulations as any other soldiers in the Roman army. If it had been the other way round, then I'd have insisted that the Iberian be punished the same way.'

'You might well insist, but do you think for one moment that Rhadamistus would agree to that? I bloody well doubt it.'

Cato had already been feeling tired and now he sensed the exhausting pit of despair he had only recently emerged from creeping up on him again. 'Listen, Macro, what choice do you think I have? Both sides here need each other if there is to be any hope of Rhadamistus reclaiming his throne, and Rome reclaiming its influence in the region. Ever since we marched out of Syria there's been no love lost between our men and his. We've suffered the consequences of being divided once. If I refuse to have Glabius punished then we'll risk that happening again. Right on the cusp of preparing for the decisive moment of the campaign.' He gestured to the far bank of the river. 'Artaxata is four days' march in that direction. If the Iberians see Glabius walk free then I'd be as good as driving a wedge through the column.'

'And if you execute Glabius, what effect do you think that will have on the morale of our lads? They'll happily follow you into battle. But if you side with the Iberians and put one of our men to death, then it will cost you the loyalty of the Praetorians and the slingers.'

'I'm not siding with anyone. I'm applying the regulations.'

'But the regs are wrong in this situation and you know it.'

'The regulations are the regulations,' Cato retorted. 'Regardless of the situation. And in this case, in this precise situation, it is vital that we stick by them, or we risk ruin. Macro, I've made my decision and I will not change it. There's an end to the matter. Do not dispute with me any further. That's an order.'

Macro made to reply, then stiffened into a formal posture as he responded in a tone laced with contempt: 'As you order, sir.'

'Precisely.' Cato looked past Macro to the surgeon. 'Have you done with Glabius yet?'

'Just tying off the dressing, sir . . . There!' The surgeon leaned back to admire his handiwork. 'As neat a set of sutures and dressing as you'll ever find, sir.'

Cato ignored him. 'Glabius! On me!'

The slinger came trotting over and stood in front of the two officers. Now that Cato was about to pronounce sentence on him, he suddenly became far more aware of Glabius as an individual, as opposed to merely a face in the ranks. The slinger was a well-built man in his thirties, dark hair, streaked with grey, tied back with a leather thong. His face was broad, with deep-set brown eyes either side of a nose that looked as if had been broken more than once. There was a scar across the cheekbone beneath his right eye and his beard was neatly trimmed. Despite the beard, his lips were set in a natural smile that promised innate good humour. But there was no shred of any humour in Cato's heart as he cleared his throat and forced himself to speak in a matter-of-fact tone.

'Auxiliaryman Glabius, you are aware of military regulations regarding fighting in the ranks?'

'Yes, sir.'

Cato's heart sank a little further as the slinger unwittingly added to his culpability. If he had claimed that he was not aware, there might have been slim room for manoeuvre.

'Then you know the penalty for killing another soldier.'

'Another Roman soldier, yes, sir.'

'The regulations clearly state Roman or allied soldier.'

Glabius shook his head. 'It says Roman soldier, sir. I know, because I read them when I joined up.'

One of the rare literate auxiliaries in the army, Cato mused. And still only a ranker? He should have been an optio by now, at least. He had not made the most of whatever potential he had ever had.

'Then you will recall the terms of the preamble to the regulations, where it states that the regulations extend to all allied soldiers marching alongside Romans. So, you'd be facing the same penalty for killing an Iberian as you would a Roman.'

244

Glabius's mouth sagged open but he did not dare to name the sentence himself.

'Death.' Cato nodded slowly.

'But, sir, it was an accident. I swear it, on the life of my children. I never meant to kill him. He attacked me and I struck a blow in self-defence. It ain't right that I should die for that.'

'It doesn't matter,' Cato asserted. 'The regulations apply under any and all circumstances. You have admitted being familiar with the rules so you should know that there is no basis for excusing the killer. You should have thought about that before you struck the fatal blow.'

'But . . .' Glabius shook his head helplessly. 'But what was I supposed to do, sir? Let the bastard stab me?'

'You should have backed off.'

'And let him walk away with the money he owed me?'

'Yes. Then come and report it to your centurion to take action. As it is, you stabbed the man and have condemned yourself as a result. All for the sake of a handful of silver.'

'Sir,' Macro interrupted. 'This ain't right. I'd have done the same thing in his place. And so would you.'

'Then I would have you face the consequences, just as I would expect you to make me face them. Exceptions cannot be made, for anyone, for any reason. Otherwise the regulations will be worthless. They have to be obeyed if discipline is to be upheld. Without discipline no army can function. You have served long enough to know that what I say is true . . . Well?'

Macro gritted his teeth and nodded. 'Then have him flogged, sir. Anything but executed. It'll go down badly with the rest of the men.'

'It will go down badly with our allies if Glabius is permitted to live.'

Cato felt exasperated. He no more wanted this situation than Macro did. It dismayed him to have to lose one of his men in addition to one of Rhadamistus's. It was an utter waste, when every man was needed to ensure the success of the campaign. He was sorely tempted to do as Macro said and punish the man severely, but that was precisely why the regulations were as draconian as they

245

were. If every officer exercised his discretion towards leniency then there would never be any meaningful sanctions.

'We have no choice in the matter.' Cato drew himself up and fixed his gaze on the slinger.

'Glabius, by your own admission, and in contravention of army regulations, you did draw your dagger and stabbed a comrade and caused his death. Therefore, as the senior officer present, it falls to me to decide your punishment. I sentence you to death in a manner yet to be decided.' He paused, then added, 'Do you wish to say anything?'

Glabius shook his head. 'Sir, you can't do this to me. I know the regulations, but I was defending myself.'

'That's irrelevant.'

'But I have family who depend on me in Antioch. A wife and kids. What will become of them?'

'I will see to it that they get your savings.'

'This ain't bloody right, sir . . . It ain't right . . .' His voice trailed away.

'You've had your say.' Cato gestured to Macro. 'Take hold of him and follow me. But don't speak out of turn.'

They made their way back to Rhadamistus, who regarded them coldly. 'Well? What is to become of this murderer?'

'I have condemned him.'

'Good. Then hand him over to me. I'll see that he is put to death in a suitable manner.'

Cato recalled the manner in which Rhadamistus had executed his own men after the Parthian raid on their camp. Even though the auxiliary was to die, Cato balked at the idea of handing the task to the Iberians. Some deaths were far worse than others, he knew, and he was not willing to have Glabius suffer unduly. If only because it would further enrage his comrades in the slinger cohort. 'No, Majesty. Glabius will be punished according to our code. He will be put to death by his comrades, in front of his entire cohort. The execution will take place at dawn.'

'You dare to defy my will? This scum murdered one of my men. Therefore he should be answerable to me. I demand that my men carry out the execution. You will hand him over.'

246

'I will not,' Cato replied firmly. 'If you wish, you can bear witness to his execution at dawn. You, and the men of his unit. But no more than that, given the tensions between your soldiers and mine, Majesty.'

Rhadamistus barked an order to his followers and two of them stepped forward and moved towards Glabius. At once Macro drew his sword and pushed Glabius behind him. Raising the point towards the Iberians' throats, he growled: 'You heard the tribune. The prisoner stays with us.'

The Iberians looked to their leader for guidance and Rhadamistus repeated the order and thrust his hand towards Glabius to reinforce his will. At the same time Cato had been swiftly weighing up the situation. His initial fury at Macro vanished the moment he realised that his friend's action had committed them both, whatever the outcome. Now he drew his own sword and took his place beside Macro.

'Call your men off. We are not handing Glabius to you.'

Rhadamistus smiled. 'You are two. My immediate followers outnumber you five to one. If you want to fight, then you will lose.'

'We'll see about that,' Macro retaliated with a dangerous glint in his eye. 'Who's first, eh?'

The Iberians paused and Cato seized the chance to try to head off the fight. 'If any harm comes to us, then my soldiers will turn on you and none of us will survive.'

'I will not say it again, Tribune. Sheathe your swords and leave your man to us.'

'No,' Cato refused, keeping a careful watch on Rhadamistus's followers, who had spilled out on either side. 'Just keep edging back, Macro.'

Aiming their swords high, the two officers backed away, while Glabius retreated behind them, never too far that he got separated from the two officers. Now some of the Romans from around the nearest campfires edged forward, some with swords drawn. The Iberians kept pace with the two Roman officers and their prisoner for a short distance before Rhadamistus called out a command and they halted, glaring at the Romans as they retreated to the safety of their lines. As soon as he felt safe, Cato returned his sword to its scabbard and ordered Macro to do the same. Then, with Glabius between them, they quick-marched to headquarters to make the arrangements for the following morning.

CHAPTER TWENTY-SEVEN

'The men are ready, sir,' Macro reported as Cato stood in front of the punishment party. With him were the standards of both cohorts, and four Praetorians formed up around Glabius. The auxiliary had been stripped to his loincloth and stood barefoot in the rosy light of dawn. In front of them, on three sides, were ranged the cohort of slingers, each man in his leather cap, cape, tunic and boots. Their capes were swept back on one side to expose their sword handles. Optios and centurions stood in front of their denuded commands. Rhadamistus and his senior officers and eight men from the dead man's unit waited behind the punishment party, ready to bear witness to the execution. The rest of the column had already crossed the river and formed up on the far bank, waiting for the order to resume the advance, once the execution was over.

Cato and Macro exchanged a salute before the latter stood beside the prisoner. Cato paused a moment to look round at Glabius's comrades, trying to gauge their mood, but their faces were impassive and their discipline seemed unaffected by the plight of their comrade. Glabius had spent the night under guard outside Cato's tent. He had not slept, but begged Cato plaintively to spare his life, until Cato could stand it no longer and told him to keep his mouth shut if he wanted to avoid being gagged and bound. After that, the auxiliary had muttered miserably to himself in an undertone.

Cato remained alone through the night, his sleep disturbed by the occasional moans of anguish from Glabius as the night remorselessly consumed what little time was left to him. As the first glimmer of dawn appeared on the horizon Macro brought some food for him but the auxiliary had no appetite and instead begged Macro to help him escape.

'Can't do that. Sorry, lad. The tribune's word is the law and there's no getting round it.'

'But I have a family, Centurion. What's to become of them?'

'How am I supposed to know? Now come on, try and eat something. A little food in your belly ain't going to do you any harm.'

'Ain't going to do me much good either.'

'Suit yourself.' Macro set the bowl down. 'I'll be back when the morning assembly is sounded.'

Once he was sure that Macro had gone, Cato rose from his bed and put on his boots before emerging from his tent. Glabius looked up, then automatically stood to attention.

'At ease,' Cato ordered, then gestured at the bowl of gruel. 'Centurion Macro is right. That might do you some good.'

Glabius ignored the food and met his commander's gaze directly. 'Why are you doing this to me, sir?'

'You know why. You committed an offence that is punishable by death.'

'That's your interpretation, sir. I doubt whether it would hold up in front of a magistrate back in Rome.'

'But we're not in Rome.'

It was a glib comment and Cato felt guilt and pity stir in his breast. 'Look here, Glabius, you killed a man. That is the bald fact of the matter. Then I have the Iberians' account of what happened, and yours.'

'And the optio's account, sir. Besides, we told the truth. The Iberians are lying bastards.'

'Maybe,' Cato conceded. 'But the two versions do not agree. So all I know for certain is that there is the body of Rhadamistus's man, and that you admitted killing him. On that basis I am obliged to carry out the punishment laid down in the regulations. You will die within the hour, Glabius. The question you must ask yourself is: in what manner do you choose to die? Will you die like a coward, crying and protesting your innocence? Or will you die like a Roman soldier? Proud and defiant in the face of death.'

'Why should I care, sir? I'm dead either way.'

'Yes, but how do you wish your comrades to remember you? More to the point, how do you want those Iberian bastards to remember you? It might not seem like much, but there is a small measure of revenge to be had here. Show them how a Roman dies. Head high, staring Charon in the face and showing his contempt for his enemies. If what you say is true then the man you killed was a coward. His comrades have dishonoured themselves by lying about him. They will be looking at you and hoping that you dishonour yourself by showing your fear and crying for mercy. Deny them that and you will have won a small victory over them, and you will leave an example behind to encourage your comrades . . . Do you understand?'

Glabius sniffed with derision. 'I understand that my own commanding officer has betrayed me for the sake of cosying up to his Iberian friends.'

Cato felt anger surge through his veins, but restrained himself from snapping at the man. Glabius's point hit home more acutely than he could know.

'There are no further words to be said then. I'd suggest you eat that food. Like I overheard Centurion Macro say, it might help. Otherwise, make your peace with whichever gods you worship. Your time is short. It might be a good idea to make your last words count. Goodbye, Glabius. I'll see you in the afterlife.'

'Sir?' Macro prompted quietly. 'The men are waiting.'

Cato stirred, suddenly aware that he had been staring at the assembled auxiliaries in silence for some time while his mind had been recalling the earlier hours. He nodded and cleared his throat before he ordered: 'Very well. Escort the prisoner to the centre of the formation.'

'Yes, sir.' Macro saluted and took his place in front of the men guarding the prisoner. 'Punishment party . . . Advance!'

They made their way out into the open space, Macro and the Praetorians marching while Glabius did his best to keep up as they crossed the stony ground.

'Punishment party, halt!' Macro called out and the six men

stopped beside a small pile of rocks that had been prepared for the occasion.

There was a brief pause before Cato stepped forward and drew a breath. 'Comrades! We are assembled here in accordance with the military code to bear witness to the execution of Gaius Glabius for the crime of killing a comrade. Glabius has freely confessed to the crime and therefore, by virtue of the power vested in me by the Senate and People of Rome, I have condemned him to death by stoning. Sentence to be carried out by his section of the second century of the cohort. Proceed!'

Macro turned and took Glabius firmly by the arm and led him a few paces away from the Praetorians, then shoved him down on to his knees.

'Execution party, advance!'

At Macro's order, seven men stepped out of the ranks of the auxiliary cohort, strode towards the pile of rocks and took one in each hand before forming a shallow crescent in front of Glabius. None would meet his defiant gaze for more than an instant. When the last of them was in position Macro spoke in a voice loud enough to be heard by all those gathered to witness the execution.

'Gaius Glabius, do you have any last words?'

Cato felt his stomach tighten anxiously as he looked on, praying that the auxiliary would do his best to die with some dignity, especially in front of Rhadamistus and the small group of Iberians standing with him.

Glabius swallowed, then straightened his back and raised his chin defiantly. 'Sir, I wish it to be known that I hold no ill-feeling towards my commanding officer, who is carrying out his duty . . . To my comrades I offer my thanks for the companionship of the many years we have served together, for all that we have shared. As we have grieved for fallen comrades before, I would ask that you grieve for me now. I . . . I ask that you bear news of my death to my family in Antioch and tell them that though I was put to death, I did not dishonour myself . . .' He paused, then gulped and lowered his head and Cato feared that his nerve had failed at the last moment and that his dignity might crumble into abject despair. He gestured quickly to Macro to bring things to an end.

252

'Execution party . . .' Macro began.

Glabius snapped his head up and shouted, 'Long live the emperor! Long live sacred Rome!'

'Begin!' Macro bellowed as soon as the condemned man's final words died on his lips.

His comrades hesitated, no one wanting to cast the first rock.

'Do it!' Glabius cried out. 'Now, brothers! Let's show those barbarian bastards how a true Roman dies!'

The man on the extreme right hurled his rock with all his strength, sacrificing accuracy as a result, and the missile glanced off Glabius's hip. He opened his mouth to cry in pain, then snapped it shut. Another rock flew at him, striking him on the chest, then another, cracking against the skull just above his ear. Then they were all throwing rocks at him in earnest, desperate to get the deed done as swiftly as possible and spare their comrade by granting him a quick death. Cato looked on with gritted teeth as a rock gashed Glabius's forehead and blood flowed over his brow and streaked down his face to spatter his breast. Another hit him on the eye and he tumbled back on to the ground. The execution party snatched up more rocks and threw them at his body as Glabius instinctively curled into a ball. The sound of the impacts reminded Cato of a laundry he had visited in Rome where men beat wet cloaks with great wooden paddles. Now and then Glabius lurched and spasmed as blood flowed from the gashes in his skin. Then he lay still, his body moving only under the impact of the rocks still being thrown at him.

Macro allowed it to continue for a little longer before he gave the order to stop and the men drew back, some still holding rocks, as their chests heaved with exertion and their faces were fixed in masks of anguish. He paced over to the body and stood over it. Glabius still lay in a ball, his knees drawn up to his chest. The curve of his back was a mass of bruises, cuts and streaks of blood. His collar bone had been shattered and a bloodied shard of bone projected through his skin.

'Glabius?' Macro spoke softly. When there was no response he used the toe of his boot to turn the body over so that Glabius flopped on to his back. Macro's breath caught in his throat as he saw that the jaw had been smashed and in the mangled remains of the mouth broken teeth fringed the stump of his tongue where Glabius had bitten through it. Then Macro saw that Glabius's chest was still rising and falling, and a moment later a hideous gurgling moan came from his throat.

'Right, lad, you've had quite enough,' Macro muttered as he drew his dagger. He kneeled beside the body and placed the point of the blade in the soft tissue under Glabius's chin and rammed the dagger home, twisting it from side to side as blood gushed over his knuckles. Glabius's limbs trembled violently as his toes and fingers stretched to their fullest extent. With a grunt of effort, Macro jerked the blade free and eased himself upright. The stink of urine and shit came from Glabius's loincloth and Macro wrinkled his nose as he found a clean patch of cloth to wipe off as much of the blood as he could from the dagger and his hands. Then he sheathed the blade and stood up, turning towards Cato.

'Beg to report that the prisoner is dead, sir!'

Cato crossed over to Rhadamistus. 'I trust that Your Majesty accepts that justice has been done?'

Rhadamistus's face betrayed no emotion as he gave a curt nod. 'I am satisfied.'

Then he turned and walked away, his men following behind like a pack of cowed hounds. Cato regarded them with contempt for a moment and then filled his lungs to give the order for the cohort to be dismissed. The auxiliary slingers broke ranks and filed back to take up their packs and make ready to march, while the colour party made for the ford to cross the river. At a quiet command from Macro the men from Glabius's section who still had rocks in their hands let them drop and stood silently by his body as Cato approached. He glanced briefly at the mutilated features of the dead man before he addressed Glabius's comrades sternly.

'There's no time to give him full funeral rites. Get him on the pyre and make sure it's alight before you catch up with your cohort. I know that some of you feel that Glabius should not have been executed. That's too bad, and there's nothing that can be done about it now. There will be no further trouble with the Iberians and no attempts at avenging Glabius. If there is, then I will hand the

254

individuals responsible over to Rhadamistus to deal with. And we already know how harshly he deals with those in his own ranks who fail him. Imagine what he might do to one of you . . . Now, pick up the body and get it on the pyre.'

He and Macro stepped aside as the auxiliaries stooped to lift Glabius from the bloodstained ground, and as they made off his head lolled back, so that he seemed to stare directly at Cato, forcing him to suppress a shudder.

'A pity that.' Macro clicked his tongue. 'I had a word with his mates before the execution. Seems that Glabius was a good sort. And a decent soldier. Such a waste.'

'Yes,' Cato conceded. 'At least he faced his death with courage. I'm grateful to him for that.'

'Grateful?' Macro shook his head slowly. 'Ain't going to do him much good now, is it?'

'Not him. But I swear before Jupiter, Best and Greatest, that I will ensure that his savings reach his family, and that I will match whatever sum he leaves them from my own purse.'

'If that's what it takes to make you feel any better about this.'

Cato felt pricked with irritation by his friend's remark. 'We have finished our business here, Centurion.'

Macro stood to attention. 'Yes, sir.'

Cato indicated the smears of blood still on Macro's hands. 'Get yourself cleaned up and join the column. Dismissed.'

As the column marched away from the river along the road to their goal at Artaxata, Cato glanced back down the shimmering ranks of the Praetorians, over the baggage train to the men of the auxiliary cohort, and wondered if the loss of Glabius was more keenly felt than those men they had lost in combat. An execution always hit the men's morale hard and it was poor timing given that the decisive encounter of the campaign was imminent. Glabius's death weighed heavily on Cato's conscience, even though he had done his best to conceal the depth of his misgivings. What else could he have done? he asked himself. In war, a commander must always weigh the cost of his men's lives against the desired outcome as sparingly as possible. The certainty of the death of one man was a lesser evil than the risk of the death of many. It seemed like a sound enough policy, until a face was put on the man who was required to die. Then the obvious thought formed in his mind. What if it had been Macro? What would he have done then? Try as he might, Cato could not imagine ever giving the order to condemn his closest friend to such a death. And that self-knowledge concerned him deeply. Not just for the shaming depth of the hypocrisy of having Glabius executed while Macro would have been spared, but also because it proved that Cato lacked the necessary steel that he believed a man of his rank should possess. It was a hard truth, and it echoed in his mind as he led the column to face the enemy and decide the fate of the kingdom of Armenia.

CHAPTER TWENTY-EIGHT

The character of the landscape changed dramatically as they approached the Armenian capital. The hills gave way to undulating terrain, watered by tributaries of the Araxes river, where sprawling farms and orchards spread out either side of the road. The surface was free of the rocks and irregular ruts that had hindered steady progress before, and the column was able to cover a good fifteen miles each day before constructing a fortified camp. The fertile ground was easy to break up to form a rampart and ditch and there was no shortage of food to replenish the stores that had been depleted while crossing the mountains.

Word of Ligea's fate had spread far in advance of the marching column, and the local people hurried forward to proclaim their loyalty to Rhadamistus and offer the best of their food and wine to him and his soldiers, as well as the Romans marching with them. The advance soon took on something of a carnival appearance as farmers, villagers and the folk of small towns thrust bright blooms into the hands of the soldiers and many of the men took to turning them into wreaths to wear about their heads. Wineskins and haunches of meat were bought from the locals for a handful of bronze coins and shared freely because they were so cheap. Though there was still dust in the air along the road, the men chatted and joked, and occasionally bursts of marching songs were picked up by one century after another and the soldiers sang lustily, as was their wont when their individual voices were magnified into such a rousing volume.

'They're in a good mood.' Macro grinned as he joined Cato, who was sitting in the shade of a copse of cedar trees as the column halted for a rest at noon on the third day since crossing the Araxes river. He lifted his canteen and took a swig of the watered wine before offering it to Cato.

'Thanks.' Cato took a swallow and for once he found that Macro had diluted the wine just enough to make it pleasurably palatable. Or was it that he had simply become used to the brew? he wondered.

'It's just as well,' he remarked on Macro's comment as he handed the canteen back. 'We should reach Artaxata tomorrow. Late in the day, I should think, so we'll make camp and start the siege the next morning. Once Tiridates is removed the rest of Armenia should fall in behind the people of the capital, and swear loyalty to Rhadamistus.'

Macro nodded, then scanned the surrounding countryside. Distant patrols of Iberian horse-archers dotted the landscape in an arc two miles ahead of the column. 'Funny, I would have thought that we would have seen some Parthians, given how close we are.'

'I was thinking the same thing. You'd think that Tiridates would want to attempt some kind of harassing action to unsettle our men before they reach the capital. That's what I'd do in his place.'

'Perhaps he's as cocky as our friend over there.' Macro nodded to the last of the trees lining the road, where Rhadamistus was sitting with his cronies, feasting on some snacks his slaves had set out for them. 'Maybe Tiridates thinks the city walls will keep us out.'

Cato shook his head. 'I think we can be certain he knows about our siege weapons. And from what Rhadamistus told us, the walls are no stronger than those of Ligea. So it's surprising that he hasn't harassed us all the way from the river. At some point his men were bound to get in amongst the wagons of the siege train and have the chance to burn some, if not all, of our onagers. Then we'd have had no hope of breaching the walls of Artaxata. Not without digging mines under the towers, and you know how long that can take.' Cato rubbed his jaw. 'It's a puzzle all right. I'd love to know what the Parthians are up to . . . Better double the watch on the ramparts tonight. And have Nicolis's century on stand-to behind the rampart.'

258

'You think that's necessary, sir?'

Cato thought a moment. 'Best to be safe, since we know the enemy must be up to something. I'd rather be cautious and not need to be, than need to exercise caution and fail to do so.'

Macro blinked as he digested this and made a neutral grunt. 'I'll let Nicolis know.'

They were silent for a moment, each giving himself to an interior train of thoughts. Macro was thinking about the end of the campaign. Once the Armenian capital was taken and Rhadamistus was securely back on the throne then the Second Cohort would return to Syria and he would see Petronella again. Macro smiled. He had never felt this way about any woman before, not even that fierce Iceni lass he had briefly been involved with. Petronella was bold and held her own in an exchange with any woman or man who crossed her path. And smart too. Perhaps too much so, as often she was at least one step ahead of Macro. And fierce as a lioness when she needed to be . . . And in bed as well. Now don't let yourself be thinking of that again, he mentally chided himself. The truth of it was she was a good friend too. They laughed at the same things and could match each other drink for drink.

He took a healthy swig from his canteen and fixed his attention on the routine duties he must carry out when the column halted and made camp.

Cato's thoughts were of a more anxious and sinister kind as he fixed his gaze on Rhadamistus and his entourage. He had never been comfortable in the Iberian's company, even before Bernisha's revelation about his responsibility for the death of Petillius and his men. Since then, being in the presence of Rhadamistus made him feel sick with suppressed anger and anxiety. He feared giving himself away and becoming a target for the Iberian's scheming. And there was Cato's wider concern for his men, given what Rhadamistus had proven himself capable of. At present he needed the Romans to back up his claim to the throne. But once he was safely installed in Artaxata, what then? Would he be content to allow them to return across the frontier, or would he demand that they remain as his 'guests'?

The longer Cato was forced to remain, the greater the risk that

Rhadamistus would discover what he knew. He was desperate to complete the mission and quit Armenia as soon as possible. If there had not been so much at stake, then he would have taken his own revenge and nothing would have given him greater satisfaction than putting Rhadamistus to death in the same way that the Iberian had killed Cato's soldiers.

It was a pity, he thought. There was as much to admire about Rhadamistus as there was to despise. He was bold and brave and led from the front. He was also ambitious, ruthless and cunning – fine qualities for any despot, Cato supposed. But the same qualities made him perilous for any person who dared to thwart his ambition. Such were the rulers that Rome was required to treat with in order to maintain the balance of power over her vast empire and sprawling frontier. At times Cato was astonished that Rome could exercise such influence with a relatively modest number of soldiers, even allowing for the weight of her reputation in the minds of her allies and enemies. They could be sure that if Rome entered into an alliance, then she would never permit an ally to be worsted. On that guarantee her reputation hung. That was why it was Cato's duty to ensure that Rhadamistus triumphed over Tiridates and his Parthians, and why he must bear the burden of knowing about the treachery of Rome's ally. For the present, at least.

He stirred and rose stiffly to his feet. 'It's time to move on. Have the assembly signal sounded.'

'Yes, sir.' Macro stood, slipped the canteen strap over his shoulder and went to find the cohort's bucina player amongst the fringe of trees. A moment later a series of brassy notes cut across the gentle hubbub of conversation and there was a rumble of groans as the Praetorians and auxiliaries climbed to their feet, took up their marching yokes and shuffled back into formation along the road. Cato crossed over to the soldier holding his horse and swung himself up into the saddle. Further along, Rhadamistus and his followers were only just stirring, and their leader paused to finish a goblet of wine at a languid pace before he rose to his feet and led the way to their horses. The Roman soldiers and the Iberian spearmen watched them impatiently until they had all mounted and walked their horses to the head of the column. When they were finally in position, Cato pointed to the bucina player.

'Sound the advance.'

The following evening, once the camp's fortifications had been completed, the rampart was lined with curious soldiers anxious to survey the defences of the Armenian capital less than a quarter of a mile away. Artaxata was constructed in the loop of a minor river, just wide and deep enough to provide a useful natural defence on two sides of the city. While it served to make Artaxata easier to defend, it also meant that it was easier to contain the defenders as well. Macro and Cato climbed on to the platform above the gate that faced the city. The sun was still above the horizon and the long shadows of the rampart stretched out across the open ground towards the wall that surrounded Artaxata. Around the city he could make out Rhadamistus's mounted patrols sent out to discourage any attempts to escape from the capital. Like many cities, it had outgrown its defences and a handful of neighbourhoods were clustered along the main routes leading out of it. Some attempt had been made to demolish the buildings nearest the walls to deny the attackers any shelter within bowshot of the wall, but there was still plenty of cover, Cato noted, as he pointed out some structures near the main gate.

'We'll get men into those tonight and fortify them. From there the slingers can keep the enemy's heads down while we start the siegeworks.'

Macro nodded. 'I have to say I'm surprised that the Parthians seem to be gifting us the chance to establish bastions so close to the wall. And given the height of the city's battlements we could easily build up to the same level and sweep the walls clear of defenders before an assault is made. Makes you wonder what kind of fool is in command over there. Unless it's supposed to be a trap of some kind.'

Cato scanned the buildings and the ground around them closely before he replied: 'I don't see how it could be a trap. But we'll find out when we go in tonight.'

' I assume that means you'll be leading the party?'

Cato looked at him sharply. 'Yes, what of it?'

Macro was not happy raising the subject, and sucked in a breath through his teeth before he continued. 'After Ligea, it might be best if you stayed back. The men need you, sir.'

'I was not myself at Ligea,' Cato said quietly. 'I was deceived, I . . .'

'Deceived?'

'It doesn't matter.' Cato hurriedly collected his thoughts. 'As I said, I was not myself. But I am recovered now and ready to lead my men into action again. Given what happened to Glabius, I think I have ground to make up in their eyes.'

Macro shook his head. 'You have nothing to prove. It's true that they were brooding over the execution, but that's just soldiers for you. But they've put that behind them. You saw how they were these last few days. Raring to get stuck in. And what they need is to know that the man commanding them is the best man for the job. That's you, lad. I'd be a poor replacement.'

Cato smiled. 'No you wouldn't, brother. Anyway, I've decided. I will be leading the party. I need to see their defences close up.'

'As you wish, sir,' Macro conceded. 'It's your funeral.'

'Trust me, I'll be careful.'

The ladder beneath the watchtower creaked and a moment later Narses climbed on to the platform, breathing hard. Cato regarded him coldly, briefly wondering how far the courtier was complicit in his master's actions.

Narses bowed his head before he spoke. 'His Majesty requests your company for a feast tonight, to celebrate our arrival at his capital. You and Centurion Macro, sir.'

'A feast?' Macro rubbed his hands together. 'And why not? Best way to mark the end of a long march, I always say.'

'Do you?' Cato arched an eyebrow, then considered the invitation. 'At what hour?'

'At sunset, sir.'

This far into the summer the days were long, but there would be plenty of time to eat and then organise the men for the night's operation, Cato decided. But he'd need to make sure he did not drink heavily, or overeat. And if he refused the invitation then he risked causing offence.

'Tell His Majesty we would be delighted to attend.'

Narses looked relieved and nodded quickly. 'I will tell him at once, sir.'

With that he swung himself back on to the ladder and hurried down and away before Cato could change his mind.

The Iberian encampment was livelier than ever before. Some of the soldiers had taken out the wooden instruments they called duduks and were playing in pairs, one man droning an almost constant low note while his companion blew the notes of the main song, and others joined in by humming along as they shared their food and wine around the campfires. It was quite different to the raucous laughter and ribald doggerel coming from the Roman tents, Cato noted curiously. Allies they might be, for now, but their language and culture were as alien as those of any far-flung barbarian.

Somewhere, during the march from the river, Rhadamistus had managed to obtain more luxurious accommodation and was able to entertain at least fifty guests in comfort inside the largest tent. As Cato and Macro entered he greeted them with a broad smile and indicated the cushions in the place of honour to his right.

'Welcome, my friends! Welcome. Be seated.'

Cato bowed his head, and Macro followed suit as his friend answered formally: 'We thank you, Majesty, for the invitation and—'

'Spare yourself the polite protocol, my friends. We are all comrades in arms here. Tonight we dine as brothers on the eve of battle. Once those Parthian dogs are cut down Artaxata will be mine, and my beloved Zenobia will be at my side once again. Come, sit and eat with us.'

The two Roman officers did as they were bid, settling on to the fine material of the soft cushions. Another recent purchase, Cato guessed, and almost obscenely comfortable compared to the thin bedroll stuffed with horsehair that lay across his campaign bed. Servants hurried through a side flap and set an array of dishes and two flasks of wine in front of them. Macro eyed the spread hungrily then reached for a dish of lamb cutlets before pausing guiltily to wait for his superior to start eating first. Cato was mindful of his plans for later that night and plucked a small glazed loaf from a basket and nibbled the corner.

Rhadamistus laughed. 'Why, Tribune, someone might think you were afraid I was trying to poison you! If you would like my taster to sample your dishes before you eat, I'd be happy to oblige.'

Cato shook his head. 'I apologise, Majesty. It's just that Roman soldiers are not used to such fine foods while on campaign. We believe that our soldiers march further and fight better on plain fare. Is that not so, Centurion?'

Macro eyed the lamb and a basket of figs sorrowfully before he reached for a loaf from the same bowl that Cato had chosen from and agreed, in Greek for their host's benefit: 'That's right, sir. Although, of course, when in Armenia, and all that.'

'A very healthy attitude!' Rhadamistus nodded. 'I see you have spotted the spiced lamb. A true delicacy of this region. You must try it.'

Macro grinned cheerfully, while steadfastly refusing to meet Cato's stern glare. 'Indeed I will, Your Majesty!'

He popped one of the larger chunks of lamb in his mouth and chewed vigorously for a moment, before his jaw stopped working and then hung open as he muttered, 'Spiced? The bloody thing's on fire.' He swallowed carefully, then poured a goblet of wine and downed it swiftly before pouring another as sweat pricked out from his brow.

Cato clicked his tongue disapprovingly. 'Centurion Macro is just demonstrating why Roman soldiers need to maintain a plain diet, Majesty.'

Rhadamistus chuckled as he leaned forward and helped himself to a chunk of mutton and chewed happily as he stared Macro straight in the eye. 'Perhaps our food is sometimes too much of a challenge for those with a more delicate palate. Never mind, Centurion. Stick to the bread, just like Tribune Cato, eh?'

Macro scowled slightly as he looked away and drew cooling air over his still tingling lips.

'How will you open the siege tomorrow?' Rhadamistus directed his question at Cato.

Cato swallowed the mouthful of bread he was chewing thoughtfully and cleared his throat. He had already decided not to brief the Iberian on the night action as he did not trust his host to be discreet. If word spread, and reached the enemy, then the Parthians might have the opportunity to set a trap, or at the very least to launch a spoiling attack. It was better to seize the outlying buildings under cover of darkness and inform Rhadamistus in the morning.

'Majesty, the first step will be to send a herald forward to demand the surrender of the city. I suggest that you offer the people of Artaxata clemency in return for opening the gates to you.'

'Clemency? I would sooner deal with them in the same manner we dealt with those treacherous dogs in Ligea. It is a pity that I cannot kill all my enemies.'

Cato stifled his anger at the memory at being manipulated into the destruction of Ligea and forced himself to respond in a neutral tone. 'As a general principle, it is better for a king to at least spare some of those he intends to rule. So it would be best to offer clemency.'

'And if the people of Artaxata refuse to take advantage of my generosity? What then?'

'Then we do as we did at Ligea. We use the siege weapons to batter our way into the city. Then we kill Tiridates and his Parthians and place you on the throne.'

'You make it sound engagingly simple, Tribune.'

'It is simple enough in principle, Majesty, but of course it will entail a considerable amount of digging to throw up fortifications for our siege weapons. Fortunately, that is what Roman soldiers are good at, even if they are not particularly enamoured of the hard work and danger that go with it.'

'I can imagine.'

Cato paused a moment before he came back with the question he wished to put to Rhadamistus. 'And you, Majesty. What are your intentions once you have recovered your throne? What do you intend to do in order to secure your position?'

Rhadamistus regarded the Roman officer shrewdly. 'I imagine that my friends in Rome would prefer that I exercise moderation in order to win the affection of my people. We have already discussed this, you and I, and my position is clear and unchanged. The people need to be cowed into obedience, so that they obey my will as swiftly and unthinkingly as a whipped cur obeys its master. There are many in Armenia who are ill-disposed to me. Those I already know of and those whose hearts are not yet known to me. The former, I will hunt down and kill, so that the latter may be spared, if they learn by example. If not, then they too will be eliminated.'

'I see,' Cato responded thoughtfully. 'And how will Your Majesty determine what is in the hearts of others? If they have a mind to hide their feelings, that is. How will you know if a person is ill-disposed towards you if they do not profess it? Surely there is a risk that you might execute a loyal subject?'

'That is true . . .' Rhadamistus pursed his lips. 'But that is a risk I am willing for them to take.'

Cato puffed.

'You disapprove, Tribune?'

'It is not for me to approve or disapprove of the actions of a king. I merely carry out the orders dictated to me by my superiors.'

Rhadamistus smiled slightly. 'Nevertheless, I sense you disapprove. Still. Even after your actions at Ligea? At the time, it seemed to me that you embraced the notion of the punitive example meted out to the townspeople.'

Cato felt his guts churn with anger and sudden bitter hatred for the Iberian and it required every strained sinew of his self-control to conceal his true feelings. It took him several heartbeats before he spoke in a flat tone: 'What happened at Ligea was unfortunate. I will not let it happen again, Majesty.'

'Are you saying we were wrong to do as we did?'

'I admit that it seems to have produced a certain amount of useful trepidation so far . . . But I would urge you to consider very carefully how you act when the throne is yours once again.'

Rhadamistus struggled to restrain himself as he composed a reply. When he did speak, there was no mistaking the cold disdain in his voice. 'Rome is my ally. Your emperor is my friend. And you, Tribune Cato, I respect. However, I find your advice somewhat presumptuous. You are a mere cohort commander, a soldier. You are not a ruler of a kingdom, as I am. Statecraft is my area of expertise,

266

not yours, and I would be grateful if you remember that in future, before you consider offering me any such advice.'

'Majesty, you asked me for my opinion about what happened at Ligea. I merely offered a soldier's view, but I will desist in offering opinions about such matters from now on, as you command.' Cato brushed the crumbs from his tunic and rose to his feet. 'I thank you for your hospitality, but I have preparations to make for the opening of the siege at first light. With your permission?' He gestured towards the entrance to the tent.

Rhadamistus's expression was dark and ominous for a moment and Cato wondered if he would refuse to let them leave. Then the Iberian waved his hand dismissively and turned his attention to the nobles seated to his left and raised his gold goblet in a toast.

'Come on, Macro, let's go.'

Macro cocked an eyebrow at Cato and then, with a plaintive expression, he gestured at the food spread out before him.

'Oh, bollocks . . .' With a quick glance at Rhadamistus to make sure he was not being watched, Macro hurriedly stuffed a small honey-glazed pie into his mouth, then grabbed a lamb haunch and shoved it in his sidebag as he scrambled to his feet and followed Cato out of the tent.

CHAPTER TWENTY-NINE

Using the point of his sword, Cato sketched out a rough plan of the buildings, the city's main gate and the section of the wall on either side in the soil beside the campfire outside his tent. The signal for the third hour of the night had sounded shortly before and the soldiers selected for the task were filing by in the darkness as they made their way to the gateway on the side of the camp facing away from Artaxata. Even though it was a moonless night and thin skeins of cloud were threading their way across the starry sky, Cato was anxious to take every precaution to ensure his party was not spotted prematurely. He had picked Centurion Ignatius to act as his second in command, and an optio from the auxiliary cohort, Lycus, to command the thirty slingers who would be defending the buildings once the Praetorians had seized them. Macro and his century were to stand to behind the camp's main gate in case the party ran into trouble and needed to be reinforced, or rescued.

Cato sheathed his sword and moved to one side to ensure that his rough diagram was easily visible to the others. He indicated the boxes he had drawn in the earth.

'These buildings seem to suit our needs best. Since the enemy have demolished the houses between them and the wall, we'll have a clear view of the wall at first light, and the range is good for your slingers, Lycus.'

The optio stared at the diagram, then spoke. 'If we could get a couple of bolt-throwers on top of the buildings that would be even better, sir. The Parthians wouldn't dare even risk a peep over the walls then.'

'I agree,' said Cato. 'I've already given orders for two of the weapons to be brought forward the moment we've captured and fortified the buildings. You'll be in charge of the crews. Centurion Ignatius will be in overall command of the party once things are set up.' He paused as he leaned forward to draw out another box to one side of the buildings, directly in front of the gate. He then drew a zigzag leading back from the box towards the outline of the camp.

'Centurion Nicolis, you will be in charge of the work party. While we take the buildings I want you to mark out the lines for the approach trench and the battery. We'll start digging before dawn. By the time there's enough light for the enemy to see, I want them to be in no doubt about our intentions. They already know we have siege weapons, and they'll know we'll be using them on the main gate. They'll also see that the fortified buildings will mean we can sweep the defenders from the wall opposite, and cover the men digging the approach trench and the battery. I'll let that sink in for an hour or two before I send a herald forward to demand their surrender.'

'Do you really think they will surrender?' Macro asked doubtfully.

'They'd be fools not to,' Cato answered. 'Rhadamistus has already shown them what happens to those who defy him. And once they grasp that there's not much they can do to prevent us taking the main gate, then I'm hoping they'll see sense and surrender while they have the chance. It's their best chance at coming out of the siege alive. And our best chance of making sure we don't have to lose any more men from either cohort.' He looked round at his officers to make sure they heeded his next words. 'We need to surprise and shock them tonight. When they see what we have managed to achieve by first light, I want them to be convinced that it is only a matter of days before we break into Artaxata and let our men, and those of Rhadamistus, off their chains. We do this right and we'll scare them into surrendering before we even start bombarding their walls . . . Are we clear, gentlemen?'

Macro and the others nodded and muttered their acknowledgement.

'Good. It may be that we can take the buildings without a blow being struck tonight. But if we encounter the enemy then we go in hard and give no quarter. Now, join your men and wait for the order to move. Good fortune go with you all.'

Cato led the men out of the fort and headed away from the wall for a mile or so before he turned towards the barely discernible outline of the city gate rising up against the slightly fainter night sky. His plan was to come in towards the buildings at an indirect angle in case the Parthians were expecting any force sallying out from the camp. The Praetorians would seize the buildings and deal with any defenders before the slingers occupied them. Then the men of both cohorts would fortify their strongpoints as best they could in the remaining hours of darkness. In addition to the weapons they carried, they had been issued with rations for the next day and ordered to fill their canteens, in case the enemy attempted to retake the buildings or cut them off.

As Cato felt his way over the dark ground he could not help recalling the night attack on Ligea, and had to stop himself thinking about what had followed. This time, if all went as he hoped, lives would be saved. Armenian as well as Roman. There would be no excuse for Rhadamistus to visit death and destruction on the people of Artaxata. It would be different for Tiridates and his supporters, of course. Cato had no doubt about the grisly fate Rhadamistus had in mind for his enemies. But there was nothing he could do to save them.

He halted his men a hundred paces from the nearest of the buildings and then took five men forward with him to scout while the rest were quietly ordered to sit down and keep still and silent. Cato approached in a half-crouch, unhurriedly, watching ahead for any signs of movement and frequently glancing down to ensure he did not stumble over any obstacles. Directly ahead was a low building and the tang of manure gave away its function, but there was no sound of movement from the stables and Cato guessed that the animals must have been taken inside the walls. They passed the opening to the yard and stayed close to the wall as they made their way towards the cluster of buildings that the enemy had not yet torn down. Beyond the barn there was a patch of open ground around a well, and then a two-storey structure, the largest, with awnings running around three sides. An inn, Cato guessed.

Turning to the others, he whispered his orders. 'I'll take that building. You each take one of the others close by. Search them thoroughly and watch for any sign of the enemy. Then report back to me beneath the awning at the corner, over there.'

They padded over the open ground and fanned out. As Cato closed on the building he had chosen, he saw benches and tables beneath the awnings. There were even clay cups still left on some of the tables. He picked his way towards the arched entrance of the inn, ears straining for any sound of voices or movement, but all was quiet. Pausing outside, he forced himself to breathe as quietly as possible and then stepped inside. Although his eyes were accustomed to the night he could make out only the barest details of the interior. A counter ran along one wall, opposite more benches and tables, all of which would provide plenty of material to fortify the building, he decided with satisfaction. He felt his way along the counter until his hand came across a sticky patch. He caught the unmistakable odour of garum and wiped his fingers on his tunic before he proceeded. At the far end of the room, beyond the counter, was a narrow staircase. Bracing one hand on the rough plaster of the wall he climbed to the second storey.

A corridor stretched out in front of him. On one side there were storerooms, now empty of anything of value, and on the other side several small cells furnished with simple beds, where prostitutes plied their trade beneath shutterless windows. A ladder led up on to a flat roof, where Cato crouched as he looked around him. There was a low parapet running around the roof, no more than waist height. Not ideal, he mused, but an adequate base upon which to construct protective hoardings. The other buildings he had chosen were close enough together to permit the easy construction of linking walls, and the whole would provide exactly the kind of bastion he had been hoping for: close enough to the city gates to harass the defenders while the siege weapons created a breach.

Something clattered down below and Cato froze. The noise came again, a soft scraping sound this time. He drew his short sword and crept back to the ladder and eased himself down each rung until he was standing on the floorboards of the second storey. The sound

271

was louder now, but still coming from below, on the ground floor. He listened for any other sounds, but there were no voices, no whispering and no sound of footsteps. If there was someone else in the inn, then it seemed that they must be alone. Moving carefully towards the stairs, Cato eased his weight down on each step and bent low to see into the heart of the inn. All was still and then the scraping started again. He could hear it clearly enough now that he could identify it as the scraping of a clay pot across the flagstone floor, and it was coming from behind the counter. Hardly daring to breathe, he edged round the end of the counter, holding his sword out to one side, ready to strike.

A shape lurched out of the shadows, low and fast, and flew up at Cato's chest before he could react. The impact drove him back and he lost his balance and tumbled to the floor with his assailant on top of him, pressing into his chest. His sword slipped from his fingers and Cato instinctively raised his hand to protect his face. Hot, stinking breath puffed across his cheek and then something wet and warm curled over his fingers while his other hand reached round what he thought was a fur cloak but turned out to be fur. Cato eased himself back and sat up as the dog continued to lick his fingers, and then he caught the odour of garum again and could not help a nervous chuckle. It seemed that the piquant sauce was valued as highly in the canine world as it was in the human. He felt for his sword and returned it to its scabbard.

'Easy there.' Cato spoke softly and stroked the dog's broad head with his spare hand. He could just make out the proportions of the animal, large and solid. There was a rope halter around its neck with a short length that ended in frayed tatters. It seemed that the dog had been left tethered and chewed its way free. Cato stood up and let the dog continue licking his fingers for a moment, and it wagged its tail happily.

'You gave me the fright of my fucking life, my hairy friend,' Cato said in a low voice as he patted the dog's flank. 'And now, if you don't mind?'

He withdrew his hand and made his way cautiously to the entrance of the inn, anxious that the sound of his fall might have alerted any enemy lurking nearby. But no alarm was raised and he sat down on a bench to wait for the other men to return. The dog had followed him outside and sat beside him and then dropped its head on to his thigh and nudged his arm until Cato stroked it again. A soft, blissful moan sounded in the dog's throat. Then its head snapped up and there was a low growl. Cato glanced round as one of his men approached.

'One of ours,' he said to the dog and patted its flank.

The soldier hesitated as he heard the growl. 'Is that you, sir?'

'Yes, damn you. Keep it down. There's a dog been left behind here. That's all. Anything to report?'

'Building's empty, sir. But it's good and solid and suits our needs.'

'Excellent. Right, go back to Ignatius and have him bring the rest of the men forward.'

The soldier trotted away from the buildings and a moment later another arrived. One by one they came and made their report and each time the dog growled warily until Cato reassured it. When the last man had made his report, Cato decided to have a quick look at the approach to the city gates before the rest of his men turned up. He gave the dog a gentle shove.

'Go on, you brute. Go . . .'

The animal retreated a step then came forward again and rubbed its muzzle against his hand.

'Go, I said.' Cato pushed more urgently this time, forcing the animal to retreat a few paces. It stood in the darkness, head cocked to one side, uncertain. Cato gestured to the others. 'On me.'

They set off, along the street to the house standing at the end. After a moment the dog padded after them, then went on a short distance ahead of Cato before he could grab the end of its tether.

'Blasted animal,' he muttered. If only it had been the kind of abused stray that knew better than to come too close to people.

The dog was near the corner when it stopped dead and let out a low growl. Then Cato heard voices muttering and the crunch of boots on the gravelled street and he swiftly drew his sword and whispered over his shoulder, 'Blades out.'

A shadow came round the corner, a large man with a club in one hand and holding a bundle over his shoulder with the other. He saw the dog first and drew up as it growled again. Then he saw the

Romans along the wall. There was a beat as all stood still, then the man dropped his bundle and swung his club back to strike as more men came round the corner.

'Get 'em, lads,' Cato hissed urgently. 'Before they give us away.'

He sprang forward as the leading figure swung his club at the dog. The animal darted aside just in time and scrambled off to a safe distance. Cato slashed at where he judged the man's arm was and felt the point tear through cloth before the man lurched back. The other Praetorians rushed forward as more men came round the corner, dropping their bundles as they made ready to fight with a mixture of clubs and daggers. Lowering himself into a balanced crouch Cato thrust his point at the nearest opponent, who still held a bundle under one arm as he waved a club wildly with the other. The point of the blade caught his opponent high in the chest and penetrated a few inches until it struck bone. There was a gasp of pain an instant before the club struck above the elbow of Cato's sword hand. It was a jarring impact and then agony exploded up and down his arm. He managed to hold on to his weapon but his arm was numb and limp and Cato knew it would not serve him in the fight. Blood trickled from torn flesh and he realised that his opponent's weapon must be studded, or spiked. He transferred the sword into his left hand and rushed headlong into the man who had struck him, stabbing wildly and feeling his blows land again and again as warm flecks of blood spotted his face. His opponent stumbled back and staggered around the corner out of sight.

Cato flattened against the wall, his right arm hanging uselessly as he kept his left hand up, ready to strike again. In the darkness it was difficult to discern who was Roman and who wasn't, unless he caught sight of the glimmer of a short sword in the furious melee being fought without a voice raised on either side. A figure was down on the ground, curled up in a ball and moving feebly. Another was staggering away towards the city walls. Just in front of Cato a man raised a club and brought it down savagely on his opponent's skull with a sharp crack and the man collapsed. At once the attacker turned towards Cato as he raised his club again. There was little time to react as the club swept down. Cato threw up his sword and there was a dull clang as sturdy wood clashed with the flat of the blade.

His clumsy parry saved Cato as the head of the club lost its impetus before striking a glancing blow off his right shoulder.

Sensing his advantage the man struck again. Cato ducked and the blow struck the wall behind him, showering him with fragments of mud plaster. But now he was down on one knee and he knew that if the next blow connected with his head then he would be out of the fight, even if the blow was not fatal. There was a throaty snarl and a dark shape leaped at Cato's attacker, growling and snapping as it bit into the man's arm and locked its jaws as it savagely shook its head. The man cried out in panic before suddenly cutting the sound short. He struggled back, wrestling with the dog, striking out with his spare fist, with no effect at first. Then a lucky blow caught the animal on the snout and it released its grip with a sharp whine and slunk down at Cato's side.

With a rush of pounding boots Centurion Ignatius and his men came running forward. One of the others called out a warning to his comrades and they gave ground, snatched up some of the bundles they had dropped and ran back over the open ground towards the city. With difficulty Cato sheathed his sword with his left hand and leaned back against the wall, trembling with the excitement of combat. He swallowed as he picked out the crest of Ignatius's helmet.

'Sir?' the centurion called out as loudly as he dared. 'Tribune Cato?'

'Here,' Cato replied huskily. He cleared his throat. 'Over here.'

Ignatius approached and stopped dead as the dog growled again.

'It's all right,' Cato chuckled at the centurion. 'I *think* the beast is on our side. Get the wounded men inside the inn over there. Then set your men to work. Ten in each building. Station the slingers on the roofs.'

'Yes, sir. By the way, who were those men? Why aren't they raising the alarm?'

Cato stepped over to one of the remaining bundles and prodded it with his toe. There were some bolts of cloth, and the rattle of metal goblets and dishes. 'Looters. From Artaxata. That's why they kept quiet.'

He was interrupted by the braying of a distant horn, of the kind used by the Iberians. A moment later there came faint shouts and the thin whinnies of horses and the clatter of weapons.

'Get to work!' Cato ordered sharply. 'I want this area securely fortified by first light. Move!'

CHAPTER THIRTY

'Now, that is a really ugly dog,' said Macro as he looked over the animal sitting beside Cato as Bernisha bathed the punctures and cuts on Cato's right arm where the club had struck him. The thin light that came before the dawn provided enough illumination for Bernisha to go about her work, and for the features of the dog to be revealed. He was not handsome to be sure. A tawny coat covered most of his skinny body and there were patches of bare skin where puckered scars were exposed. He had long, powerful limbs and a large head with a long snout, and a furry ear on one side was mismatched by the torn stump on the other. He leaned against Cato's side and panted gently as his gaze flitted warily between Macro and Bernisha.

Cato had tried to shoo the dog away as he oversaw the initial work being carried out on the bastion, but the brute stayed close and then followed him as he returned to the camp. By the time he reached the gate, he had relented and took up the frayed leash. After all, the dog had saved him, and the least he could do was to see that it was watered and well fed before he decided whether to cast it loose or keep it. Almost as if it had read his mind the dog nuzzled his hand and licked his fingers and gave a plaintive whine until he stroked its head.

'Oh, I think it's love at first sight, as far as he's concerned.' Macro grinned. 'What are you going to do with him?'

'Haven't decided yet.' Cato looked down. As Macro said, he really was quite ugly, a bad cross between a hunting dog and the runt of a litter of the scraggiest of jackals, Cato reflected. And yet, as he regarded the dog, it looked up at him and began to wag its bushy tail, sweeping it happily across the gravelled ground. Something like affection stirred in Cato's breast and he patted its flank. 'Oh, he can stay for now.'

Macro's nose wrinkled in distaste. 'He stinks. He needs a bath.'

'Bernisha can see to it,' Cato decided. 'As soon as she has finished cleaning and dressing my wound. But he needs some food first.'

'Here, let me,' Macro intervened, delving into his sidebag for the remaining scraps of the meat he had smuggled out of Rhadamistus's tent the previous evening. There was some gristle, and a few strips of meat still attached to the bones, and he tossed them to the dog. The beast leaped up and bolted down what was immediately edible and then settled to chew on a bone, one paw pinning it down while his jaws and tongue worked furiously.

'Bloody hell,' Macro mused. 'Poor bastard's starving.'

Bernisha tied off the dressing securely. Cato nodded approvingly and then indicated the dog and made a scrubbing motion. She scowled but took the dog's leash and gave him a harsh tug before leading him towards the camp gate closest to the river.

'The dog needs a name, if you're going to keep him,' said Macro. 'But if he's going to be a nuisance I can take care of it. I'll make it quick. Don't like to see animals suffer. Parthians on the other hand . . .'

'Well, yes, naturally,' Cato concurred as he watched the dog trotting beside Bernisha. It felt like a monstrous act of betrayal to allow Macro to put down the dog who had saved his life. 'I think I'll keep him. Feed him up and train him well and he'd make a decent hunting dog, I dare say.'

'A hunting dog?' Macro arched a brow at Cato. 'Since when were you a hunting man?'

'There's always a time to take up a new interest,' Cato said defensively. 'And I'll begin with . . . Damn, he needs a name.' He stared after the dog once again. 'Looks lean and hungry . . . Cassius is as good a name as any.'

'Cassius?' Macro pursed his lips. 'Why not? Cassius then.'

Cato stood up and flexed his elbow gently. There was a sharp stinging from the wound, but aside from a little stiffness it felt serviceable enough. He reached for his helmet and turned to Macro. 'It's time we formally announced the start of the siege. Let's go.'

They strode through the camp and out of the gate to where the bucina-man and Cato's bodyguards were waiting beside their mounts. As Macro clambered on to his saddle, Cato fastened the straps of his helmet under his chin and mounted his own horse. From the slight vantage point he surveyed the night's progress with satisfaction. The forward redoubt was coming on well, and the sound of hammering and sawing came from within as the work party continued constructing its defences. The gaps between the buildings had already been sealed with abandoned wagons and carts and doors and shutters nailed to the outside of the vehicles to act as a makeshift palisade. More men were visible on the roofs, erecting hoardings opposite the city walls to protect the slingers and provide shelter for the bolt-throwers once the pieces had been hauled up the internal stairs and the weapons assembled.

To one side of the buildings, no more than twenty paces away, another party of men were busy putting the finishing touches to a crude earth rampart facing Artaxata's main gatehouse. It would provide shelter for the construction of the rest of the siege battery once the approach trench was completed. A third party was toiling away on the first angle, just out of bowshot from the city walls, picks chinking into the stony soil to break it up before it was shovelled to each side to protect those passing along the trench. Around the walls the Iberian patrols kept watch for any attempt to break out of the city.

Cato nodded with satisfaction. 'Let's hope that our efforts impress the other side as much as they impress me.'

Macro clicked his tongue. 'They'll be even more impressed when the battery is complete and the first rocks start flying over their heads.'

They were interrupted by the sound of horsemen and turned to see Rhadamistus and his nobles trotting out of the camp gate towards them.

'Oh, wonderful,' Macro growled. 'His nibs does not look pleased.'

Cato turned his horse towards the Iberian and raised his hand in greeting. 'A fine morning, Majesty. I was about to offer terms to King Tiridates.'

'Were you, indeed?' Rhadamistus frowned as he gazed towards the redoubt and the other preparations for the opening of the siege. 'Would you mind explaining this activity? I was not notified about it.'

Cato affected surprise. 'I apologise. These are merely the routine actions of any Roman army besieging a town. I had not thought to inform you. But, as you can see, we are making good progress.'

'I would have preferred to have been told about your routine actions, Tribune.'

Cato dipped his head. 'Of course, Majesty. I will inform you of each step I take in future. As it happens, I would also like to be informed about the reports given to you by your patrols. Last night, while I was supervising our work parties, there was some kind of disturbance from further along the wall. I heard the blast of one of your men's horns. Might I enquire as to the cause?'

Rhadamistus glanced away towards the city gates to try and conceal his guilt. 'A small matter. One of my patrols came across a party of enemy horsemen. A few blows were exchanged before the enemy bolted into the desert. One of my men received a flesh wound. I did not accord it sufficient significance to inform you.'

'I see,' Cato persisted calmly. 'And did this enemy party come from the city, or from outside?'

'Does it matter?' Rhadamistus asked airily. 'They were bested by my warriors and driven off. That is all that matters.'

'I hope so, Majesty.' Cato gestured towards Artaxata. 'You have timed your moment well. Do you wish to accompany me as I ask for the surrender of your capital?'

Rhadamistus looked towards the walls. Here and there, a helmet glinted briefly in the early-morning sunlight as defenders risked a brief glimpse over the battlements before ducking back out of sight of the slingers on top of the redoubt. He returned his gaze to Cato and smiled thinly.

'There is nothing I would enjoy more than ordering that those dogs surrender Artaxata to me. However, the last time I stood outside these walls and demanded the surrender of the city I was obliged to deploy a ruse to win the day. I fear that some of my former subjects might be tempted not to honour the rules of parley.'

'Ah yes. I recall that you bribed the Roman garrison to hand over the previous king, your uncle, and that you promptly murdered him and his family.' Cato paused, as if in reflection. 'I can see that such an action might undermine some people's trust. You are right, Majesty, it might be best for you to leave negotiations to me.'

Cato took up his reins and urged his horse forward. Macro and the others followed on and the small party of horsemen made its way towards the city gates. Some of the men in the work parties looked up as they passed by, before their officers snapped an order and they hurriedly continued their duties. The sun was well clear of the horizon and almost in their eyes so that Cato and his men had to squint as they approached the capital.

'I hope they don't give us the same treatment they might want to give Rhadamistus,' Macro said quietly.

'We'll know soon enough. Let's hope there's enough respect left for Rome that they wouldn't dare trick us.'

'If not?'

'Then I hope you'll accept my apology when we meet in the next life.'

Macro laughed loudly and shook his head. 'You're a proper caution, Tribune Cato. Anyone ever tell you that?'

'Not until just then. Now, what's this?'

They had just passed between the redoubt and the forward rampart set up for the siege engines when there was a dull rumble as the city gates began to open. Cato reined in and raised a hand to halt Macro and the others. Before the great studded timbers stopped swinging a party of men on foot emerged and conferred briefly as they glanced towards Cato. Then one of them, dressed in a plain black tunic and cap, was given a gentle shove before he paced warily towards the waiting horsemen. As he drew closer Cato and the others could see that the man was tall and gaunt and advanced in years. His eyes flicked from side to side anxiously as he warily observed the men on top of the redoubt and the sentries keeping watch from behind the rampart. There was no point in letting the enemy see too much, Cato decided, and he cupped a hand to his mouth and called out in Greek, trusting that the language was as

281

widely used in Artaxata as it was across the rest of the lands that had once been ruled by Alexander the Great.

'Stop there! Come no closer.'

The old man halted and clasped his hands together in front of him. Cato clicked his tongue and urged his horse forward. He wondered if the enemy had also decided to discuss surrender terms. In which case it might be better to put them off their guard. A moment later the mounted Romans halted in a shallow curve in front of the man.

'Who are you, and what do you want?' Cato demanded. 'Be quick about it, as we don't have time to waste on pleasantries. We have a siege to begin.' He gestured towards the work going on at the battery. 'We'll have your walls down in a matter of days, and then sack the city. So speak up, what do you want?'

'Begging your pardon, Excellency.' The old man bowed deeply and straightened up quickly. 'I am Arghalis, the chamberlain of the royal palace. I have been sent by the Armenian nobles of the court to speak for them.'

Cato's ears pricked up. The nobles? Not Tiridates?

'So? What do they have to say?' he asked tersely.

The man swallowed. 'Excellency, the tyrant, Tiridates, has fled the city. He escaped last night with his remaining Parthians. Only a handful of palace guards remain.'

Cato and Macro exchanged a look of surprise before Cato interrogated him further. 'Why did he leave?'

'Tiridates did not have enough men to resist you. As soon as he had news of the approach of your army he sent to Parthia for help. None came. Most of the Parthian soldiers were recalled by Vologases months ago, Excellency. There are rumours that the Parthians need every man to deal with a rebellion in Hyrcania. He had no hope of resisting your army. And so the people of Artaxata rejoice at the return of King Rhadamistus.' He leaned to one side and looked past Cato to where the Iberian and his advisers were waiting just outside the camp. 'I assume that is His Majesty over there?'

Cato ignored the query. 'So who is in charge of Artaxata? The nobles?'

The chamberlain nodded.

'They wish to surrender?'

The old man made an anxious face. 'They wish to discuss terms, Excellency. In return for the surrender of the city the nobles demand that you guarantee their safety, and mine, from reprisals.'

'Reprisals? It's hardly surprising that the Armenian people might want revenge against those who collaborated with the Parthians. But their fate is not a matter for me to decide. That will have to wait on the word of King Rhadamistus.'

The expression of anxiety that had formed on Arghalis's face took on a new intensity as he wrung his hands. 'Excellency, it is not the wrath of the common people that we fear, but that of His Majesty. I wonder if you are aware of the circumstances under which he was forced to quit Armenia when Tiridates seized the throne? Loyalties were somewhat . . . divided, one might say.'

'I imagine one might,' Cato replied coldly. 'That is a matter between you, the nobles and your king. Once you have surrendered. And let me tell you this . . .' He leaned forward in his saddle and stared intently at the chamberlain. 'There will be no guarantees for the safety of you and your friends over there. You will surrender Artaxata to Armenia's rightful king, and you will do it immediately. If you don't, and I have to take the city by force, then I guarantee that I will hunt down you and those noble men, and their families, and I will have your heads mounted on spikes around the walls of the city to feed the crows.' Cato straightened up and stared at the man with disdain. 'Those are the terms. The only terms on offer. Take them or leave them. I give you until noon to decide. If you surrender, then you will open the gates and I will lead my men into the city. If the gates remain closed then my men will batter your walls down and bring fire and the sword to you and your people, without mercy. Is that clear?'

'Yes, Excellency.'

'Then begone!'

The chamberlain turned abruptly and scuttled back to those waiting outside the gate.

Macro chuckled as he watched the old man stumble and pick up his pace, glancing back over his shoulder in terror.

'Well, lad, you'll put the fear of the gods into that lot. They'll be

283

shitting themselves when he tells them what you said. Nice touch, that, about the heads feeding the crows.'

'I meant every word of it. If we lose one more man than we have to then I will make those responsible pay for it.' Cato wheeled his horse around and trotted back towards the camp to report to Rhadamistus. Macro stared after him briefly and puffed his cheeks before he urged his horse to follow. He had hoped that his friend had put his troubles behind him and been restored to the man Macro knew before. But there was an edge to him now, almost all the time, a world-weariness that permitted only a glimpse of the usual banter that had passed between them. It was as if Cato were hiding something from him, something he dared not reveal to Macro. And that smacked of a lack of trust that the latter found hurtful after all they had been through together. But one thing Macro had long since learned: there was little point in trying to coax it out of his friend. Cato could be an obdurate bastard at times and was prepared to take the burdens of the world on his shoulders rather than risk being seen as unequal to such an impossible task. The lad was a vine cane for his own back, Macro concluded. All he could do was stand at his friend's side and do what he could to keep Cato out of harm's way whenever it could be avoided. That was what friends and comrades did for each other.

As far as Macro was concerned, the soldier's world was charac-terised by hardship and violence, at the behest of scheming statesmen with no more integrity than a half-starved rat. In such a world the greatest treasure of all was the men around you that you could depend on. The men you would trust with your life, unhesitatingly. Cato was one of that rare breed.

CHAPTER THIRTY-ONE

Macro screwed his eyes up at the sun, then tapped his vine cane against the side of his greave as he paced up and down at the front of the column. The first four centuries of the Praetorian cohort were formed up in close order, three hundred paces from the city gates. Rhadamistus and his small group of nobles, with his bodyguard, were sitting on horses in a gap between the second and third centuries, where they would be well protected once the column entered the city. Cato and the colour party and ten picked men would march at the head with Macro.

'It's time,' Macro announced. 'Noon, I'd say. Or just after.'

Cato was standing still, feet braced apart, hands clasped behind his back, and had not moved for nearly half an hour, much to the irritation of his friend. Close by, Cassius was gnawing happily on a bone as he tried to get at the marrow. It was important to Cato to try and recover the unflappable persona he had presented to his men before his world collapsed in on him at Ligea, as he cringed with shame at the thought of being considered weak-minded and unable to cope with the strains of command. An officer, especially one of his rank, must earn the respect of his men if they were to follow him confidently. For a man as plagued by self-consciousness as Cato, the very idea that his men would regard him with contempt, or, worse, pity, made him feel nauseous. The tapping of Macro's vine cane interrupted his introspection and he stirred.

'Patience,' he said gently and cocked an eye at the sun gleaming in the heavens. As best as he could estimate it, Macro was right. It was noon. But there was nothing to be achieved by pig-headed punctiliousness and giving the order to dismiss the men and continue with the siege. Better to give the people of Artaxata the benefit of the doubt for a little longer.

'They'd better stick to their side of the deal,' Macro said sourly. 'Not that you can expect much honesty from these bloody easterners. Treacherous dogs, the lot of them. I like my barbarians to play straight. Like those Germanian bastards. They may look like upright hunting dogs, but they fight fair and stick to their word.'

'Really?' Cato looked at him. 'I seem to recall a certain Arminius leading General Varus up the forest path, and that didn't end so well for Rome.'

Macro frowned. 'Well, Arminius was an exception, obviously. But my point about this lot here in the east holds true and I defy anyone to prove otherwise.'

Given what Bernisha had revealed to him, Cato was inclined to agree and the thought soured his spirits.

'Ah!' Macro stopped tapping his vine cane and craned his neck. 'And about bloody time.'

Cato turned to see that the gates were swinging open once again and a moment later a small squad of soldiers, no more than twenty men, he estimated, emerged from the entrance and formed up on either side of it. After them came what looked like the same party of nobles that had thrust the hapless Arghalis forward to ask for terms.

A thudding of hoofs caused Cato to glance over his shoulder and he saw Rhadamistus, robes flying, galloping to the front of the column. He reined in sharply, his horse kicking up a small dust storm that caught in Cato's throat and made him cough. Cassius stirred and his muzzle wrinkled as a low snarl rumbled in his throat.

'Majesty,' Cato tried not to splutter. 'You see, your people welcome your return.'

Rhadamistus grinned. 'Indeed! Armenia is mine again.'

'Yes, Majesty. You have your kingdom, and your throne returned to you. And I imagine that you are to be reunited with your wife very soon.'

Rhadamistus's lips lifted into an amused smile. 'Yes. I shall be with her again. Now, let us not delay a moment longer, Tribune. Order your men to march into the city.'

Cato nodded. 'At your command, Majesty. But, for safety's sake, may I ask you to return to your bodyguards?'

'No. I will march at the head of my army, like any king returning in triumph should. You may ride directly behind me, in the place of honour, as my trusted ally and servant.'

Cato made himself smile. 'I thank you, Majesty.'

'Then let's be quick about it, and begin!'

Cato had one of the headquarters clerks take the dog's leash and then mounted his horse and gave the nod to Macro. The latter filled his lungs and faced down the column of Praetorians, four abreast, in neat ranks that would have graced the parade ground back in Rome.

'Second Cohort of Praetorians! Prepare to advance at the steady pace . . . Advance!'

At once the stillness was broken as the column stepped out, nailed boots crunching on the stony ground in a regular rhythm as each century rippled towards the city. Rhadamistus tapped his heels into his mount's flanks and the horse walked ahead, with Cato half a length behind and just to the right of the Iberian. As the column approached the gatehouse Cato could see faces appearing along the wall on either side. The majority of them appeared to be civilians and therefore presented little danger. He felt his innate suspicion begin to ease. He should be feeling elation, he chided himself. After all, the campaign was over. It had been a success. Rhadamistus was on the verge of reclaiming his throne, and without a rock or bolt having to be shot at the city. But equally Cato knew that those who rushed to celebration often had cause to regret it. Until Rhadamistus was safely seated on his throne and Artaxata was in the hands of the Roman soldiers, and their Iberian allies, Cato would leave nothing to chance. He turned in his saddle to address Macro.

'Keep the formation tight, Centurion.'

'Yes, sir.'

It was, perhaps, an unnecessary order, but Cato needed to feel reassured that the men would be ready to fight if there was any trickery. The closer they drew to the gates the more he felt the familiar icy tension in the back of his neck.

As Rhadamistus reached the soldiers either side of the gate, they snapped to attention, staring straight ahead. Beyond them the chamberlain and the handful of nobles went down on their knees and bowed their heads. The Iberian stopped his mount just short of them so that the nearest flinched at the proximity of the horse's hoofs. Behind him, Cato raised a hand to halt the column and Macro bellowed the order. Then, in the stillness, the chamberlain's plaintive voice rose.

'Your Majesty, we greet you in the name of the people of Artaxata, and all of Armenia. The kingdom welcomes the return of our true and only ruler. All hail King Rhadamistus!'

'Hail the king!' the nobles and soldiers echoed. 'Hail King Rhadamistus!'

As the echoes faded off the city walls, Rhadamistus surveyed the men in front of him with a stern eye before he responded to the greeting. 'Yes, I have returned. There is much to be done, so let us waste no more time. What is your name and title?' he demanded.

'Arghalis, Majesty.' The chamberlain's voice trembled. 'I am the royal chamberlain.'

'Ah, yes. I remember you. You used to run the kitchens. Is that not so?'

'Yes, Majesty.'

'And after I was ousted, you were promoted by Tiridates, I suppose?'

'Yes, Majesty. After he executed your chamberlain he needed a replacement. He selected me. I had no choice in the matter, Majesty,' he pleaded.

'So you say. I'll find out the truth soon enough and there will be many changes in the royal household. For now, you may remain my chamberlain.'

'I thank you, Majesty. With all my—'

'Later, Arghalis. I want to return to my palace at once. You and these others can lead the way, and clear the welcoming crowds aside before me and my army. On your feet, all of you!'

The chamberlain and the others scrambled up and hurried back through the gates and into the city as Rhadamistus walked his mount under the arch, and Cato and the rest followed at a respectful distance, yet near enough to spring forward and protect Rhadamistus if there was any sign of danger. On the other side of the gate was an open area, with a nymphaeum to one side where water ran clear from spouts inside the mouths of sculpted lions. On the other side were a guardhouse, stables and the stalls of the tax collectors ready to assess the tariff on those entering the city, and on the goods brought in by merchants. Ahead lay a relatively broad avenue, lined with columns, stretching into the heart of the city. At the end, the avenue climbed up to an acropolis upon which the palace had been built and where the rulers of Armenia could look out over the capital and the teeming multitude that lived within its walls. But, glancing round, Cato could see no sign of any welcoming crowd. The small number of civilians on the walls either side of the gatehouse looked down at Rhadamistus in silence. A handful of people were abroad on the streets, but as soon as they spied their king and his soldiers they melted away, shutting themselves behind doors and disappearing up side alleys rather than risk attracting his attention.

Macro, who was marching at Cato's side, could not help feeling a little anxious about the brooding stillness around them, as he spoke softly. 'A suspicious man might well think we were being led into a trap.'

'It had crossed my mind too,' said Cato, then he gestured towards the chamberlain and the nobles, walking a short distance ahead of Rhadamistus. 'As long as they're still with us I reckon we're safe. That lot don't strike me as the kind who willingly put themselves in any danger.'

He stared at the figure of the Iberian prince who would be king. Rhadamistus sat stiffly in his saddle and stared directly ahead. The excitement and cheerfulness he had shown as the gates opened had swiftly died away. 'I think they may be in more danger than they realise.'

'What do you mean?'

'This is not the triumphant homecoming our friend has been expecting.'

'I was under the impression he was keen to be hated and feared.'

Cato shrugged. 'I imagine that's what all despots claim, until they need to be loved, and then it's too late. Mark my words, he will take this as an insult and that means someone is going to pay for it.' He

289

glanced down at his friend with a wry smile. 'It's the same the world over. We've seen it often enough back in Rome. When the powerful feel hurt and frustration and unleash their rage, then the rest of us have to find a safe corner to shelter in, until it blows over. Something tells me there's a storm brewing.'

The motley procession reached the foot of the ramp leading up to the palace without incident. Ahead, the road rose a short distance then turned to one side to begin a two-stage zigzag before reaching the palace gates at the top of the acropolis. Close to, Cato could see that it was no more than half the height of the Capitoline Hill in Rome, but it still provided an easily defended strongpoint that dominated the city. A handful of guards grounded their spears as the new king rode through the arch under the gate tower. Possibly the same guards who had stood to attention as the previous occupant of the throne fled several hours before, Cato mused. It was also likely that many, if not most, of the servants of the palace were those who had waited on Rhadamistus before he had been forced into exile. In which case their reaction to his return would reveal much about the nature of the king and his kingdom.

A low wall ran around the line of the rock upon which the palace had been built and the ground within had been levelled to provide plenty of space for the accommodation, gardens and storerooms. Despite the opulence of the buildings and their setting, Cato was surprised to see so few servants in evidence. Those that were there dropped to their knees and bowed their faces to the ground as soon as they caught sight of Rhadamistus and did not stir again until he had passed by and progressed another fifty feet or so. The chamberlain stopped outside a columned portico and the nobles drew aside and bowed their heads as their king dropped lightly from his saddle and strode through into the entrance to a lofty hall beyond. At once the chamberlain and the others scurried after him.

Cato dismounted and handed the reins to one of his men before he glanced round the interior of the palace compound, rapidly filling up with Praetorians and the first of the Iberian cataphracts to enter the palace. He turned to Macro.

'Your first section is to come with me. The rest can fall out, but I don't want them wandering around. They stay here. I know how light-fingered some of them can be. But we're guests, not conquerors. Make sure they don't forget that.'

Macro raised his vine cane and winked. 'You can rely on this.'

'I'm counting on it. Meanwhile, take some men and see what accommodation there is for us here. And somewhere for Cassius to be kept?'

Macro glanced over to see the dog straining at the leash as it raised its nose to sniff the scents of the palace compound. 'Don't know what you see in that mongrel.'

'Maybe he'll make a nice pet for Lucius when this is over.'

'I'm thinking maybe Lucius will make a nice snack for him.'

Cato smiled, then turned the conversation back to the business at hand. 'I'd rather we had both cohorts and the baggage train somewhere safe. If there's not enough room then find some quarters as close to the ramp as possible. If you need me, I'll be in there with the king.'

'Sooner you than me, lad,' Macro responded with feeling. Then he turned to order the first eight men of his century forward to act as the tribune's escort.

Cato checked his helmet was on straight, adjusted his sword strap so the scabbard hung neatly at his side, then drew a deep breath. 'Right, let's go.'

He led them out of the sunlight into the shaded portico and thence into the reception hall, a modest space by comparison to the imperial palace in Rome, but imposing nonetheless as the columns along the wall supported a vaulted ceiling painted dark blue and pricked out with golden stars and a large silver crescent so that it was like looking up into a clear night sky. Corridors opened on both sides and ahead lay a doorway, three times the height of a man, and ten feet across. The doors were open and as Cato strode through them he noticed that they were of a dark wood inlaid with ivory and silver designs that depicted hunting scenes. Beyond lay the royal audience chamber, the ceiling towering even higher than the reception hall, and tall windows letting light and a breeze flow into the chamber. Cato quietly ordered his men to guard the door and took his position to one side and slightly apart from the group of nobles. A moment later those who had accompanied the king on his march from Syria, together with the dismounted cataphracts of his personal bodyguard, entered the chamber and formed a separate group.

Rhadamistus had already mounted the dais set against the far wall where a tapestry covered with more gold stars against a rich dark-blue cloth hung behind the throne. The throne itself was constructed from ebony inset with geometric ivory patterns, and a large silk cushion covered the seat. Rhadamistus inspected the throne for a moment, under the anxious gaze of the chamberlain and the small party of nobles and courtiers, no more than twenty in number.

'It stinks of Tiridates,' he announced in Greek as he plucked the cushion from the throne and tossed it to one side of the dais. 'Burn that and have a fresh one brought at once.'

The chamberlain hurried to the cushion to pick it up.

'Not you, you dolt!' Rhadamistus snapped. 'Have a servant deal with it.'

'Yes, Majesty.'

Rhadamistus looked round the chamber as he sat down on the bare wood. 'Where are they all? The servants?'

Arghalis lowered his head so that he would not have to meet his master's gaze as he replied: 'Many of them have left the palace, Majesty.'

'A king cannot live without servants. Send for them and tell them I command them to return.'

The chamberlain flinched. 'Majesty, they have left the palace and Artaxata. As have many of its people when they heard of your return and the fate that befell Ligea . . . Only the most loyal of your subjects have remained at the palace.'

'Only the most loyal?' Rhadamistus repeated with heavy irony. 'The same subjects who remained loyal to Tiridates as recently as yesterday?' He glared at the nobles who had met him at the city's gates. 'You served that usurping dog. All of you. You are traitors. Hardly two years before, you chose him over me.'

'Majesty,' one of the noblemen began to explain, taking a pace forward, 'we had no choice but to humour the tyrant Parthia imposed on us. All the time we were loyal to you. That is why we are here now to greet you. I swear this is true. On my honour. Before all the gods of Armenia, I swear that I am loyal to you until death.'

'Really? Until death?' Rhadamistus leaned back in the throne and rested his hands on its ivory arms as he stared at the nobleman. 'I am deeply touched by your loyalty, Petrodenus. Deeply touched. Such a fine sentiment deserves to be put to the test.' He turned to the captain of his bodyguard. 'Cut off his head. Let's see you profess your loyalty as you die.'

The nobleman's eyes widened in alarm and he rushed forward on to the dais and threw himself at his king's feet. 'Majesty, I implore you. Spare me and let me prove myself to you. I am loyal, I swear it. More loyal than any man here who calls you master.' He gestured desperately to the others in the group who had been with him at the city gate.

Rhadamistus looked at him with contempt and raised his sandalled foot to thrust the nobleman away. Then he glared at those who had remained at the palace. 'It seems our friend here casts doubt on the degree of your loyalty to me.'

The nobles dared not speak but some shook their heads, while others flinched. Meanwhile the captain of the guard and two of his men had climbed the podium and seized the noble cringing in front of the throne. While the cataphracts took his arms and forced him to bend forward on his knees, their captain drew his curved blade and looked to the king for instructions.

'What are you waiting for? I said cut off his head.'

'No!' the noble screamed. 'Majesty! I beg you. I am loyal! I—'

The blade slashed down and caught in the awkward angle where the man's neck bent as he looked up imploring the king. The muffled *tchunk* as the blade cut through gristle and bone made Cato shudder. But the horror was not over. The captain's sword had cut only half of the way through and now his victim's head hung to one side as blood spurted from the wound and an anguished gargling still came from his throat.

'Do it properly, you fool!' Rhadamistus raged.

The captain raised his sword and cut again, then again, and only on the fourth time did the mangled head drop from the body and splash into the blood pooling below. The soldiers released their hold and the corpse slumped forward before suddenly spasming and spattering blood across the king's robe and face.

'Get that filth out of here! And have the head mounted on a spike on the palace wall where everyone in the city can see it. Now!'

The captain snapped an order to one of his men and the soldier clenched his fingers in the hair of the head and hurried out as he held it to one side, dripping.

Then there was silence in the room as Rhadamistus, with a look of disgust, used a sleeve to wipe the blood from his face. He turned his gaze to the captain and pointed out the men clustered behind the chamberlain. 'Kill the rest of them. Their heads can keep the first one company. Not him, though! Not Arghalis. He lives.'

The nobles cried out in panic and protest as the soldiers clustered around them with drawn weapons. The chamberlain staggered to one side before his knees buckled and he collapsed and covered his face. Behind him the captain pointed towards the door.

'Not outside,' said Rhadamistus. 'Here, where I can see . . . Kill them.'

No sooner was the order given than the soldiers closed in, stabbing and hacking with their blades. Cato watched helplessly as the nobles raised their hands to try and protect themselves as blood sprayed through the air and bodies and severed limbs fell to the floor amid bloodied robes and puddles of gore. One of the nobles managed to duck out of the massacre and limped across the chamber directly towards Cato, arms outstretched as he begged to be saved. But before he could reach the Roman one of the cataphracts dashed after him and slashed at his head and struck him down.

The flurry of blows and the cries of the mortally wounded came to an end and the soldiers, covered with blood and chests heaving, stood over the bodies heaped at their feet. The only sound was the quiet sobbing of the chamberlain as he lay curled on the ground to one side. Rhadamistus stood up, crossed over to Arghalis and kicked him.

'Stop weeping! Get on your feet!'

The chamberlain let out a wail and began to tremble violently.

'On your feet, I said! Or I'll cut your head off myself where you lie.'

At once the man rolled aside and clambered to his feet, half crouching in mortal terror as he looked up at his king.

Rhadamistus pointed a finger at him as he spoke. 'You will send a message to every nobleman in Armenia. And to the leader of the council in every city and town. You will inform them of what happened here. If they do not present themselves at my court within thirty days, and swear an oath of loyalty to me, on the lives of their families, then I will have them condemned as traitors, and their heads, and those of their wives and children, will be added to the others on the palace wall. Thirty days only. I will accept no excuse for any delay. Now go, you dog, and send the messages out, before I change my mind and add your shrivelled little head to the others.'

Arghalis shuffled away, bent low, and then turned as he drew close to the door and rushed from the king's presence. Rhadamistus raised his chin imperiously as he turned to his cronies. 'You may help yourselves to the riches and estates of these traitors. And you, Tribune, what reward does my loyal Roman ally ask of me?'

Cato felt numbed by the display of butchery, but he controlled his expression and made himself reply clearly and tonelessly.

'There is no need to reward me, Majesty. It is my bounden duty to serve you. This land is your kingdom alone, and no Roman should ever be a part of it. Now, with your permission, I must see to the quartering and provisioning of my men.'

Rhadamistus wafted a hand towards the entrance. 'You may leave us for now. But there will be a feast tonight, Tribune. We must celebrate my homecoming. And my reunion with my Queen.'

'As Your Majesty wishes.' Cato bowed his head and turned to march from the room as steadily as he could, desperate to get outside into the fresh air and away from the tang of blood and the urine and shit of those victims who had loosed their bowels as they were cut down for the pleasure of the king.

CHAPTER THIRTY-TWO

Terror was a powerful motivation, Cato conceded, as he entered the palace that evening in the company of Macro and the other centurions and optios from the column. The chamberlain had managed to organise an elaborate banquet in a matter of hours, and the chamber where the nobles had been cut down had been transformed. Gone were the pools of blood and gobbets of flesh, and in their place were low couches arranged in rows either side of bowls and platters heaped with delicacies and freshly cooked meats and baked bread. Flowers and ribbons of brightly coloured cloth decorated the walls and columns of the chamber. To one side a small group of musicians were playing jaunty tunes on duduks accompanied by cymbals and some stringed instruments.

Rhadamistus was sitting alone on the dais, propped up on a large divan heaped with cushions. One of his bodyguards stood at each corner of the dais while his taster sat below his table and was careful to sample each dish and glass of wine that was set before the king. For a man who had just been returned to his throne, Rhadamistus did not exude an air of celebration and delight, thought Cato. Instead he wore a brooding expression as he gazed out over his guests. Not many of them appeared to be enjoying the event either, and while Cato recognised the faces of most of the king's closest followers and the senior officers of the Iberian troops, the rest of the guests must have come from Artaxata: rich merchants, minor nobles, tax farmers and the like. And all of them clearly anxious not to attract the attention of Rhadamistus or his cronies.

As the Romans entered the chamber, Cato noticed Arghalis standing close to the entrance as he oversaw the servants to ensure

296

that his master had no excuse to berate him. The chamberlain raised his staff and rapped it on the marbled floor three times to draw attention to the new arrivals.

'His Majesty welcomes Tribune Quintus Licinius Cato and his officers. True allies of Armenia, and heroes who have fought at the side of the mighty Rhadamistus!'

His introduction was met with a chorus of cheers from those who had marched from Syria, and a less hearty welcome from the other guests, who no doubt resented the Roman interlopers almost as much as they dreaded the king who had returned from exile. On the dais, Rhadamistus raised his cup, smiled, and toasted Cato and his officers, and those in the chamber hurriedly followed suit.

Cato acknowledged the greeting with a formal bow. All the same he was conscious that the Romans would stand out in their plain woollen tunics and sturdy leather belts and boots, while the Armenians and Iberians would be wearing their finery, scents and make-up. Since there was no way of competing with the wealthy appearance of the nobles, Cato had decided that it would be better to make a virtue of being plain-speaking, hard-fighting soldiers, and left his best tunic and toga in his travel chest. He had hoped to have his tunic brushed for the feast, but Bernisha was nowhere to be found. The last time he had seen her was before the cohort formed up to enter the city. None of the headquarters clerks or guards knew where she had gone, and Cato assumed she had chosen to disappear into the city before finding her way back to her family. He felt a keen sense of hurt at the girl's abandoning of him, and guilt that he had prompted it by being too suspicious of her motives.

'Your seating is over there, Excellency.' The chamberlain indicated two rows of empty couches to the side of the hall. 'Take your places and I will have food and wine brought to you as swiftly as possible.'

Macro raised an eyebrow. 'Seems we are no longer good enough to dine with His Majesty, or even near him. You'd think his allies deserved better.'

'Maybe it's important for him to show these people that he is not too dependent on Rome,' Cato speculated. 'Besides, I'd rather concentrate on filling my boots than making small talk tonight.'

'And now you're talking my kind of small talk.' Macro patted his stomach.

Cato nodded his thanks to Arghalis and led his officers around the feast towards the couches. As the senior officer he took the spot nearest to the king, with Macro opposite, and then the other centurions sat before the optios. Looking at his men, Cato was struck by their casual demeanour, then it occurred to him that as soldiers of the Praetorian Guard they would be used to such entertainments, unlike the men of the legions and auxiliary cohorts garrisoning the frontier. But this was a feast like few others. Despite being a celebration to mark the return of Rhadamistus, the mood was subdued and anxious. Most of the other guests were making a show of eating and barely picked at their food, as if they were fearful that it was poisoned but were even more afraid of causing offence by giving the appearance of fearing that it was poisoned. Only a small group seemed to be enjoying the food and the bonhomie: those who had returned from exile, and the others who had remained loyal to Rhadamistus in his absence, or were recent converts to his cause and swift to declare their loyalty and offer him gifts of gold and silver. Some, no doubt, hoping to profit from the new regime, or at the very least save their own heads.

There seemed to be no rush to feed the new arrivals and Cato turned his attention towards more professional matters.

'How are the arrangements for the men's accommodation going, Macro?'

'Very nicely, as it happens. That fellow that showed us in just now couldn't have been more helpful.'

'That comes as little surprise. Go on.'

'As you know, the officers have quarters in the wing of the palace closest to the stables and stores where the rest of the men are. The first four centuries have cleaned out most of the stables allotted us and are making themselves comfortable. Our friend the chamberlain has provided them with rations. Good stuff too. And wine.'

'Make sure there's not too much of that going round. At least not until we find our feet here.'

Macro nodded, making a mental note, then continued. 'The last of the men were tasked with bringing in the wagons. I had left orders to raze the marching camp, but that Iberian, Narses, said the Iberians want to use it to corral their horses. I didn't see any problem with that.'

Cato thought a moment. 'It makes sense. Better than our lads having to give up the stables.'

Macro grinned. 'That's what I thought, sir. Anyway, the wagons are parked in a merchant's yard below the acropolis, under guard. Those men we have no room for in the palace are billeted in houses near the yard. That's Ignatius and Porcino's centuries, and the auxiliaries. Their rations have been arranged, or so that chamberlain says.'

They glanced at Arghalis, hovering at the rear of the chamber, anxiously watching over it to ensure that the guests' needs were catered for.

'I think we can rely on him to be as good as his word,' Cato said, with a wry smile. 'That's one job I'd be happy to give a miss.'

'Ah, about time!' Macro's eyes lit up as a line of servants approached, carrying platters and wine jars. They set them down before the Roman officers and hurried back to the door leading to the kitchens. Macro ran his gaze over the food and reached out towards a glazed capon, and then paused to look at Cato to take the lead.

'Go ahead, lads,' Cato grinned. 'Tuck in.'

His officers needed no further encouragement and fell upon the food and drink laid out for them with all the gusto of men who had put up with simple marching rations, leavened by occasional looted fare, for most of the campaign. Cato's approach was more restrained as he was conscious of the need to set a refined standard of behaviour appropriate to his rank. He picked out a few small pies and munched steadily as he reclined on his couch and surveyed the other guests and their host. The strained atmosphere that hung over most of the chamber was palpable, and Cato decided that he and his men would stay for only as long as was necessary and then make the excuse that various duties demanded their attention. He had no desire to remain and witness any further displays of Rhadamistus's cruel despotism.

And just then the demeanour of Rhadamistus changed dramatically. The sour, brooding expression gave way to a broad smile as he sat up and stared towards the entrance. Cato followed his gaze and saw that a new party had arrived: four women in veils and flowing gowns of brilliant colours and designs. Behind them came another woman in a dress made of a rich dark-blue material. She carried herself imperiously, and her eyes were surrounded by kohl, so that they were even more striking above the veil that covered her nose and jaw with slender chains of gold and silver over the fabric. There was more gold on her arms: bejewelled bands that stretched from her wrists almost up to her elbows. The hubbub in the chamber quickly subsided as all eyes turned towards her.

Macro swallowed hard and muttered, 'By the gods, that woman's a walking king's ransom.'

Cato nodded, realising at once who she must be, even before the chamberlain announced her. The rapping of his staff echoed off the surrounding walls to demand the silence that she had already won with her dazzling entrance.

'Her royal Majesty, Queen Zenobia . . .'

There was a rustling of robes as the guests hurriedly rose to their feet and bowed their heads respectfully. The servants in the middle of the hall stood aside and bowed low as Zenobia's companions proceeded ahead of the queen at a stately pace. As they approached the dais Rhadamistus rose to his feet and held out his hands. The other women moved to the side to take their place at a small table set there for them, while Zenobia climbed the steps to the dais and took her husband's hands.

'My dear wife,' he intoned. 'It brings great joy to my heart to have you at my side again.'

She dipped her head before replying in a clear voice: 'And to my heart also, Majesty.'

'Come, sit at my side.' Rhadamistus indicated his couch and she eased herself down carefully so as not to let the folds of her voluminous gown catch awkwardly beneath her. Once she was seated, the guests resumed their places, and the conversation, such as it was, slowly swelled in volume.

'How very touching,' Macro said quietly. 'Seems the Iberian lad's got a soft side after all.'

But Cato was not smiling as he stared towards the dais. The pleasure of eating good food and drinking fine wine in the company of Macro and the other officers turned to ashes as his stomach knotted with anxiety and shame over the exposure of his wretched stupidity. Macro regarded him with amusement.

'Cato? Lad, what's wrong? You look like you've just lost a denarius and found a sestertius shoved up your arse . . . Cato?'

When Cato failed to respond to his attempt at humour, Macro's smile faded on his lips. 'What in Hades is wrong? Poison?'

He looked down at the food in horror, and let the pastry he had been about to eat drop on to his plate.

'No,' Cato told him coldly. 'Not that kind of poison at least. Look at her . . . Look closely.'

As food was brought to the queen she reached up and unhooked the veil and set it down beside her before leaning forward to pick up a fig.

'Fuck me . . .' Macro shook his head. 'It's her. Bernisha.'

'Yes . . . Though I doubt that was ever her name.' Cato gritted his teeth as the full scale of her deceit crashed down upon him. 'Zenobia, then.'

'But what in bloody Hades is going on?' Macro demanded. 'What was all that business about her being a captive of Rhadamistus? Of her being afraid of him? What's their game?'

'I don't know.' Cato shook his head, still struggling to think it through, and then he was struck by the cold, numbing fear of what might happen to him if her husband knew about the night she had slept with him. Men had died for far less egregious wrongs done to Rhadamistus. Men had been burned alive and beheaded for incurring his wrath one way or another. He had already proved that he was willing to murder Petillius and a score of Praetorian guardsmen to achieve his aims . . . Or had he? Perhaps that was a deceit too? Maybe they had been killed by the Parthians all along. Or . . . or was there some still deeper game that had been played against Cato? He frowned as he tried to think it through. Perhaps Rhadamistus had been suspicious of his allies. After all, Rome was inclined to use various princes and kings as playing pieces in the great game of imperial influence against her enemies. A client king could be easily held in check if he knew that Rome could replace him with one of the hostages living as 'guests' of the emperor. What if Rhadamistus had schemed to have Cato take Bernisha – Zenobia – into his tent? She would be perfectly placed to eavesdrop on Cato and his officers and report back to her husband if she discovered the Romans were playing Rhadamistus in order to win back Armenia for him before deposing him and seizing the territory for the Empire. There were many things she could glean from Cato, especially if she seduced him. But why tell him what she had about Petillius? What was there to gain in that? He had been on the point of throwing her out, Cato reasoned. She would need to do something desperate to retain her place in his tent. So she told him a story so shocking yet convincing that he would buy into it, and it would fool him into 'protecting' her from Rhadamistus.

Cato was appalled by his naïvety. He felt used and worthless and disgusted with himself.

'Cato?' Macro's expression was troubled beyond words. 'What did that bitch do to you?'

Cato shook his head. 'Not now. Not here.'

His head was swimming and the chamber suddenly seemed far too hot and suffocating. He swallowed and rose from the couch. 'I need a piss. Stay here. I'll be back soon.'

Moving unhurriedly in order not to attract attention, Cato edged round the chamber and slipped out through a side entrance. He came out in a narrow service corridor. To one side he could see servants coming and going from a kitchen, taking empty platters out while fresh food headed into the feast through another side entrance. There was no sound or movement from the other direction and he strode that way, anxious to get into the cool night air. At the far end of the corridor was a door, and he opened it to see that it gave out on to a yard behind the stables. A handful of Praetorians were playing dice on the far side of the yard, and he kept away from them as he left through the gates into the open ground in front of the palace. Opposite him was a pillared pavilion overlooking the city, and he made for that. The only other people in sight were the figures of sentries further along the low wall of the acropolis. The muffled hubbub of the banquet vied with the carousing of Roman soldiers in the stables. Below him lay the city, sparkling with the flickering glare of torches and from which rose the cries of drinking men, the occasional wail of infants and outbursts of angry exchanges. He leaned his head back and stared into the starry sky for a while, where a sliver of moon hung. He breathed intensely while trying hard to make sense of the treachery of those it was his duty to treat as allies.

'I bid you a good evening, Tribune Cato.'

He turned quickly, hand reaching for the hilt of his dagger, but she was alone, dimly visible in the faint light of the stars and moon. Her face looked smooth and silvery, like the belly of a snake, he thought bitterly. Her dark eyes were fixed on him as she took a step closer, but he retreated, keeping a safe distance between them.

'Can it be that you hate me?' Her lips lifted in a slight, seductive smile. 'After all that we have shared while on the road to Artaxata? You were not so unwilling to be close on that cold night.'

'We have shared nothing,' Cato snapped. 'It was all a complete fiction. A lie. You are as treacherous as a snake. I should kill you now with my bare hands.'

'But of course you won't. Not if you wish to live and return home to that young son of yours.'

Cato felt his flesh creep with the urge to strangle this woman who had played him like a cheap lyre. He lunged and took her by the arms and thrust her against the wall and pushed her so that she was bending back over the void and the rocks below.

Zenobia laughed in his face, her expression flushed with excitement. Cato held her there for a few beats then drew her back and released her, his heart pounding.

'Does Rhadamistus know?' he demanded.

'Does he know that I told you what he did to Centurion Petillius? Or that I fucked you?' She ran her tongue across her lips. 'Of course he does. He just hasn't decided what to do about it yet. Fortunately, he is just intelligent enough to listen to me and heed my advice that it would be foolish of him to have you killed. For now.'

'Why did he send you to spy on me?'

'Why do you think? Rome cannot be trusted. You pretend to be his ally, and all the while, Rome serves no interests but its own. Who knows what secret orders you had been given? Only a fool

303

would not have wanted to try and discover what your true purpose was. Now Armenia is in our hands and there is no need for further subterfuge. And so Bernisha becomes Zenobia.'

Cato shook his head. 'But you didn't just spy on me. You went further than that.'

'True. You are not an easy man to read, Tribune. I needed to get close to you, under that hard shell you present to others. They say that the way to a man's heart is through his stomach. But what do "they" know?' She reached down and pressed her hand against Cato's groin and he stepped back hurriedly.

She laughed again. 'Besides, I have needs, like anyone else. Like you. Oh, come now, Tribune. Was it so bad? You seemed quite content at the time.'

Cato shook his head. 'Macro is right. You're a bitch. A slimy, calculating, evil bitch . . .'

This time there was a crack in her composure and she glared at him with open hostility. 'You had better be careful, Tribune. You are living under my roof now. My rules. And if you think how well I played you, then you'll have to trust me when I say I know how to play my husband even more ruthlessly and effectively. He really thinks that *he* is the ruler of Armenia. I made him what he is. He thinks we are partners. He trusts me because it serves his interests to. Together we have achieved all this.' She waved a hand towards the city. 'He is king and I am his queen. Something that would have taken years if we'd remained in Iberia and been content to wait for his father to die. That dotard seems set to endure for ever . . .' She paused a moment then wagged a finger at Cato. 'Never forget, it serves Rome's interests at the same time to have Rhadamistus on the throne, so spare me your anger and outrage, Cato. Your emperor needs this as much as I do, and it is your duty to serve him.'

Cato felt trapped by her words. She was right. This was the goal of Nero's policy here in Armenia. His mission was a success. All that remained now was to quit Artaxata as soon as Rhadamistus's reign was secure.

He drew himself up and pointed a finger at her. 'Stay away from me.'

She tilted her head to one side and shrugged. 'As you wish. Enjoy the rest of the feast, Tribune. No doubt our paths will cross again another time. Goodnight.'

She turned and strolled comfortably back towards the palace. Cato watched her until she disappeared inside, then heaved a deep, calming sigh and went to rejoin his comrades.

CHAPTER THIRTY-THREE

Cato stayed away from the palace as much as he could over the following days. There was plenty to occupy him at first. The defences of the redoubt that had been built outside the city were dismantled as the owners returned to their homes and businesses. Now that his soldiers were comfortably billeted, they could rest and make repairs to their kit. The wounded were cared for in one of the palace's empty grain stores, and the cohort surgeon's daily reports were encouraging. Most of the sick and injured were recovering well and would soon return to duty. Some were not so fortunate: they were either maimed or crippled and would never return to the ranks. They would have to be discharged when the column returned to Syria. A grim prospect for most of them, Cato reflected sympathetically. Some men, bitter at the loss of a limb, or left with a debilitating limp, frittered away their discharge gratuity and spent what was left of their life as street beggars. Others were fortunate enough to have family to return to, and if they husbanded their meagre resources, they might eke out a simple life. That was as good as it got for the vast majority in their predicament. Life in the army was tough enough. Life outside of it, in such circumstances, could be very harsh indeed.

Idleness was the main enemy of soldiers in comfortable billets when there was no campaigning to be done, and Cato gave orders that the duty roster was to be maintained, with one century always keeping watch from the walls of the acropolis while the other units were inspected, paraded and sent on patrols around the city. While the rankers grumbled and cursed him for it, the Praetorian centurions and optios had no complaint. The enforced leisure of the cohort was a fine opportunity to get back to the spit and polish of the barracks routines in Rome that had been sadly lacking on the march. For the first time in months the Second Cohort of the Praetorian Guard was turning out immaculately each morning and being drilled with inch-perfect precision in the palace courtyard.

Cato spent much of the time catching up on the minutiae of administrative tasks. The wills of those who had been concerned to make such arrangements had to be unsealed and read through. Some men had left their savings for their families back in Rome and their wills had to be carefully set aside until the cohort returned. Others had left their possessions to their comrades and these wills could be executed at once, producing small windfalls for the individuals concerned. Money that was swiftly spent in the drinking houses and brothels of Artaxata.

However, it seemed to Cato, on those occasions when he ventured out to walk Cassius, that the Roman and Iberian troops were amongst the few who were enjoying the delights of the city without restraint. The mood of the people was fearful, and King Rhadamistus was doing little to assuage their fear. Worse, he seemed to provoke it with reckless glee. Hardly a day passed without the execution of another group of people who had been denounced as having collaborated with Tiridates and the Parthians, or simply as having failed to display unquestioning loyalty to the king. Cato witnessed these wretched individuals being dragged through the streets to the platform in the middle of the great market, where they were put to death one by one, according to the method pronounced by Rhadamistus. The fortunate ones were beheaded. The others were made to endure the torments of flaying, burning and strangling. Afterwards the bodies were carted out of Artaxata and piled into a common grave, minus their heads, which were added to those already adorning the spikes that Rhadamistus had ordered to be set up along the city walls.

Cato could see the fear in almost every face as he walked the streets of the capital with Cassius trotting at his side. Few dared meet his gaze or do anything that might incur his displeasure since, as a Roman, he was seen as a close ally of the tyrant living in the palace. Inevitably those people who could afford to began to leave the city, packing their belongings on to carts and trundling off to farms they owned away from the capital, or to the homes of distant family and friends in other cities and towns. Only the poor could not afford to leave, but as long as they kept their heads down and made no complaint they were safe enough. After the numbers of those leaving began to increase, Rhadamistus decreed that anyone who tried to flee the capital would be treated as an enemy and put to death. As for those who had already left, he announced that they too were traitors and that their homes and any other property remaining in the city would be confiscated and sold at public auction, and the proceeds added to the royal treasury.

The day before the deadline Rhadamistus had set for the nobles to come to pay homage to him, Cato was resting on his bed, looking out through the open doors of his balcony towards the distant mountains. His dog lay stretched on his back beside the bed as Cato stroked his belly. Although the height of summer was a month or so away, the hours around noon were hot and the streets airless, and Cato preferred to remain in the cool shade until later in the afternoon. Besides, it decreased his chances of encountering Zenobia. The merest thought of her caused him to feel sick with anxiety. She held his life in her hands and could bring the wrath of Rhadamistus down on him in an instant.

So far, not one noble, or representative of the kingdom's towns and cities, had entered Artaxata in answer to the king's ultimatum, and there were rumours that rebellion was brewing. If so, then Cato feared that it would take months, if not years, before Rhadamistus was secure on his throne and the Romans would be able to return to Syria. The prospect was daunting and depressing, and Cato's mood was bitter indeed, even as he gazed out on the fields and hills of the surrounding landscape set against the backdrop of the mountains, the peaks of which still glistened with snow.

There was a knock on the door, and Cassius rolled over and pricked his remaining ear up. A moment later Macro entered. 'You'd better come quickly, sir. There's trouble brewing in the town.'

The brothel was located in a large yard. A portico ran along one side, giving out on to the city's main avenue. Opposite was a wine shop with benches and tables set outside, most of which had been overturned and were surrounded by shattered wine jars and clay beakers. On either side of the yard stretched buildings with shabby hangings covering the entrance to cubicles where prostitutes plied their trade. Several bodies lay amid the upturned benches and tables, and others who had been wounded sat or lay nearby, moaning and crying out in pain.

By the time Cato and Macro reached the scene a large crowd of Armenians had gathered in the avenue outside, and there were angry shouts and hostile looks as the two officers at the head of the squad of Praetorians forced their way through the mob and entered the yard. One of the duty patrols was holding the crowd at bay and the optio in charge looked relieved as he saw that his commander had arrived to take charge of the situation.

'What in Hades is going on here?' Cato demanded.

The optio turned and gestured to a group of off-duty Praetorians standing in a corner of the yard. 'That lot are to blame, sir. They came in here, got drinking and kicked up a fight with the locals. Blades were drawn and it got out of hand.' The optio nodded towards the bodies and Cato gritted his teeth at the euphemism.

'I'd say it got more than out of hand, Optio.'

'Yes, sir. I suppose.'

Macro sniffed. 'You suppose? I take it that lot aren't just lying stretched out in all that blood for their health.'

'No, sir.'

Macro put his hands on his hips. 'So what exactly happened?'

The optio rubbed his chin nervously. 'We heard the commotion while I was leading the patrol further along the street, sir. The lads and I came running and when we got here they was all over the place. By the time we'd knocked a few heads together and put a stop to it there were a number of dead and wounded. That's when I sent a man for you.'

Cato looked round and saw several men and heavily made-up women in another corner guarded by two men from the optio's patrol. He felt a weary frustration that once again the tension between his men and those they were supposed to call allies had led to bloodshed.

'So who started it?'

'Once I'd stopped the fighting I questioned the Praetorians, sir. They reckon the owner of this place had cheated them on the wine bill. When they refused to pay he called in his heavies. The owner pulled a knife out. One thing led to another.' The optio shrugged. 'You know how it goes.'

Macro nodded. 'Aye, that's what happens all the time. Bloody easterners try to gouge our lads every chance they get.'

'What did the locals say happened?' asked Cato.

'I tried to find out, sir, but all I could get was their jabbering away. Couldn't get any sense out of them and told them to shut up.'

'You told them to shut up?'

'In a manner of speaking, sir,' the optio agreed uncomfortably. 'They needed a bit of encouragement . . .'

'I see,' Cato said flatly, keeping his temper under control. 'Wait here.'

He strode over to the Armenians and they regarded him warily. 'Any of you speak Greek? Well?'

One of the men half raised his hand. 'Me, sir. Some Greek.'

'What's your name?'

The man's eyes narrowed suspiciously. 'Why?'

'Just tell me your name,' Cato spat impatiently.

'Philadates, sir.'

Cato doubted that was true, but it made no difference. He just needed to give the man some confidence to speak. 'Philadates, tell me what happened?'

The Armenian thought briefly and then began. 'We see Romans here many times now. They drink and use our whores. So far they pay for what they get. But today, these men came. We have not seen them here before. They come early in the day, and drink, and drink. They use the women. Then the owner tells them, you pay me now. They laugh at him, they say they are guests of the king and will not pay. They go to leave and he stops them. Calls his men to help him. One Roman takes his sword and tells him to move. The owner says no, and draws knife.'

'Wait,' Cato interrupted. 'Where is he? Which one of you is the owner?'

'There.' Philadates pointed to a body near the upturned tables. Cato saw a fat man spread-eagled on his back. His throat had been torn open and his tunic was saturated with blood.

'What happened? Who killed him?'

'That man there. Close to portico,' Philadates said warily, not willing to point him out publicly. 'He stabs owner as soon as he sees knife. Then there is fight. And . . .' He gestured to the carnage and destruction in the yard.

Cato nodded. 'Right. Stay where you are.'

He crossed to the far corner where the auxiliaries were waiting and Macro fell into step beside him. 'So what excuse did that one give?'

'He says our lot caused this.'

'He would say that,' Macro sniffed. 'You know what they're like. That incident with Glabius was proof enough.'

Cato did not respond. He fixed his gaze on the man that Philadates had indicated, a lean soldier with a slim face and dark curly hair tied back with a thong. Then he looked over the rest briefly before he addressed them. 'The optio says the locals started the fight. Is that right?'

A few heads nodded and there were murmurs of assent. The lean man made no response, Cato noted, before he continued, with a smile: 'And once they started it, you showed 'em what we're made of, eh lads?'

This time there was more agreement, and no small measure of drunken arrogance that they had taught the locals a lesson.

'The optio tells me that the fat bastard who owns this dump was the first to draw a blade.' Cato shook his head with contempt. 'Doesn't surprise me. That lot would stick a knife in your back as soon as smile at you.'

Macro shifted uneasily beside him and muttered, 'Sir, I don't think—'

Cato ignored him. 'The scum got what was coming to him. I'd do the same in your place, lads.'

The Praetorians smiled openly now, at ease with their commanding officer's attitude. Cato smiled back. 'So who stuck it to him, eh?'

Instinctively some of them glanced towards the thin man, then

311

realising what they had done they cast their eyes down. Cato turned to the guilty party, who gritted his teeth as he shot a look of contempt at his comrades.

'You, step forward.'

The Praetorian heaved a sigh and advanced two paces and stood to attention as well as he could, given his drunken state.

'Name?'

'Titus Borenus. Second Century, sir.'

'Borenus. The locals say you and these others were responsible. They say you refused to pay, and when the owner confronted you, it was you who struck the first blow and killed him.'

'If that's what they say, then they're liars, sir. Like I told the optio, he drew a knife on me. I had to defend myself.'

Cato pointed towards the fat corpse. 'That's him, right?'

'Yes, sir.'

'I can't help noticing that his dagger is still in the scabbard on his belt.'

A brief look of alarm flitted over Borenus's face as Cato continued addressing him.

'So you claim he drew his blade first?'

'Yes, sir.'

'And you stabbed him in the throat in self-defence. At which point he then carefully replaced his dagger in its scabbard before he fell dead. Is that it? . . . Well?'

Borenus opened his mouth to reply, but no words came. He refused to meet Cato's gaze now and cast his eyes down at the ground between them.

'Look at me, damn you!' Cato snapped, and the Praetorian reluctantly obeyed. 'What the fuck do you and these other idiots think you were doing? Have you already forgotten what happened to Glabius? We were sent here by the emperor to win Armenia back to our side. We're supposed to be their allies. We are not their conquerors, we are here to be their friends, whether they like it or not. That means we pay our way and treat them nice. But now you fools have spilled their blood, and they want yours. Listen to them.' Cato gestured to the mob outside in the avenue. 'I've a good mind to throw you out there and let them deal with you.'

312

Now he saw fear in the faces of the Praetorians, and he let it feed on them for a moment longer before he turned to Macro. 'I want this lot to have their hands bound behind their heads, where the crowd can see it. Then we'll march them back to the acropolis and deal with them there.'

'Yes, sir!' Macro saluted and turned to the men. 'I'll have one bootlace from each man. Right now!'

Cato left his friend to deal with it and returned to the optio. 'We're marching back to the acropolis the moment the centurion's done. I want your men closed up tight around the prisoners. I want them protected, but I don't want any more of the locals harmed. Tell your men they are not to strike out, or even strike back, unless I give the order. Is that clear?'

'Yes, sir.'

'Then form them up.'

Cato crossed over to Philadates. 'I believe you told the truth. Those men will be punished, and you will be compensated for the loss of life and damage here. You have my word on it.'

'Your word?' Philadates said mockingly.

'Yes. And I stand behind my word.' Cato nodded a brief farewell and returned to the optio and his men, who were formed up in two lines with a space between for the prisoners, who were shoved in that direction by Macro as he bound each man's hands. When the last of them was in place, Cato and Macro closed up the rear of the small formation.

'Optio, let's get moving.'

The optio nodded and then braced himself to call the orders loudly enough to be heard over the din of the mob outside the yard.

'Shields up! . . . Advance!'

At a steady, measured pace they marched towards the portico and then out into the street. Those closest fell back to give them space but were prevented from giving much ground by those behind, and the optio had to push and shove people aside before his patrol and the prisoners could make any progress. All around was a sea of angry shouting faces and waving fists. Some tried to thrust past the Praetorians to strike the prisoners, who were forced to keep their heads down and take the blows on their shoulders and the hands and

313

arms tied across their necks. Some in the crowd had sticks and beat at the shields as the Romans edged by.

'Don't strike back!' Cato shouted. 'I'll have any man who does flogged!'

They pushed on, struggling through the crowd along the avenue, and now stones and dung were hurled at them as well. Macro swore out loud as a piece of shit struck him on the nose and he reached for his sword. Cato grabbed his arm.

'No! Leave it!'

His friend glared back and growled incoherently as he shook Cato's hand off, and then kept his helmet lowered as they continued forward. Ahead, the crowd began to thin out as they reached the fringe of the screaming mob and then, to Cato's relief, they emerged into the open and quickened their pace as they pulled away. The more ardent of the local people followed them, hurling insults and jeering as they threw the last of their soiled missiles after the Romans. Then, from the direction of the acropolis, he saw more Praetorians trotting towards them and recognised Centurion Ignatius at the head of his men.

'Tribune? Sir?'

'We're here!' Cato raised his hand. 'Have your men keep the crowd away and then follow us back to the acropolis. But make sure no one gets hurt.'

'Yes, sir! My lads can handle them easily enough.'

'I meant make sure none of the locals get hurt.'

'Oh . . . Yes, sir.'

As Ignatius's men formed a shield wall across the avenue, Cato and the others hurried on, relieved to have escaped from the enraged crowd. But Cato's relief quickly faded and turned to anger as he glared at the Praetorians, bloodied and bruised and covered in filth. The tensions that were simmering in the streets of Artaxata had been dangerous enough already. Now he would have to find a way to punish these men that would satisfy the anger of their victims and help repair the damage they had caused.

That evening, as the prisoners languished in a storeroom at the end of the stables, Cato was summoned to the palace to account for what

314

had happened that afternoon. Rhadamistus sat on his throne, leaning slightly forward as he listened to Cato's report. At his side, on a divan, lay Zenobia, playing with a cat as she glanced up occasionally and gave Cato a knowing smile. He did his best to ignore her, and when their eyes did meet fleetingly the familiar chill filled his heart. When Cato had finished, the king sat back and folded his arms.

'What do you intend to do about these men of yours, Tribune?'

'They will be punished, Majesty.'

Rhadamistus cleared his throat. 'I hear that seven of my subjects were killed, and another six were wounded. How many of your men were killed in the incident?'

Cato shifted his weight on to his other foot. 'None, Majesty. And those who were injured received only superficial wounds.'

'None,' Rhadamistus repeated with heavy emphasis.

Cato shrugged. 'My men are trained to fight. The civilians were not.'

'Quite. My people are angered by what happened. And so am I. They want blood for blood. And so do I. We demand justice.'

'There must be justice, Majesty. On that we agree. Justice tempered by consideration of the circumstances that gave rise to this unfortunate incident.'

'As far as I am aware, and your own words confirm it, the circumstances were that your men entered the inn, got drunk, used the women there, refused to pay, and when confronted they drew their swords and butchered several of my subjects. Those are the circumstances, are they not?'

Cato could only nod his assent.

Rhadamistus sighed. 'I understand that you want to defend your men, Tribune. But if I allow them to be spared, then you and I may win your men's approval, but that will outrage my people. However, if I condemn your men then I will win my people's approval, while your soldiers will be angered.' He shook his head. 'It is a problem. But the truth is that in a year's time I will still need the loyalty of my people, while you and your men will almost certainly have left Armenia. I have more to gain by executing these soldiers than if I do not. Don't you agree?'

The question was rhetorical and Cato did not consider it deserved a reply. Instead he posed a question of his own, and delivered it in a tone tinged with contempt: 'Don't you think that you have murdered enough of my men already?'

There was a sudden awful tension in the chamber. Zenobia's hands stilled as she stopped stroking the cat and stared at Cato. The king clenched his jaw, but Cato saw no anger in his expression at first, then he recovered from his shock and rose swiftly to his feet in order to tower over the Roman officer.

'How dare you speak to me in such a manner?'

Cato did not flinch. 'Do you deny it?'

'I am the king of Armenia! I will not be spoken to in such a way by a mere Roman officer. You will go on your knees and beg for my forgiveness.' Rhadamistus stabbed his finger towards the floor directly in front of the dais. 'Kneel!'

'I will not kneel to *you*,' Cato said deliberately.

The king's bodyguards on either side of the dais began to edge forward.

'Then you will pay for it with your head.'

'Before you even consider harming me, you might want to remember that there are nearly a thousand of my men just outside your palace. If you kill me, then I assure you they will kill you and all your followers. It would be better that you sat down and listened to me . . . Majesty.'

The two men glared at each other, and then the king resumed his seat, his face drained of blood as he gritted his teeth. Cato took a moment to steady his nerves and continued to speak calmly.

'I will see to it that the family of the innkeeper is compensated for his death and for the damage to his property. The soldiers responsible will be flogged and their ringleader will receive twice as many blows as the others. The punishment will be carried out in the great market for all to see that justice has been done.'

'Roman justice, you mean,' said Zenobia.

'It is the only justice my men and I will answer to.'

'And if His Majesty refuses, and insists on *his* justice? What then?'

Cato did not answer, and as Rhadamistus stirred he feared that the queen was on the cusp of making the confrontation even more dangerous.

Before anyone could speak again there was the sound of running feet and Narses raced into the room, breathless and agitated.

'Majesty!'

'How dare you interrupt us?' Rhadamistus roared. 'You dog! I'll—'

Narses was anxious enough to speak on. 'It's the nobles, Majesty. They have come. All of them. And their followers.'

At once the king's expression changed and he grinned in triumph. 'I knew it! I knew those cowards would bend the knee and come crawling to me to ask for mercy. Where are they?'

Narses glanced at Cato and his nerve began to fail him. 'Majesty . . . They are approaching the city even now.'

'Then we must meet them. Send for my cavalry commander. Tribune, have your men called to arms.' Rhadamistus clapped his hands together in delight and turned to Zenobia. 'There! It is all just as I said it would be.'

But the queen already sensed the truth as she scrutinised Narses' anxious face.

'You fool,' she muttered. 'They're not coming to surrender to you.'

Rhadamistus looked surprised. 'What do you mean?'

But Zenobia had turned her attention to Narses. 'Tell him. Tell His Majesty.'

Cato saw Narses swallow before he dared speak again. 'Majesty, they are coming. At the head of a host. I fear they have come to destroy you.'

CHAPTER THIRTY-FOUR

From the highest tower of the palace there was a fine view over the capital and beyond to the rolling landscape that surrounded Artaxata. Away to the west, some five miles distant, there was a great haze of dust. Before it advanced a line of horsemen, and every so often the afternoon sun glinted off a helmet as the nobles' army advanced. The leader of the patrol which had spotted the enemy early that morning had been sent for, and now he emerged from the stairs to be questioned by his superiors.

'How many men do they have, Majesty?' asked Cato.

Estimating the size of any enemy force was always a fraught issue, Cato knew. Inexperienced men often vastly overstated the number, and then there was the question of how much of the total force they could see. In hilly landscape, or dusty conditions, judging the size of a marching column was difficult even for experienced eyes. The horse-archer officer standing before him looked very young and his beard scarcely amounted to more than a few tufts of dark hair. He thought for a moment before he responded to his king.

'He says four, maybe five thousand in all. No more than a thousand of those are mounted,' Rhadamistus translated.

'All the same, it's impressive that they managed to gather so many people willing to take up arms,' Cato mused as he shaded his eyes and stared towards the dust cloud as he considered the soldier's report. The rebel nobles had gathered together barely enough men to match the forces at the king's disposal, and Cato had little doubt that Rhadamistus's men and the two cohorts were of better quality than the forces facing them.

'No siege weapons, I take it?' he asked the king.

'He says not.'

Cato frowned. He had to admire the courage of the Armenian nobles in taking on their king with the odds against them. Or were they acting out of desperation rather than courage? After all, most of them were condemned men and their choices were limited. They could wait in their estates or fortified towns to be destroyed one by one, or they could flee Armenia and throw themselves on the mercy of the rulers of neighbouring kingdoms, like Parthia. Instead they had chosen to take the fight to Rhadamistus in the hope that they could crush his army and force him to flee once again, if they could not hunt him down and kill him first. Cato could easily follow the train of thought that had led them to this course of action, desperate as it was.

'They would be foolish to attack the capital without siege weapons, Majesty. I cannot believe they would throw merely themselves at the city's walls. That would be little better than suicide.'

'I agree.' Rhadamistus stroked his chin. 'Then what is their intention, do you think? To offer battle outside the city?'

'Or to surround the city, encircle it with fieldworks and try to starve us into submission.' Cato considered the river flowing around the capital. While it provided Artaxata with water and drainage, the swiftness of the current and the patches of shallows and rocks rendered it impossible to navigate. There would be no chance of relief or resupply from that quarter and so a prolonged siege might well succeed. After all, Caesar had managed to contain a greater force at Alesia, and fight off an even bigger army sent to relieve the Gauls.

'Then we must not give them the opportunity,' Rhadamistus decided. 'We must march out to meet them, and crush them decisively. That will put an end to any thought of rebellion or challenge to my rule. And it will serve your emperor's ends as much as my own, eh?'

'Yes, Majesty.'

'Then we must decide when to strike.' He looked up at the sky. 'It will be dark before they reach the city. It would not be wise to risk attacking under the cover of night.'

Cato nodded with feeling. While a raid or other small-scale

319

operation was possible in darkness, a battle was an action on an altogether greater scale and required clear oversight of unfolding events. Even with well-trained and disciplined men with experience of night-fighting, it was a risky endeavour that resulted in disaster far more often than it delivered success.

'We should bring in the men and horses from the marching camp, Majesty.'

'Abandon the camp? And let those traitors take it?'

'We could defend it, but that may just cost us the lives of the men sent to hold the camp. Even if we hold it, what use will it serve? If we use it for the artillery then the enemy will simply move back out of range before standing their ground. I say we abandon it. It's too far from the city wall to present any threat. It's not worth fighting for. Better we concentrate our forces for the battle, Majesty. If we want the best chance of victory.'

'You think there is any doubt about the outcome?' Rhadamistus laughed. 'Tribune, I expected more from you.' His amusement faded. 'After the way you stood up to me in my audience chamber, I thought you fearless. Maybe I was mistaken.'

Cato refused to respond to the jibe. But there was something to be won from the arrival of the rebel army. 'Your people have a new matter to distract them, Majesty. Their attention will shift to the threat posed by the rebel army that threatens to sack Artaxata. They will look to those who defend them. Now is not the time to punish my soldiers. You have my word that they will be disciplined as severely as the regulations permit, but there is no need for their fate to come between us any more.'

Rhadamistus thought a moment and nodded his agreement. 'Very well. I will put the matter aside, for the present. Who knows? With luck maybe those men will die in the battle as heroes, and save me the trouble of having them executed, eh?'

'Indeed,' Cato responded flatly. 'That would be a solution.'

'Good!' Rhadamistus clapped his hands together. 'Then we must prepare for battle! Ready your Praetorians and slingers. Tomorrow, at dawn, you will march at the head of your men, and I will ride at the head of mine, and together we will crush those dogs. By nightfall, there will be many more heads decorating the walls of my capital!'

the king concluded with a look of cruel satisfaction.

'Yes, Majesty,' Cato responded simply, even as he offered a prayer to the gods that the heads would not be those of himself and his men.

Even before the first glimmer of dawn crept over the mountains to the east, the walls of the city were crowded with civilians keen to get the best vantage point to witness the spectacle of the coming battle. Behind the city gates, and along the length of the avenue beyond, the infantry and cavalry of the king's army formed up and waited for Rhadamistus to emerge from the palace and lead his men out of the city. On the tower of the gatehouse, Cato and Macro looked to the west, where the rebel army was already extended in a line, just over a mile away. Their main strength was a large block of infantry armed with a motley selection of weapons and armour, as far as Cato could make out as he strained his eyes to pick out the detail. On each wing was a body of cavalry, about five hundred strong, horse-archers for the most part, but small groups were armed with lances and wore the scale armour of cataphracts.

'I reckon there's no more than four thousand of 'em, if that.' Macro shook his head. 'And they look more like a village militia than trained soldiers. Got to hand it to them, they have balls to challenge our lot like this.'

'There's also the men in the camp,' Cato cautioned.

'That lot?' Macro chuckled. 'How in Hades do the rebels think that's going to help them? They'd be better off deploying them in the main battle line.'

They switched their gaze to the marching camp, which had been overrun during the night. A handful of the king's horse-archers, who had remained too long, had been surprised as the rebels rushed out of the darkness through the open gates and killed several of the Iberians before the others fled. Now the enemy had invested the camp with a modest force of archers who stood on the ramparts ready to harass any of Rhadamistus's men who ventured out of the city and passed by them. Some of them were keeping watch on the city while the others rested on some of the large piles of feed that had been abandoned when the king had ordered his cavalry to fall back behind the walls of Artaxata. On careful inspection Cato doubted there were more than a hundred archers there. Barely enough to be a nuisance. They would be easily dealt with once the main rebel force was defeated, or even if they were foolhardy enough to attempt to intervene in the battle.

'All the same,' Macro continued, 'I'd prefer they were dealt with before we took on the main rebel force.'

Cato nodded. But there were other considerations: the time it would take to eliminate the men in the camp, and the disproportionate losses that would have to be taken in any assault on the fortification. 'I don't like the idea of leaving them there, but they can be dealt with after we've defeated the others, if they don't surrender first.'

'I suppose so.' Macro regarded the archers for a moment longer before turning his attention back to the distant rebel army. 'Either way, I can't see them coming out of this on top.'

Even allowing for the small force in the camp, Macro's assessment was correct, Cato decided. The rebels barely matched the king's army in number, had less than half the cavalry fielded by Rhadamistus, and had a large proportion of poorly equipped men whose morale might not even endure beyond the first charge by either side. Cato felt pity for them as they stood waiting for Rhadamistus and his army to approach. It was not difficult to imagine the desperate courage of men determined not to be ruled by a king who had already proved himself unfit to reign over Armenia and whose return could not be endured. In truth, his sympathies lay with the rebels and he would rather have been fighting with his men at their side than for the murderous tyrant terrorising the people of Artaxata. But Rome had chosen the side of the tyrant and Cato must do the bidding of the emperor, and the sour taste of bad conscience stuck in his throat.

There was a cheer from the Iberian troops, and Cato and Macro turned to see the king and his entourage trotting down the avenue. Ahead of them the infantry and horsemen moved to the side to let the party pass by. Very few of the people on the wall echoed the cheers. Most looked on in silence and Cato had no doubt that they would be grateful to see the king defeated and killed on the battlefield in front of the city. Their reaction to Rhadamistus was a reminder of Cato's prudence in deciding to leave the gatehouse in the charge of Centurion Nicolis and his men to ensure that the people of Artaxata did not take advantage of the king's brief absence to lock him out.

'Cuts quite a dashing figure, doesn't he?' Macro commented as the king approached the gates. Rhadamistus looked magnificent, Cato conceded. His already impressive physique was swathed in black robes glittering with silver braid. A black cuirass inlaid with a gold star encased his chest and a conical helmet added to his towering height.

'Let's go,' said Cato and led the way down the stairs and out into the street, where the Roman infantry were waiting to one side in a long column stretching back towards the palace. On the other side the Iberians stood by the horses, waiting for the order to mount. The plan was for them to lead the advance, spreading out to cover the infantry before taking up their final position on the flanks. Cato kneeled down beside Cassius, who he had left leashed to a ring bolt close to the gate house, and gave his head a gentle stroke. 'You're going to have to stay here, boy. Can't be having to look after a dog in the middle of a battle. Even a brave one like you, eh?'

Cassius raised his nose and licked Cato's face, and Cato smiled as he wiped his cheek. He turned to one of Centurion Nicolis's men tasked with defending the gate. 'Take care of him until we return.'

'Yes, sir.'

Cato would be leading his men on foot, and he took the helmet held for him by one of Macro's men. He pressed the skullcap down firmly on his head before easing the helmet into position and fastening the straps beneath his chin as he stepped into the street. Cassius gave a keening whine and Cato turned and pointed to the ground. 'Down!'

The dog sat obediently but continued a low whistling noise through his nose. By the time Cato had finished the last adjustments to his helmet and armour, Rhadamistus had reached the open ground beside the nymphaeum and reined in as he gestured towards the clear skies.

'A fine day for battle! The gods are kind to us.'

'I hope they will be, Majesty.'

'Pah, we have two thousand mounted men and over fifteen hundred infantry. All well-trained and armed. They will scatter that rabble like chaff in the wind. Do you always sour your spirit with such thoughts, Tribune?'

Macro clicked his tongue and muttered, 'See? Not just me who thinks that.'

Cato bowed his head apologetically. 'There are some who say I am cursed with a cautious nature, Majesty.'

'Is that so?' Rhadamistus did not try to conceal his amusement. 'I cannot think why. You should be rejoicing, Tribune. Today we will exterminate those traitors who refuse to bend to my will, and who frustrate the interests of Rome. Before the day is out we will have our victory and will celebrate with a feast and the finest wine as we survey the heads we have taken in battle.'

'An alluring prospect indeed, Majesty.'

Rhadamistus pointed in the direction of the enemy. 'I saw that they are already formed up for battle.'

'Yes, Majesty.'

'Then we must not keep them waiting. Open the gates!'

Centurion Nicolis repeated the order to his men and a moment later, with a section of men hauling on the thick ropes fastened to the iron rings on the back of each gate, the heavy timbers rumbled on their giant hinges and the vista of open ground beyond was revealed. At once Rhadamistus spurred his horse forward and cantered through the arch, followed by his men and then the rest of the cavalry as they swung nimbly on to their mounts and raced after the king. The air filled with the din of hoofs on cobbles and the choking swirl of the dust they kicked up. The contingent of Iberian spearmen quick-marched after them. When the last of the spearmen had cleared the gatehouse, Cato nodded to Macro and the latter coughed to clear his lungs and then barked the order to advance, and the order was relayed by the centurions further down the avenue.

With Cato at the head of the colour party, and Macro's men tramping in perfect time just behind them, the Praetorians and auxiliaries emerged from the city and followed the road leading west towards the enemy. The camp was set off to the right, two hundred paces away, and they would pass by at extreme range for the archers lining the nearest rampart. A small band of Iberian horse-archers was dashing across the front of the camp to harass the defenders and kick up dust to obscure the rest of the king's army marching out to do battle. Even so, Cato could see the odd arrow shot high into the air, slowing at the top of its arc before it dipped and plunged swiftly towards the Romans. Most fell short, struck the ground and quivered briefly before taking on the appearance of a slender desert flower. Only one of the Praetorians was hit, halfway down the column, as a shaft pierced his calf and forced him to drop out and sit at the side of the road as a medic raced back from the colour party to treat the wound.

They were soon out of range and had a clear view of the ground ahead. The enemy line stretched across a low rise, and, closer to, Cato could see no sign of any reserve formations behind them. The cavalry, mostly horse-archers, were standing by their mounts on each flank. The right flank extended to a thick belt of reeds that grew along the river, while the left hung on a stretch of open ground. Away to the left, half a mile beyond, was a thin line of fruit trees. Cato saw that there was plenty of space for Rhadamistus's cavalry to sweep round the enemy flank and strike them from the rear and cut off any hope of escape once the Iberian spearmen and Romans had broken through in the centre. As soon as the bulk of the king's cavalry drew close to the enemy they halted and began to deploy in a long line facing the rebels. The spearmen formed up just behind the centre, where Rhadamistus and his bodyguards sat on their mounts. The cover was taken off the new royal standard and a moment later the long silk pennant rippled out lazily in the faint breeze, the morning sun making the red lion design bright and fiery.

Macro quickened his pace to catch up with Cato. 'Looks like Rhadamistus wants his Iberians to win this one on their own, sir.'

'That's fine by me,' Cato replied. 'I'm in no rush for our men to pay a heavy butcher's bill, if that can be avoided.'

Macro sighed. 'Not sure the lads will be happy about standing by and looking on.'

'That's as may be, but this is Rhadamistus's show. If he wants to claim his victory without our help, then that helps him look stronger in his people's eyes, and, more importantly, to the Parthians.'

'And it means that he and his men will get the pickings from the battlefield loot,' Macro responded from a somewhat less strategic perspective.

Cato did not reply as he made a quick estimate of the distance to the spearmen and halted the column. 'Centurion, we'll deploy right and left. Slingers to advance fifty paces ahead of the Praetorians in open order. Send a runner to Centurion Keranus to let him know.'

'Yes, sir.'

As the centuries reached the colour party they deployed to the right and left in turn and turned to face the rear of Rhadamistus's line. They stood four deep, to form a compact body of reserves compared to the extended Iberian battle line. The dust stirred up by the horses and the rear ranks of the spearmen totally obscured the rebels beyond and Cato doubted that he and his men would see much, if anything, of the clash before the enemy inevitably gave ground and then were routed. It would be frustrating not to be able to follow the course of the battle, but that was often the plight of those in the rear echelon, who suffered a degree of anxiety as a result. It could not be helped, Cato knew, but his men were disciplined veterans and unlikely to let their imaginations unsettle them.

When the last of the king's men were in position, the trumpeter close to the king raised his instrument, and blew a series of notes. As the signal died away, a roar ripped from the throats of the Iberian horsemen and the horse-archers galloped ahead all along the line. The cataphracts trotted forward, keeping in close formation and husbanding their mounts' strength for the charge to ensure that they struck as one, at speed, when they crashed into the enemy line once that had been disrupted by the archers. Dust swirled and swiftly a pall hung in the wake of the horsemen and hid them from view, and a moment later the spearmen had followed them into the gloom. The periodic sound of the trumpet and the drumming of hoofs clashed with the muffled drums of the rebels and the occasional dull clatter of weapons along with whinnies from horses and shouted orders.

326

'Going our way, do you think?' asked Macro.

Cato gestured towards the bank of dust stretching beyond them. 'Your guess is as good as mine.'

'Perhaps we should move closer, sir. In case we're needed.'

Before Cato could answer, there was a fresh blast of trumpets, but from some greater distance than the battle raging before them. After a brief pause they were answered from behind and the two officers turned to look back towards the camp. A dull cheer swelled up from that direction and was echoed a moment later from the river and then the direction of the trees away to the left. Figures were already emerging from the treeline: men leading horses, which they mounted and galloped towards the battle. On the other flank, more men spilled out of the reeds and surged towards the Iberian flank.

'It's a fucking trap,' Macro snorted bitterly. 'Clever little bastards, ain't they?'

As Cato looked back towards the camp he saw that the gates had been flung open and a horde of men were heading straight for the rear of the Roman line. Not the handful of archers he had seen earlier, but hundreds of infantry armed with spears and swords.

'Where in Hades did they spring from?' Macro demanded. 'From under the bloody ground?'

'Not quite,' Cato replied in barely concealed despair at the realisation that they had been fooled by the enemy. 'From under piles of straw.'

It was a finely worked trap. Rhadamistus's patrols had been shown the main body of the rebel army, and then under cover of darkness the rest of their men had been marched forward and hidden all round the area where Rhadamistus had been lured into deploying his own army. Any prospect of an easy victory over the rebels had vanished. Now all that was left to Cato and his men was to fight their way out of the trap and get back to the city. Cato could see his men looking anxiously around at the enemy closing in on them from the rear and both flanks. He had to steady their nerves.

And prepare them to fight for their lives.

CHAPTER THIRTY-FIVE

Cato grabbed a deep breath and cupped his hands to his mouth. 'Second Praetorian Cohort will form square! Colours to the centre!'

He allowed a beat for the centurions to prepare and then roared, 'Form square!'

As his officers echoed the order and controlled the manoeuvres of their centuries, Cato's mind was racing to grasp the relevant details of the surrounding ground and the likely disposition of forces, friendly and enemy. Rhadamistus and his men must by now be aware of the trap and Cato had to trust that the king would be trying to escape it as swiftly as the Romans. Already he could see some of the spearmen emerging from the dust, falling back towards the city and the slingers.

Cato felt a surge of panic as he rushed forward. 'Centurion Keranus!'

The auxiliary centurion looked back towards his commander.

'Get your men back! I want them on the rear face of the square! Move!'

As Keranus gave the orders to his men, Cato paused to look round. The city gates were nearly a mile distant and between the Romans and Artaxata stood the camp and the rebel force that had been concealed within. He estimated their number at over a thousand. The force emerging from their concealment in the reeds was roughly twice the size, the same as the cavalry approaching from the opposite flank. The latter were mostly horse-archers, as far as Cato could make out at the present distance. Both flanking forces were angling towards Rhadamistus and his Iberians, Cato realised.

That left him with a dilemma. Should he advance to support the king, or hold his men together and cover the retreat to the city? The battle was already lost, he decided, as he saw yet more spearmen running back towards the Romans, and now the first of the Iberian cavalry. The sight of the fleeing Iberians persuaded Cato towards the latter choice.

While Macro's men formed the rear of the box, two more centuries formed each side. Shortly afterwards Centurion Keranus and the auxiliaries filled the gap at the head of the formation. They were the most lightly armed of Cato's men but he was confident their slingshot would clear a path through any rebels that were to block their retreat to Artaxata. On either side streamed the Iberians. Some had already thrown down their shields and spears and those already beyond the Romans now realised the danger closing in on all sides. Blindly driven by fear, some changed direction and made for the diminishing gaps between the rebel forces. Others slowed and stopped and looked on in anguish. Cato saw an officer jogging towards the box, trying to rally more men to a small band still following him. As he got closer, Cato called out to him, waving his arms to attract the officer's attention. The Iberian looked up and beckoned to his men to join the Romans. As Macro's men moved aside to let them through, Cato saw that the officer was Narses. His sleeve was torn and bloody above his left elbow.

'Where's Rhadamistus?' Cato demanded.

Narses shook his head. 'We got separated when he charged the enemy line. The last time I saw him, he had broken through their centre. I thought we were on the verge of victory. Then there was a signal and the rebels came back at us like wild animals.' He lowered his gaze in shame. 'That's when my horse was piked. I rolled clear and when I came up I got cut. Then I tried to find my way to the rear, saw the men fleeing and tried to stop them.'

'You haven't seen the king since?'

Narses shook his head.

Cato gritted his teeth and then pointed to the slingers. 'Take your men and form up behind the auxiliaries. If the enemy get too close, you'll have to defend the front of the box. Clear?'

'Yes.'

'Then go.'

Cato looked up and saw that the formation was closed up and ready to move. Macro came trotting up.

'I saw that Narses fellow. Does he know what's happened up front?'

'The Iberians have broken. The king was cut off. We've lost.' Cato nodded towards Artaxata. 'That's our only chance. Let's get going.'

Macro shouted the order to move and then began to call the time to keep the men in pace as the box pulled back towards the city. Ahead of them the rebels from the camp had formed a rough line and their leaders were stirring them up into a frenzy as they brandished their weapons and their battle cries filled the air. More Iberians fled past the Romans, some on foot, but many were mounted, and a chorus of jeers rose from the Praetorian ranks.

'Shut your fucking mouths!' Macro screamed at them. 'I can't hear myself think if you bastards mouth off! Shut up!'

Chastened, the soldiers fell silent again and Macro resumed calling the pace in a steady parade-ground voice.

Centurion Keranus came up to Cato as he marched along beside the colour party. 'Do you want me to try some shot at the rebels ahead of us, sir?'

Gauging the distance between the box and the enemy line waiting for them Cato saw that the range was long. He wanted to save the full impact of the slingers until they were close enough to unleash a devastating series of volleys.

'No, wait for my order. But when I give it, I want your lads casting shot as quickly as they can.'

Keranus managed a grim smile. 'They'll do their job, sir.'

'If they don't then you're all on fatigues for a month.'

They exchanged a quick grin and the auxiliary centurion hurried back to his men as the box trudged closer to the city. The king's men fleeing the battle were now streaming across the open ground as the rebels came in from the flanks, desperate to run them down before they could escape. The first of the rebels from their original battle line were emerging warily from the dust, and as soon as they could see their enemy routed before them they let out a triumphant

330

cry and rushed forward. Amongst them were individual Iberian horse-archers and cataphracts, and some small groups, trying to cut their way free.

Cato ran to join Centurion Keranus and Narses and saw that the rebels between them and the city were edging forward now, as they built up their courage to charge. Although Cato heard no order given, a roar swelled up and the enemy rushed ahead. The archers held back and let their shafts fly in a high arc, over the heads of their comrades. Cato shouted a warning but most of the arrows fell short as the range was long. Only a handful reached the head of the Roman formation, lodging in the shields of the Praetorians on the side of the box and striking two of the slingers. One was pierced through the collar bone and the barb tore down into his vitals. He staggered a few steps and then slumped to his knees before rolling on to his side and writhing as he bled out. The other was struck in the shoulder and he fell back and called for one of the medics.

There was time for one more ragged volley that wounded three more of the auxiliaries and then the charge was too close for the archers to risk any more arrows. At fifty paces' distance Cato ordered the formation to halt and turned to Keranus. 'Your turn.'

'Third Balearic! Ready slings!'

The men expertly slipped lead shot into their pouches, then the front rank stepped forward two paces and began to swirl the cords round and then up over their heads.

'Loose!' shouted Keranus.

Even as the lethal missiles whipped over the open ground towards the rebels, the front rank of the slingers slipped back to the rear, while the next rank stepped forward and unleashed their volley just as the first smashed into the oncoming enemy. Although Cato had seen slingers in action before, he was still impressed by the impact of the simple-looking weapon. While it was easy to see javelins and arrows, slingshot were almost invisible and that added to the terror of their effect. At least a score of the rebels stopped dead in their tracks, as if they had run into a wall, as the lethal shot ripped through flesh and crushed bone. Rebels tumbled to the ground and those behind tripped over them, and the leading ranks were in immediate disarray. Those not facing the slingers charged on heedless of the slaughter of their comrades and raced towards the Praetorians on either side of the box.

Cato allowed the slingers to shoot several more quick volleys and saw that the path ahead was clear of any enemies still standing, although the ground was covered with the bodies of the dead and wounded cut down by slingshot. He quickly ordered Narses to move his spearmen in front of the slingers and then called out the order:

'Formation! Advance!'

With Macro again calling the time the box edged forward as the first of the rebels reached the flanking centuries and a running skirmish enveloped the Praetorians. At the front of the box the Iberian spearmen began to stab the rebels wounded by slingshot, sparing no one, despite their pitiful cries for mercy. The slingers, then Cato and Keranus, made their way over the bodies and blood-splattered ground. The slingers now stooped to picking up rocks and weapons and hurling them over the heads of the Praetorians into the enemy massed on each side.

The formation was slowing as the men fought off their attackers and Cato looked ahead to gauge the distance to the city gates. They were still open and he could see Centurion Nicolis and his men formed up across the entrance. It was too soon, Cato raged. The box was not close enough to the city for the gates to be opened for them yet. Nicolis was just offering the enemy a tempting target. And already the rebel archers had turned on them and had started to loose arrows. A dark shape dashed from between Nicolis's men and darted between the rebels before disappearing from sight and Cato cursed the man who was supposed to be looking after his dog. But there was no time to spare Cassius any further thought.

'Sir, look there, the king!' Macro had thrust his arm out and pointed in the direction of the battle. The dust still swirled and there were many figures visible in vague outlines, some still fighting. A party of riders had emerged from the gloom and Cato saw the towering figure of Rhadamistus amid several of his bodyguards. The standard was not with them. As soon as they sighted the box they galloped towards it. Macro called for his men to let them pass, and they stood aside briefly as the horses thundered by, and then closed ranks. Cato hurried over to the king and saw patches of blood glistening on the black of his robes and armour, and smeared on the flanks of his horse. Some of his companions were wounded and one was hunched over his saddle horns as blood dripped from his fingertips.

'Majesty! Are you injured?'

Rhadamistus looked dazed, then glanced down at his robes and felt his limbs and chest and shook his head. 'No . . . Nothing.'

Cato could not help wondering if the gods were saving the reckless king for some purpose, so charmed was his life.

Rhadamistus looked round, taking in the situation now that he was in no immediate danger. 'What are you doing, Tribune? Why are your men retreating? Turn them about and charge the enemy.'

'Majesty, the battle is lost. It was a trap, the enemy outnumbers us. We must save what we can. And fight another day,' he added to help reassure his ally.

'No. We must strike now, while we can sway the battle in our favour.'

'The battle is lost,' Cato said firmly. 'It was lost before it began. Stay here, with us.'

He turned to the men guarding the standards. 'Take their reins. Don't let them leave the box.'

Cato moved off before the king could protest at his orders and saw more of the enemy closing in on them from the flanks and the rear. Soon they would have exhausted their bloodlust on the Iberians and would move in for the kill against the Romans. The city was over half a mile away, and Cato feared that his men would not make it. They might not even make it as far as the abandoned camp if the rebels managed to arrive in sufficient numbers to surround them and halt their progress. Already a number of wounded Praetorians had fallen out of position and were being helped along by the medics inside the formation, but soon, Cato knew, they would be forced to leave the wounded behind.

He quickly gauged the distances and the slowing pace of the box and made his decision. The camp offered the nearest protection and they could take shelter there and then attempt a breakout towards the city when it was dark. If they attempted to reach the gates now, there was a good chance that they would never make it. He made his way to Macro to quickly explain his plan, in case he was struck down and needed his friend to see it through.

'The camp?' Macro looked doubtful. 'There'll only be a ditch and a rampart between us and them.'

'Better defences than we have now.'

'True.' Macro sucked a breath through his teeth as he considered the situation. 'You're right. Best chance we have.'

Cato clapped him on the shoulder. 'Be ready for it when I give the order.'

'Yes, sir.'

The formation continued slowly along the road as more and more of the rebels closed in and forced them to fight every step of the way. Over at the city gates the archers and a swarm of mounted men had forced Centurion Nicolis back inside the capital and, as Cato watched, the gates were closed. The sight caused a moment's despair, then relief. At least the gates were safe and the centurion had not risked his men in some foolhardy attempt to hold the route open. There was certainly only the slimmest chance for Cato and his men to cut their way through to the city. The camp was much closer now, the nearest entrance no more than a hundred paces away. As yet the enemy did not appear to have realised the opportunity it presented to the Romans. It would be difficult and time-consuming to attempt to pivot the formation, Cato realised, and he decided the solution would be to continue the advance, then halt opposite the entrance and simply lead with the left-hand centuries and continue to advance at a right angle.

The horsemen who had driven Nicolis and his Praetorians back into the city were now approaching the Iberian spearmen at a canter, in front of a mass of infantry. The slingers flung their shots over the heads of the spearmen into the attackers, striking down more of the enemy. Timing the moment as best he could, Cato ordered a halt and then a change of face as the men on the perimeter held their shields up in a continuous wall and stabbed at the rebels attempting to hack their way through. As soon as the formation was ready he gave the order to move again and the box edged towards the camp.

At first the change in direction confused the enemy and there was alarm from those facing the two centuries that now formed the front and thrust the rebels back. Those closest to the Romans backed away but were caught by the ranks compacting behind them and presented easy targets for the Praetorians' thrusting spears tearing at their exposed flesh. Cries of fear and panic rose up and the first of the enemy turned from the rear of the press and edged back and then began to run. It was not a rout. Most still fought on, but the box was able to press a steady pace. By now Cato could see that the rebels around them numbered in their thousands and it was clear that any attempt to make for the city would have ended in failure and massacre.

They were almost at the ramp over the outer ditch and the next part of the manoeuvre was going to be difficult, as so much hung on the situation inside the camp. Cato crossed over to Centurion Ignatius and indicated the camp entrance.

'When we get close, you break off with your men, go through the gate and then secure the other entrances. Don't stop to deal with any of the enemy you find inside. Just take and hold the other gates.'

'Yes, sir.'

As soon as the rebels realised they were caught between the advancing Romans and the ditch, a fresh panic ensued as men tumbled down the steep incline and some were impaled on the short sharpened stakes that had been driven in at an angle to hamper the progress of any attackers. Cato halted the box at the edge of the ditch and gave the order to Ignatius. At once the centurion called on his century and they charged over the ramp, through the open gates, letting out a loud war-cry to unnerve any rebels still inside.

'Keranus!' Cato called to the auxiliary commander. 'Your men next. Get them on the rampart and have them shoot at will.'

'Yes, sir!'

As soon as the slingers had entered the camp, and then Rhadamistus and his bodyguards, Cato began to feed more men across the ramp, taking every fifth man out of the line as he went round the rest of the formation, so that it shrank progressively until only Cato, Macro and fifty men remained, closed up around the end of the ramp. Behind and above them, the slingers were laying down a barrage of shot into the rebels pressing hard against the Romans still outside the camp. It was impossible to miss such a target at that range, and Cato saw rebels constantly being struck in the head, or on the limbs holding their weapons high, as blood sprayed over those around them.

He tapped a man on the shoulder. 'You. Fall back. Over the ramp!'

The Praetorian thrust his shield forward, then stepped back, and the men on either side closed up and the tiny perimeter shrank a little bit more. Cato continued pulling them out one man at a time until there were just enough left to hold the end of the ramp, four men either side of Macro.

'Centurion! When I give the order, you and your men turn and run for it.'

'Don't keep us waiting,' Macro called out, not daring to look back.

Cato ran across the ramp and into the camp. A quick glance round the interior showed that his men were in command of the defences. The remaining gates were closed and sections of slingers lined the ramparts to keep up a steady barrage on the enemy beyond. He turned to the soldiers beside the gate.

'I want that shut as soon as the last of our men are across the ramp.'

The Praetorians nodded, and three picked up the locking bar and stood ready. Cato turned to see the rear of the Praetorians as they braced their studded boots and leaned into their shields as they were pressed back.

'Macro! Now!'

'Go, lads!' Macro bellowed and then lunged forward, slashing wildly with his sword to drive the enemy off. Then he turned and bolted after his men. The slingers above the gate unleashed a fresh hail of shot to cover the centurion, and several more of the enemy went down. Then, from the swirling ranks of the rebels, someone hurled an axe. It spun end over end as it flew after Macro and the blunt head struck him on the back of his helmet. He staggered on two steps and then collapsed on the ramp, halfway to the gate, and lay still.

CHAPTER THIRTY-SIX

Cato was running forward even as Macro went face down on the ground. There was no thought of the responsibility to his other men, or the need for a commander to accept one loss for the greater good. All he saw was Macro sprawled and vulnerable, and the first of the rebels surging forward, mouths agape with triumphant roars as they raised their weapons to kill the Roman centurion. Cato's sword scraped from its scabbard as he charged the few paces it took to reach his friend and stood over his body, teeth gritted and lips drawn back in a snarl as he squared up to the enemy and prepared to defend Macro.

The first of the rebels came at him with a levelled spear, desperate to claim the honour of killing a senior Roman officer. Cato cut down on the broad iron spearhead with a ringing blow and knocked it to the side. Then he snatched at the shaft with his spare hand and grabbed hold and wrenched it towards him, pulling the rebel off balance just as he slashed at the man with a savage back-handed cut that laid open his face from cheek to cheek in an explosion of blood, bone fragments and teeth. The rebel released his grip and reached his hands to his face as he staggered to the side of the ramp and fell into the ditch.

Two more men ran up, armed with long curved swords and shields. Cato knew that he could not keep them both at bay. As the first feinted and Cato moved to block the blow, the other moved against his exposed flank, sword raised to strike. But before he could make the blow, he let out a cry of surprise and pain as Cassius burst through the rebels behind and clamped his jaws around the man's ankle, pulling him off balance. The rebel fell back, almost on top of

337

the dog, who released his jaws and leaped to the side, then turned quickly as he crouched beside his master, hackles raised and teeth bared in a ferocious snarl that caused the rebels to hesitate for one brief, decisive instant that saved the lives of Cato and Macro.

'Move, sir!' a voice cried out and Cato was roughly shouldered aside as a Praetorian took position just ahead of him, shield to the enemy and sword raised. Another man joined them, just as more rebels came forward, swinging curved swords at the Roman shields. Cato reached down to grasp Macro's harness with his spare hand and tried to drag him towards the gate.

'Damn you for being so bloody heavy,' he grunted as he heaved and only managed to lurch a short distance. Cassius gave one last growl and padded after his master.

Two more Praetorians came rushing forward. The first joined the two men fighting the rebels, while the other sheathed his blade and grabbed Macro's arm. 'Pull, sir!'

Working with the other man, Cato managed to draw Macro's inert body the remaining distance across the ramp and into the camp. Then he let go and called out to the three men still covering the rescue. 'Fall back!'

They did not need any further encouragement and retreated from the enemy, cutting and thrusting as they went. As they passed under the sentry walk above the gate, the slingers dispatched a volley into the faces of the rebels and struck down the nearest men. An instant later the Praetorians stumbled into the camp and their comrades closed the gates and thrust the locking bar into its brackets as the first of the enemy crashed against the timbers.

'Shoulders to the gate!' Cato ordered, pressing himself against the bar to keep it in place as the iron hinges began to protest. From the other side he could hear the grunted efforts of the rebels and dust shook from the gate as they struck at the outside in frustration. He could hear the continuing cracks and clatter as the lead shot crashed against helmets and armour. The enemy took the punishment for a little longer before their losses unnerved them and they fell back across the ramp and retreated to whatever scant cover they could find to shelter from the slingers.

Cato eased himself away from the gate and hurried across to

Macro, who had been turned on to his back as a medic squatted beside him and looked over him for signs of wounds.

'There are a few cuts and scratches but I can't see anything else.'

'He was hit on the helmet, from behind,' Cato recounted as he undid the straps and eased the helmet and skullcap off Macro's matted hair. He saw a shallow dent in the back of the helmet and showed it to the medic. 'There.'

Macro's eyes fluttered and he let out a low moan. Then his head rolled to the side and he vomited. The medic eased him over to prevent him from choking and wrinkled his nose at the acrid stink. 'Proves he's alive at least.'

Cassius came over and eagerly sniffed the vomit, and with a feeling of disgust Cato thrust him away before the dog was tempted to lap it up. Cato turned to the medic.

'Look after the centurion, and keep an eye on my dog,' he ordered and then stood and clambered up on to the sentry walk. The sounds of battle had all but ceased, and as he surveyed the ground surrounding the camp he saw that the rebels had pulled back from the ditch. Keranus gave the order to his men to lower their slings and conserve their ammunition. The enemy's archers had also ceased shooting and retreated out of range. The only movement on the ground immediately to Cato's front came from the injured amongst the bodies strewn about the route the Praetorians had taken as they fell back. Most of them were rebels, but there were many Romans and Iberian spearmen out there as well and Cato spared them a moment's pity; there was nothing he could do to help them. They were fated to be finished off by the enemy when they began to pick over the battlefield looting the bodies. More dead were scattered over a far wider area and these, Cato knew, were mainly the victims of the routed Iberian forces. In the distance, a rough band of corpses marked the original battle line, up to the point where the trap had been revealed.

He sighed and found that his limbs were aching slightly after the intensity of combat, and it took a moment before his mind had calmed enough to think carefully about the situation he and his men were now in. A quick look over the interior of the camp revealed that most of the men of the two cohorts had survived. Besides them the only Iberians remaining were the survivors of the contingent of spearmen and Rhadamistus and his bodyguards, no more than thirty men in all. Together with the three hundred Praetorians and just over two hundred slingers, that was not enough to defend the ramparts of the camp if the enemy decided to mount an attack from all sides simultaneously. Of course, there was also the handful of men still under Centurion Nicolis, Cato reflected, glancing towards the city. Then he saw that the gates were open and a party of mounted rebels casually entered under the arched entrance. He felt his spirits sink at the sight. Nicolis and his century must have been betrayed from within the city and now Artaxata was in the rebels' hands. There was no hope for the survivors now. They were trapped, outnumbered and cut off from the refuge of the acropolis in the city. There was no hope of being relieved either – the nearest Roman troops were hundreds of miles away. They were without no food, and only had the water carried in canteens. All was lost, he realised bitterly.

Cato turned away and sat down on the rampart overlooking the inside of the camp. Close by were the scattered remains of the feed piles where the enemy had been concealed. The sight wounded his professional pride. He should have guessed something was awry when he and Macro had scrutinised the camp from the walls earlier that morning. That already seemed like a long time ago, Cato thought. But there was no time for such indulgent self-recrimination, he told himself. He had to come up with a plan, any plan. His men expected it of him. Looking over the camp he quickly decided that there was no chance of defending the entire perimeter. They would have to construct some kind of redoubt in one corner, but the only tools to hand were their weapons. Their picks and shovels were with the wagons and siege weapons in the palace stables. All of which had fallen into enemy hands.

Cato considered their few remaining options. They could defend the camp until the enemy inevitably found a way over the ramparts and swamped them, or, if the rebels were wise, they would wait until thirst and hunger drove the defenders into submission. There was another possibility Cato considered. He and the others could attempt to break out and fight their way back to the frontier. The futility of the idea made him shake his head mockingly. In the end, it came down to surrender or fighting to the death. With the stark clarity of those choices ringing in his mind he returned to Macro and found his friend sitting propped up against one of the posts supporting the sentry walk. The medic had left him there while he attended to the other wounded. Cato undid the straps beneath his chin, took off his helmet and stretched his shoulders before squatting down on his haunches.

'How are you feeling?'

'Bloody awful,' Macro winced. 'Head feels like it's a blacksmith's anvil. Your bloody hound keeps licking my face, and everything's spinning and . . .' He bent and retched.

'You had a bad blow to the head, brother,' said Cato. 'What do you expect?'

Macro wiped his mouth on the back of his hand and then reached round cautiously and flinched as his fingers encountered a lump the size of a hen's egg. 'It's always the bastard behind you that knocks you down.'

He shut his eyes a moment and continued. 'What's the situation, lad?'

Cato shook his head. 'This time, we're truly fucked. There is no way out. We either die in here or we give up.'

'Surrender? No bloody chance. After what our Iberian friend's done to the locals they'll want our heads along with his. I'd rather take my chances and die with a sword in my hand.'

'What chances?' asked Cato. 'We're done for either way. In any case, you're in no shape to fight now.'

'No?' Macro grumbled. He thrust himself up and on to his feet, then stood a moment swaying, before he slumped against the post and slid back down on to the ground with a frustrated groan. 'Fuck . . . Fuck . . . Fuckity-fuck.'

'Quite,' Cato agreed with feeling. He wanted to offer his friend some words of comfort, but there were none. It was tempting to sit down beside Macro and give in to circumstances, but that was a luxury no commanding officer had a right to indulge. He must look after the men as best he could until the very end. Only then would his duty to them be fulfilled.

'Stay here, Macro, until you're fit to fight. That's an order.'

Cato reached up and mopped a lock of perspiration-drenched hair away from his forehead before he replaced the sodden skullcap and then his helmet. Then striding off he called out:

'Officers! On me!'

Having ordered the optios to provide strength returns and assigned each centurion a stretch of rampart to defend with his men and apprised them of his gloomy conclusions about their situation, Cato made his way over to where Rhadamistus was sitting on a pile of straw a short distance from the remainder of his men. His sleeve had been cut away and a dressing tied about his arm. His expression was bleak as he looked up at the Roman officer and then he forced a smile.

'I would imagine that the brevity of my reign will win me a special place in history, eh?'

Cato smiled back. 'More than likely.'

The king's smile faltered. 'There is no hope then?'

'None that I can see, Majesty.'

'Majesty?' Rhadamistus shrugged. 'Some king I turned out to be. If Zenobia could see me now she would surely sneer.'

Cato doubted it. Even if Zenobia had not been captured yet, she would be dreading her own fate at the hands of the rebels.

'What happens to me now, Tribune?'

Cato felt a stab of contempt. Where was Rhadamistus's compassion for the men he had led into a trap, the men whose bodies lay scattered over the ground before the capital, or those others still living, being hunted down by the rebels? Where was his concern for Cato and his Praetorians, compelled to follow him to defeat? He cared for none but himself, and Zenobia. This was not a man who should be king, Cato judged. Rome had chosen the wrong ally. He tried to clear his mind of such considerations as he made his reply: 'You can try to escape. You have a fine horse, but if I were a betting man I would not give good odds on outrunning your enemies. But if you stay here, your choice is the same as the rest of us. Surrender, or fight to the end. Some might argue that an honourable king would choose the latter.'

342

Rhadamistus considered this for a moment. 'And what do you advise?'

'It's not my place to advise you in such matters. The choice is yours alone.'

'I see.' Rhadamistus fixed Cato with a searching stare. 'You've never really admired me, have you?'

'Admired?' Cato was unprepared for the observation. Until now he had lived in fear of what this man might do to him and others, on a whim, or as a result of some cynical calculation. 'You have some admirable qualities, sure enough. You have courage. And strength, and that is enough to inspire others to follow you . . .'

'But?'

'But you are a man who is prepared to use treachery and murder to get his way. The lives of others carry no weight in your choices. You are also cruel and foolish. And you are a man who is guided by one even more self-serving than you.'

'Zenobia?'

Cato nodded. 'For all that, I pity you. But not as much as I pity all those who have had to suffer because you are the man you are.' He paused. 'I have a son. A little boy, who I may never see again, thanks to you. And there are many amongst my men who will leave widows and orphans because of you.' It was a relief to unburden himself of all these thoughts; a cold pleasure to present the naked truth to a powerful man wreathed in the conviction of his own infallibility and the flattery of servants, until defeat had stripped him of all his finery and high self-regard. At the end he was merely a man after all.

Rhadamistus frowned. 'You dislike me, Tribune.'

Even now, he lacked the awareness to see the bare truth, Cato realised, and he laughed bitterly.

'What is so funny?' Rhadamistus demanded.

'You are, Majesty,' Cato said simply. 'You are beyond even pity. Dislike is too feeble a word for all that I feel about you.'

They stared at each other a moment, and Cato could see anger vying with reason in the other man's expression. At one point he was sure that Rhadamistus was about to spring up and try to strike him down in rage. But before that could happen, a cry went up from the sentry walk above the gate.

343

'Sir! Tribune Cato!' Centurion Keranus was waving to attract his attention. 'There's something happening. Over at the city gate.'

Cato was grateful for a chance to turn away from the king and hurry over to the rampart and climb up to join Keranus and the slingers spread out either side of him. A compact group of horse-archers had emerged from the gate and were approaching the marching camp. At their head rode two men. One raised a horn and began to blow a series of notes, while the other was dressed in a nobleman's robes and wore a breastplate and helmet. Beyond the wall a column of smoke was rising into the sky in the direction of the royal palace.

'Want me to give them a little encouragement to turn round and run back into the city?' asked Keranus.

'No. Let's hear what they have to say. At least it will buy us some time.'

The party approached to within a hundred paces before they halted and the two riders continued towards the ramp and stopped. The noble looked up at Cato and addressed him in Greek. 'Are you the Roman officer in command?'

'I am. What do you want?'

The noble smiled slightly. 'I have been sent by the high council of Armenian nobles to demand your surrender.'

For a moment Cato was tempted to brazen it out. 'What are your terms?'

'Very favourable, I think you will find. We will allow you and your men to leave the camp, and return to Syria unmolested. Armenia has no quarrel with Rome. We merely seek to govern our own affairs, without interference from Rome, or Parthia. We regard Rome as a friend of Armenia.'

'Friends don't kill each other.'

'Nor do friends impose tyrants on each other.' The nobleman's smile faded. 'Your emperor made a grave error when he attempted to force Rhadamistus on us once again. The Iberian is a foreign usurper, and we will not tolerate him. Any more than we will tolerate another ruler imposed by Parthia. If the gods were to grant us justice then we would take Rhadamistus into the great market of Artaxata and visit every cruel torment on him that he has used on his victims and grant him as slow a death as many have endured at his hands. However, our proposal does not permit us to dispose of the tyrant.'

'Oh? Why not?'

'Our rebellion is supported by Iberian gold and Iberian weapons. In exchange, King Pharasmanes has also offered us a ransom for the safe return of his son. He has sworn to us that Rhadamistus will never be allowed to enter Armenia again.'

Cato struggled to control his reaction to the news. This was a strange turn of events indeed. What game was the king of Iberia playing? Why would he offer to help the rebels topple his son when it was through his support that Rhadamistus had become king in the first place? He drew a breath.

'What precisely is your proposal?'

'You will surrender the camp, and Rhadamistus and any of his men, to us at once. Your men will lay down their arms and be our prisoners until you, and an escort of Roman soldiers, convey Rhadamistus to the frontier and hand him over to the Iberian governor of the town of Iskerbalis. When you return, the rest of your men will be released. Your weapons will be returned and then you will march back to Syria, taking with you a letter for your emperor stating that we will remain allies of Rome. The actions of the last few months notwithstanding. Are the terms clear to you?'

'Why are my men needed to escort Rhadamistus to Iberia? You could do that yourselves. You don't need us.'

'King Pharasmanes does not trust us to hand his son over alive. A Roman escort is his guarantee of safety.'

'I see.' Cato nodded. 'And how do you know that I would not take Rhadamistus to Syria so that a fresh attempt can be made to place him on the throne of Armenia?'

'Roman, I trust you even less than the king of Iberia trusts us. That is why we will hold your men hostage until you return from delivering Rhadamistus. If you fail in that task, for any reason, then we will kill your men. Those in the camp with you, and these we captured in the city.' He turned and shouted a command. The horsemen moved aside to reveal a group of men in the tunics of Praetorians. They had been stripped of their shields, weapons and

345

armour. There was one other figure with them, a woman, and Cato knew at once who she must be. The horsemen gestured to the prisoners and motioned towards the camp. The prisoners moved forward warily.

'These men, and the queen, we return to you as a sign of our good faith,' the nobleman continued. He glanced up and shaded his eyes. 'I give you until noon to agree to our terms. If you do not, then we will wait and let thirst weaken you. When the moment is ripe, we will enter the camp and kill anything still alive within, except Rhadamistus. Until noon, Roman.' He bowed his head, turned his mount away and trotted back towards the city, passing the prisoners as they hurried by in the other direction. Cato waited until he could clearly recognise Nicolis and some of the others to make sure this was not a trick. Then he turned away and saw Rhadamistus standing halfway up the rampart staring at him.

'I assume you heard it all?' Cato said.

'I did . . .' Rhadamistus cleared his throat. 'And what will you decide to do about their proposal?'

Cato drew himself up and looked down at the other man. 'I have already decided.'

CHAPTER THIRTY-SEVEN

A month later Cato was sitting in the garden of the governor's villa in Iskerbalis, a town just beyond the frontier with Iberia, where he and the others had been held for the previous twelve days. The section of Praetorians he had brought with him were playing dice in the shade of a cedar tree in the corner of the garden. It was a hot summer's day and the air was still and stifling, and he would have preferred to be out riding or walking in the hills that surrounded the town or swimming in the cool waters of the river that flowed past its walls and which marked the boundary between Armenia and Iberia. However, the governor was under firm orders to ensure that his guests, as he addressed them, were to remain in the villa under close guard. They were treated well enough, with ample food and drink and comfortable living quarters, but the entrances were locked and they resorted to making their own amusements within the walls of the villa, while the sounds of the streets beyond served only to remind them of their confinement. It was as well that Cato had left Cassius in Artaxata; the dog would have hated being cooped up and would surely have outworn the governor's hospitality very swiftly.

Cato made a routine of exercising and drilling his men each morning before dismissing them and heading to the villa's bathhouse, where he enjoyed the steam room before plunging into the small pool that was refreshed daily from the river, which fed off mountain streams, and so the water was delightfully cold. After that he walked round the courtyard garden until noon, when the governor was pleased to invite him up to the roof terrace for a light meal and amiable conversation about Cato's experiences of travel and conflict across the Empire. The governor was a friendly-seeming man with an appetite for knowledge of the wider world and he had a library, modest by Roman standards, in a room leading off the terrace. Most of the manuscripts were written in languages Cato had not seen, but there were enough works in Greek for him to while away the hours until the evening meal. This was the least pleasurable part of the day, as the governor insisted on entertaining Rhadamistus and Zenobia along with Cato, and the exchanges were often stilted, except for the spells when the Iberian prince's optimism fed his ambition and he talked of his plans for future conquests, the moment his father saw fit to furnish him with fresh soldiers. All the while the governor listened politely and even seemed amused at the hubris of Rhadamistus from time to time. Cato, by contrast, affected to ignore the prince and refused to get drawn into any protracted conversation with him, or Zenobia. Especially as there was already a palpable tension between the erstwhile king and queen of Armenia, following his humbling defeat.

As the days passed and his frustration at inaction increased, his thoughts turned to the unavoidable prospect of reporting to General Corbulo when the column returned to Syria having failed to carry out its mission. Rhadamistus's short reign was over and Armenia was ruled by a council of noblemen for the present. Cato could not see that enduring for long. Neither Rome nor Parthia would tolerate a neutral Armenia. Control of the hapless kingdom was all that would satisfy either great power. That Tiridates had been driven out, along with his Parthians, would be scant comfort, and the Armenian offer of de facto neutrality would be taken as a setback when word reached Rome. And then there was the matter of the loss of the baggage wagons and the siege weapons. At least they had been denied to any potential enemies, Cato reflected with some small satisfaction. As soon as he had seen that the battle was lost, Centurion Nicolis had taken the initiative, withdrawn his men from the gate and rushed back to the palace to set fire to the baggage train and siege equipment. All had been destroyed, along with much of the palace, once the flames spread, before Nicolis was forced to surrender.

Macro had been left in command of the remaining troops, and

the rebels had assured Cato that they would be well looked after until his return. Even so Cato dreaded that they would not honour their promise to treat their hostages fairly. Especially as they had taken all the Iberian soldiers to one side after the surrender, and then shot them down with arrows. Only Rhadamistus and Zenobia had been spared, since that was all that was required of the rebels to comply with the deal they had struck with the king of Iberia. The day after, Cato, his escort, and the deposed king and queen rode out of Artaxata and took the trade route to the border and the city of Iskerbalis. There was no need to guard against escape since Rhadamistus was eagerly anticipating his return to Iberia and the opportunity to pursue fresh dreams of power. The greater danger came from the Armenians as they journeyed through the land, and Cato did his best to avoid towns and large villages where he and his men might be overwhelmed by angry mobs stirred up by memories of Rhadamistus's first reign. In truth, he had grown sick of the sight of the man, and his scheming wife, and could not wait for the chance to leave the governor's villa and return to Artaxata.

His one immediate cause of anxiety was the refusal of his host to permit the Romans to leave until the king of Iberia gave his permission. The king, Cato was told, had been sent a message announcing that his son had reached Iskerbalis safely and a royal courier had galloped back to inform the governor that His Majesty was coming to meet his son in person. Which raised the question, why did he simply not send for his son instead? Nor was it just Cato to whom this question occurred. At the cordial evening meals Rhadamistus raised it from time to time, only to be politely deflected by the governor, who insisted he was merely obeying instructions and had no insight into the king's reasoning.

On this fine morning, a month after the defeat outside Artaxata, Cato was stretched out on a couch in the warmth and had closed his eyes to doze briefly when he sensed a shadow had fallen across his face. He blinked his eyes open and saw Zenobia looking down at him, her expression cold and calculating for an instant before it was masked by the sweet smile that Cato was now certain she used on any man she wished to manipulate into serving her purposes.

349

'A fine morning, Tribune Cato,' she said sweetly.

He swung his legs over the edge of the couch and sat up, regarding her warily. 'It was, until a moment ago.'

She affected a hurt look. 'I hardly think such an ill-mannered comment is justified.'

'Look here, I am tired of your games, and you cannot play me as you do your husband.'

'Is that so? I seem to recall that I managed to persuade you to bring me into your tent . . . and your bed.'

Cato frowned. 'That was a mistake. I shan't make it again.'

He glanced round.

'If you are looking for my king, he is still asleep, or was, when I left him but a moment ago. I know how to exhaust a man.' She shot him a coquettish look before she continued. 'So we can talk in peace.'

'I have nothing to say to you.'

Without waiting for an invitation, she sat down beside him and covered his hand with hers. Cato shook it off angrily. 'Enough!'

'Very well.' Her expression hardened. 'I will not play any games with you for the moment. But I must ask your opinion on something. Speak freely or not, as you will.'

Cato's chest heaved in a bitter sigh. 'What is it?'

Zenobia folded her hands in her lap and thought a moment before she spoke in a low voice. 'I do not understand why we are being held here. What reason could Pharasmanes have for keeping us waiting? Why not just send for Rhadamistus at once? I fear that he does not trust his son.'

'Can you blame him? And after all that you, and he, have put me and my men through, I can't find it within myself to trust you either. I'd sooner trust a scorpion.'

'That is uncalled for, Tribune.'

'I beg to differ. I have known you and Rhadamistus long enough to realise just how calculating and dangerous you both are. King Pharasmanes must have an even deeper understanding of the treacherous nature of his son. If I were him, I would not permit Rhadamistus free movement within Iberia. He's already proved himself capable of betraying and murdering his uncle in Armenia. It is not such a large step to take from murdering one member of his family to murdering another. I'd rather Rhadamistus was somewhere contained, and where I could keep an eye on him.'

Zenobia looked at him thoughtfully. 'Then you are saying that this place is to be our prison?'

'It seems that way.'

Her shoulders sagged fractionally as she took this in. 'You echo my thoughts, Cato.'

There was a brief silence between them before Cato spoke again. 'The question that I am asking myself is why my men and I are being kept here with you.'

'Yes . . . I wondered that. Now that you have brought us to Iskerbalis there is nothing to stop you returning to your cohort.'

'I am sure King Pharasmanes has a good reason. I hope we'll discover what it is soon. I tire of such hospitality very easily.'

She smiled at his ironic tone. 'Yes. We'll find out soon enough, I'm sure.'

The answer came later the same day, at dusk, as there was a sudden commotion in the street outside the governor's villa, with the sound of a large group of horses drawing up and shouted exchanges in the local tongue. Cato was in the library and set down the scroll he was reading to step out on to the terrace to investigate. One side looked over the large courtyard at the front of the building and he saw several servants dashing about, and then the governor hurrying to the doors that opened on to the street. When the servants were in position around the edge of the courtyard and his guards lined up on either side of the door, the governor gave a nod to his major-domo and the man slipped the large iron latch and swung the doors inwards. Light flooded the entrance from the street outside and then shadows fell across the mosaic floor, followed by a score of soldiers in green tunics and black cuirasses. They filed to the sides and there was a pause as another shadow appeared, and then a tall man entered. He wore simple blue robes and a gold diadem with a large ruby mounted above his forehead, holding back his grey hair. At his entrance all but his guards went down on their knees, including the governor. There was a brief exchange before the governor climbed

351

to his feet and led the king in the direction of the wing of the villa used for official matters.

Cato went downstairs into the garden and saw that his men were in a group muttering anxiously at the commotion.

'It's the Iberian king, lads. He's finally arrived to fetch his son. With luck we'll soon be on our way back to rejoin the rest of the cohort.'

That brought some looks of relief and a few smiles. One of the men puffed his cheeks. 'We've been wondering how long we'd be kept here, sir. Been starting to feel like prisoners, if you know what I mean?'

Cato nodded. 'Although, as prisons go, it's not so bad.'

'You speaking from experience there, sir?' another soldier piped up.

'No.' Cato wagged a finger. 'And if you ask me questions like that again, Guardsman Plautius, you will be.'

The men laughed and he was pleased to see that their anxiousness had gone. 'Stay here, lads, I'll go and see what's up.'

Cato turned and headed towards the entrance to the corridor leading through the house. As he emerged into the courtyard he saw Rhadamistus and Zenobia angrily confronting the captain of the royal bodyguards. The latter was impassive, and he and his men refused to give way as they blocked the entrance to the wing of the house where the governor and king had gone shortly before. They turned at the sound of Cato's boots crossing the courtyard and Rhadamistus gestured towards the armed men with a look of contempt.

'These dogs refuse to let me see my father! I'll have them flogged when he finds out about this outrage.'

Cato noted that Zenobia looked far more subdued, and there was a calculating expression in her eyes as she stood to one side.

Even though Rhadamistus was no longer a king, he was still susceptible to arrogance, Cato decided, 'I am sure there is a good reason for it, Majesty. These men are only obeying orders. It would be wrong to insist they be punished.'

A month earlier, Rhadamistus might have flown into a rage at such thwarting of his will, but defeat and the loss of his throne had humbled him to a degree, and after a moment's reflection he sighed. 'You are right, Tribune. I will not have them punished, on this occasion.'

He stepped aside and placed a hand on his wife's shoulder. 'My father will be delighted to see me again. To see us both.' He smiled at Zenobia. 'He always told me that he thought you a beautiful and intelligent woman.'

She smiled back, as if with pleasure at the flattery, but Cato saw that it was no more than a perfunctory expression.

'The king will welcome us to his court. He will find me new soldiers to make new conquests for the glory of our royal line. In time, I will be a king again. And I will not forget your loyalty, Tribune, nor the debt of gratitude I owe to Rome, despite how things turned out.' He drew himself up. 'I am a man who is loyal to his allies.'

Cato was struck by his defiant, superior tone. Had he forgotten all that Cato said to him in the camp before the surrender? Was it that he did not guess how perilous his predicament was? Were his confidence and arrogance such that he truly believed King Pharasmanes would welcome him like a doting father and heap further honours and opportunities upon him? Or was it simply bravado, intended to conceal the fear and uncertainty gnawing at his heart?

Cato forced himself to bow his head in gratitude. 'I am delighted to hear it, Majesty.'

A voice called from down the corridor and Cato saw the governor standing at the entrance to his modest audience chamber, beckoning to the captain of the guard. With the armed men on both sides, Rhadamistus, Zenobia and Cato were escorted into the presence of King Pharasmanes. The chamber was no more than forty feet across and there was no dais, or throne-like chair, merely a marble-topped table and a carved wooden seat behind, from where the king regarded those he had summoned. His guards filed into the chamber and stood on either side, as if to emphasise that the three were prisoners.

The king's gaze fixed on Cato as he addressed him in Greek. 'It is important that you understand what I have to say. The governor tells me you speak Greek well.'

'Yes, Majesty.'

'That is good.' The king turned his dark eyes to Rhadamistus. 'It warms my heart to see you, my son.'

Rhadamistus smiled and took a step forward: 'Father, I—'

Two of the guards lowered their spears to stop him approaching any nearer to the king. There was a heavy silence as Rhadamistus's jaw hung slackly, then the king rose stiffly and made his way round the table to stand a short distance in front of his son. Up close, Cato could see that his face was heavily lined and his sunken eyes were grey and glinted like silver. His lips lifted in a smile as he spoke. 'You were always my favourite child. From the moment your mother presented you to me. You were bold as an infant, always first to say what you were thinking, first in every race you ran. And years later the best student my swordmaster ever taught. You rode like you were born in the saddle. So strong, so handsome, so loved by all and so feared by some. Rhadamistus, no father could be more proud of your qualities.'

He reached out and rested his wrinkled hands on his son's shoulders and then drew Rhadamistus forward to kiss him on the forehead before he embraced him. He held his son for a moment and over Rhadamistus's shoulder Cato thought he saw the glimmer of tears in the old man's eye. Then, abruptly, the king drew back and retreated a pace and his expression became stern. 'I rightly praise your qualities. But there are also faults in your character, chief amongst them ambition. Long before you had grown into manhood I knew that you desired to take my place on the throne of Iberia. But you swore loyalty to me and were content to wait for me to grow old and die. But I grew older and did not die, and your impatience was there to see. That is why I gave you soldiers to go and take Armenia for your own and slake your thirst to rule. It was that, or regard you as a rival for the Iberian crown.' He paused and shook his head sadly. 'But you proved yourself unfit to rule and were forced to flee and go and beg Rome for help to reclaim Armenia. And that was when I finally accepted that your ambition overruled all other considerations. You are not to be trusted, Rhadamistus. You are treacherous and you are dangerous. Such men are not fit to be kings, and if they are not content with what else life has to offer, then they are not fit to live.'

Rhadamistus's eyes widened in dread. 'Father, my king, I am your servant. I swear on my life that I am a loyal son.'

'You are no man's servant but your own. I am sorry, my son. My child. You leave me no choice. I am not safe while you live. Nor are your brothers or sisters.'

Rhadamistus clasped his hands together. 'I beg you. Give me a chance to prove my loyalty.'

'You have had plenty of chances. More than any man has a right to expect.'

Rhadamistus turned towards Zenobia and stabbed a finger at her. 'She made me this way! It was her, always her, filling my mind with whispers and promises of things to be. Scheming, always scheming.'

Cato saw the shocked expression in her face, and then fear and then cold fury, all in a heartbeat, as her lips twisted into a sneer. 'You accuse me of scheming? Me? I was as loyal to you as you never were to your father. If I schemed, then it was only because I was forced to.'

'You lie! I never forced you. Father, she lies!'

'Quiet, you fool,' she snapped. 'Yes, fool . . . Too stupid to see that the king has already decided your fate. Too stupid to realise you would have achieved nothing without me cajoling you into doing what was necessary, and constantly battling to prevent your cruel nature undoing all that I had made you achieve.' She shook her head. 'It is all over now. Majesty, it is true what you say. Your son has a bad soul, and I did all that I could to guide him to what was right. If I have done wrong, it was only in trying to make Rhadamistus do what was best for him, and you. I do not deserve to share his fate. I beg for mercy.'

Rhadamistus trembled with rage at her words. Then before anyone could react, he sprang at her. She turned, her mouth opened to scream, but only a gasp escaped her lips. Cato dashed forward and slammed his fist into Rhadamistus's jaw. The Iberian prince staggered back, dazed, and two of the guards quickly took his arms and pinned them behind his back. In his hand was a small dagger with a fine blade, smeared crimson. Cato turned to Zenobia. She looked down and saw a red blotch spreading across her tunic.

'He stabbed me . . .' she said softly with a look of stunned surprise. Then she stumbled back and sank to the ground. Cato hurried to her side, unwinding his neckcloth. There was a neat hole in the blood-drenched cloth and he pulled it apart to reveal her skin. He wiped the blood aside and saw the entry wound briefly, before more blood welled up out of it. Turning her he saw another hole and realised that the blade had only pierced flesh and muscle and not damaged any organs. He tore his neckcloth into two and pressed the bundles into the wounds, making Zenobia cry out.

'You'll probably live,' he said. 'Just a flesh wound.'

Cato looked up and saw the shocked expression on the king's face as he regarded the injured woman, then his wild-eyed son. He swallowed and took a deep breath to calm his nerves before he spoke.

'Prince Rhadamistus, I sentence you to death . . .'

'For what reason?' his son demanded.

'Does it matter? Given all that has been said here.' The king shrugged. 'Very well, then. Plotting against your king, murder of your uncle. Attempted murder of your wife. Those alone are sufficient reasons.' Pharasmanes turned to the captain of the guard and issued brief instructions. Before Rhadamistus could protest again he was dragged from the room and down the corridor out of sight. Cato could hear him struggling and cursing the guards as he went, fighting until the very end. There was a final pitiful shriek.

'Father!'

Then silence.

King Pharasmanes closed his eyes tightly and clenched his fists for a moment, then sighed heavily as he turned to Cato.

'Tribune, you will take his head back to Artaxata to show the people. You will tell them that I will leave Armenia in peace. When you eventually return to Rome, tell your emperor that I humbly suggest he does the same. No good will ever come of wasting so many lives and treasure attempting to win power over Armenia. Do you understand?'

'I understand, Majesty. But I cannot speak for the emperor.'

King Pharasmanes stroked his creased brow. 'I have heard that the new emperor is no more than a boy. I hope he is wise beyond his years, for the good of us all. Neither Rome nor any other kingdom can long endure a foolish braggart running its affairs . . . Take my son's head and make your preparations to leave at once. You Romans are not welcome in Iberia. Begone.'

CHAPTER THIRTY-EIGHT

Tarsus, October

The change of season was evident in the leaves falling from the trees in the walled gardens of Tarsus and carried into the streets by the cool breeze. The men of the two cohorts Cato had led into Armenia were setting up camp under Macro's watchful eye while Cato entered the city to report to General Corbulo. He had taken the time to think carefully about it before committing himself to a written record. The mission had been a failure insofar as the man Rome had sent to rule Armenia was dead and the kingdom was in the hands of a group of rebel nobles who had yet to choose a successor. Despite their protestations of neutrality there was no guarantee that the next king would decide to be an ally of Rome. And if, instead, he chose to align himself with Parthia, then Armenia would once again know war. The mission's failure was compounded by the losses suffered by the two cohorts, as well as the destruction of the siege weapons. The fact that they had been destroyed rather than allowed to fall into Armenian hands was not likely to win Cato any approval.

When he reached the general's headquarters Cato was informed that Corbulo was out hunting in the hills and was not expected back before nightfall. Cato handed over his written report and told the clerk where he could be found and then left the building to make for the silversmith's house near the Forum. Despite the prospect of being reunited with his son, Cato's heart was heavy as he strode through the streets with Cassius's leash in his hands. The dog was much improved in appearance since the time Cato had adopted him. Most of his fur had grown back over the bald patches and now covered his scars. There was nothing that could be done about his missing ear and it lent him a lopsided appearance which might have occasioned laughter had he been a smaller animal and not looked quite so ferocious. As it was, people steered well clear of him as they passed the Roman officer and his shaggy beast.

Cato was oblivious to the impression he and Cassius were making. His thoughts were deeply troubled. Corbulo's disapproval would be relayed to Rome and Cato had little doubt that his failure to bring Armenia back into the Roman sphere of influence would be seized on by his enemies in the palace to strip him of his command of the Second Cohort. That would leave him languishing in Rome, waiting for a new posting. But with several officers of similar rank and greater experience vying for each vacancy there was little prospect of an appointment to a new command.

He crossed the Forum and turned the corner into the street where the silversmith had his small workshop and house. His heart rose at the familiar sight and he smiled to himself as he strode up to the door of the house. He stopped outside in the street and leaned down to fondle Cassius's good ear. The dog wagged his tail happily.

'Now then, boy, you are going to cause a bit of a stir when we go inside. No biting. Or jumping up. You're likely to flatten Lucius, and likely to get flattened by Petronella if you try it on her. Licking is fine, provided you don't drown anybody in that stinking drool of yours. Do you understand?'

The dog looked up at him blankly and then gave his tail another wag as if to test the water. Cato smiled. 'You're right. I'm just trying to put the moment off. Come on then.'

He turned and rapped sharply on the door. He waited, but there was no response and he pounded with the flat of his fist.

'All right!' Petronella yelled from within. 'Coming!'

The bolt slid back and then the latch and the door opened a fraction as her face appeared. Then her tired expression vanished and she beamed as she threw the door open. Then she froze.

'What in Hades is that thing?'

'This thing is called Cassius. He's kind of a pet,' Cato explained, and then continued in a more ingratiating tone. 'For Lucius to play with.'

'Play with?' Petronella cocked her head to one side as she examined the beast. 'Ride on, more like. Is he tame?'

'Define tame.' Cato stepped over the threshold and Cassius followed, looking up at Petronella warily as Cato spoke reassuringly. 'She's also tame, boy. Doesn't bite.'

'Oh thanks.' Petronella made a face, then anxiously looked past Cato into the street. 'Where's my man? Where's Macro?'

'He's fine. Just seeing to the camp before he comes here.'

'Seeing to the camp?' Petronella frowned. 'He's been away for months and he's not bothering to come and find me until he's put up a few tents.'

'Exigencies of army life, I'm afraid. He won't be any longer than he has to.'

'He'd better not be.'

'So, where's my son?'

Petronella nodded towards the interior. 'I only just got him down for a nap. Little bugger's been a right nightmare last few days, begging your pardon. He's been stroppy and difficult to feed. Up half the night and then bad-tempered the next day. I've been teaching him his letters. Or trying to.'

Cato laughed. 'Then you should be glad Macro and I are back to instil a little discipline.'

'You?' She sniffed. 'You two wind him up worse than ever.'

They turned at the patter of feet and then Lucius let out a squeal of delight and ran across the room. 'Dada!'

Cato swept him up and planted a big kiss on his cheek and Lucius pulled away at the touch of his bristles. Then let out a scream as Cassius jumped up and rested his big paws on Cato's waist and licked Lucius's feet.

'Wolf!' Lucius cried out. 'Eating me!'

'He just wants to be your friend,' Cato explained. 'Although if you don't start behaving for Petronella he may just eat you.'

Lucius looked at him earnestly. 'I'll be good. Promise. Please don't let the wolf eat me.'

'All right then.' Cato gave him a hug and sat him on the edge of the table beside the entrance. Then he handed the leash to Petronella and shut the door. 'Take Cassius to the yard for now.

He can be fed a bit later, after I've had a chance to say hello to Lucius properly.'

Petronella narrowed her eyes. 'And do I look like a kennel slave? Oh, all bloody right.'

She leaned down and wagged a finger at the dog. 'Cassius, eh? Well you better behave yourself if you don't want any trouble.'

Before she could react he licked her face and wagged his tail.

'I think you've made a good first impression,' said Cato.

'Well, he bloody hasn't.' Petronella yanked the leash and headed towards the rear of the house. 'Come on, you.'

Cato hunched down in front of his son. 'So, Petronella says you've been a naughty boy. I hope that isn't true.'

Lucius kicked his feet loosely in mid-air and lowered his head, looking at Cato from under his brow as he smiled mischievously.

By the time Macro reached the house dusk was falling and a few lamps had been lit to provide light inside. Cato let him in, and as Macro took off his cloak and hung it on a peg by the door, Lucius leaped up and rushed over to him. Macro crouched and gave him a hug and then ruffled his wavy hair.

'That's way beyond regulation length, lad. Needs a cut. And I know just the lady to see to that. But where is she? Where can Petronella be, eh?'

'Right here . . .' She stood on the threshold of the atrium, hands on hips. 'And why have you kept me waiting so long?'

'Waiting?' Macro looked to Cato helplessly.

'Oh! You fool. Come to me!' She laughed.

Macro gently eased Lucius aside and rose to his feet before Petronella rushed forward and wrapped her arms around him and kissed him hard on the lips. Then she drew back and held his hands. 'I need a word with you, alone.'

'If that's all right with you, sir?' Macro turned to Cato.

'Indeed.' Cato grinned. 'I'm sure there's plenty for you two to, ah, talk about.'

Macro winked and then led Petronella upstairs and a moment later the bed creaked and there were gasps and cries from Petronella and muttered affectionate blandishments from Macro.

Cato and Lucius were sitting in the corner playing with some wooden gladiators and the boy stopped for a moment and looked up at the ceiling as they listened to the noises from above.

'Uncle Macro and Petronella are wrestling again, aren't they, Dada?'

'Yes, they are. I am afraid it might be quite a long bout.' Cato smiled and decided it might be a good time to change the subject. 'So, tell me what you've been doing since we've been away.'

To the accompaniment of Macro and Petronella's amorous reunion, which lasted longer than Cato would have thought possible before all went quiet, he listened with growing pleasure and affection as Lucius told him of their daily lessons, which he liked sometimes, and their walks through the town to the market, where he counted out the money for the food they bought, which he always liked. He also spoke of their attempts at fishing and how he was better than Petronella. How he did not like the girl in the house next door, who always seemed to be sitting on her step when Lucius went out and smiling at him. All of it was a kind of soothing poetry to Cato's ears, as he became immersed in a world without soldiers, without war, without death or mutilation, without politics and treason, without fear. For a moment he felt the poignant longing for the simple pleasures and innocent curiosity of childhood that all adults felt at times.

A fist pounding on the door broke into Cato's reverie. He patted Lucius on the head and pointed to his toy basket. 'I think you should put those away now. It's time for bed.'

Lucius pouted. 'Must I?'

'I'm not Petronella. You'll do as I say.'

Cato stood and went to the door. There was a soldier standing outside with a torch. Behind him stood another man with the hood of his cloak raised. The soldier stepped aside respectfully as the man entered and closed the door behind him. He slipped his hood back and Cato stiffened as he saw General Corbulo looking around.

'Are we alone?' Then he spied Lucius quietly putting away his wooden gladiators. 'Who else is in the house?'

'Centurion Macro and his woman are upstairs, sir. The silversmith keeps to the far end of the house.'

'Good.' Corbulo went and stood over Lucius. 'Your boy?'

'Yes, sir.'

'A fine lad. You must be proud.'

'I am.'

'And I'm sure he will make a fine soldier one day.'

Cato did not respond and then he leaned down and set Lucius on his feet. 'Off to bed with you, now. Dada needs to talk with his guest.'

Lucius looked up. 'Are you a friend of Dada?'

Corbulo smiled thinly. 'Something like that, young man. Now do as your father says, eh?'

After Lucius had padded out of the room Corbulo sat at the table and his expression hardened. 'I went over your report when I got back from hunting. It did not make for good reading.'

Cato had prepared himself for such a moment, and met his superior's gaze steadfastly as Corbulo continued: 'I don't imagine our masters in Rome will be very pleased with the outcome of your mission. Not that it was carried out on their orders, admittedly. The mission was my initiative. When word reaches Rome that we have lost a valuable asset in Rhadamistus, there will be a demand that someone is held accountable for his death. However, I will be able to defend myself – as will you – on the basis that Armenia had already fallen under the sway of Tiridates and the Parthians and that it was essential to at least attempt to strike before the enemy consolidated their hold over it. We might even argue that a neutral Armenia should be considered something of a success, even if we lost a client king in the process. But you know how these things tend to be twisted for political ends.'

'Indeed I do, sir. The death of Rhadamistus will be presented as an affront to Roman prestige and power and one of the senatorial factions will demand your recall so that a new man can be sent out to teach the Armenians a lesson, as well as the Parthians.'

'Quite.' Corbulo nodded. 'And it is bound to be some half-witted favourite of Nero with limited experience who wants to make a reputation for himself. The situation is dangerous enough without making it worse by having some idiot blundering about in the desert just like Crassus. I will not permit that to happen.

Therefore we must recover Armenia, and then strike at Parthia, and we must do it soon, before my enemies back in Rome have a chance to work their mischief.' He leaned forward. 'You haven't spoken to anyone at my headquarters about the contents of your report, I hope?'

'No, sir.'

'Excellent. Then I suggest you keep your distance from the headquarters staff, and I will file your report away amongst my personal papers and neither of us will speak about the mission, at least until I lead my army into Armenia in the spring.'

'But, sir, how can we keep this a secret? My men will talk the moment they visit the city's taverns and crack open the first jar of wine. And I can hardly forbid them to say anything. That's the surest way of starting gossip.'

'I agree. So we say nothing. If your men talk, then word will inevitably reach the ears of an officer, or a spy working for a rival senatorial faction. Then they will write a report and send it to Rome, where it will be discussed and a message will be sent back demanding a detailed report from me. I will of course send a message back saying the matter of Rhadamistus's death will be investigated. With any luck I can drag it out for long enough to make it irrelevant. But you must play your part too.'

'My part, sir?'

'. . . is to keep your mouth shut. If pressed you say you got your man to Artaxata and got him on the throne and then returned to Syria, as ordered. If it means leaving a few details out, it's going to take a long time before the full story is known. By then, we have to hope that we'll be well into the campaign and have a victory or two to celebrate. And we both know how easily good news flushes out the stench of bad news.'

Corbulo paused to let Cato take stock and then stood up. 'You're a fine officer, Cato. From what you say in your report, you were a victim of circumstance and Rhadamistus's mistakes. But that won't save you being censured by the Senate, and howled down by the mob. You owe it to yourself and Rome to have a chance at redemption. And that chance will come when the army marches in the spring.'

'Yes, sir.'

Corbulo raised his hood again and made for the door and pulled it open. The soldier was still waiting outside and the light of his torch lit up the general's face, blood red. He paused on the threshold and tapped Cato on the chest.

'Don't get too comfortable here in Tarsus. I need to toughen the men up. I'll be taking the army up into the mountains for training during the winter. It'll be hard, and they'll hate me for it, but when we strike at Parthia I want men at my back who I can count on. Are you such a man, Tribune Cato?'

'Yes, sir.'

Corbulo gave him a hard stare. 'Good. Now enjoy your time with your son as much as you can. War is coming. War with Parthia. And when it comes, you and the rest of the men in my army will be tested as never before. Count on it.'

AUTHOR'S NOTE

I t is difficult for someone living now fully to appreciate the challenges facing the Romans in what is blithely refered to as the 'Middle East'. What is it the middle of, exactly? And east of where? Like so many terms casually used it tends to hide its assumptions and thereby lure policy-makers into actions based on false premises, or just plain ignorance. We've seen plenty of evidence of that in recent decades and it is rather tempting to make easy judgements about history repeating itself with respect to western intervention and Rome's incursions two thousand years earlier. However, history does not simply repeat itself. Although, as we shall see below, there are certain homologies between then and now which speak more to policy models than to specific characters and events.

The Blood of Rome deals with Rome's rivalry with Parthia over the kingdom of Armenia. The struggle between the two empires endured for hundreds of years with no decisive outcome. The first official encounter between the two powers came early in the first century BC when the Roman general Sulla met a Parthian embassy close to the River Euphrates. From the outset relations between the two sides were characterised by suspicion and ignorance. This was primarily because of the huge cultural differences between Rome and Parthia. The latter had no standing army, and was ruled by a despot. By contrast, the Romans at that time had largely professionalised their army, and the state was governed by vying political factions. While the Parthians viewed the Romans as aggressive landgrabbers, the Romans regarded their opponents as effeminate, untrustworthy and barbaric. These mutual stereotypes were to shape

366

relations between the two powers ever after, at huge cost in treasure and manpower for both sides.

Not only were Rome and Parthia different culturally, they were – more significantly – different militarily. It has often been pointed out that the Roman military was ponderous and therefore generally tied to their lines of communication, which necessarily limited the range and speed of operations. The Parthian military was mainly based on horsemen – archers and cataphracts – with nobles being responsible for supplying a body of men to serve the ruler of Parthia when the need arose. This meant that the Parthians could advance swiftly and were very effective at fighting in a hit-and-run style. The result was that when the Romans met the Parthians on open ground, the Romans were at a disadvantage. It is worth recalling that Crassus and his legions came to grief at the hands of a far smaller Parthian force primarily composed of horse-archers, who were able to stand off and whittle down the helpless legionaries. What this meant was that later Roman commanders decided to forsake an advance across the open landscape of Mesopotamia and chose to advance over the mountainous ground of Armenia to the north, which was much more favourable to their infantry.

Unluckily for the people of Armenia, they found themselves astride the main campaign route between the two powers. Rome needed control of Armenia to provide a route into Parthia, and to secure their northern flank. This is why Armenia came to assume such vital importance in the Roman mind. From the Parthian perspective, the significance of Armenia was based on a long history of loose control over the kingdom, and far closer cultural ties than Rome ever had with the people of Armenia. As is often the case, the perceived significance of the prize grew out of all proportion to its actual strategic significance.

Once Rome had been worsted by Parthia, the enemy assumed an almost mythic status as the supreme rival to Rome. Roman generals saw war against Parthia, and control of Armenia, as an opportunity for personal aggrandisement and vied with each other, and their antecedents, to win glory by humbling Parthia. In doing so, they needed to present Parthia as a threat that was out of all proportion to the actual dangers posed by the enemy empire. As noted above, the Parthian military was geared towards short-term mobile warfare, and there was never any serious intent to invade and conquer the eastern Roman empire. However, for the Romans to recognise and accept that would have robbed them of the justification to partake of glory-seeking that was a key aspect of their character. A dangerous enemy was needed, and so a dangerous enemy Parthia became, and remained.

If we indulge a taste for making historical parallels, this tendency is a feature of much policy-making in recent decades, as was the case with the infamous 'Domino Theory' that led to the disastrous war and the defeat of the US in Vietnam. Certainly, a realistic appraisal of any threat posed by Vietnam and Parthia might have ensured that the vast costs expended by both the Romans and Americans were avoided. A diplomatic solution in both cases would have saved very many lives and would have been more effective in the long term. But populist leaders have never shied away from sabre-rattling to excite the nationalist fervour of the masses. It is a much easier sell than the protracted diplomatic negotiations and compromise that peace entails. Indeed, Emperor Augustus was frequently criticised for coming to a diplomatic arrangement with Parthia rather than waging war.

Which brings us on to the matter of the challenges faced by Roman commanders that were so different to those faced by modern armies conducting operations in the region. In the first place there was the slow dissemination of news. Today, any event can be reported to a global audience in a matter of minutes. Two thousand years ago, it could take years for Rome to become aware of the succession of one ruler by another in the lands to the east of the frontier. Then there was the nature of the terrain itself. In the absence of Google Earth or even maps, Roman commanders literally had no idea what lay ahead of them. Where a route might lead, what water supplies were nearby, what towns lay ahead was all a mystery until the legionaries actually marched over the ground in question. Marching blindly into terra incognita was made more perilous still by the unreliability and treachery of local guides, who often led Roman armies into traps or inhospitable terrain that whittled down their numbers. The sheer scale of the Parthian empire meant that any plans for long-term conquest would have required far more troops than the Romans could have concentrated for the task. Like the coalition forces in a much later Mesopotamian incursion, they were spread too thinly to maintain any more than nominal control over the ground. This then led to the usual intractable political problem of not being willing to invest in sufficient manpower to achieve a decisive result, while at the same time not being able to afford the political costs of withdrawal. The inevitable result of this, as we have seen all too often throughout history, is a protracted and costly occupation that ultimately ends in retreat and damage to reputation.

Despite my earlier caveat about drawing easy parallels, there is much that Roman soldiers, like Macro and Cato, and modern soldiers like my son, would recognise in each other's situation. I have little doubt that they would share a fatalistic sigh at the burden laid on the shoulders of soldiers by their political masters who, all too often, are oblivious to the bodies buried beneath the foundations of the posterity they crave for themselves.